for the real Bertie

Prisoner At the Bar

A Midge Carrington Mystery

by
Margaret Suckling

Copyright – Margaret Suckling 2016

The right of Margaret Suckling to be identified as the Author of the Work has been asserted in accordance with the Copyright, Designs and Patents Act 1988.

All rights reserved. No part of this publication may be reproduced or transmitted in any form or by any means, electronic or mechanical, either current or in the future, including photocopying, recording or by any information storage or retrieval system, without prior written permission from Margaret Suckling, except for the inclusion of quotations in a review. No part of this publication may be otherwise circulated in any form of binding or cover other than that in which it is published and without a similar condition being imposed on the subsequent purchaser.

This book is a work of fiction, and the characters in this book are entirely fictitious and any resemblance to any real persons, living or dead, is purely coincidental.

Prelude

"It is the prosecution's case that you, the accused, are guilty of this dreadful crime. Moreover, you have compounded your hideous act by a betrayal of the very ideals which you once swore to uphold. There is little excuse for any man who turns to violence to escape his troubles, but for you, a member of the legal profession, to do so is a shocking breach of trust."

The bewigged speaker kept his eyes sternly on the defendant in the dock for a moment longer, before theatrically spinning round to the twelve men and women gathered to try a man for his life.

"Ladies and gentlemen of the jury, if you turned to your vicar or priest for advice and he lied to you; if you asked your solicitor for help and he stole from you; if you begged your doctor to save your life and he gave you medicine to hasten your end, then you would be betrayed, just as the victim in this case was vilely and treacherously betrayed. It is my job, as counsel for the prosecution, to set out for you exactly what the defendant did; and it will be your job, as the jury, to deliver your verdict upon this sorry wretch."

I

Adagio

Chapter One

Yawning, Midge Carrington pushed the newspaper away. Early mornings held little attraction for her at the best of times and depressing news from Germany did not enliven matters. She contemplated the crisp toast in the silver rack for a moment, toying with the idea of another slice, before returning her gaze to the newspaper in the hope of finding something more uplifting than the latest negotiations with Herr Hitler.

As the grandfather clock in the passage intoned ten, an elegant middle-aged woman bustled into the breakfast room, carrying a vase filled with roses.

"Really, Midge!" she exclaimed as the sight of her niece dawdling over breakfast met her eyes. "How have you ever managed on your own in Cambridge? Lectures start at nine o'clock, not eleven!"

Midge grinned lazily. "I did buy several alarm clocks to help me, but just at the moment I'm enjoying not being expected to be anywhere. You've no idea how pleasant it is to waken and then go back to sleep again, rather than rushing around trying to get to the correct place on time and failing miserably!"

Alice Carrington shook her head, while attempting to look disapproving.

"If I were to do that, not only would I miss breakfast with your uncle, but I'd never get anything done in the garden before luncheon." Then, with a rueful glance outside at the lowering Suffolk sky, she added, "Or, indeed, before it begins to rain!"

"Never mind, Aunt Alice," consoled Midge, "when Jenny gets here, she'll be sure to want to be energetic; maybe she'll join you for some pre-breakfast gardening. Think what a splendid example you can both set me."

Mrs Carrington laughed. "If Jenny's been working as hard as she claims, she's more likely to want to lie in as well. Do you think that she really will end up being a lawyer? She could easily come out instead; she's a pretty little thing and there's plenty of money in the family. Isn't her father quite well-connected, too?"

Stirring her tea thoughtfully, Midge nodded. "The thing is, Jenny would soon get bored doing the season. Obviously, she'd enjoy the dances and the dresses and that sort of thing, but, for all that she can be frivolous, she wants to achieve something with her life. Being a barrister is the only thing she's ever wanted to do."

"It's not an easy life for a girl."

"No career is easy for a girl," growled Midge. "Joan Handley at our school won the top scholarship to Newnham, came high up in every maths exam she took at Cambridge and all that happened was that the men sneered at her. So what's she doing now? Teaching!"

"Teaching is a worthwhile task," pointed out her aunt in a placatory tone.

"Yes," agreed Midge, "but there's a war coming; Joan should be using her brain for something more important than instructing dim twelve-year-olds in arcane branches of geometry."

"You were one of those dim twelve-year-olds, once."

"I know! Which is precisely why I think it's an utter waste of Joan's time and her talents. Surely there must be something better she could do?"

"I suppose that she'll free up a man to go into uniform if it does come to war."

"A man!" snorted Midge with contempt. "When Mr

Chamberlain and the powers that be stop thinking of women as low-grade substitutes for men and start using women's real abilities, then we might get on a lot better. Russia seems to be happy to use women's brains; why can't Britain?"

"What use would your Latin and Greek be in wartime?" enquired Alice Carrington, with the suspicion of a smile on her face.

Midge laughed. "Probably not a great deal, although Latin might come in handy for explaining to the local priest what our troops were doing. 'Bless me, father, for I have sinned. I've blown up a bridge and need more dynamite.' "

Watching her niece struggle upright and limp across the room, leaning heavily on a stick, Alice winced inwardly. It was all very well Midge casually suggesting that she could act as an army interpreter (and indeed, rather more usefully than Latin, her command of German was fairly sound), but what use would a girl crippled by polio be in wartime? If it came to that, what were Midge's chances of carving out a happy life for herself in peacetime? Even going up to Cambridge was something of a risk. What if Midge's health gave way under the strain?

Sensing her aunt's eyes on her, Midge grimaced. She had a shrewd idea as to what her aunt was thinking, but did not want to start an argument. Cambridge might not work out, but at least it was an escape from the alternative: being stuck at home with nothing to occupy herself and no-one to talk to apart from her uncle and aunt. Deliberately altering the subject to the vexed question of why Mrs Peabody, the doctor's wife, had insisted on changing the flower arrangements in the church when it was not her turn to do so, Midge was able to guide the conversation into safer channels. The iniquities of the flower rota led naturally on to the suspicions that the new curate was worryingly Low Church and the scandalous rumour that he had been seen emerging from a Methodist chapel in Ipswich.

"Mrs Gregory swears that it was Mr Walters," ended Alice.

"What was she doing near a Methodist chapel, anyway?" enquired Midge lazily. "Surely she's so High Church she's practically a devotee of Rome?"

Her aunt laughed. "I know you don't care about the village gossip," she remarked, "but if I don't keep at least partly aware of what's going on, I'm liable to make the most embarrassing gaffes, such as offering the colonel's wife cake *two weeks* after she had started some exceedingly odd grated-carrot and nut diet. She rejected my Victoria sponge with such exaggerated horror that you might have thought that I'd offered her poison."

"You probably had," Midge pointed out. "Some of those diet sects preach that the wrong foods harm not just your body, but your mind as well."

"Quite," agreed Mrs Carrington. "Her latest fad is to eat twice as much as she actually wants to eat so that her body becomes sickened of food, and her will to eat very little becomes stronger and stronger."

"That must make serving at dinner rather challenging. Perhaps she has two places laid for her?"

"Or even three," concurred Alice. "And to answer your original question, it wasn't actually Mrs Gregory who saw the poor man; it was her cook, who was visiting her sister in Ipswich."

"Ipswich, home of unforeseen, unmentionable evils." Midge grinned. "I do hope that Jenny manages to change onto our little branch line without being abducted or force-fed carrots."

"No danger of that; John's collecting her from the railway station at Ipswich."

"John?" queried Midge in surprised tones. "I assumed

he wasn't coming down for another week."

Mrs Carrington sounded mildly embarrassed. "I thought that it might be nice if he came a little earlier and we would have more time together. After all, he'll be going to Austria shortly after Christmas."

Midge returned some harmless remark, but underneath she was not altogether pleased that her cousin was returning to the family fold a week earlier than she had expected. Along with life at Cambridge, Cousin John was another subject which Midge did not wish to have to address at the moment, and she suspected that it would be far harder to ignore his existence when he was actually present in the same house, rather than happily ensconced in his rooms in Trinity.

Hence it was that, shortly after three o'clock, the Lagonda crunched over the gravel and drew up by the front door. A slim, elegant figure descended from the motor, laughing at the driver's compliments that she was not scared by his driving. Alice Carrington, who knew Jenny of old, greeted her with pleasure, expressing surprise at how little time it had taken them to travel from Ipswich. A few minutes later, the door to Midge's sitting-room was flung open and Jenny blew in tempestuously like a whirlwind. Having kissed Midge on the cheek and thrown her toque carelessly on the settee, she leaned back elegantly.

"Darling, simply too divine to see you again! I want to know absolutely everything!"

Midge gazed at her old school friend rather miserably. Jenny seemed to have become most horribly sophisticated since she had left school. Naturally, living in London might be expected to have its effect on one's fashion sense, but, as she took in Jenny's impeccably-tailored suit, her silk stockings, her smart black shoes and her elegantly cropped head, Midge could not help mentally comparing the overall effect with her own camel-coloured wool skirt and leaf green twin-set. If she were to live in London for a decade she would not achieve the same distinction as Jenny appeared to achieve with no effort whatsoever.

A mischievous grin flickered over Jenny's face.

"Midge, sweetie, I know that I am hopelessly overdressed for the country, so don't sit there with that petrified look as if some wicked Bright Young Thing had floated into your snuggery all ready to drag you off to a simply shocking dive of a nightclub. You have indeed taken receipt of the expected Fletcher, Jenny, putative barrister-at-law, but tomorrow you shall see me in much more suitable attire. I should hate to shock the vicar were he to see your little friend from school in this current transformation."

"Well, I haven't seen you for months," retorted Midge, "so how am I to know whether you've taken to nightclub living or not?"

"Would my revered papa allow me to haunt such dens of iniquity?"

"Knowing you, it wouldn't make much difference if your father disapproved; you'd find some way to persuade him!"

"The case of the diamond clips does spring to mind," admitted Jenny.

Midge shot her a suspicious glance.

"My said parent," stated Jenny with a grin, "had suggested in the most tactful of terms that I might be just a touch too, shall we say?, decorative for his chambers. Apparently, peacock blue is not normally the colour of choice for aspiring barristers, even if the suit was accompanied by simply *the* most fetching hat. So, in an attempt to prove my case I pointed out that I had to brighten the place up or my spirit would never withstand the strain. James and Ronald are simply too musty and fusty to be true, more like fifty-year-old members of a golf club than clever young men."

"Ronald?" queried Midge in some confusion.

"One of the boys in chambers. Quite sweet, but, my dear, his ties! Anyway," continued Jenny, temporarily throwing off her impersonation of a gracious lady, "Daddy started being almost as stuffy as a golf-club bore himself and said that he didn't want the boys to be distracted by me. He suggested that they needed to work even if I didn't. So I pointed out that I could distract them just as much in a severely-cut black suit as I could in bright blue and that there were some advantages to being decorative. He expressed doubt to this interpretation of the utility of the female form, so I challenged him to take me to a legal dinner. I bet him that he would show up every other barrister in the room because they'd either be accompanied by fearfully dowdy women or frightfully earnest young men from their chambers."

"And did you win?"

"Of course I did – there was a pair of diamond hair-clips riding on it, not to mention my personal pride!"

"What would you have done if you'd lost?" enquired Midge curiously.

"There would have been a horrible hole in my allowance for several months because I'd already bought the clips!"

"You are an idiot!" laughed Midge. "No wonder your father thinks that you are a distraction in his chambers." She paused. "Are you actually doing any work, or are you floating round London enjoying yourself?"

"Such suspicion!" complained Jenny, before suddenly becoming much more serious. "Actually, I'm working jolly hard, but I need some frivolity to keep my spirits up."

"Why? Is the work difficult?"

"It's not learning the law that's the problem, it's people who don't think that I ought to be learning it! I've only being studying for a term, but I'm already sick to death of being asked why a pretty little thing like me wants to get involved in law. If a man asks, he normally follows it up with wondering whether a girl could possibly learn all the necessary information. And if a woman asks, she generally makes a snide remark about me stopping playing at being a lawyer once I get married. They like to hint that I must meet lots of nice young men whilst training." Jenny snorted contemptuously. "No-one asks men why they want to become lawyers; no-one spends all their time hinting that men only go into law to meet eligible young women. So why do they insinuate it about me?"

Midge looked sympathetically at her friend. Now that Jenny had become worked up, she seemed much more like her friend of old, rather than an alien fashion-plate.

"What you need is a women's college of law," she suggested. "Women dons wouldn't question your desire to learn; they'd be only too keen to insist that you did more and more."

Jenny ran a speculative glance over Midge, wondering whether there was more to Midge's remark than she had intended to imply. For the moment she forbore from pursuing the issue, merely remarking that women's colleges tended to have unreasonable rules about nightclubs and other essential places of modern living.

"Imagine if I had to be cosily tucked up in my room by ten o'clock each night! I'd probably spend most of the first term being gated and be sent down in my second. Not really the approach I have in mind for emancipated womanhood."

Midge grinned appreciatively.

"I can see that you might find Newnham's regulations a bit tiresome, but for goodness sake don't say too much at dinner about gadding about town at all hours. My uncle doesn't really approve of emancipated womanhood. In fact, I'm not sure he really approves of women working."

"Huh!" grunted Jenny in unladylike tones. "Your uncle would employ me soon enough if I had a story to sell. Disapproval would fly out of the window, particularly if he could do one of his competitors in the eye over it."

Noticing Midge's unconvinced expression, Jenny changed the subject.

"What about tea? Ought we to be joining the others?"

"Don't worry. Aunt Alice said that she would get Ellen to bring something up for us. She was sure that we would have lots to catch up on, and she thought that it was warmer up here."

Jenny grinned. "Are you still complaining about how cold it is compared to India?"

Midge responded with a rueful sigh. "Everyone teases me about how much I hate the cold, but I can't help it! Cambridge doesn't seem to be any warmer, despite being further inland."

"In that case," suggested Jenny, "I shall have to risk hideous damage to my suit and hurl a few more logs on the fire, rather than chance you catching cold." She made her way towards the basket near the fireplace, before remarking in pretended shock, "Good lord, woman, do you burn whole trees here?"

"Naturally; this is the country, not the Old Bailey, and don't you forget it!"

Chapter Two

Back in London, Patrick Fletcher, K.C., was not exchanging frivolous jokes. Instead, he was grimly discussing a problem which had been causing him considerable anxiety.

"I have an appointment with Forrest this afternoon – how he responds will dictate the action which I then take. I suspect that I know how he will react."

"You mean he will not agree?"

"Exactly. And, if he does not, then there is only one possible course left." Fletcher shrugged. "Clearly, there are dangers associated with taking such decisive action, but it is the only way in which to deal with Forrest for good."

His interlocutor nodded. "I agree. The man must be stopped before he does more damage."

Chapter Three

While Jenny and Midge were catching up on what had happened to various school friends, mother and son were discussing Midge downstairs.

"She looks terribly pale and worn out," worried Mrs Carrington. "Do you think that Cambridge is too much for her?"

"Anyone might well be tired after their first term," John pointed out. "Give her a chance to recover before you draw any conclusions."

The unspoken thought that Midge was not anyone hung heavily in the air between them. There were several dons who limped round Cambridge with a constant reminder of their service in the Great War, but John had seen no other girls from Girton or Newnham who had been crippled by polio.

"Can't you check up on her more often?" fretted Alice, forgetting that John was, if anything, far too inclined to feel responsible for Midge's welfare, since she had caught infantile paralysis while visiting Greece with him five years earlier.

"I don't think so, Mother," frowned John. "Midge is an independent type and she would detest it if she thought that I was watching what she was getting up to. It's one thing Midge visiting me when she feels like it and quite another for me to demand to see her regularly and to badger her about her work. It would undermine her confidence dreadfully."

Mrs Carrington was inclined to argue the point, but John, mindful of the manner in which Midge had fired up when he had asked how she was coping with varsity life, maintained his position valiantly.

"It won't help Midge to find her feet socially if people think that she's always running off to see me," he maintained. "It's like when a boy goes to public school; it doesn't do him any good if his brother is always fighting his battles for him. He should be able to turn to his major if he really needs him, but not be dependant upon him."

Having been to neither public school nor Cambridge, Alice was forced to accept her son's view, but she was not entirely reassured.

"I'm glad that Jenny is here; she may help to cheer Midge up and make her look a bit more like herself."

By the evening, Jenny was thoroughly settled in. She had had a conducted tour round the old farmhouse and had insisted on penetrating all the rooms which she remembered from previous visits, not even neglecting the dusty attics or the stables. Eventually Midge glanced at her watch. "Don't you think that we ought to change for dinner? Aunt Alice will fuss if I don't give you enough time to bathe."

"And as I have my reputation for sophistication to maintain, I don't want to turn up at dinner with damp hair and a general air of having crawled into my dress at the last minute."

"That sounds rather more like me than you," agreed Midge. "It was frightfully embarrassing when I came into Formal Hall late in my first week at Newnham."

"Lying on your bed reading a book when you ought to have been putting on your best bib and tucker?" suggested Jenny knowledgeably. "Or were you busily grooming Bertie-the-Cat, rather than yourself?"

"There's some truth in that," acknowledged Midge. "But the main problem was that I got lost and kept following one wretched corridor after another, until I finally pushed open a heavy door expecting to find the Hall, full of feasting students."

"But?"

"But I had reached the dim and august portals of the Senior Combination Room instead."

"Ouch," sympathised Jenny. "Was there anyone there?"

"Yes." Midge grinned. "An incredibly aged don sent a piercing glance in my direction and addressed me as Miss Umm Err, before asking me to be seated. At that point I fled."

"I'll let you loose in Middle Temple," suggested Jenny. "You could really get lost there, with all the lanes and funny little staircases leading up to misshapen rooms and crooked passageways."

"So lost," countered Midge, "that I should end up as one of the Temple ghosts, constantly wailing and calling your name in the hope that you might lead me back to the world. Do you think that it would encourage people to give you briefs if they kept hearing a mournful call of Fletcher, Fletcher, Jenny Fletcher?"

Jenny laughed. "As barristers aren't allowed to advertise, that might make an interesting case in court. Could I be held responsible for my friend's ghost whom, when living, I had introduced into Temple? And would calling for help constitute advertisement?"

"More likely you'd get prosecuted for wilful abandonment," suggested Midge as they made their way upstairs.

Nearly an hour later, the whole party except Geoffrey Carrington were assembled in the drawing room. Jenny, resplendent in a rather daring creation of teal green marocain which hugged her body as closely as a sheath, had finished the ensemble with a gossamer-thin silver lace wrap draped negligently from her shoulders. Alice was wearing a black velvet dress which, as she was busily explaining to Jenny, might not have a fashionably low-cut back, but had the benefit of being warm. "So often when I go to visit people for dinner, I discover that I am sitting in a draught and I do simply detest that. And when you reach my age, you have to be so careful if you wear colours. You look simply delightful, my dear, but you are young enough to carry it off. If you could have seen what I saw last week, you would realise what I meant – a woman of nearly seventy dressed in flame-red velvet and wearing scarlet lipstick."

Midge grinned. "She was sitting on a maroon sofa, too."

Alice winced at the memory. "To be fair, anyone who wasn't in black or white would have clashed with the sofa, but, really, flame-red is not the colour to wear at that age. It's so unforgiving."

Jenny now asked a question, unconnected with fashion, which had been puzzling her. "I thought that Mr Carrington was supposed to be reporting on negotiations at a conference. If he has returned home earlier than expected, does that mean that international diplomacy had given up all hope of peace?"

Alice's mood darkened. She had been delighted at the prospect of her husband joining them that evening, but, as Jenny suggested, the omens might not be good.

"Why does Herr Hitler have to be so unreasonable?" she sighed fretfully. "General Whitlock was telling me at dinner last week what a wonderful man he is and how he has done so much for Germany and helped sort out the unemployment problems. That's all very well, but I shouldn't like to live on the German border; it would be like sharing a house with a wolf – it's probably very friendly when it's been fed, but what happens when it gets hungry?"

"I shouldn't like to be in Italy either," agreed Midge. "I had a letter from Alix last week. Obviously it's been through the censors but, reading between the lines, things are pretty tense there. Apparently one of the men on the dig has just disappeared. Getting the trains running on time isn't worth that sort of price."

"Cocktails," ordered John, noticing that his mother was looking upset, "and then I want to hear exactly what Alix is digging up at Cerveteri. There's been a lot of interesting stuff come from that region, although I had heard that the local archaeologists thought that most of the Etruscan tombs had probably been found by now."

Etruscan archaeology and the correct interpretation of bronze mirrors found in graves lasted until Geoffrey Carrington's arrival. Apologising for having delayed the company, he asked them to begin dinner whilst he changed. The mulligatawny had just been removed when Geoffrey entered the dining-room.

"What a relief to be back, even if I do have to return to London tomorrow morning." He sank down onto the carving chair at the head of the polished mahogany table. "I feel as if I have heard so many people talking so much drivel that I never want to hear any discussion on any subject again."

"That might put a bit of a dampener on tonight's dinner," commented John, with a laugh. "Seriously, though, do you think that there was any point in the conference?"

"There is always point in talking if you have two sides who want to come to an agreement," suggested Geoffrey as he drew the roast beef towards him and began to carve it. "The problem with this conference was that there were six nations represented and not one of them wanted the same thing. We shall never avert war; all we can do is to try to put it off until we are more ready."

"Mike is applying to transfer to the Air Force," remarked Jenny. "He thinks that we shall need as many fighter-pilots as possible when war starts. He wants to get trained now so as to be prepared for it."

"Will Tom join him?" enquired Midge. Jenny's brothers were twins and what one did, the other copied.

Jenny wrinkled her nose reflectively. "It's the first time that they've disagreed on what to do. Tom thinks that it is a waste of his army training to leave the regiment, but Mike believes that the Air Force will need pilots who understand what the men on the ground are trying to achieve. I think that Tom might have followed Mike, but he's already been selected to go on a tank course. He'll go on it once he returns from Alexandria."

"What does your father think about their plans?" asked Alice.

"He was frightfully sarcastic about Tom," replied Jenny with a grin. "First of all, he questioned whether Tom knew how slowly tanks moved, and then he enquired whether Tom was 'pursing this unprecedented course' because Tom had run out of excuses to give the magistrates when he appeared before them on a summons for dangerous driving. Mind you, Daddy isn't at all mechanically-minded, so he doesn't sympathise with Tom's obsession with speed."

"Your father is one of the pre-eminent legal minds of his generation," remarked Mr Carrington, somewhat repressively.

Jenny smiled sweetly at the equally eminent correspondent. "I know; that's why I am so lucky to be able to train in his chambers."

If Jenny had been looking for a red herring to distract the conversation from the possibility of war, she had succeeded admirably. Geoffrey was an intelligent, well-read, thoughtful man but, as his niece had remarked earlier that day, he had considerable reservations about the Modern Girl, particularly some of those varieties which were encountered through the medium of his newspaper office.

"While I have no wish to disparage either your intelligence or your interest in the law," he began, "do you really believe that you will ever practise it? Are you not taking the place of a man who could be training for a profession which he will continue to follow until he retires?"

"And what will happen when you marry?" pointed out Alice. "Your husband won't want you to work. And if you were to have children, you would be unable to work."

Repressing the desire to say that any putative husband might have to take her wishes into account, rather than merely dictate his own, Jenny searched for a more emollient answer.

"I can see that young children might present a problem but what would happen if I gave up the chance to study law on the assumption that I should marry and have children, and then I never married? Wouldn't that be rather a waste? If I have ability, oughtn't I to use it? And if women make up half the population, might some women not feel more at ease being represented by a woman solicitor or – if things went to court – a woman barrister?"

"Exactly," agreed Midge. "The female chorus in Euripides' *Medea* understands Medea much better than a male chorus would."

"I'm not sure that a child-murdering witch is quite the best argument for lady barristers," observed Geoffrey sardonically. "But, Jenny, what do you have to say against my second point? Aren't you depriving a man of the chance to learn a skill which will support him and, quite possibly, his wife and children?"

"I haven't deprived anyone of anything," replied Jenny, trying to keep her temper under control; after all, if she really were to practise law she would face harder questioning than this, with perhaps a man's life at stake. "I'm studying at my father's chambers and he can do what he likes. Anyway, he wouldn't have given me a place unless he thought I was worth it."

"Surely that would suggest that you might not have won a place elsewhere?" demanded Geoffrey. "You have been able to train because of your father's position; would you have been accepted into other chambers?"

"If I hadn't, it would have been because I am a girl, not because of my ability. Surely it is better to look at people's inclinations and abilities, not whether they are male or female? Daddy tried to persuade Mike and Tom to follow him into the law, but they were uninterested and chose the army. If he had made them study law that would have deprived two people – male or female – who wanted to read for the Bar from doing so. People ought to be able to study if they have the ability and the interest."

"Pioneers are needed in all areas," agreed Midge. "Look where women's education would be if Miss Beale and Miss Buss hadn't tried to create decent girls' schools which taught meaningful subjects, not just how to run a home or 'accomplishments'. I don't see why Jenny shouldn't be a pioneer in the field of law. Even Plato said that women ought to be trained to rule, if they had the capacity to do so. If Jenny has all the attributes of a lawyer, why should blinkered prejudices prevent her from becoming one?"

Geoffrey laughed. "Ideals and reality are two rather different matters. Anyway, I don't know what your father would think about sending you to Newnham if he knew that you would come back a radical campaigner for the cause of women."

"Don't tease the child," warned Alice, seeing that Midge looked uncomfortable. "He doesn't mean it, my dear; all of us, including your father, are very proud of the fact that you are at Cambridge and we are delighted that you have the opportunity to go there."

Alice's reassuring remarks left Midge feeling more uncertain than her uncle's had. It was very kind of her aunt to say that she was proud of her, but Midge's first term had left her feeling distinctly unsure whether she was really up to the demands of college life. And if she could not cope with Newnham, what could she achieve in life?

Chapter Four

The man seated at his desk in Duke's Buildings yawned and gathered his papers together. He glanced at his watch and stiffened in shock. He had let things run on too long – his whole schedule for the evening was in danger of being disrupted. Hastening along the corridor, he knocked on the end door for form's sake, before bending down and glancing through the keyhole. Then he retreated hastily.

Standing on the steps of the office building, he looked round. Surely there would be a policeman – he normally came along just before the hour. Where was he? Where the devil was he? Suddenly, a shiny blue helmet came into view. The watcher sighed. Thank goodness. He ran down the steps towards the policeman. "Officer," he gasped. "Officer, I've found a body."

Chapter Five

The next day dawned bright and surprisingly warm for December. True to Midge's prediction, Jenny had risen early and, after breakfast, joined Alice for a stroll in the gardens. Despite studying the subject for several years at school, Jenny's knowledge of botany was limited and her inability to distinguish lime tree from ash was matched by her profound ignorance of the names of most of the plants which Alice was proudly describing to her.

"I've had the greatest trouble trying to establish cistus here," remarked Mrs Carrington. "All the books say that it enjoys direct sun, but the only place where it has taken properly is in semi-shade by the elm-tree."

Jenny nodded intelligently, enjoying the sweep of the lawns and the silhouettes of the trees whose leaves now lay in crackling heaps upon the ground. In her experience, garden-lovers, like golf-players and fishing fanatics, were perfectly happy with the semblance of understanding on the part of their auditors. Actual comprehension and response would get in the way of their story. Jenny had perfected her technique of simulated intelligence when listening to her father talk about mighty battles on the Test and the Itchen and, while she was quite happy to allow him to tell tall tales of giant trout of demoniacal cunning, her only complaint was that he would not reciprocate in pretending comprehension of her views on hats, hemlines, or whether the latest Schiaparelli design was a success.

Eventually the difficulties of over-wintering cyclamen and the vexed question of whether the annoyance of stray bluebells spreading over the western border was too much to pay for the glories of the bluebell wood in spring had been thoroughly aired. At that point, Alice turned for the house, and changed the topic to one which was worrying her far more than the state of the garden.

"I wanted to talk to you about Midge. She looks dreadfully tired and she's rather taciturn. I do hope that she's not exhausting herself trying to rush around too much." Alice snapped off a dead twig to conceal her emotion. "By the time we had finished dinner she looked positively gaunt. I wish she'd never gone to Cambridge if that is what it's going to do to her!"

Jenny pondered for a moment. "The thing is, Midge has had to adjust to a new environment this term. When she returned to school after her polio attack it must have been exceptionally difficult, but at least she knew everyone there and knew the surroundings. At Cambridge she's having to adapt to everything: people, places and new work. I suppose it is only to be expected that it's all a bit demanding at the moment."

"But she looks so white and thin; what if she makes herself ill?"

"Midge is pretty sensible," argued Jenny. "In any case, I've seen her go grey with pain at school, so she's not necessarily getting worse."

Alice stared thoughtfully at a rose bush. Surely it could not be getting mildew in winter?

"I know that Midge hates being pestered with questions about how she is feeling," she continued, "but if she speaks to you about things, please do try to find out whether she really is coping or just putting on a brave face."

"Of course," agreed Jenny, somewhat unwillingly. She understood that Mrs Carrington was worried about her niece, but, equally, she knew that Midge loathed being badgered about her leg. In fact, Jenny wondered whether part of Midge's apparent loss of self-confidence might be attributed to precisely that. It could not be much fun having to repeatedly explain to people that you walked with a stick because you had been struck down with infantile paralysis as a girl. Since Midge had been meeting a lot of new people, presumably she might have also have been making a lot of explanations. Jenny kicked the turf moodily, unaware that she was scarifying Alice's feelings by her assault on the hallowed sward. Midge practically never even mentioned being crippled; what must it be like arriving at Newnham and discovering that people wanted to ask about your withered leg, not which subject you were reading?

Meanwhile, Midge was still lying cocooned in her blankets, wondering whether she had to get up yet. She had had one of her bad nights where she had been unable to get comfortable owing to the pain in her leg. Bertie, who did not believe in sleeping downstairs when there was a soft, cosy bed inhabited by his mistress upstairs, had kept her company all night but, despite the comforting presence of her cat, Midge had lain awake for hours. When she finally emerged from her bed, one rapid glance in the looking-glass showed her that the ravages of the previous night were clearly stamped upon her face.

"Blast," murmured Midge, reaching for her wrap. "I'd better wear the navy twin-set this morning, even if the sweater is starting to look a bit aged. Any other colour will make me appear even worse. At least it's only Jenny who's staying at the moment – another guest might wonder what on earth I'd been up to!"

When Midge eventually made her way downstairs, she found John ensconced in the morning room, but no sign of Jenny or her aunt. The cousins greeted each other and then there was an awkward pause, eventually broken by Midge.

"Has Uncle Geoffrey already gone back to London?"

"Yes." John folded the newspaper and tossed it on a table "How are the quiet folds of the country suiting you

28

after the high life of Newnham?"

Midge shifted uneasily. She was sure that John was leading up to something. Blast Jenny; why did she have to abandon her to her cousin's tender mercies?

"They're fine."

"That's good to know; I wondered whether you might find Brandon a bit boring and staid these days, just as you said I am."

John's tone was perfectly friendly, but Midge turned scarlet.

"Dash it, John! Can't you forget about what I said?"

John caught the note of unhappiness in the midst of Midge's anger and his annoyance with her evaporated.

"I suppose it was rather too tempting to throw my wicked past in my teeth when I started quizzing you. But you might also remember that worrying about you is not the same thing as accusing you of not working hard enough or of being feeble. I am your cousin; I have a right to worry about you."

Midge blushed vigorously. She could hardly explain that half the reason she had snapped at John was because he so clearly worried about her only in a cousinly capacity. Emancipated womanhood certainly had not reached as far as telling a man that you were keen on him.

Fortunately, at this point Alice and Jenny returned. Alice looked concerned at Midge's appearance, but avoided asking whether she was feeling all right. "Ah, my dear, there you are! Have you had breakfast?"

"All I want, thank you," replied Midge jesuitically. She knew that her aunt would fuss if she skipped breakfast, but she was in no mood for food.

Jenny grinned conspiratorially, but maintained a tactful silence. Midge, who had something of a turn for natural history, had once explained to her how lizards were sluggish and unable to digest food until they had warmed up their body temperature by basking in the sun. Midge claimed to be similarly cold-blooded and Jenny had often happily swiped Midge's bacon at school. Clearly, a term at university had done little to change her friend's attitude to morning activity.

Meanwhile, Midge had had time to take in Jenny's appearance. Although the fledgling lawyer was now much more suitably attired for the country, Midge felt shabby beside her as she noted the elegant coral twin set and the lustrous black pearls hanging round Jenny's pale neck like a string of glistening grapes.

Jenny's hand went up to touch her pearls, mildly embarrassed by Midge's attention.

"Admiring my beads?" she murmured. "Daddy said that it was about time that I had them; they were Mother's and I don't think that he's trusted me to look after them properly before."

Midge flushed. Jenny's mother had died shortly after Jenny's birth; how dreadful to have been coveting something which must bring Jenny pain as well as pleasure.

"What's the plan for this morning?" she demanded, eager to change the subject. "Is there anything you had in mind?"

Midge often rested after lunch and Jenny was sure that she would want to that afternoon – particularly since they had all been invited out to dinner in the evening. Hence Jenny was ready with an excuse to let her friend rest. "I hope you don't mind, but John said he'd take me out riding this afternoon."

"Of course I don't mind," Midge replied. "It'd be a shame if you didn't get out on such a nice day."

"In the meantime, can you help me to choose what to wear this evening? I don't know how cold the house will be, or how much people dress up or anything."

Midge nodded and, after checking that Mrs Carrington

did not need them, the two girls made their way upstairs to Jenny's room.

Ruthlessly grabbing a row of hangers from the wardrobe, Jenny spread the selection out on the bed. Midge's eyes widened. A year in London with what must clearly be a substantial allowance had certainly enabled Jenny to indulge herself. Thrusting aside the teal green marocain which she had worn the previous night, Jenny held up a glittering silver lamé dress which dropped straight as a column down to the floor.

"What do you think of this?" she demanded.

"It's hardly fitting for a dull law student," giggled Midge as Jenny twirled the dress round. "Apart from those cross-over straps, there's hardly a back at all."

"Backs, my dear," observed Jenny, "are OUT!"

"Possibly, but you'll freeze if you wear that. Anyway, it looks more like a dance frock than a dinner dress."

"I thought you'd say that," mourned Jenny, "but it's brand new and I'm dying to wear it. However, I asked for guidance and never let it be said I rejected your thoughtful words. What about this one?"

"Flame red," commented Midge. "The dining-room at the manor is a Victorian masterpiece. Plum curtains, maroon Turkey carpet and red velvet chairs to go with the mahogany table."

"Does it have still lifes on the wall too?" enquired Jenny. "Now do you see why I wanted your advice? Something warned me when I was packing to make sure that I had a decent selection to choose from. Pity, because I rather fancy myself in that one."

While Jenny had been peacocking in front of the mirror, Midge had been rummaging among the litter of frocks on the bed.

"Oooh," she sighed with envy as she picked up a jade-green shantung silk of classic, almost severe, cut. "What gorgeous fabric!"

"Try it on," urged Jenny, "we're pretty much the same size."

Midge shook her head vehemently, "No, I'd look silly."

"You wouldn't; you'd knock everyone's eyes out."

"No. It's very kind of you, but I'd rather not."

Jenny repressed a sigh. She knew that Midge was very sensitive about her appearance, but she thought that her friend followed the wrong approach. Rather than trying to hide herself away in dark colours in the hope that her withered leg would thus become less noticeable, Jenny believed that Midge ought to sparkle like a diamond. People's eyes would not linger on her leg and her sticks if there was a dress and jewellery to distract them.

"Shall I be traditional tonight?" asked Jenny, turning the subject back to her choice of dress. "Which do you think – black velvet or midnight blue satin?"

"My aunt will be in velvet," commented Midge. "Show me the satin."

Jenny held the dress up against her body, letting the fabric fall down to her ankles.

"Traditional, but beautifully cut," Midge remarked. "I like the way it hangs in slight folds at the hem."

"Just as well, it cost me – or, rather, Daddy – a ridiculous amount. But as I said to him, if James takes me out one night, and Ronald demands the favour two nights later, and Dickie from the next door chambers asks me to come dancing on Friday evening, then a girl needs to have more than one evening frock."

Midge giggled. "Your father is very indulgent. I can't imagine my uncle stumping up like that, even if I had the nerve to ask him."

"Nerve can get one a long way," remarked Jenny with a smirk. "Look at me!"

"I am," agreed Midge. "And what I want to know is,

which of these boys do you like best?"

Jenny cocked her head to one side and began to enumerate their merits. "James makes me laugh, Ronald can always find a taxi and Dickie dances like a dream, better than anyone I know."

"Is it so important that they can dance well?" asked Midge, with a twinge of bitterness.

"My dear chump, if Dickie were the right man for me, it wouldn't matter if he had two left feet or no feet at all. The point is that he isn't, nor is Ronald, nor anybody else, but there's nothing to stop me enjoying their company until I choose to settle down. And think how useful it will be if my first case is against one of them. Instead of being petrified that I am drawn against a ferociously effective campaigner, I'll know that I'm only facing James who blenches every time he thinks my father is going to ask him a question about the law of criminal libel."

"Does your father do that to all of his pupils?" enquired Midge, wondering whether this was similar to her supervisor's disconcerting habit of introducing questions of Greek history into the middle of a Latin supervision.

"Not exactly," admitted Jenny. "James is qualified, but he once made a complete hash of examining a witness and Daddy wants to ensure that he never gets it wrong again. I'm terrified that he'll find out how little I know about torts because then I'll face a grilling every breakfast until I can pass muster." She cast a glance at her friend. "Have you met anyone you like in Cambridge?"

Midge blushed. "No."

Jenny regarded Midge thoughtfully. Over the last year, John's name had cropped up in Midge's letters and conversation more than was strictly necessary, and Jenny had a strong suspicion than Midge had fallen for him. It wasn't particularly surprising – tall, good-looking John would be a catch for any girl. But it was unclear how he felt about Midge. Jenny sighed. She didn't know whether to be jealous that Midge had someone she was keen on, or whether to be grateful that, at the moment, she did not have to cope with such complications herself.

The rest of the morning passed in luxurious idleness.

"I wish this sort of moment could last forever," sighed Jenny, as she stretched out lazily in front of a crackling fire, admiring the shape of Bertie's paws. "Nothing to do apart from enjoy myself."

Midge laughed. "You looked as if you were going to fall asleep a few minutes ago; are you saving up all your energy for riding?"

"Are you sure you don't want to be a barrister, Midge? You could invent such splendid excuses for pleas of mitigation."

"It's all the practice I had at school explaining why we were so bad."

Jenny grinned. "I'm glad I enjoyed a giddy youth – it makes Daddy so much more appreciative of my solemn, steady industriousness now."

At luncheon, Jenny was in the middle of a deep discussion with Mrs Carrington about whether hemlines were going to fall in spring when the tinkle of the telephone interrupted the conversation.

"Who on earth could be ringing at this time?" demanded Alice, exasperated. "If it's the butcher, I shall be furious; I gave him perfectly clear instructions about tonight's joint."

"Don't worry, Mother," replied John as he rose from the table. "I'll deal with it." Thirty seconds later, he returned to the dining room in some surprise.

"Jenny, there is someone called Ronald Thornley who wants to speak to you; apparently it's very urgent."

Looking perplexed, Jenny hurried out into the hall.

When she re-entered the dining-room five minutes later, she swallowed hard, before stammering, "My father. He... he..."

"My dear child," began Mrs Carrington, sure that Jenny had received the worst possibly news.

"There's been a murder," Jenny continued abruptly. Then she added in a voice of complete disbelief, "The police suspect that Daddy may be involved."

"Suspect?" repeated Midge breathlessly. "Do you mean he has been arrested?"

Jenny nodded. "Please, Mrs Carrington, would you mind if I went to my room and packed? I must return and see what I can do."

"Of course you must," urged Alice. "Would you like one of us to come with you? I don't like the idea of you being alone in that barrack of a house."

"I suppose the servants will still be there," remarked Jenny somewhat shakily. Then she turned to Midge appealingly. "Midge, would you come? I know you have work you need to do and there's Bertie, but…" Her voice tailed off.

"Don't be silly, of course I'll come! Just give me time to grab some clothes."

Meanwhile, John had been looking at a Bradshaw. "If you girls can be ready in half an hour, I ought to be able to get you to the station in time to catch an express."

Sitting, surrounded by suitcases, in an otherwise empty first-class compartment an hour later, the two girls stared at each other as the express thundered nearer and nearer towards London.

"I still don't understand why the police have arrested Daddy just because a client of his has died," stated Jenny in bafflement. "Ronald couldn't say much over the telephone, but he was explicit that the police are charging Daddy with murder. Just because Daddy had a meeting with the client earlier in the day, why does that mean that Daddy is involved?" Her face took on a determined expression. "Immediately we get home, I'm going to chambers to find out what's happening, and then I'm going to visit Daddy. You do think that I'll be allowed to see him?"

"I don't know," responded Midge, "But John told me to warn you not to dress too smartly when you do."

"Does John think that I would care whether I get my clothes dirty or not when my father's being held in some foul gaol?" demanded Jenny, with a suspicion of tears in her voice.

"Of course not," reassured Midge. "What he meant was that the police will take less notice of you if you are dressed soberly and discreetly. You don't want to put the inspector in charge of the case on guard."

"Sorry," replied Jenny. "Actually, that's pretty bright of John. I hadn't thought about talking to the police. If they think that I'm meek and mild and harmless they may let something slip."

"Exactly," Midge agreed, hoping that this idea might bring some comfort to her ashen-faced friend. For her own part, she wondered what Jenny could possibly do to help her father now that he was enmeshed in the net of the Law.

II

Andante poco accelerando

Chapter Six

Jenny's natural desire to rush off to see her father immediately was frustrated by several factors. First, Mrs Field, the housekeeper, wanted to pour out her woes to Jenny and then, when Jenny had finally pacified her, Midge persuaded Jenny to change into something less noticeable than a coral jumper and a tweed skirt with orange and green flecks. When they finally set off through the teeming streets towards Middle Temple, Jenny kept twisting round and glancing out of the back of the taxi-cab in which they were travelling.

"What's up?" hissed Midge, concerned as to her friend's behaviour.

"I've got this ridiculous feeling that we're being followed," whispered Jenny. "Do you see that grey Austin Seven, three cars behind us? I'm sure it was parked near the house when we left. Do you think that it's a police car?"

"It doesn't look much like one. Perhaps it's a reporter."

Jenny groaned. "Oh glory, I'd forgotten about them." She leant forward and gave the taxi-driver some new instructions, before explaining her change of plan to Midge. "We're going in through the neighbouring chambers. It's got a back exit which links into our chambers. We might manage to get in unnoticed."

Midge removed the silk scarf which she was wearing. "Tie that round your hair and put your hat on top."

Jenny looked with disfavour at the scarf. "What a beastly combination the two'll make," she remarked, "but

37

you're quite correct, it may help to disguise my yellow mop."

"If you'd like, I'll go round the front and try to distract any reporters."

"That's very decent of you," replied Jenny, touched by Midge's offer. She knew that the last thing which Midge would want was to appear in the newspapers as a mystery female visiting the chambers of the chief suspect. "Let's see whether we can get in unobserved and we'll worry about alternatives later."

As the taxi swept past the crowded front of the chambers of Patrick Fletcher, K.C., and on to the deserted entrance of the next set of chambers, it was clear that Jenny's strategy had been successful. Slipping into the gloomy doorway with its painted list of the residents, Jenny led Midge along the passageway, down an uneven flight of steps and through another archway into a stone-flagged court.

"This way," urged Jenny, hurrying to the right and into another dull, badly-lit hallway.

Breathing heavily, Midge followed her friend. "Run on ahead," she hissed, "they won't take any notice of me if they see me on the staircase, but they might recognise you."

Feeling guilty at abandoning Midge, Jenny took her advice, flitting along the passageway like a wraith, before racing up the stairwell. Following as fast as she could, Midge paused before lunging at the stairs. She could hear noisy remarks from the reporters clustered by the entrance, but although the office-boy standing guard gaped at her as she went past, Midge toiled upstairs to where Jenny was waiting unnoticed by the reporters.

"Miss Fletcher, thank goodness you have come," exclaimed a middle-aged man with grizzled hair. "We had no idea at first where you were."

"This is my friend, Miss Carrington," explained Jenny, before turning to Midge, "and this is Mr Thomson, Daddy's clerk."

After greetings were exchanged, Jenny turned towards a tall oak door.

"Wait," cautioned Thomson. "The police are still searching through your father's papers. We must talk in another room – shall we go to mine?"

Jenny blenched at this piece of information, before leading the way across the dark corridor to another panelled door.

"Let's use Ronald's room – I'd rather not risk being spotted by journalists."

Ronald Thornley, a tall, cadaverous man with a lopsided smile, rose to greet Jenny as she entered.

"You've made good time," he commented. He hauled out a chair for Midge and perched himself on the desk to make more space in the crowded room. Midge glanced round with interest. Heavy bookcases lined three walls, crammed with law reports. She could just make out the titles of some of them. What did King's Bench mean? And what did the Admiralty Division handle? It was hard to imagine colourful, flippant Jenny inhabiting this gloomy room and poring over tomes like the one open on Ronald's desk. Midge shrugged. If it came to that, most people would find her taste for Greek history strange.

After introducing Midge, Jenny demanded to know what had happened.

Thomson took up the tale.

"Yesterday, William Forrest, a solicitor from Forrest and Creech, saw your father by appointment. They were together for nearly an hour, during which time tea was brought to them. Later that evening, Forrest was found dead in his office at Duke's Buildings in Holborn. He appears to have been poisoned. Forrest's confidential clerk said that Forrest returned to Duke's Buildings directly from visiting your father. The police inference is that whatever poisoned him must have been in the tea which he may have drunk here."

"But why do they suspect my father? Surely this Forrest may have had enemies? How do we know that he didn't take the poison himself?"

"Exactly what we asked," remarked Ronald. "The police aren't yet disclosing what the poison was, but I don't see how they can be so certain that whatever it was had to be taken here."

"Forrest," mused Jenny. "Forrest and Creech. Where have I heard that name before?"

Ronald looked uncomfortable. "I'm afraid that's one of the points that the police inspector made. Forrest and Creech are a rather shifty outfit in the City with an insalubrious name. Nothing actually illegal, but about as close to the bone in terms of legality as you can go without actually being struck off. Inspector Groves made a great deal about a man of your father's standing dealing with a firm like Forrest and Creech."

"Why?" demanded Jenny impatiently. "Surely Daddy had a good reason. After all, every barrister meets dubious specimens in the course of his work; I can't see why it is so important."

"Perhaps not," agreed Ronald. "However, the really damaging point is that, according to Forrest's clerk, Forrest said that he'd had a row with your father and that your father had sworn to get even with him."

"If Daddy were going to murder someone, why would he be so stupid as to threaten him and leave him alive for long enough to go running around telling everyone?"

"Groves didn't discuss that," replied Ronald.

"Had my father mentioned this man to you?" asked Jenny, looking distinctly worried.

"No, Miss Jenny," replied Thomson, unconsciously slipping into the mode of address which he had used when Jenny had been a schoolgirl, visiting her father in chambers. "The police inspector questioned me about it and demanded to see all of our appointment books for the last two years."

"It's all utterly frightful," declared Ronald, with one eye on Jenny's white face, "but I don't think that Inspector Groves is going to change his mind."

"Surely the case is a bit weak?" queried Midge rather hesitantly. "I mean, if this man had died here, the connection to Mr Fletcher would be stronger."

Ronald scowled gloomily. "The trouble is, Groves hasn't revealed the whole case yet. All we know is that he's got some reason for suspecting Fletcher other than the fact that Forrest drank tea here. I don't know whether the police found some incriminating documents at Forrest's offices, but they've been going through everything they can lay their hands on here."

"I don't believe that there could possibly be anything incriminating," stated Jenny flatly. "Are you suggesting that my father is a criminal and a murderer?"

"Of course not," Ronald returned hastily. "But we have to face facts; there must be some evidence which has led Groves to arrest your father. We may be able to believe in your father's innocence because we know his character, but a jury won't."

This blunt assessment of the situation rather took Midge's breath away and she glanced at Jenny in concern. Her friend's head drooped momentarily and Midge thought that she saw the gleam of tears in her eyes. Then Jenny raised her head proudly, like a warhorse scenting battle. "In that case, we must find out what this so-called evidence is and disprove it."

While Thomson returned to keep an eye on the policemen currently searching Patrick Fletcher's room, Ronald summoned James Parry, the other junior barrister, in to join them. With his slick dark hair and his matinee idol good looks, Midge could see why Jenny enjoyed going out to dinner with James. Any girl would enjoy the admiring glances which such a handsome couple would attract, and Jenny had said that he was witty as well. Midge grimaced. Right now, what Jenny needed was people who were kind, rather than good-looking. Ronald seemed pretty supportive so far, as did Thomson. Would James be equally helpful?

Jenny glanced at her gold wrist-watch. "When do you think that I can go and see Daddy?"

"They're probably still questioning him," pointed out James. "I'll get Thomson to find out and then one of us can run you over to wherever they're holding him."

Jenny's face tightened, before she forced herself to concentrate on what Ronald was saying. Drawing up a piece of paper, he began to make notes.

"This Forrest chap had an appointment at three o'clock. Thomson says that he was five minutes late, but that he stayed until nearly four. Thomson's sure of the time because Major Rowland was due at four and Thomson wanted to get your father to sign something in order that it could be taken round to Arbuthnot and Smythe before the end of business. Major Rowland is a stickler for punctuality and Thomson only just had enough time to get your father's signature before the Major turned up."

"Did Forrest go off the premises?" demanded Jenny.

"One of the secretaries saw him leave," James stated. "I don't think that he could have returned without being noticed. And, in any case, if he was back in his office before five o'clock, he wouldn't have time to lurk round here."

42

"As regards the tea," Midge began thoughtfully, "what evidence is there that he drank it?"

"Miss Ellis, the junior typist, brought some in around three thirty and poured it. She removed the tray when Forrest left and, I'm afraid, washed everything up."

"Did she see anything odd about the tea-cups?" asked Jenny fearfully.

"No," reassured James. "I asked her immediately after she'd been quizzed by the inspector. She's a bit imaginative, and I wouldn't put it past her to invest perfectly ordinary sugar particles with some fateful significance, but she swore that there was nothing in the least bit odd about the cups. Apparently Groves offended her by questioning her as to why had she washed the tea things up immediately. She told him that he might leave dirty cups lying around his house, but that wasn't how she'd been brought up and she wasn't about to start bringing slum habits into this building, which anyone but a common policeman could see was a gentleman's chambers."

James' mimicry brought a brief flicker of a smile to Ronald's face before he remarked soberly, "It's negative evidence, but it might help to sow doubt. The trouble is we still don't know what sort of poison was used. It might not be one that leaves a sediment."

"So much for the teacups," commented Midge. "Do we know whether Forrest left on foot or by taxi?"

Ronald shook his head. "No, I'm afraid not. However, we know that he left here at four and, according to his clerk, he was back in his Holborn office in Romberg Street before five. He may well have walked if it took him forty or fifty minutes to get back."

"What's to prevent him having stopped for a drink on the way and being poisoned at that point?" Midge demanded.

43

"Nothing," agreed Ronald slowly. "I suppose the police will question all the publicans along his supposed route to see whether he did go in for a drink."

"Maybe he did," suggested Jenny hopefully. "He must have been walking frightfully slowly if it took him fifty minutes to get from here to Holborn."

"The police will suggest that that is evidence for Forrest starting to feel ill," pointed out James. "Our best hope is if they discover a publican who saw him."

"I don't think that we should rely on the police," stated Jenny determinedly. "They think that they got their man already. Why should they bother checking pubs for evidence which will disprove their case?"

"Do you mean that we ought to turn ourselves into private detectives and investigate things ourselves?" questioned Ronald in some surprise.

"Yes. Why not?" retorted Jenny. "At least we'll *want* to find new evidence. And there's lots that we can do easily enough. You and James can question barmaids and check up how long it takes to walk to Duke's Buildings.

"And you?" asked Ronald, with a slight touch of sarcasm. He did not fancy himself as an undercover investigator, suspecting that the role hid an inordinate number of possibilities for embarrassment.

Jenny cast around for something which she could do. "I'm going to make sure that Miss Ellis has not left out anything important. Midge can come with me."

True to her word, Jenny's first action when leaving the conference was to hurry to the typists' room. Miss Jenkins, the elder typist, greeted Midge politely, before clucking over Jenny sympathetically.

"My dear, such dreadful news! I could never have believed it when that police inspector marched in here, demanding to see your father. And, would you believe it, his sergeant even interrogated poor Ethel for an hour!"

Jenny turned to the junior typist. "How ghastly for you, Miss Ellis. I do hope that he was polite."

Ethel sniffed. Naturally, she was sorry for Mr Fletcher, who was always punctiliously courteous to her, although – in her view – frighteningly austere. However, she often felt rather unimportant compared with the clerks and barristers, and she was determined to extract the greatest possible amount of enjoyment from the attention which was now focussed on her. Why, Charlie the office-boy had actually offered to run an errand for her at lunchtime, rather than grumbling as he normally did.

"I couldn't answer for a policeman's manners, never having had one in the family, but if he thought that he could ride rough-shod over a girl I soon showed him his error."

"Good for you," remarked Jenny.

"Well then," continued Ethel, "we established who I was, and where I lived, and how old I am – which to my way of thinking is a cheek to be asking. I mean, what difference does it make to my evidence whether I'm twenty or sixty?"

"Quite," interrupted Miss Jenkins, feeling that Ethel was exhibiting rather too much enthusiasm and needed to be brought down to earth. "Neither of us is going to see twenty again, so we are clearly old enough to make sensible statements."

"I thought that it wouldn't help poor Mr Fletcher," remarked Ethel, underlining her loyalty to chambers, "if I were to worry about my own feelings, so I tried to ignore the inspector's manner and answer his questions."

"How very decent of you," replied Jenny, wondering if she were overdoing the best butter. "What did he want to know?"

Ethel who, for all her foibles, was not a stupid girl,

45

decided to speed up her tale. "He wanted to know who asked for the tea; who made it; who brought it; who removed it; and what was done with the cups."

"Pretty comprehensive," Jenny noted.

"And then his sergeant confiscated all of the tea, the tea-pots and the rest of the crockery," complained Miss Jenkins bitterly. "He told us that if we wanted tea we could borrow things from next door. As if we would with that nosy parker in their chambers, busy telling everyone's business to anyone who is prepared to listen to her."

Jenny looked blank.

"I'm sorry, Miss Fletcher," apologised Miss Jenkins. "You wouldn't know about Miss Burnham; she came as a temporary typist in October and, if Sir Eustace Leadbetter's head clerk had any sense, he'd've let her go at the end of the month. But he thinks that he knows better than the head typist and he's insisted on keeping her. And he a married man with five children!"

Midge, who was watching from the sidelines, deduced from this somewhat abstruse statement that the temporary typist was presumably pretty. She made a mental note to suggest to Jenny that Ronald or James might be asked to take the talkative Miss Burnham out and try to discover whether she knew anything useful.

"We certainly can't do without tea," agreed Jenny, "so, please, do use some of the petty cash to buy what we need. You normally make the tea, don't you, Miss Ellis?"

"Yes," agreed Ethel. She could never decide whether it was a menial task or a handy break from her labours. After all, it did get you noticed by the younger members of chambers; Mr Parry was always chaffing her. "And I made it yesterday, same as usual. Mr Thomson came in here and said that Mr Fletcher wanted tea. I brought it in to him and left it there."

"What time was this?"

"Just after half past; I thought it was maybe a bit earlier, but Miss Jenkins reminded me that we commented on the fact that the new kettle has such a loud whistle that it nearly drowned out the bell from the church."

"Was Miss Jenkins in the pantry with you?"

"No. I slipped back in here to finish some urgent typing while the kettle boiled." Ethel scowled. "That sergeant seemed to think I shouldn't have left the tray for an instant, but there was no-one near the pantry, either before I filled the kettle or when I made the tea."

"Did you pour out the tea when you took the tray in?" Jenny enquired, hoping that Ethel had.

Ethel shook her head. "I just laid it on the table and went out."

Jenny sighed. If the typist had poured the tea and passed the cup to Forrest, then her father could not be accused of having adding poison to it or deliberately choosing a cup which did not have poison in it.

"The inspector kept on and on about that," added Ethel. "He even made me show me where I'd laid it down. Then he asked whether Mr Fletcher had said anything and whether he looked his usual self. So I told him that, being a gentleman, Mr Fletcher had said 'Thank you, Miss Ellis,' and that he looked exactly like himself. Mind you, that's more than could be said of his visitor."

Jenny sat rigidly, while Miss Jenkins, who had not heard this piece of information previously, demanded to know more.

"What do you mean, Miss Ellis? You haven't mentioned that before."

"Well, I've only just remembered it," replied Ethel sulkily. "What with the shock of Mr Fletcher being arrested, and then being questioned until I didn't know whether it was night or day, I hadn't thought about that Forrest."

Swallowing nervously, Jenny slipped in a question before Miss Jenkins could tell Ethel off. "What did this man look like?" she enquired gently.

"Like he'd seen a ghost," returned Ethel. "I remembered thinking to myself, 'Well, you haven't just been told about a legacy from a long-lost uncle in Australia. More like that all the money's been left to a cats' home and probably better use they'd make of it, too, than you, you great mannerless thing!'"

Although fascinated by this insight into what the typists might think of the eminent and not-so-eminent clients who came through the doors of her father's chambers, Jenny managed to keep to the point. Ignoring the fact that barristers did not deal with legacies, she asked, "Why do you call Mr Forrest mannerless?"

Ethel blushed. "Sorry, Miss Fletcher, I got a bit carried away; I shouldn't have said that."

"No, no, please tell me why you thought it."

"He was very abrupt and offhand when he came in. He behaved as if it were my fault he was late. And he glared at me when I brought in the tea."

Jenny pondered this information. Clearly her father had said something to upset Forrest. Was this evidence in her father's favour – or further evidence against him?

"Can any of you remember what sort of mood Mr Forrest was in when he made the appointment?"

The two typists exchanged glances. In view of her seniority, Miss Jenkins spoke up. "Mr Forrest didn't make the appointment, I'm afraid, Miss Fletcher; your father did."

"*Daddy* made the appointment?" exclaimed Jenny, startled. "But he never makes appointments for people; they have to go through Thomson."

"Nevertheless," stated Miss Jenkins, "Mr Forrest's appointment was written in your father's appointment book in your father's handwriting, and neither we nor Mr Thomson remember having anything to do with making that appointment."

"The police have taken the book away with them," added Miss Ellis gloomily. "They don't seem to consider that we need that book to…". Her voice tailed off as she realised that telling her employer's daughter that his clients had to be informed that he was in gaol and would be unable to see them was hardly tactful.

Chapter Seven

Although Miss Jenkins had volunteered to stay on at the office to keep Jenny company, Jenny had turned down her offer. The office staff had already stayed past their usual hour and, while grateful for their loyalty, she did not want to delay them any further. James Parry had gone to Lincoln's Inn in the hope of speaking to Fletcher's solicitor, and Thomson had refused to leave until he had heard more news. Jenny left Thomson prowling round the entrance, while she and Midge retreated to the tiny room which she shared with Ronald. Ronald was working on a brief for Roderick Staunton, one of the senior barristers in the chambers, but he pushed it away with a sigh.

"I'll be glad when I get some more briefs of my own, rather than constantly devilling for Staunton."

"You'll probably pick up a few of my father's clients," commented Jenny, before adding gloomily, "unless they decide to shift chambers altogether."

"It's a bit early to be thinking like that," urged Ronald, fearing that Jenny was probably correct, but not wishing to depress her spirits still further. "What did you find out from La Ellis?"

Jenny frowned. "Quite a lot, but I'm not sure how useful it is. Nor am I sure whether we ought to tell the police what Miss Ellis observed." She proceeded to outline Ethel's information.

"There's no reason for us to tell the police," averred Ronald. "Ten to one they'd use it against your father and it's not as if it's a concrete fact – for all we know, Ethel could have been imagining Forrest's expression because she took a dislike to him. We're not keeping a witness up our sleeve – Groves had the chance to question her."

"If only Miss Ellis had poured out the tea!" groaned Jenny. "Then there could be no possibility that Daddy added poison to it."

Ronald disagreed. "The police could still claim that Mr Fletcher poisoned Forrest when refilling the cup or something like that. Or the poison could be in the milk or sugar. That's why the police have taken everything away to be tested in a laboratory for traces of poison."

Midge interrupted rather hesitantly. "If they do find traces, presumably it won't be in the tea-caddy. After all, if it were full of poisoned tea, then your father would have been poisoned too. So that leaves two possibilities. Either the poison was in the milk or sugar, or it was added to the tea in your father's room. If it were in the tea then Forrest must have added it himself, because clearly your father didn't put it there. And if the poison were in the milk or sugar then someone else in chambers added it."

"You're quite right, Miss Carrington," began Ronald, before being urged by Midge to call her by her first name. "Logically, if Forrest was poisoned, he must have taken poison either here or elsewhere. If the poison was administered here, then any of us might have done it."

"But why?" asked Jenny in perplexity.

"I've no idea," replied Ronald, "but I don't think that we can afford to neglect any possibilities." He gave a twisted grin. "You're the only one who is definitely innocent because you were away in Suffolk and couldn't possibly have been tampering with milk or sugar."

Jenny looked green as the realisation struck that Ronald, or Thomson or Miss Jenkins might be a cunning, ruthless murderer. The idea seemed only marginally less ludicrous than the idea that her father was one.

"It seems to me," commented Midge robustly, "that the sooner we get some actual facts the better. When are the police likely to find out where the poison was?"

"It could take days," Ronald explained. "And don't forget that while tests may clear the tea-caddy, the milk-bottle and the bag of sugar, since La Ellis washed everything up so efficiently, the actual tea-pot, milk-jug and sugar-basin which were used on the tray cannot be tested."

"Maybe she's the murderer!" declared Midge hopefully.

"Why?" enquired Ronald with interest. He found the junior typist irritatingly lively, but had never before entertained thoughts of her possible homicidal tendencies.

"Forrest had dallied with her sister and betrayed her; he had embezzled her mother's life savings; he lied in court and sent her brother to gaol," suggested Midge rapidly, before sighing. "We're going to have to know an awful lot more about Forrest before we can supply motives."

"Why would anyone here want to kill a complete stranger?" persisted Jenny.

"Don't forget that the crime doesn't have to have been committed here," Midge pointed out. "And even if it were, someone might have broken into the office and added poison to the sugar."

"Given there are so many possibilities," suggested Ronald, "let's start by working out where the poison might have been and who might have had access to it."

"The little pantry off the typists' room is hardly the Bank of England," remarked Jenny gloomily. "Anyone in the building could have had access to it."

"Agreed, but it would be pretty odd if anyone had seen Roderick Staunton, for example, hanging around the tea caddy."

The picture of the pompous and overweight barrister lowering his dignity sufficiently to make his own tea raised a slight smile from Jenny.

"Since your father had tea as well as Forrest, it's most likely that the poison was in the sugar," guessed Ronald. "La Ellis confirmed that both cups had been used and both had taken milk, but your father doesn't take sugar in his tea, does he?"

"No," confirmed Jenny. "But Miss Ellis said that she tipped the unused sugar back into the bag before she washed up the sugar-basin. Surely if the police find poison in the sugar it won't be possible to tell whether it was in the basin or in the bag?"

"'She says'," repeated Ronald. "That's the problem, isn't it? We don't know whether we can trust anyone's evidence."

"If all the poison were found at the top of the bag that might make it more likely that someone added poison to the sugar-basin and Miss Ellis had poured it back into the bag," suggested Midge. "After all, if it were added to the bag they could have no idea who might use it."

"Especially with Charlie around," agreed Jenny. She turned to Midge. "Charlie's our office-boy. He's always drinking tea, and he takes about three spoonfuls in every cup. If you wanted to poison off a visitor, you'd be running a distinct risk of poisoning Charlie as well."

"A homicidal maniac in chambers," groaned Ronald. "That'd be all we need!"

"Moreover," commented Jenny enthusiastically, "most people know that my father hates having sugar in his tea. So if someone wanted to poison off Forrest, it would be a worthwhile risk. Miss Ellis said herself that she left the tray for a few minutes. Anyone could have slipped something into the sugar."

"Half-three," mused Ronald. "That would definitely let Charlie out. He was delivering papers and Thomson was annoyed because he returned late. I think it would let me and Parry out, too. He came in to ask me something about Statute Law and stayed for around twenty minutes. I know it was just after quarter past when he came in because he made some joke about having five bob on Kent Lad in the three fifteen and wishing he was there to see it run."

"Did you check the time?" demanded Midge.

53

Ronald's eyebrows shot up, before he nodded thoughtfully. "You're right; I suppose I oughtn't to take anyone's word for anything. However, Parry had dug up a most interesting point about the 1911 Act." His eyes glistened momentarily. "It must have taken us at least twenty minutes to decide the answer, and I know for certain that he went back to his room at twenty to. I still had to finish something off for Staunton and I wanted to get away early last night, so I glanced at my watch to see how much time I had left."

He scratched his head meditatively before concluding, "Of course, I could be lying, and we might be wrong about poison being added to something on the tea-tray, but I don't see what else we can work on at the moment."

"No," murmured Jenny, "I don't either."

It was at that point that James Parry returned. Normally debonair and cool, he was looking distinctly harassed, with an unaccustomed frown on his face.

"Thomson said that you were in here," he remarked as he hurried across to Jenny. "I managed to speak to Cottrell's clerk." He turned to Midge politely, "Cottrell is Mr Fletcher's solicitor."

"What did he say?" Jenny demanded.

"Your father wants to retain Sir Everard Denys. Denys has agreed."

"Good," commented Jenny. She had seen Sir Everard in action in court and had a high opinion of his ability. If the case did come to trial she wanted to have a really good advocate on their side.

"Where is Cottrell?" asked Ronald. "I thought that he was going to come here."

"He's still at Scotland Yard," explained James. "Apparently he intends to stay there until Groves finishes his questions." He turned apologetically to Jenny. "I'm afraid it doesn't look as if you'll be able to see your father before tomorrow." He paused, not looking forward to adding the next piece of information. "After the police have finished questioning him tonight, it seems that he will be charged, then transferred to Wandsworth prison and held there."

Determined to preserve a brave front, Jenny nodded her understanding of this news, before asking in a voice which only shook slightly, "But you think that I'll be able to see him tomorrow?"

"Yes," agreed James, hoping fervently that there would be no last-minute change of plan. "Now, if you'll excuse me, I need to go and see Staunton. He left orders for me to report to him when I returned, but I thought that I'd slip up here first."

Ronald grimaced. "Staunton's very much the acting-head of chambers, isn't he?" As Parry left the room, he turned to Jenny. "Do you want to wait here to see Cottrell, or shall I run you both home?"

"I should prefer to wait," replied Jenny, feeling that she would go mad if she were to return without having heard the most up-to-date news.

The next two hours were a dreadful strain. Ronald busied himself with his neglected paperwork. Jenny, after talking further with Thomson, persuaded the clerk to go home, and attempted to contact her brother Mike. Since the regimental adjutant told her that Lt Fletcher was on manoeuvres in Wales and currently uncontactable, Jenny was forced to rely upon a plea that Mike be asked to telephone her as soon as he received her message. As she put down the telephone, she turned angrily to Midge.

"I don't know why I bothered to hide up what's happened. It will be all over the papers tomorrow and Mike will probably see them before he gets my message."

Midge remembered what Jenny had said about her

other brother being in Alexandria. "Do you have any means of contacting Tom?"

Jenny shook her head. "I don't even know where he's been sent."

"Your father will know. Or Mike will – he won't stay in Wales for ever."

Jenny and Midge then retreated to James' room where the three of them kept going over and over what little information they had. James smoked one cigarette after another, while Jenny paced around the confines of the tiny room like a caged leopard which could scent baboons out of reach on the other side of the fence. When Hubert Cottrell finally arrived, Jenny looked sheet white with exhaustion.

"My dear child," ejaculated Cottrell, "you should be at home, not here!"

"I wanted to hear everything as quickly as possibly," answered Jenny, unwilling to explain that she shunned returning to the family house, suddenly alien without the reassuring presence of her father.

"In that case," Cottrell replied, "if I may usurp Parry's room, I shall tell you exactly what I know."

"Do you mind if Miss Carrington stays with me?"

"I'm afraid that is impossible." Cottrell bowed in Midge's direction. "I hope you will understand that it would be something of a breach of trust for me to discuss matters of such gravity with someone who is not a member of the family."

"Daddy wouldn't mind. He knows Midge well."

Midge could see that the solicitor was not going to give way. "Don't fret, Jenny. I'll be fine. Concentrate on what you need to find out."

Jenny yielded and Midge and James left. When they were out of earshot, James apologised to Midge.

"Don't worry about what Cottrell said. He's very

punctilious about professional matters."

"I quite understand. It's just like doctors not talking about their patients."

James looked relieved at this evidence of comprehension from a non-legal mind. "I didn't want you to think that Cottrell was being unfriendly."

"Everyone's got quite enough to worry about without my taking offence over things." Midge eyed James speculatively. He certainly seemed to be sorry for Jenny, and, to judge from her comments in Suffolk, Jenny obviously liked James. Would that encourage him to tell her a few things? It was worth the attempt. "I say, James, do the police normally arrest people quite so soon after a murder?"

The barrister shrugged. "It depends upon the circumstances. As I said, they must have more evidence than just the alleged quarrel."

"But Mr Fletcher's a member of the legal profession. Wouldn't that make them a lot more careful?"

"Potentially." James glanced at Midge. "Look here, I know you want to support Jenny, but for goodness sake don't let her run away with the idea that this will get suddenly resolved. It won't. I've heard of Groves. He's a decent, hard-working type. He certainly isn't the sort of man to arrest the first person he can lay his hands on – particularly not in a case of murder."

Midge swallowed. "That's what I was afraid of."

Nearly three quarter of an hour later, Jenny bid Cottrell goodbye and rejoined the others. The elderly solicitor had the gift of clear exposition, but his information had left Jenny despondent, particularly as he had confirmed that Mr Fletcher had been charged with wilful murder. Ronald looked at her expression and intervened before Jenny could say anything.

"I'm going to take you both home. You can fill us in tomorrow; what you need now is to have something to eat and then rest."

Jenny tried to argue, but James backed Ronald up.

"Your brain will be clearer tomorrow and we can plan what to do then."

"Very well," sighed Jenny, too tired to pursue a fruitless argument. "Cottrell has warned me that Inspector Groves wants to ask me some questions tomorrow morning, but he hopes that I shall be able to see Daddy later."

James smoothed his already-slick hair nervously.

"I say, you will be careful when Groves questions you, won't you?

"I'm supposed to be learning the law," muttered Jenny bitterly. "And I don't even know anything – I wish I did." She forced a smile. "Actually, I was hoping that if I look frightfully weak and defenceless, Groves might relax his guard and I might just pick up something useful."

"Crafty," approved James, well aware of the importance of appearances in the witness-box. Presumably the same considerations might apply during police questioning.

Ronald soon had the girls packed into a taxi. The three sat in silence as the taxi drove through the steady rain. Jenny stared out at the black pavements slick with moisture and the smoky yellow of the street lamps which cast their bold glow upon the pedestrians hurrying homeward. It was difficult to observe such normal, natural scenes and to realise that, for the rest of the world, life was following the regular path of events: work, supper, maybe an outing to the flicks. Whereas for her there was merely a murky black cavern of impossibility crammed upon impossibility. Impossible that her father was involved in any illegality; still more impossible that he would have resorted to violence to escape from the consequences of illegality. However, that was the crux of the police case against him. Jenny struggled hard to battle down a sense of deep panic as she recollected what Cottrell had said to her: "Do not think that this will be an easy case to defeat; the police appear to be very confident that they have got the right man."

When they reached Jenny's home, Ronald insisted on accompanying them up the short flight of stone steps to the door. Only after Field the butler had cautiously opened the door and had confirmed that there had been no further events which required immediate action did Ronald raise his hat and slip back to the waiting taxi.

Field looked grave when he ascertained that neither Jenny nor her friend had eaten. Too tired to argue, Jenny agreed to his suggestion of an *omelette aux fines herbes* and fresh rolls. When this duly arrived in the dining room, Field had taken it upon himself to bring two glasses of burgundy. Jenny had grimaced at the thought of carousing whilst her father lay in gaol, but Midge was relieved to see the wine bring a trace of colour to Jenny's cheeks. When the girls retreated to the comfort of the drawing room, Jenny curled up in a large chair by a brisk, roaring fire, looking particularly small and vulnerable. She fiddled with the tassel of a cushion, separating out the different strands of silken colour, before eventually bursting into speech.

"Cottrell's really worried. He tried to hide it, but he is. He warned me that the police have a good case." Staring into the dancing flames which devoured the coal in the grate as they leapt up towards the chimney, she steadied herself. "The thing is, they've got more evidence than the poison."

Midge attempted to reassure her. "We thought that they must have," she pointed out.

"Yes, but not anything as bad as this. Apparently, a

letter from Forrest arrived this morning at Scotland Yard accusing my father of attempting to extort money from him. It said that Daddy had threatened him with all sorts of things if he did not do as he demanded, and that Daddy had told Forrest that a complaint against Daddy would not be believed because Forrest's reputation stank, whereas Daddy often acted as a prosecutor for the Crown, so would be trusted by the authorities."

"What did your father say about the letter?" demanded Midge.

"He denied it absolutely. But, basically, it's Daddy's word against Forrest's. The police would probably believe Daddy if they were both alive, but Forrest is dead. Someone must be responsible, so they think that it was Daddy because he was in dispute with him."

"What was it about?" asked Midge curiously, before adding hastily, "Don't tell me if you'd rather not."

"Don't be silly; of course I'm going to. After all, I want your ideas on this as well as mine. What happened was this. There's an eminent German professor of law whom Daddy knows quite well. He's come to dinner several times, and he and Daddy have immensely learned, technical discussions about Roman law, the Edicts of Justinian and jurisprudence. In fact, they talk until all hours about anything. Well, Professor Schulmann is a Jewish refugee and, naturally, he's knows a number of other refugees. So when it came to his ears that one of those refugees had fallen foul of an extortioner, he wanted to ask Daddy's advice."

"Because your father is a lawyer?" suggested Midge intelligently.

"Not only that, but because some of those ghastly rags like *Action* keep saying that Jews club together and help each other at the expense of Englishmen. The Professor was worried that, if the case came to the attention of the newspapers, it might be weakened if he was obviously behind it. Can you imagine what it would be like if Maule Ramsay or Mosley were busily claiming that one filthy representative of the international conspiracy was helping another who had entered this country illegally?"

Midge noted with interest that Jenny's political awareness had become considerably heightened over the previous twelve months. However, she was still somewhat confused as to why exactly Mr Fletcher had become involved with Forrest.

"Do you mean that the Professor's friend had entered this country illegally?"

Jenny nodded. "Yes. Herr X was smuggled into this country and given false papers but, after he found a job, Forrest began to blackmail him. He said that, unless Herr X gave him half of his earnings, he would report him to the police and get him sent back to Germany."

Midge blenched. "But he would be dispatched to one of those camps if that were to happen."

"Exactly," agreed Jenny grimly. "So, of course, the poor man did as he was told, but a friend of his found out, or guessed, what was happening and turned to Professor Schulmann for advice, and the Professor told my father."

"Wasn't that a little risky?" asked Midge hesitantly. "I mean, if this man is here illegally, couldn't your father be accused of condoning a breach of the law?"

"Perhaps, but it's far worse to let a solicitor – a man who has sworn an oath to uphold the law – get away with extortion." Jenny shrugged. "I think Daddy would be dashed sorry for Herr X in any case, but if there's one thing which angers him above all else it is seeing the guardians of the law break the law." She gave a brief smile. "I don't mean that he'd throw Ronald out of chambers if Ronald broke some silly licensing restriction, but he simply could not ignore something as wicked as Herr X alleged."

"What did he do?"

"He decided to summon Forrest to his chambers on an excuse and then confront him with the evidence."

"Did he have any? And what if Forrest had reported the refugee to the police?"

Jenny gave a small smile. "There was nothing to stop Professor Schulmann from arranging for Herr X to be sent up to Manchester or Glasgow after he had given a signed statement. Moreover, I don't suppose that Daddy hoped that Forrest would confess; I think that he expected that Forrest might bluster a lot but then stop trying to persecute Herr X."

Midge frowned. "I can see why the police swooped on that letter from Forrest, but why do they believe it, particularly if your father has explained what happened?"

"To the police way of thinking, the problem is that if Daddy didn't kill Forrest, then who did?"

Chapter Eight

The next morning, dark shadows like bruises under Jenny's eyes testified to how little she had slept. Midge was also tired, having kept Jenny company until late into the night. Neither was talkative at breakfast and neither felt any more optimistic about events. Jenny toyed miserably with her bacon and eggs, pushing them round her plate before abandoning them scarcely touched.

"I suppose we'd better get Field to find a cab," she eventually commented. "I'd rather see Inspector Groves at Scotland Yard than have him here."

Midge ran her eyes over Jenny's outfit. Today she was dressed in a coat and skirt of sober hue, but Midge felt that she would not achieve her stated aim of lulling the police into assuming that she was ineffectual and harmless.

"Look, old thing, I don't want to badger you, but if you want to appear defenceless I think that you ought to change. That suit is too well-cut and sophisticated."

"Not quite the innocent village maiden?" asked Jenny rather listlessly.

"No." A rueful grin crept over Midge's face. "If you want to look like the village maiden, why don't you borrow the navy twin-set which I was wearing yesterday? It would create the correct unsophisticated, rural effect."

An hour later, Jenny and Midge were in Inspector Groves' office at Scotland Yard. The Inspector had accepted Jenny's request that her friend stay with her – it was only natural that a young woman would not want to be alone when being questioned and it was not as if she were an actual suspect. Indeed, when Jenny had slipped off her coat and sat down, Inspector Groves had been mildly surprised at how young and defenceless she looked. He had expected Miss Fletcher, who by all accounts was as sharp as you like, to be, well, a bit more striking, a bit more decorative. This girl looked more like a little country mouse than a lively lawyer-in-training.

"Now, Miss Fletcher," he began, "it's very good of you to come here. As you know, I want to ask you some questions merely to clarify a few points; you yourself are not a suspect."

Jenny was momentarily surprised by the policeman's paternal tone. However, other considerations swiftly fled as his questions began. It soon became apparent that Groves was pursuing two threads: first, did her father have any money worries, and second, had Jenny ever heard of Forrest before the day of the murder. Although Jenny returned an emphatic 'no' on both points, the Inspector continued to probe at her answers. Finally, he asked her whether she had anything she wanted to say.

"Yes," she declared defiantly, "I believe that you have made a terrible mistake. My father would never have murdered this man Forrest. Moreover, even if you think that he might have done so, because you don't know him, I don't see that the evidence against him is anything more than circumstantial. It hasn't been shown that the poison was administered at my father's chambers and, even if was, that wouldn't necessarily mean that my father did it."

"Well, Miss Fletcher," responded the police officer heavily, "I admire you for your loyalty, but there doesn't seem to be anyone else in that office who is linked to Forrest, whereas your father not only knew him, but was accused by him."

"You're assuming that no-one else knew Forrest because you haven't investigated whether they did," Jenny retorted hotly. "I think it's just as reasonable that... that...." She faltered for a moment, before remembering Midge's inventive suggestions, "That Forrest might have jilted one of the secretaries, or embezzled someone's savings or lied about a shared client. But you won't find that out unless you look properly."

Groves was irresistibly reminded of his wife telling off their small son for not searching hard enough for a lost schoolbook. Did all women regard men as inherently incompetent, no matter their age or status? Frowning down a grin, he tried to reassure the girl sitting bolt upright in front of him, like a youthful Britannia.

"We shall, of course, investigate all leads, including continuing to question other members of your father's chambers. However, I am afraid that the evidence which we have so far appears compelling enough to charge your father."

There was a short still pause, before Jenny forced herself to ask when she might visit her father. Groves looked at her compassionately, wondering whether criminals would avoid committing crimes if they were to realise how much their families suffered when they were caught. He thought it unlikely, not least because, in his experience, so few criminals seemed to think that they would ever be caught.

"If you don't mind travelling in a police-car, I could take you out to Wandsworth now," he suggested. "That way you'll avoid any trouble with newspaper men – have you been pestered by them at all?"

Midge fully expected Jenny to mention her fears that she had been followed, but Jenny merely returned a non-committal reply that there had been rather a lot of them in Middle Temple.

Groves made a brief telephone call to warn the prison that he would be visiting shortly, before conducting the two girls downstairs to where a police car, complete with driver, was waiting. On the inspector's advice, Jenny and Midge sat in the back where they were less visible to any lurking journalists. Little was said as the car snaked its way through the London traffic before finally arriving at its destination. Jenny looked in horror at the huge tall gates which loomed menacingly above them. There was no chance of mistaking the forbidding message which the architecture of Wandsworth gaol spelled out: power lay with the incarcerators, not with those who were incarcerated.

Groves showed the guard on duty his police card and the three were ushered through the gates and into the inner courtyard, where a further check and another grim doorway awaited them.

"Questioning a suspect, Inspector?" asked the guard, casting a thoughtful look at Jenny and Midge. "You know where to go, don't you, sir?"

Groves nodded conformation, while Jenny winced inwardly at the description of her father as a suspect. A straggling walk across the yard, followed by a right turn, led them inside the prison proper. The harsh smell of antiseptic caught Jenny's throat as they made their way along a corridor painted in two shades of institutional grey. She began to fear that they were being led towards her father's cell, but the policeman soon stopped at a grey metal door which had a small window set into it, with three iron bars over the window. A warder in his uniform sat outside on a stool, but rose to greet the inspector.

"Morning, sir."

"Morning. I've come to question the suspect in the Forrest killing."

"Fletcher, wasn't it, sir? We got your message from the Yard and he's in there waiting for you."

Jenny felt that her blood ought to boil with rage at her father being spoken of in this way, like a common criminal. Instead, she was struck numb and chill with dread. What if they were unable to find any evidence of her father's innocence? What if the police case convinced a jury? What if her father were kept inside this inhuman place until one day he was led out to the scaffold?

"I'll tell your father that you're here," explained Inspector Groves as the warder jangled his keys, before selecting the correct one. "Then I can let you speak to him, but for no more than half an hour, I'm afraid."

Jenny nodded her thanks, too full of emotion to speak. However, once the cell door clanged shut behind her, she had to blink away her tears as she caught sight of her father standing in front of her, looking exhausted and worried.

"Daddy!" she exclaimed, before kissing him.

"Thank you for coming, Jenny," replied the barrister. Then he frowned. "Are you sure that you are up to this... prison-visiting?"

Jenny laughed rather bitterly. "If I become a lawyer, I may have to get used to visiting prisons," she declared, before taking in the fact that, although her father was wearing a suit, he was without a tie or braces. "Didn't Field pack any ties? I thought he was supposed to have put up a bag for you."

Mr Fletcher explained his inelegant attire.

"The police don't want me hanging myself before the trial. They've taken my shoelaces away as well." Jenny's appalled expression prompted him to add, "It's a common precaution, but don't worry, my dear, I have no intention of giving up the fight yet."

Jenny pulled herself together.

"Cottrell gave me a full explanation of what's happened so far, but what happens next?"

"The first thing is that I'll be brought before a magistrate today to enter a plea. I'd rather that you didn't come; it's a formality and Cottrell will be there to represent me."

"Bail?" whispered Jenny, without much conviction.

"On a charge of wilful murder? I'm sorry, Jenny, but there's no hope of bail. I'll be remanded and returned here.

Then it will be a matter of waiting for the case to reach court. I calculate that we have at least a month before it can do so, perhaps longer."

Jenny gulped. A month was a very short time in which to try and untangle whatever had happened to Forrest.

"Whom has Groves questioned in chambers?" asked Fletcher.

"Everyone," replied Jenny. "Even me."

"What has Groves asked you?" demanded her father, angry that she should have been questioned.

"He wanted to know if I had heard of Forrest, and whether you had any financial worries."

Fletcher frowned. "That's the line I suspected he was following. Cottrell warned me that Scotland Yard would investigate my bank account and all of the financial transactions at chambers."

"Surely they won't be able to find anything?"

Fletcher allowed himself a dry riposte. "If you mean, will the police find evidence of anything untoward, then no, I have no fear of that; not unless Thomson has been interpreting tax regulations in a rather idiosyncratic manner."

"Thomson cooking the books?" repeated Jenny in a high-pitched voice. "Surely he's probity personified?"

"That had always been my view of him," agreed her father, "which is why I doubt that Inspector Groves or his minions will find anything of much interest in the chambers accounts." He grew more serious. "However, the difficulty is that the police case is not based on my having illicitly acquired monies over several years from extortion; it is that I saw an opportunity to extort money from Forrest and, when he threatened to reveal what I was doing, I killed him."

"It's all supposition based on Forrest's letter."

"Exactly; that's what makes the case against me so

difficult to disprove. The prosecution can argue that the very lack of evidence is as suggestive of my guilt as it is of my innocence. Take the first accusation: I attempted to extort money from Forrest. The defence – I trust – will be able to show that there are no traces of income from unexplained sources in my bank accounts. However, the prosecution can retort that this was the first attempt and so no money had yet been paid over. They will argue that Forrest's letter is evidence of threats of extortion: why would a man write to the police admitting his own wrongdoing unless he were fearful of a greater danger? Is it coincidence that he named me as his blackmailer on the last day of his life? Is it coincidence that he approached the police for help on the very evening of his death? Is it coincidence that he visited me hours before he died?"

Fletcher shrugged his shoulders. "I could make a very pretty case for the prosecution with no trouble at all."

"But what about the defence?" urged Jenny. "We've got to find flaws in the prosecution case, not help them."

Hearing the pain in his daughter's voice, Fletcher attempted to smile.

"Oh there are flaws in it, my dear, but I don't want you to imagine that it will be easy to convince a jury."

"I know," answered Jenny impatiently. "Cottrell's already made that abundantly clear to me."

"The first flaw is that there is no evidence that I needed or received money. How far that will persuade the jury of my innocence I am doubtful – they will assume that everyone needs money, so why shouldn't I? The second flaw in the prosecution case is that Professor Schulmann will confirm that he consulted me in regard to Herr X. However, while that may strengthen the case that Forrest was a dubious specimen, it does not prove that I did not suddenly decide to acquire an extra source of income by blackmailing Forrest, perhaps even as revenge for what he had done to Herr X."

Fletcher sighed momentarily. "If the accusation were merely one of blackmail, I would feel relatively confident that my word would be taken against Forrest's. The difficulty arises because he is dead and, what is more, he died shortly after seeing me."

Jenny grimaced. It was probably a result of years of forensic debate that her father could discuss his own case so dispassionately, but she was feeling rather less clinical about the matter.

"Surely a major flaw in the prosecution case is why you would be so stupid as to take the risk of trying to extort money from Forrest?"

"It applies less to the murder charge. However, I'm inclined to think that the police have not thought through the implications of suggesting that I poisoned Forrest on the very day that I brought him into chambers to demand money from him. If I felt so unsure as to Forrest's reaction that I had already laid in a stock of arsenic or prussic acid in case he refused to pay up then surely – as you say – I would have resisted attempting to extort money from Forrest."

Fletcher paced backwards and forwards.

"If it weren't for that damned – sorry, Jenny – that wretched letter, I don't suppose that I should be incarcerated here. But the letter points the finger of suspicion at me and me alone. Hence the police will be satisfied with a cursory look at Forrest's associates."

"But surely the prosecution can't base their entire case purely on the evidence of one letter?" protested Jenny. "Would a jury really convict just on that?"

"They might," grunted Fletcher. "And it depends who's leading for the Crown how convincing it sounds. In a poisoning case, it may well be the Attorney-General."

"Somervell?" queried Jenny. "There are others who are

more dangerous."

"He's quite dangerous enough," warned Fletcher. "Anyway, it may not be Somervell. There's McClure or Hilliard." He sighed momentarily, fearing that he had to warn Jenny of possible complications, but not relishing the task. "Now look here, Jenny, don't run away with the idea that that letter will be the only evidence against me." He held up his hand as his daughter began to argue. "I have an unpleasant suspicion that the police may not have revealed all their cards yet. So don't go getting your hopes up that this will be laughed out of court at the inquest."

Jenny gazed at him despondently. If her father thought that there might be further problems ahead then he was probably correct, but what further evidence could the police have possibly discovered which suggested that her father was guilty? An angry thought that it was Forrest who ought to be in the dock, not her upright and honourable father, prompted her next remark.

"Ronald said that Forrest had an unsavoury reputation," commented Jenny. "Do you think that we ought to investigate in case we can discover anything which might show why someone else would want him dead?"

Fletcher halted directly in front of Jenny.

"Listen to me, Jenny," he commanded. "When you gaily talk about 'investigating' Forrest, you do not realise the potential dangers involved. Forrest did indeed have a dubious reputation and he almost certainly knew a number of people still worse than himself."

Jenny protested, but her father overrode her interruption.

"You are only nineteen," he pointed out, before hastening to sweeten this somewhat squashing statement. "I know that you are intelligent, sophisticated and training to be a lawyer, but you do not have my years of experience of criminal types. Don't forget that I prosecute as well as defend, and I have been instrumental in sending some very unpleasant characters behind bars. Catching criminals is not a game and you are not a policeman. You're a girl and I forbid you from getting involved with the criminal fraternity, as you almost certainly will do if you start investigating Forrest."

"But it might help," argued Jenny, angry at being dismissed as some callow youngster, too naïve to perceive danger.

"Without the resources available to the Yard, it is highly unlikely that you could uncover anything related to the case. If you did discover anything about Forrest's contacts, it would almost certainly be unconnected to his murder." He added grimly, "How do you think that some criminal financier is going to respond to a fresh-faced young woman sticking her nose into his business?"

Jenny flushed, feeling rather humiliated. She could understand her father's point that the manner in which Ronald or James might react to being questioned was somewhat different from how a fraudster might respond, but surely she ought to do something rather than leave her father to be convicted?

After another five minutes' talk, there was a tap on the window. Swivelling round, Jenny caught sight of Inspector Groves pointing to his watch.

"Oh Lord," she ejaculated in exasperation, "my time must be up. I'll come again as soon as I may."

"Do the twins know what's happened?"

"Mike's on manoeuvres in Wales – I've asked the adjutant to contact him. I don't know how to contact Tom."

"There's a telegraphic address noted down in my diary. But remember that it takes a long time to get back from Egypt, and he may not be able to get compassionate leave in any case."

Jenny nodded.

"And don't forget," warned Fletcher, "don't run any silly risks."

"Of course not," promised Jenny, with her fingers crossed behind her back. "Are there any things which I can bring you? Clothes or books?"

"You might bring my Vergil," replied her father with a dry smile. "There are some very apposite phrases about the unjustly condemned in it."

Biting back a sob, Jenny gave her father a swift hug. "Keep your spirits up," she whispered. "I don't care what anyone says. I know you could never do anything wrong."

Chapter Nine

After Jenny bid her father goodbye, the inspector explained that he would escort them to the police car, where the driver would take them back to Middle Temple. After they had left, he would question Mr Fletcher again before the magistrate's hearing. Jenny nodded, finding it difficult to speak, and she and Midge set off back to the main gate in Groves' wake.

Having left the gloomy portals of the gaol behind them, Midge turned to her friend.

"How was your father?"

"All right, thank you," replied Jenny, before gesticulating at the driver's back. Midge, realising that she did not want him to overhear anything, sank back in silence. What Inspector Groves had said to her was not so important that she had to pass it on to Jenny immediately. In fact, Midge was uncertain that she wanted to pass it on at all.

After around ten minutes, the driver spoke.

"Where can I drop you, miss? The Yard's a bit public and the inspector said to take you back to your office. Would that be right?"

"Thank you," replied Jenny, wondering why Inspector Groves was taking care of her so conscientiously. Was Midge correct in thinking that a fragile appearance would convince a hardened police officer that she was unable to look after herself? Or had the inspector taken pity on Midge's bad leg, rather than on her? Did it even matter?

When Jenny and Midge had made their way past the three patient reporters who were still staking out her father's chambers, they gathered in Ronald's room, where he and James were failing to complete the *Times* crossword.

"Did you survive your interrogation?" enquired James.

"Yes, and I've seen my father."

"How was he?"

In reply, Jenny burst into tears. She fumbled in her bag and eventually found a small lace-edged handkerchief – decorative, costly and useless in the present circumstances. Ronald produced a much larger affair and passed it to her silently. There was an embarrassed silence, before Jenny pulled herself together and apologised.

"I'm sorry; I can't imagine why I was being so silly."

"Shock," replied Ronald comfortingly. "Don't worry about it. I nearly wept when Staunton bawled me out this morning."

Jenny rather doubted this statement, but dutifully asked why the older barrister had been annoyed with Ronald, who was generally regarded as a promising man who would go far.

Ronald gave his lopsided grin. "Our revered Staunton's view of my devilling was that it was unfit for his august eyes. Apparently his son could draw up a brief better than I can."

"Drivel," snorted James. "The last I heard of his precious son was Staunton complaining about 'paying ridiculous fees to keep a boy in idleness at public school'."

Ronald laughed at James' accurate mimicry of the querulous tones of the senior barrister, but Jenny was more concerned with what she had learned in Wandsworth.

"Apparently, the inquest is on Monday. Will any of you be able to come with me?"

A frown crossed James' face. "There are going to be a great number of reporters there, Jenny. Do you really think that it's wise to go? If I, or Ronald, go it won't cause anything like as much fuss with the photographers."

Jenny looked mutinous, but Ronald backed up his colleague.

"Imagine the headlines, Jenny. 'Barrister's daughter attends inquest. Miss Jenny Fletcher, the glamorous

75

daughter of Patrick Fletcher, K.C., is here pictured leaving the inquest into the killing of William Forrest, a well-known solicitor. We understand that Mr Fletcher is currently helping police with their enquiries.'"

"Surely they will say the same about you?" countered Jenny.

"James is fairly suave, but hardly glamorous," pointed out Ronald. "It's a matter of hats. A picture of me leaving court wearing a fedora or James in a trilby is very dull compared with you in a smart black hat." Then, as Jenny appeared disposed to argue, he added, "I don't believe that you have any hats which aren't smart." This tribute made Jenny smile briefly, so Ronald pushed home his attack. "Come on, Jenny, don't be silly. The press have already latched onto the story; you don't want to give them further ammunition."

"All right," sighed Jenny wearily, "but I don't want to be left out of anything else. I want to help, not sit around here wondering what to do next."

"What we're doing next," stated James, "is going to lunch at Dmitri's. It won't do you any good to starve yourself. No-one will disturb us in Dmitri's private-room, so we can talk properly at the same time as eating."

Ronald glanced at James in surprise. "Aren't we a bit early?"

"It's nearly one."

Ronald looked back at his watch and then held it to his ear. "This wretched thing's playing up again. I'd have made us all late. Sorry, Jenny."

Dmitri's lay in a narrow passage-way off the Strand, the entrance to which snaked under a low arch bearing the weight of a further two storeys and an attic hidden under tall, steeply-pitched roofs. Midge was reminded of a scene out of Dickens' London; had there been fog she could have imagined a ghostly tatterdemalion sweep's boy looming out in front of them or an insubstantial wraith of a lamp-lighter offering to light them on their way. It was something of a relief to discover that the narrow frontage of the restaurant with its tiny window-panes criss-crossed into a checker pattern appeared to be entirely of this world. Admittedly, the front of the restaurant, although clean and freshly painted, did not suggest an especially thriving establishment. However, to Midge's surprise, once they had entered, she saw that nearly every table was taken. It was just as well that the private room was reserved, although Midge groaned inwardly as she saw the narrow flight of stairs leading up to the first floor, so typical of London houses. She gritted her teeth and struggled upstairs, grateful that neither James nor Ronald remarked upon her ungainly effort.

Having conquered the stairs, Midge sank into a padded chair covered in claret-coloured velvet. After a few minutes, she felt up to taking stock of her surroundings. To judge by the effusive welcome which had greeted their entrance, Jenny and the others were well known at Dmitri's and it was interesting to see the sorts of places which her friend frequented. Glancing round the small, slightly overcrowded room, decorated with pictures of the Russian tundra and frontispieces of scores of Tchaikovsky's works, Midge found it difficult to fit Jenny's tales of evening dissipation to this environment. She mentally shrugged her shoulders; perhaps Jenny patronised different places in the evening; Dmitri's did not give the impression of being a nightclub.

Meanwhile Ronald was looking with longing at the window.

"I do wish we could open it, but Dmitri would have a fit. He believes in keeping people parboiled."

"Midge will approve," commented Jenny. "She hates

English winters, don't you, Midge?"

"Yes!" returned Midge vehemently. "I can never get warm."

"In that case, try Dmitri's special goulash," suggested James. At this point the restauranteur entered, followed by another man, who hurried over to the girls.

"Jenny! I've been worrying about you."

Jenny gave a brief smile. "Thank you, Dickie. Midge, this is my friend, Dickie. He's in Sir Eustace Leadbetter's chambers, next to ours. Dickie, this is Midge. She's at Cambridge."

As she greeted Dickie, Midge remembered that Jenny enjoyed going dancing with him. Moreover, judging from the way in which Dickie's eyes kept straying to Jenny, it was obvious that he was keen on her. That suggested that he would be prepared to help Jenny investigate things – if only they knew what to investigate. Admittedly, Midge was sure that Jenny had once said that the neighbouring chambers rather looked down upon criminal work, but this third legal expert was bound to know a lot more than she did.

Once Ronald had finished a technical discussion about wine with Dmitri, Jenny proceeded to outline to what had taken place since the previous day. In particular, she explained what her father had told her that morning: that Forrest had claimed to have helped Herr X gain false papers out of pity.

"It strikes me," commented Dickie thoughtfully after Jenny had concluded, "that the police view of what happened can be summarised into five points, each of which we shall have to break down. One, Forrest came to your father seeking advice about this German refugee. Two, your father demanded money from him. Three, Forrest was terrified because he feared what your father could do to him, and promised anything to keep your father quiet. Four, Forrest returned to his office and, realising that he could be blackmailed forever if he gave in to your father's demands, wrote a letter to the police setting out what had happened and admitting that he had supplied false papers to a refugee out of compassion. Five, Forrest died."

"That's a fair summary," agreed Jenny. "How do we tackle the five points? The first one must be susceptible to what Professor Schulmann has to say. After all, he spoke to my father about Herr X long before Forrest had the meeting."

"I agree," replied Dickie. "It's a weak point for the prosecution but, equally, what proof have we that your father summoned Forrest in to question him? As far as I can gather, the only evidence available is your father's appointment book with Forrest's name written in by your father. That may be a sign that the appointment was made in an irregular fashion, but it doesn't prove that Forrest didn't approach your father privately for the appointment which, given the sensitivity of the subject, he might have done."

"I wonder whether the police have searched Forrest's office for any sign of his appointment book?" mused James. "I don't suppose that it would be of much more use than your father's book, but perhaps they might also question Forrest's secretaries to see whether they know anything about the appointment."

"The trouble is," pointed out Jenny, "that Daddy deliberately rang up after office hours. Apparently, Forrest often worked late and Daddy wanted to catch him off guard and force him to make an appointment. If he hadn't made one, Daddy was planning to go round to his office immediately because Forrest couldn't possibly claim that he was seeing clients well after six o'clock."

"Blast!" responded James. "Still, you never know

whether the typists mightn't know something. Ours seem to spend a lot of time gossiping; why should Forrest's be any different?"

"What we need to do is to plant a spy in Forrest's office," suggested Jenny eagerly, with memories of a book she had once read coming back to her. "She could search through his papers and perhaps find out something important."

"Be realistic," pleaded Ronald. "How are you going to create a convenient vacancy – abduct half of the staff? Anyway, you can't type!"

Jenny scowled as she recognised the validity of his argument. Dickie, seeing signs of a storm, hastily interrupted.

"As regards points two and three, I don't see how the police can prove that your father demanded money or that Forrest agreed to pay up. There was no witness to the conversation. It is entirely Forrest's word against your father's and the police know about his claims only through his letter."

"Similarly with point four," agreed Ronald. "In fact, point four's pretty fishy. Given Forrest's reputation for being a tricky customer, I can't imagine him acting out of compassion, and certainly not for a penniless refugee. It's completely out of character. Moreover, why did he admit to a crime which could have seen him struck off? He must have had a motive. My guess is that he was admitting to a lesser crime in the hope that the police would ignore the graver one of extortion."

"Exactly," James nodded. "I persuaded Cottrell to let me read a copy of Forrest's letter. Forrest was very careful not to explain exactly what he had done in regard to the papers. If you ask me, he was hoping to be able to get away with admitting a slight technical breach of the law because he had been careless about not checking up Herr X's credentials. The letter certainly didn't read as if he was admitting to deliberately supplying him with false papers."

Jenny frowned thoughtfully. "So you think that Forrest was hoping to accuse my father of extortion to cover up the fact that he himself was an extortioner?"

"What other possibility is there?" demanded James. "Obviously your father wasn't trying to extort money."

"Quite! But is there anything which we can investigate in point four? Or do we have to fall back on point five and try to find out whether the poison could have been administered in chambers?"

"What I don't understand," said Midge rather nervously, worried lest the lawyers regard her contribution with contempt, "was how did Herr X know to approach Forrest for false papers? I mean, you don't just go up to the first lawyer you see and say, 'Excuse me, would you sign these false documents for me?'."

"Good point, Midge," remarked Ronald approvingly.

Jenny sat up like a dog on a promising scent. "We can investigate that!" she declared. "Even if Professor Schulmann won't tell me who Herr X is, surely he'll ask Herr X himself why he got involved with Forrest?"

"Yes," said Ronald slowly, since a flaw had just occurred to him. "However, I thought that Professor Schulmann had originally said that Forrest found out about Herr X being in the country illegally and then latched onto him, not that Forrest supplied Herr X with papers and then blackmailed him."

Jenny banged her glass down on the table in frustration. "Why does everyone and everything keep contradicting themselves?"

The unspoken answer hovered in everyone's mind – because it was a murder case and people, even innocent people, lie when they become involved in murder cases.

"It can't do any harm to ask the Professor,"

commented Dickie rather awkwardly, "but don't forget that the police will also be speaking to him. In fact, they may be able to force him to give up Herr X's name and address."

Gloomy looks suggested that no-one was sure whether this was a good thing. Midge gave a hesitant cough.

"What's up?" demanded Jenny.

"I spoke to Groves whilst you were with your father."

"What did he say?"

"He made a remark about having had one of his cases prosecuted by your father and that he had been a very efficient prosecutor."

"Then why is Groves hounding him now?"

Midge looked uncomfortable. "He said that he believed that the law should take its course, no matter who was involved. He said that he had a great respect for the legal profession, but that every profession contained men who broke the law and that it was his job to track them down." She glanced apologetically at Jenny. "I'm sorry. I hoped that he'd tell me something useful."

James attempted to cheer the party up.

"At least once the inquest's out of the way we ought to know how Forrest died. It'll make it a lot easier to investigate the poison if we know whether we're dealing with belladonna or wolfsbane. And on the subject of poison, we'd better to do better justice to the Chateau Le Clos than we have done so far or Dmitri will think that we suspect him of passing off an inferior wine as the 1933 variety!"

Chapter Ten

The days before the inquest were a time of intense frustration. Jenny had spoken to Professor Schulmann, but he had informed her that Herr X had left London. It was some consolation that the Professor intended to try to trace him but, as Jenny pointed out to Midge later, not only did that mean the Professor would be unable to attend the inquest, it meant that Herr X might have disappeared altogether.

"The prosecution will claim we're inventing Herr X if we can't produce him. It will look terrible."

Midge suspected that Jenny was correct, but did not want to say so. "What about Professor Schulmann's evidence? After all, your father never met Herr X. It was all raised by the Professor and he can swear that he told your father that Forrest was up to something."

Jenny's face lightened for a moment. "I suppose that's a point." Then she grimaced. "The trouble is, what Herr X told Professor Schulmann is hearsay and thus inadmissible as evidence. So we can't prove that Herr X actually existed or was being persecuted by Forrest."

Since the police had not yet revealed which poison had been used and whether any traces of it had been found in the tea utensils, it was impossible to consider that lead. Determined to do something, Jenny reverted to an earlier suggestion that they investigate how long it would take to walk from her father's chambers to Forrest's office, and whether Forrest had stopped to take refreshments on the way. Clearly, she and Midge could not go into the many public houses which were scattered on the route, so she badgered the men until they agreed to take on the onerous duty of drinking beer whilst chatting to pretty barmaids.

"The trouble with this idea," groaned Dickie as he set out with James, "is that there's no guarantee that we'll

83

speak to the barmaids who were on duty on the day Forrest died and we'll get very peculiar looks if we insist on speaking to every girl in the place."

"Cheer up," remarked James with a grin, "at least Forrest wasn't one of those indeterminate chaps – you know: hair middling, nose middling, height middling, eyes didn't really notice. Six foot two, muscular and with wiry black hair going grey is reasonably memorable."

"Well, you can start the talking," commanded Dickie as he pushed through the doors of the Spread Eagle. "I feel like an idiot."

"I wonder why that is?" murmured James, unable to resist the opportunity of teasing his colleague. Dickie glared at him, but followed in his wake to the bar. Leaning against the bar, James ordered two pints of mild and began a desultory conversation about the weather. Then, turning on his most charming smile, he began his task.

"Tell me, Daisy…"

"It's Rose, actually, sir."

"I knew you must be a flower," complimented James, fortunately unaware that the barmaid was mentally writing him down as 'one of that sort'. "My friend and I," he continued, gesticulating at Dickie, "were having a bet."

"Indeed?"

"He thinks that it would be harder to work in a restaurant where you're expected to remember all the customers, than to work in a bar, such as the one in this excellent pub." Seeing that Rose was looking offended at Dickie's supposed remark, James congratulated himself. "However, I said that it would be much harder working in a pub because you can't be sure whether any of the customers are going to turn into regulars until they are regulars, so you'll have far more faces to try to remember."

"That's certainly true," agreed Rose warmly. "And as often as not, you think that someone's going to be a regular and then they up and off and you never see them again."

"How do you tell them apart?" asked Dickie, feeling that he needed to take part in the conversation. "Do you go on height or colour of hair?"

"Sometimes, but most often as not it's manner. If you look at those two over by the door, you'll see that one of them is talking and talking, and the other is wishing that he would be quiet so that he could get on with picking his chances for the Saturday pools."

Two heads swivelled round to observe the men indicated.

"By Jove, I see what you mean," agreed James with warmth. "You certainly have them summed up all right!"

Rose preened herself. "I've been told I'd've been a natural on the halls," she admitted.

"Absolutely," Dickie contributed.

"So I wonder what you might have made of someone we know who was in here on Monday. A big, tall man, powerfully built and about six foot two. He's got dark, wiry hair, but it's going a bit grey at the sides."

"When was he in?"

"About four o'clock."

Rose thought long and hard. "Sorry; I can't think of anyone like that."

"Never mind," replied James. "He said it was either here or the Red Lion."

They stayed chatting for a few more minutes, making sure that no-one else had been serving the previous week, before buying Rose a drink for her trouble and leaving.

"Lord!" sighed Dickie as they came out into the fresh air. "How many times are we going to have to follow that routine?"

"For as many pubs as there are between here and Duke's Buildings."

"I've no objection to getting gloriously tight, but I can't imagine we're going to achieve a lot," complained Dickie. "It would be so much easier if we could pull out a warrant card and demand to interrogate everyone."

"But you wouldn't have any beer in that sort of investigation," pointed out James. "What's more, we'll speed up if you agree to separate."

Ronald had been delegated to stay in chambers over lunchtime in case any news came in. Midge and Jenny offered to keep him company, but he told them to leave him and pursue their investigations into tea-shops and other unlicensed establishments.

"The trouble is," sighed Midge, as she bit into an unwanted bun and stirred her third cup of tea, "I don't imagine someone like Forrest would come in somewhere like this for refreshment."

Looking at the peach walls, the cream cushions and the spindly oak chairs and tables which made up the decoration of this particular tea shop, Jenny was forced to agree. The only man in the place was a small, inoffensive creature whose wife was busily rebuking him for putting her parcels in the wrong place. "Ghastly, isn't it?" commented Jenny. "Shall we do one more and then go back?"

Midge nodded. As they set off, Jenny suddenly noticed that Midge was limping worse than usual and cursed herself. Carried away by her desire to do anything other than sitting around in chambers trying to solve what felt like a jigsaw puzzle with most of the pieces missing, she had forgotten that trailing round on a wild goose-chase was liable to leave Midge in pain. Looking frantically around, Jenny was glad to see that the next shop was nearby.

"At least that one seems to have decent cakes on display," she declared, before adding, "I think we'll get a cab back after this. I'm so full of tea that I'm swilling around like some sort of dolphin."

The fourth cake shop failed to have any knowledge of Jenny's 'friend' who had so enjoyed his meal there. Midge suspected that the others might have been equally unsuccessful. When they returned to chambers, James confirmed that he had not discovered anything and shortly afterwards Dickie floated in.

"Have you had any luck?" demanded Jenny.

Dickie shook his head. "I've been in five pubs and all that happened is that I got cursed by one of the barmaids who recognised the photograph I was showing her. She told me she'd set the police upon me if I came back."

Jenny looked very disheartened. "We're just fooling ourselves that we are doing any good," she stated. "We've no evidence to suggest that Forrest had a drink anywhere and, even if he did, why should anyone remember him. We haven't the resources to investigate properly and there are all the pubs on side streets which we haven't even considered."

"Try not to despair, Jenny," said Ronald gently. "Most investigative work consists of repetitive questioning which appears to lead nowhere. If we do discover that Forrest had a drink on his return it will be useful, but it won't be disastrous if we find no evidence of it. Apart from anything else, we can always suggest at the trial that the police ought to have checked up on the possibility."

"I'm surprised that they haven't," agreed James. "After all, Cottrell made the point to them that this is not the only place where Forrest might have ingested poison."

"After Monday, we'll know what the poison was and that will give us a timescale to work from," agreed Ronald. "There isn't much purpose in us considering whether he might have been poisoned at lunch if the poison was more swift-acting."

Chapter Eleven

On Monday, it was decided that Ronald, Dickie and Midge would attend the inquest. Ronald intended to be the representative from chambers who would serve as a sop to the press, while Dickie, who was not known to have any connections with Patrick Fletcher, made the ideal escort for Midge. Jenny had lent Midge a hat with a veil in an attempt to confuse anyone who might have seen her near chambers, although both girls knew that, if she stood up, her sticks would make her immediately recognisable.

Despite her natural fears for Jenny and Mr Fletcher, Midge, who had been a connoisseur of detective stories since her school-days, found considerable interest in the scene. She was shocked by the numbers of press-men, but Dickie explained that they were out in force partly because there had not been any interesting murders recently, and partly because this particular case offered the delightful prospect of a famous barrister, well-known for his trenchant views on law-breakers, in the dock for pre-meditated wilful murder. As a means of titillating the great British public's appetite for reading about the destruction of their fellow men, it would be hard to beat.

After the swearing in of the inquest jury and the evidence of PC Roberts, the coroner summoned Leonard Wynne.

"Please tell the court your occupation."

"I am the clerk at Forrest and Creech."

"So you knew the dead man well?"

"Yes, sir."

"Tell the court what happened on the day of his death."

"Mr Forrest informed me that he would be absent for much of the afternoon because he had to see a barrister in Middle Temple."

"Was that usual?"

The clerk hesitated. "No, not really. We don't tend to instruct counsel very often. We can handle most of our clients' business ourselves."

"I see. Now, did you observe what sort of mood Forrest was in when he left?"

"He seemed a bit nervous. He said that Fletcher was a damned hard man."

"When did he return?"

"Before five o'clock. Perhaps at quarter to or ten to."

"You are not certain?"

"I know it was before five, and I know that it was definitely some time after half-past four because I wondered whether he was going to return to the office when it was already quite late."

"Indeed. Now, after he returned, he went to his room?"

"That's correct, sir. I assumed that he was catching up on his paperwork. I had quite a lot to do myself."

"Did you speak to him afterwards?"

"Yes, sir. It must have been around six o'clock. He said that he was feeling unwell. That was why I became worried about him later."

"You say that he was feeling unwell. Did he give you any details?"

"I'm afraid not, sir. He said something about feeling a bit sick and that was it. He asked me to wait because there was something urgent he needed to complete that evening and he hoped he'd deal with it in an hour or so."

"You fetched Constable Roberts just before nine o'clock?"

"Yes, sir."

"And you told him that you had found a body?"

"That's correct, sir."

"When did you discover the body?"

"I'd been working until around eight o'clock. At that point I thought I really needed to go home. I could see that there was still a light on in Mr Forrest's office, so I waited for a bit longer. You see, I'm always the last to lock up the office."

"What time was this?"

"Around half-past eight, sir. Then I remembered what Mr Forrest had said about feeling ill and I thought that I ought to check whether he was all right. So I knocked on the door. There wasn't any answer and I wasn't sure what to do. Mr Forrest didn't like being disturbed if he had shut his door and I wondered whether he was deliberately ignoring me. So I waited a bit longer."

"Until?"

"Around a quarter to nine, sir. That was when I knocked again and called out his name. Again there was no answer, but this time I looked through the key-hole." The clerk swallowed. "I saw him on the ground. He was all twisted up. I knew that there was something very wrong, so I ran outside to fetch a policeman."

"You didn't think of telephoning for a doctor?"

"I didn't know who Mr Forrest's doctor was, sir. I thought a policeman might be able to get help more quickly."

"I see. What happened next?"

"I showed the police constable what I had seen and together we broke down the door. Mr Forrest was lying on the floor, quite dead."

"We shall be hearing evidence of how he died in a moment. Do you know of any concerns that Forrest had at the time of his death?"

"No, sir. As I said, he was nervous before going to his appointment, but he didn't give any real details other than saying that Fletcher was a hard man."

"And did Forrest have anything to eat or drink when

he returned to the office?"

"Not that I know of, sir."

"Thank you, Mr Wynne."

Sitting in the well of the court, Midge felt worried. The evidence of Forrest's final hours could certainly be taken as supporting the police claim that Forrest had been poisoned at Mr Fletcher's chambers. She turned her attention to the next witness, an experienced pathologist who was often to be found giving evidence in murder trials. Dr Brook was happy to set out his findings.

"After careful analysis of the main organs of the body, I established the fact that the vegetable alkaloid aconitine was present."

There was a hurried scribbling in notebooks from the more experienced among the reporters, whilst the coroner, Dr Winterton, requested further details.

"Could you outline for the benefit of the jury the precise properties of aconitine?"

"Of course. Aconitine is, as I said, a vegetable alkaloid. It is fatal even in small doses. The deceased had ingested a dose of around one tenth of a gram. That dose would be enough to cause death in a normal healthy male within three to four hours of ingestion."

"There was no possibility of any other poison being present?"

"No. I carried out a full check and aconitine was the only toxic substance present. There was also a small amount of alcohol, but insufficient to cause death."

"How would the dose have been introduced into the body?"

"Unless in a case of deliberate ingestion, it would be impossible to take what we might term a 'raw dose' of aconitine unawares. By this, I mean that, if the taste of aconitine were not disguised by another agent, the deceased would have been bound to notice that he was taking something unusual."

Several of the jury looked uncertain as to the significance of this reply, but the coroner had another point which he wished to establish.

"We have already heard from Constable Roberts as to his discovery of the body; can you suggest a time for when death occurred?"

"Judging by stomach contents, it was some hours since the man had eaten. I should suggest that he died between six and eight p.m."

"Can you suggest when the deceased may have ingested the aconitine?"

"It is difficult to be precise, but the most likely time is between three o'clock and five o'clock in the afternoon."

Midge's heart sank at this news; the timing placed things squarely during Forrest's visit to Mr Fletcher's chambers. Meanwhile, there was a movement amongst the jury members, and a small foxy-faced man with an unfortunate straggling red beard and wispy moustache indicated that he had a question for the pathologist.

"This here act-, acon-," he stumbled, "this poison, can it be got hold of easily?"

Dr Brook frowned. "Aconitine is used to relieve pain, particularly rheumatic pain. It is available either as a tincture or a lineament, but in each case the purchase would be recorded within a chemist's poison book."

"So, no-one could go and buy it as rat-poison and then decide to do themselves in with it?"

"No," replied the pathologist courteously. "That would be an extremely unlikely scenario. Aconitine is a controlled drug within the act and does not have ordinary household purposes."

The foxy-faced man resumed his seat with an ill-concealed air of smug satisfaction which was reflected in the expressions of the reporters. Accident seemed impossible and suicide implausible; the cry of the hounds as they scented a fresh trail was clarion throughout the court, proclaimed in their rustling notebooks and frantic pens. Their enthusiasm was increased by the entrance of Inspector Groves to the witness box. After setting out his position as the officer in charge of the investigation, the coroner proceeded to ask him several questions which delighted the reporters.

"Did you find any evidence that the deceased had bought the aconitine himself?"

"No. We have checked poison books in chemists near both Mr Forrest's residence and his place of work and have found no evidence of him buying any aconitine."

"Did you find any evidence that the deceased might have taken the aconitine by his own hand, whether wittingly or unwittingly?"

"No. As I say, there is no evidence that he had any in his possession."

"Have you discovered where the deceased was between three o'clock and five o'clock, which the medical evidence appears to suggest are the key times."

"Yes," returned Groves, with one eye on the newspapermen huddled in a corner of the court. "Between three and four, Mr Forrest had an appointment with Patrick Fletcher, K.C., and he returned to his office in Holborn shortly before five o'clock."

"Can these times be substantiated?"

"Of course, sir. We have witnesses, Mr Fletcher's own appointment book and a letter from the deceased, written shortly before he died, which gives a detailed account of his unsatisfactory interview with Mr Fletcher."

Several of the pressmen exchanged surprised glances. They had learned that the barrister had been arrested, but no information about a letter had leaked out. Those who wrote for the more lurid papers were already composing headlines about 'Sensation in Court'; for once the headlines would be deserved. When the noise died down, Groves continued stolidly as if he had not noticed the excitement.

"With your permission, sir, I should like to read this letter as an indication of the concerns of the deceased in his last few hours."

The coroner gave his permission and the inspector's deep voice dispassionately read through the damning letter, with its accusations that Fletcher had attempted to blackmail Forrest. Midge, watching the faces of the coroner's jury, realised that they had made up their minds as to what had happened. Groves now proceeded to throw a second bombshell into the court.

"May I have your permission, sir, to read extracts from further letters?"

"You may."

As if he were unaware of the vital nature of what he was saying, Groves continued in the same careful, dispassionate voice which he might have used to order vegetables from his grocer.

"These four letters were found inside a secret drawer in Forrest's desk," he explained. "They appear to be copies of letters which Forrest wrote to Patrick Fletcher over a period of time. All of them were typed by an inexpert typist. The first, which is dated to early November, states that he is appalled at what Fletcher suggested to him in his telephone call. Forrest's second letter is dated a week later and says that he will not do what Fletcher demands, however many times he telephones to threaten him." Groves paused. "I may say, Mr Winterton, that we tried to trace these telephone calls which were made to Forrest's office, but they must have originated from a call box as the Post Office could not trace them to either Mr Fletcher's chambers or place of residence."

Some of the coroner's jury appeared impressed by the

fairness of this statement, but Midge sensed Dickie tensing beside her. Clearly Inspector Groves was underlining the police view that Fletcher was the guilty man and that the untraceability of the telephone calls was no defence. Moreover, Groves had not yet finished extracting damning material from his unexpected discovery.

"While the second letter sounds somewhat blustering in tone," he declared, "the third is much more panic-stricken. Forrest states that 'the enclosed payment will be the last; I cannot give you more and you must know that your continued demands are nearly impossible to meet.' "

A whisper as light as swansdown ran through the court, and Midge watched with horror as the expressions of those who had not yet made up their minds hardened into disgusted certainty of Mr Fletcher's guilt. And still Inspector Groves had further deadly evidence to reveal.

"The final letter is dated the day before Forrest died," he intoned. "In it, Forrest agrees to meet Fletcher in his office. He closes with this remarkable statement. 'I have already given you more than five hundred pounds. I am at my wits' end – what more do you want of me? It is a harsh judgement upon me for having made a trivial error that I have fallen into the hands of a bloodsucking monster like you.' "

In the ghastly moment of silence which followed this revelation, all Midge could think was how fortunate it was that Jenny was not present, listening. Jenny had speculated wildly as to what possible further evidence against her father might be produced but never, even in her wildest flights of imagination, had she come up with something like this. Then an irrepressible wave of murmur and surmise broke round Midge, reminding her that the packed court was relishing everything which Groves had said. And, while there were further formalities to complete, there was little surprise when, following the coroner's summing up, the jury returned a verdict of murder, and named Patrick Fletcher as the murderer.

After the return of the jury's verdict, most of the reporters dashed off to file copy as swiftly as possible, but one or two tried to persuade Ronald to comment on the verdict. Leaving Ronald to deal with the newshounds, Dickie managed to grab a cab and set off back to Middle Temple with Midge. Fearful of discussing the case in public, the two waited until they were inside chambers before they poured out their news to Jenny and James.

"What are we going to do?" Jenny begged, sounding more panic-stricken than she had since the news had first broke. "How could those letters exist? Why did Forrest write them? I don't understand what's happening."

"Calm down," soothed Dickie. "The jury were bound to return a verdict against your father, given the evidence that was produced. Don't forget, that was only a coroner's court, not the Old Bailey."

"But it looks so bad," worried Jenny, unconsciously folding and unfolding a piece of foolscap as she spoke.

"Your father was already under arrest," pointed out James. "This verdict isn't going to change anything."

"What surprises me," argued Ronald, who had arrived soon after Midge and Dickie, "isn't that the police revealed those letters. The motive for doing so is obvious. Similarly, I can see why they wanted to make clear that the letters were typed by an amateur, as Forrest presumably was. But why did they let so much of the other evidence out?"

"Do you mean about the timings of the death and when the poison may have been taken?" enquired Midge.

"Yes."

"Maybe they wanted to be sure that the jury would return a true bill against Fletcher," suggested Dickie. "There could be quite a hue and cry in the legal establishment if the Yard arrested a top man without much evidence. This way they can blame the jury."

Ronald sighed gloomily. "And the press can have a field day over those wretched letters."

"The letter to the Yard was the evidence that my father feared most," agreed Jenny, in carefully controlled tones, "but the others are even worse. The prosecution can now claim that they have evidence of blackmail." She turned to the others ashen-faced. "What can we do to prove them wrong?"

Chapter Twelve

After a long and heated discussion, the team arrived at a list of things to investigate. It read:

1. Find out where the aconitine came from (check chemists' poison books).
2. Find out if anyone could have put aconitine in the tea (speak to typists again, and see if anyone was lurking near the pantry).
3. Keep trying to discover if Forrest stopped in a pub and drank something which might have contained poison.
4. Talk to Professor Schulmann re Herr X.
5. Somehow investigate Forrest and Creech.
6. Try to find out more about the letters.

Looking at the list, Ronald found it difficult not to express his honest opinion: however much they might believe in Fletcher's innocence, there was nothing that they could do which the police would not do quicker and more efficiently. Jenny could not help feeling a similar gloom, but she tried to fight it by assigning different tasks.

"I'll finish going through the tea-shops, and Midge and I are going to see Professor Schulmann tomorrow. Can you continue visiting the taverns on Forrest's route back to Holborn?"

Whilst the men were discussing the chances of them knowing someone in the City who might have a connection with Forrest and Creech, Midge was pondering the list rather glumly. She did not know the members of chambers, so could not question them, and all the other measures outlined seemed to require a lot of walking around. If trailing along to three tea-shops had tired her, she would be no good visiting chemist shop after chemist shop. It was all very well arguing with her uncle that women were just as capable as men, but she wasn't being much help to Jenny so far. Midge shook herself. This was not the time for self-pity – she needed to think of something she could do, not worry about all the things she could not. Suddenly, two ideas occurred to her. One she tucked away for further consideration, the other she raised there and then.

"The medical evidence suggests that there is quite a high chance that Forrest somehow took the aconitine when he was here, didn't it?"

"Yes," agreed Dickie, impatiently, wondering why Jenny's friend was stating the obvious. Probably, he reflected, she lacked the reasoning capacity of the trained legal mind.

"But," continued Midge, ignoring Dickie's testy tone, "if, for a moment, we assume that there was poison in the tea, how can we be sure that it was aimed at Forrest?"

"The letters Forrest wrote suggest some sort of connection," James argued.

"Possibly," agreed Midge. "Look at it this way. What if the poison were intended for Mr Fletcher?"

"Nice," applauded Ronald appreciatively. "Very nice."

"I don't think it's nice at all," protested Jenny heatedly. "Why should anyone want to poison my father?"

"Perhaps because he knew what Forrest was up to," suggested Midge.

"Quite," agreed Ronald. "Obviously, there are a number of assumptions in Midge's case, but Forrest is a more likely murderer than Fletcher. He might have tried to bump off your father, Jenny, and somehow muddled up the cups."

"Why would he write that letter after he went back to his office?" demanded Dickie.

"To cover up what he'd done," declared Midge excitedly. "If the police discovered Mr Fletcher dead after they'd received Forrest's accusations, they'd think that Mr

Fletcher had committed suicide rather than face all sorts of public ignominy." Another idea struck her. "Or maybe Forrest killed himself when he knew the game was up."

"Again, why would he write the letter?" queried Dickie.

"To take revenge upon my father for having exposed him," suggested Jenny.

"Precisely," agreed Midge. "And who's more likely to be able to lay their hands on strange poisons – Jenny's father or some crook like Forrest."

"Steady," cautioned Ronald. "You can't go calling the man a crook when you've no evidence of it."

Midge grinned. "I thought you couldn't libel the dead?"

"Shall we turn her into a lawyer?" asked James humorously.

"Never mind that," ordered Jenny. "Can we prove Midge's theory?"

"Damn proof," growled Dickie. "What's important is whether we can make it stand up in court sufficiently to cast doubt on the case against Fletcher. I agree it sounds much more convincing to us, because we know Jenny's father, but the fact of the matter is Forrest is dead and that's what the police will stick to, not fanciful arguments based on the psychology of the victim."

"In that case," stated Jenny in as determined a voice as she could summon, "we need to find something which will stand up in court." She turned to Midge. "Let's go home and plan what we need to discuss with Professor Schulmann tomorrow."

Jenny was not the only person who was making plans. While Jenny had dismissed Dickie as not being the right man for her, Dickie himself had rather different views on the matter. His head told him that he needed to make his mark in the legal world before he contemplated marriage, but every time he caught sight of Jenny his heart raced faster. Even the thought that his mother would disapprove very strongly of Jenny's wit and Jenny's preference for a glittering night-life failed to put him off. Indeed, Dickie frequently found himself day-dreaming about rescuing Jenny from peril. It did not matter whether he carried her out of burning buildings, rescued her from floods or helped her to escape from wrecked express trains, the ending was always the same – a grateful Jenny sank back into his arms as he planted kiss after burning kiss on her face and breast.

In his more tranquil moments Dickie blushed for these fantasies; he had never thought in such clichéd terms since he had been eleven and had suddenly fallen most desperately in love with the daughter of the local vicar. That passion had died a quick death after Deirdre had revealed herself to be scared of climbing trees, but the older Dickie felt that he would never be free of Jenny's bewitchment, even if she decided to spurn all that he held dear. Hence Dickie spent the early evening lurking near a certain street where his sources hinted that Miss Burnham, the talkative typist at Sir Eustace Leadbetter's chambers, was wont to have her evening repast. Guiltily, Dickie reflected that he might have more chance of gaining valuable information if he had discussed his plans with the others, but he was determined to tackle his chosen prey alone. Then he would present what he had discovered to Jenny, just like a faithful hound returning to its master with a freshly-retrieved pheasant hanging from its slavering jaws.

The chosen prey was, at this precise moment, making her way slowly back from work. The 'bus had been full and Valerie Burnham had had to stand most of the way. Her feet ached and she wondered whether she would have been better off grabbing a quick cuppa near the office before attempting the trudge home. She sighed. There was a biting wind and she could not go to the cinema; it would spoil the trip with the girls on Saturday night if she had already seen the big picture. She tried to distract herself with the thought of what she would eat for dinner. Would she have a roll and soup, or would she have sausages? Sausage and mash wasn't very genteel, but it was filling and Ernie did make a lovely gravy. Perhaps she might stop off at the newsagents and see if this week's issue of *Woman's Orbit* was in. Then she could treat herself to the latest episode of *Silent Longing* over supper.

Valerie Burnham continued to plod up the road, in a dream modelled on the sort of magazine with which she stuffed herself when the cinema was unavailable. *Woman's Orbit* was full of romantic stories in which the heroine, after dreadful trials and tribulations, invariably found True Love, preferably in the arms of a handsome young man who just happened to work alongside her as a doctor, banker or other professional man. Valerie had already eyed up the possibilities in Leadbetter's chambers, as well as those men whom she could identify as belonging to neighbouring chambers. However, much to her frustration, she had not yet encountered the slightest spark of interest in any of those who were remotely possible. Indeed, the only man who had shown an inclination to fall for her peroxide charms was Mr Usher, Sir Eustace's chief clerk, and Valerie, just as much as Miss Jenkins, recognised the impediment of him being 'a married man with five children.' Clearly he was utterly unsuitable, in which case his repeated fatherly pats on the shoulder became offensive and annoying. Maybe her cousin Doris was quite correct. Maybe barristers were a fusty lot and she would be better off trying her hand in another sort of office. But, Valerie reflected determinedly, she was not going to work for a dentist. Dentists were common and nothing would change her mind as to that, no matter how much Doris went on about Mr Priestley's blue eyes and his curly hair.

Thus Valerie was busy in her own mind disparaging the charms of Cousin Doris' employer when she turned a corner and walked slap into a man coming hurriedly in the opposite direction. The man lifted his hat politely and began to apologise, before suddenly commenting in a startled manner.

"Good lord, it's Miss Burnham, isn't it?"

"Why, Mr Purcell, whatever are you doing here?"

"I had a conference which ran late. But, my dear Miss Burnham, I'm afraid I've splashed you rather when I dropped my bag. This confounded rain!"

Valerie thanked her lucky stars that she had not cursed the – at that point – unknown man for splashing her. Mr Purcell seemed to be perfectly polite in the office, but it could not be denied that he might have reacted badly to being told off by one of the typists.

Dickie, who could be adroit when he wanted to, took the opportunity to insist on buying Valerie a hot drink to warm her up. When she hesitated, he moved in smoothly, insisting that he really owed her dinner as well.

"You must allow me to make up for being so beastly careless," he begged.

Valerie agreed. Hadn't *Paula's Promise* begun on similar lines? And Doris' silly dentist had never done more than give her a Christmas box.

Chapter Thirteen

The next day, Jenny was extremely nervous as she and Midge approached Professor Schulmann's house.

"What if Professor Schulmann can't help? What if he hasn't tracked down Herr X? What if Herr X has refused to help?"

Midge looked at her friend sympathetically. She couldn't begin to think how awful it must be for Jenny. She could still remember how cut off she had felt when she had been sent to boarding-school in England. But she had been able to write to her parents back in India; there had been no suggestion that she would never see them again. She shivered. News took a long time to filter through from India and she suddenly wished that she knew that her parents were, indeed, still quite safe.

"I'm sure Professor Schulmann will do his best," she replied rather feebly. "He's confirmed your father's statement for a start."

When they entered the Professor's house, he ushered them into a study which was crammed with files and books. A single file lay open on the desk, an envelope next to it. The lawyer kissed Jenny's hand and bowed to Midge.

"You must be the friend who is providing support to Miss Fletcher," he stated in excellent, but accented, English.

"Err..., yes."

"I am grateful that you are able to do so." With another small bow, the lawyer indicated a chair for Midge to sit in. When both girls were sitting down, he asked Jenny how he could help her.

"I wondered if you could tell us whether you have traced Herr X."

A brief frown crossed the Professor's brow. "You must understand, Miss Fletcher, that I speak to you as a representative of your father. I may also speak to Herr Cottrell."

Jenny interrupted. "Please don't object to Mid-, that is, Miss Carrington. She knows everything that's gone on so far. Please, Professor Schulmann. She's known my father for years; she wouldn't do anything to endanger his security."

"I am sure she would not wish to do so, but these things are best discussed by as few people as possible."

Midge leaned forward. "I do understand the need to be careful, Professor Schulmann. And I do realise that it is not just Jenny's father who is involved: the extortion victims have to feel that they can trust you. But I can assure you that I would not put them at risk. I swear that I would only discuss what you say with Jenny or the defence team." She shrugged. "I hardly know anyone else in London, so I couldn't."

"If you were to talk then you would endanger the defence case."

"Which is why I shall not talk."

Professor Schulmann appeared to be debating with himself. He turned to Jenny. "If I asked Miss Carrington to leave, would you tell her later what I said to you?"

"No."

Midge overrode her friend. "Of course you would, Jenny, and Professor Schulmann knows it."

The lawyer gave a dry laugh. "It appears that Miss Carrington possesses both honesty and common sense."

Jenny blushed. "I'm terribly sorry."

"You are very worried, my dear. I think that Miss Carrington may stay." The Professor picked up the envelope. "I have here notes of my conversation with Herr X. He stated that he did not approach Forrest for false papers; those were arranged for him by other people. Moreover, he swears that Forrest had been extorting money from him for some time before Forrest's death."

"That completely undermines the police claims," declared Jenny.

"Not completely," warned the lawyer. "To be precise, it undermines the allegations which Forrest made. However, it does not disprove them."

"Because Herr X could be lying?" asked Jenny flatly.

Professor Schulmann gave another little bow. "That is so."

"And you spoke to him after the letters were read out at the inquest, didn't you?"

"I am afraid so."

"Thus the prosecution can allege that his comments were concocted to counter what Forrest had written." Jenny swallowed hard. "So they're not as much use as I originally thought, are they?"

"They are of use, but they do not clear your father." The lawyer looked unhappy. "I am glad that you can see the difficulties; I do not wish you to think that the matter is easy to resolve."

Midge now intervened. "Why did Herr X not tell you this before?"

"He is currently far away from London."

"Couldn't he have left London before?"

"There were complications."

Midge waited, hoping to be told what those were. When nothing was added, she asked another question. "If Herr X gives evidence, won't he be in danger of being deported?"

"Yes."

"I don't want to appear rude, but is there anything to prevent him from refusing to give evidence, or from disappearing completely?"

"He is trying to acquire a genuine right to reside in England."

Midge shifted uneasily. "But surely that would give him further reason not to give evidence?"

Professor Schulmann glanced at both girls. Jenny caught his look.

"Please, I'd rather hear everything – even what might go wrong."

"Your friend is quite correct. I hope that Herr X will give evidence, and I shall do everything I can to persuade him. It was I who involved your father in this and I must help him in every way."

"Daddy doesn't blame you," murmured Jenny.

"Your father is the height of that which is honourable and just." Professor Schulmann sighed. "For which reason I told him of this betrayal of the law." He picked up the file. "This may help him more. It contains notes of a conversation with a Herr Lipinski, whom I myself interviewed yesterday. I have hopes that I may persuade him to testify."

"Lipinski?" repeated Jenny. "Who is he?"

"He fled to England three years ago, by use of false papers. Since then he has become naturalised. Forrest had gained knowledge of how he entered the country and blackmailed him. Herr Lipinski paid four hundred pounds to Forrest not to alert the authorities, because he feared that he would be sent back to Germany if it were learned that he had entered the country on false documents."

"Why doesn't he fear that now?" asked Midge. "Couldn't his naturalisation be revoked if he had supplied false information in the application process?"

A shadow fell upon the Professor's face. "Yes, he could be sent back, but he no longer cares. His only son died two months ago in a camp in Germany."

There was a pause, in which Jenny muttered something about murderers.

Midge cleared her throat in an embarrassed fashion. "I

know it is useful to establish a pattern of extortion, but isn't the payment different? I thought that Herr X was paying on a regular basis, not making a large single sum."

"You are quite correct, Miss Carrington. Herr X was indeed paying regularly – over half his wages, to be precise. I believe that Forrest chose whichever method would make the greatest amount in the shortest time. Herr Lipinski had investments in France which he could realise, but Herr X could not take any money out of Germany."

"Presumably it was better to latch onto someone who could pay a lump sum?" asked Midge. "After all, then it wouldn't matter it the victim did leave London."

"Yes. You have a good understanding of the situation."

After some further desultory conversation, the two girls left. They had agreed to meet the others for dinner at Dmitri's and, as the taxi crawled along the Embankment, Jenny realised that they would be late.

"I hope the boys won't mind. I hope that they'll think that we've found out something useful."

Midge nodded. She knew that Jenny was worried as to how useful Professor Schulmann's new evidence would be.

Jenny and Midge arrived ten minutes late, full of apologies, only to discover that Dickie was the sole person present in the upstairs room. Three cigarette stubs suggested that he had been there for some time.

"Where are the others?" demanded Jenny.

"I'm not sure," admitted Dickie. "I saw James at lunchtime and he said something about having a quick drink at four o'clock, but he can't still be in a pub."

Jenny muttered something uncomplimentary but allowed herself to be distracted by Dickie, who was delighted to have the chance to speak to Jenny without the other men being present. He smugly narrated how he had carefully engineered his meeting with the typist the previous evening, but was surprised to see a slight frown on Jenny's face.

"What's up?" he enquired.

"Don't you think," faltered Jenny, "that it's maybe a bit unkind to have used this Miss... Miss…"

"Burnham," supplied Dickie.

"This Miss Burnham," repeated Jenny. "I mean," she went on with an embarrassed air, "she may have thought that you took her out for dinner because you liked her, not because you wanted to pump her for information."

Dickie scoffed at this suggestion. "Don't be silly, Jenny. I'm sure she didn't think anything of it. In any case, all's fair in love and war, and we're currently at war to help your father."

Following this speech, Dickie became conscious that a chill air had descended upon Dmitri's overheated room. He was busily cursing himself for having forgotten how women all hung together whenever there was the faintest hint of romance, when Midge recalled his attention to the matter of detection.

"Did Miss Burnham have anything useful to say?"

Dickie frowned. Truth to tell, he had been so pleased with himself in having intercepted the typist without rousing her suspicions that he had rather lost sight of what he had learned from her.

"I'm not actually sure," he admitted slowly. "She certainly wasn't very complimentary about your chambers."

Jenny bristled. "Indeed?"

"Yes. She called it the Chambers of Horrors and said that your chief typist had snubbed her when she'd tried to find out what had happened."

"Miss Jenkins is very loyal," commented Jenny repressively.

Dickie shot Jenny a quick look before deciding that it would be unwise to admit that he had perhaps given

Valerie Burnham rather more wine than she was used to. Given Jenny's reaction to him taking the typist out to dinner, she would be quite likely to start seeing him in the role of a white slave-trader.

"Did she say anything else?" asked Midge.

"Did she?" groaned Dickie. "She hardly stopped, but most of it was irrelevant gossip about my chambers, not yours. The only thing that I did wonder about was a remark she made about how it was funny working next to the place where Forrest was done in – her words, not mine – when she also knew a girl who had worked for Forrest."

"Oh?" remarked Jenny alertly. "We've been neglecting the Forrest angle a bit. What did she have to say about him? Was he ever moody or depressed?"

"She didn't really say much about Forrest, more about the office. Apparently this girl she knows, a Miss Hemming, didn't much like it there – one of the partners was never present, but there were always clients coming and going at odd hours. She didn't think that it was how a normal office worked."

"How does your Miss Burnham know this other girl?" enquired Midge, to whom the germ of an idea had occurred.

"She's not my Miss Burnham," protested Dickie, before relenting. "Before Miss Burnham came to our chambers, she used to work at a solicitors' office. She's still friendly with the girls at Hargreaves, Curtis and Hargreaves, and she met Miss Hemming when Miss Hemming started working there."

"Did Miss Burnham mention anything else about Forrest and Creech apart from the odd hours?" demanded Jenny.

"Only that she wouldn't want to work for a firm where the boss got murdered and that neither did her friend. I'm sorry I couldn't find out anything else," apologised Dickie, "but honestly, Jenny, I daren't risk making Miss Burnham suspicious by asking too many questions."

"I think that you did jolly well," stated Jenny. "After all, here's a perfectly innocent woman who's prepared to say to her friends that she didn't like working at Forrest's firm. Why couldn't the police have told the coroner that, instead of producing ridiculous letters accusing my father of things that he would never do?"

"Here come Ronald and James," announced Midge, who had been staring down into the street. "I wonder what they'll make of your news."

"And ours," pointed out Jenny.

However, when the two lawyers entered the room, it was clear that they had news of their own. James greeted Jenny with a fleeting kiss which did not entirely hide his sheepish grin, while Ronald looked displeased. Ronald waited until Dmitri had brought three foaming tankards of beer before answering Jenny's question as to where they had been.

"This idiot," he declared, "got himself arrested."

James sniggered nervously. He normally got on very well with Ronald, but the other advocate had, in James' view, taken unfair advantage of his two years' seniority to express himself with considerable vigour on the subject of damned fools. Since the walk back from Holborn police station was reasonably lengthy, Ronald had had a good opportunity to practise his oratorical skills, but James felt that a rehash of these remarks in front of Jenny would be rather unnecessary. Fortunately, Jenny was more interested in facts than in opinions.

"Arrested?"

"Well, detained for questioning," admitted Ronald.

Gathering from James' grin that all was now resolved, Midge asked what had happened.

111

"It wasn't entirely my fault," argued James. "When I suggested that I go and try to buy poison, Ronald was all for it!"

"Buy poison?" repeated Jenny. "Why?"

"There are far fewer apothecaries' shops in Holborn than there are public houses," explained James. "I thought that we might discover something a bit quicker if we focussed on aconitine rather than on Forrest's putative beer-drinking."

"But the police checked to see if Forrest had bought any aconitine and he hadn't," pointed out Jenny gloomily. "What was the point in you repeating their work?"

"The police went to pill-merchants close to Duke's Buildings and Forrest's home," declared James triumphantly. "They never checked to see if he might have bought some aconitine on the way back from your father."

"If he had realised that the game was up and had decided to kill himself?" enquired Midge.

"Exactly." James sighed. "I do think that this sort of investigation is a lot easier for a policeman. They have the full force of the law behind them, we have only native wit."

Ronald could be heard muttering something uncomplimentary about James' intellectual apparatus, but James was enjoying having a rapt audience. "Picture it: a policeman enters a shop, raps on the counter and demands to see the poison book. Any argument and the shopkeeper is haled off to gaol. However, we are forced to use any number of spoils and stratagems. My first venture was unsuccessful because the girl behind the counter informed me that she wasn't allowed by law to sell poison to gents, and only her dad could be doing that, and he preferred to trade with proper rat-catchers belonging to the guild."

"You should have taken that as a warning," Ronald declared.

"I misinterpreted the auguries," agreed James. "Buoyed

up by my prentice effort, I launched myself at the next establishment which caught my eye, a rather prosperous looking affair with plate-glass windows stacked with bottles filled with coloured water, all aimed at attracting the unwary passer-by."

At this point it was Jenny's turn to mutter something about the Patent Medicine Act, but this interjection was waved away with aplomb by James.

"Dear child, when you are a qualified barrister-at-law, as I am, you will know exactly when you can make these sort of remarks and when not."

"Be quiet, Jenny," urged Midge, as her friend attempted to disabuse James of the notion that she held him in high esteem. "I want to hear what happened next."

"There was a rather superior female who blanched at the notion of selling ratsbane to me and swiftly passed me on to the poisoner-in-chief."

"Why ratsbane?" demanded Jenny.

"I had to have some sort of a cover-story," James pointed out, "so I said that I was bothered by rats in my digs and had promised to get some poison for my landlady, as she thought that it was a man's job." He coughed. "In reality, my very formidable landlady is more than capable of buying poison, whether to rid her own house, or the entire street, of rats." He took a long pull from his glass of beer. "That's where things started to go wrong. The chemist was quite prepared to sell me some preparatory compound of his own."

"And you would have got a look at his poison book when you bought it," pointed out Ronald.

James grinned ruefully. "I got a bit carried away and asked for aconitine."

"But why would anyone use aconitine for rat-bait?" asked Jenny. "The doctor at the inquest said that it was never used like that."

113

"Yes, well, quite," murmured James.

Ronald gave one of his rare smiles. "Apparently, James decided to go for the silly-ass-about-town approach. He pretended to want something a bit more fashionable than arsenic, or whatever is normally used."

James blushed. "I wasn't that bad! I merely asked whether he sold much of that odd poison which was used in the recent murder case and, when he said that he didn't, I asked him whether he might add a little to my rat-bait to ginger the whole thing up a bit. He nodded and disappeared." James pulled a face. "I thought that he'd gone to prepare the poison, but he slipped out the back door and grabbed the nearest bobby. The next thing I knew, I was detained for questioning."

"The first thing that *I* knew about it," proclaimed Ronald, "was when Roderick Staunton showed up in my room with a police constable in tow and ordered me to go and see whether the Parry currently under questioning at Holborn police station belonged to us."

"If only they had blasted well telephoned," groaned James. "They would have been dealt with by Miss Jenkins or, at the worst, by Thomson. But, of course, when they sent a policeman round to check, old Staunton had to discover all about it."

"You'll be in for a wigging tomorrow," warned Jenny.

"Don't remind me," pleaded James. "I've already heard Ronald's views on how the well-regulated barrister comports himself."

"Why didn't Mr Staunton come to bail you out?" asked Midge.

James laughed. "Ronald was hanging around with nothing to do; why ought Staunton to soil his hands by entering something so shameful as a police station?"

"I might point out that *Rex v. Oswald* is not normally categorised as having nothing to do," remarked Ronald somewhat curtly, conscious that he would have to work late into the evening to make up for lost time.

Jenny ignored this point. "What did you tell the police?"

James played with the tablecloth nervously. He had a feeling that Jenny was not going to be pleased with him. "Well, the thing is, Jenny, I had to give my real name and place of business and…" His voice tailed off.

"And?" demanded Jenny suspiciously.

"And," James continued reluctantly, "the sergeant at the station recognised where I worked and got frightfully excited about it all. He insisted on sending for Inspector Groves."

"What did you tell him?"

James cast a glance of appeal at Jenny. "He didn't believe that I really wanted rat-poison and he threatened to go round to my lodgings and interview Mrs Jones. Honestly, Jenny, I'm sure he knew exactly what I was up to."

"But you went and told him what you were doing all the same," growled Jenny.

"Be fair," expostulated Dickie. "Parry's a member of the Bar; he cannot refuse to answer reasonable questions from a police officer."

Jenny relapsed into silence, recognising the truth of Dickie's point, but wishing all the same that Inspector Groves was not aware that there were other investigators on the track of the killer of William Forrest.

Seeing Jenny's downcast face, Ronald changed the subject. "Let's order something to eat and then you can tell us what Professor Schulmann said," he declared abruptly.

Chapter Fourteen

It did not take Jenny long to summarise what they had been told by Professor Schulmann.

"That's important, Jenny," commented Dickie softly. "If nothing else, a direct contradiction of one of the statements in Forrest's letter will help to raise questions about the other statements."

"Exactly," Ronald agreed. "There's no-one quite like Denys for casting doubt over witnesses. Think what he can do with a letter which can't argue back!"

James and Dickie were adding to this professional assessment when Dmitri entered, followed by several waiters laden down by heavy trays. As the aroma of goulash wafted towards Jenny, she suddenly realised that she was ravenously hungry. She had been too apprehensive about her interview with the Professor to eat lunch, and she had had no time for tea.

Once the waiters were safely out of the room, Midge asked something which had been worrying her.

"Will the refugees' evidence be seen as entirely reliable?"

Ronald pulled a face. "It rather depends on how the jury reacts to foreigners."

"That wasn't quite what I meant." Midge hesitated. She did hope that the men weren't going to laugh at her. "What I meant was, how do we know that they are telling the truth? Think about it: Herr X has run away – maybe he has a guilty conscience. And now we've got evidence of another man being blackmailed. If there was a direct, deliberate system of extortion, then there are bound to be other victims – perhaps a large number of them. What if one of them was the murderer?"

Dickie appeared to be making a calculation. "How would this man know that Forrest was going to see

Fletcher?"

"He wouldn't need to," argued Midge. "All he'd need to do was lie in wait near Forrest's office. When he saw Forrest returning, he could beg to speak to him. He could suggest talking things over quietly in a pub. Then, whilst he was pleading for more time to pay, he could poison Forrest."

Jenny's face lit up momentarily. "That's brilliant, Midge." Then her face fell. "But how on earth would we prove it? How could we trace this man? You can't exactly advertise for refugees who have been blackmailed and resorted to murder, can you?"

Ronald could not disagree with Jenny's assessment. "I'm afraid you're correct, Jenny. But talk to Cottrell about it."

"I'm seeing him tomorrow." Jenny bit her lip unhappily. "I wish I could do something more to help."

The following morning, Midge hung around the house on tenterhooks until Jenny finally departed to see Cottrell, her father's solicitor. Immediately Jenny had left, Midge asked Field to hail a taxi for her. Once in it, she set off for Fleet Street, edgily repeating to herself that there was no reason for her uncle to be visiting the head office of his newspaper at that particular hour. She and Jenny were fully aware that – in theory – emancipated womanhood could tackle anything a man could. All the same, Midge knew that Mr Carrington would view her intended proceedings with distinct displeasure and she had no desire to meet him before she had even begun. Taking a deep breath, she walked past the commissionaire, entered the large atrium, and gave her name to one of the girls who directed visitors to the appropriate rooms.

"Do you have an appointment, Miss Carrington?"

"I sent Mr Palmer a telegram last night," explained

Midge, hoping that the newspaper's music critic would be in the building.

"Let me telephone up to his office and check."

After a few minutes, during which the girl appeared to hold several different conversations, she turned back to Midge with a polite smile.

"Mr Palmer will see you now, Miss Carrington. Please take the lift to the fifth floor where his secretary will show you to his office."

As the lift mounted upwards, Midge worried nervously as to whether the newspaperman would remember her. She had guessed that her surname would at least secure her an interview, but would Arthur Palmer actually agree to help her?

After conventional greetings were out of the way, Palmer asked what he could do for Midge. He expected that she was after tickets to some concert; what he was not expecting was a nervous request that he write a reference for Midge as a typist in the name of Mary Carew.

"What do you need a reference for? Anyway, you're not a typist – I thought that you were reading Classics at Newnham?"

Seeing the doubtful expression on the reporter's face, Midge hastened to reassure him. "I'm not asking you to lie about me; I can type and I can do shorthand after a fashion – my uncle made me learn ages ago."

"And why does my esteemed colleague not supply this reference? Does he even know that you want one?"

Midge blushed. "Err..., no. But I'm sure he'd think that I was showing the sort of initiative that journalists use. And I'm trying to help a friend."

Arthur Palmer looked at Midge closely. He had worked long enough in the newspaper business to know that scoops could come of such odd requests, but he had no intention of helping an inexperienced girl land herself in trouble.

"I think that I need to know a bit more about this," he commented gravely. "Apart from anything else, why do you intend to use a false name – you aren't doing anything silly like running away from home, are you?"

Midge's offended dignity soon reassured him on this point. "I'm not thirteen," she reminded him, before going on to point out that whilst she, personally, was proud of her name, it was an unsuitable one to use when carrying out undercover investigative work.

The reporter considered this argument thoughtfully. "Into which particular firm do you intend to insinuate yourself?" he enquired.

Midge grimaced. She had wondered in advance how she would deal with such a question and had been unable to come up with any answer other than the truth.

"Forrest and Creech," she admitted unwillingly.

Palmer's eyebrows shot up. He might spend most of his time discussing atonality, Diaghilev and Debussy, but he was not so far removed from matters of ordinary life that he had not been following the murder trial of the year. Indeed, given that the editor had cleared the front page of any other news on the day that Patrick Fletcher had been arrested, and had shown every indication of reacting in a similar method should further dramatic developments occur, anyone who worked at the *Universal Record*'s headquarters was probably better informed as to the progress of the trial than the average police constable in the West End district.

"Well, well, well," sighed Palmer reflectively. "I wonder what you've got hold of." He scratched his head. "I seem to remember Carrington mentioning that Fletcher's daughter was at school with you. Is that the connection?" Then, when Midge remained silent, he laughed. "I shan't try to steal your scoop, Miss Carrington; just remember to mention my name when the editor is handing out praise and glory."

The pair spent the next quarter of an hour concocting a suitable reference, before the reporter gave Midge a few words of advice.

"Don't trust anyone in your office; don't trust anyone you don't know; and keep your contacts with Fletcher's friends and relatives as limited as possible – you don't know who might be watching you."

Midge nodded solemnly. Now that she was launching herself into this quest she felt sick and uncertain. Apart from anything else, she did not even know whether Forrest and Creech intended to employ a new typist to replace Miss Hemming. After all, with one partner dead, there might be significantly less work than usual. However, Palmer recalled her attention.

"Are you fixed up with an accommodation address?"

"I've got lodgings near Holborn."

"Do you have a second reference?"

Midge grinned. "My cousin John will supply me with one – I hope! Having done typing for a don will explain how I know lawyer's Latin."

"Very organised," praised Mr Palmer. "However, if you get stuck, I can arrange another reference for you."

He cut short Midge's thanks to ask her a final question.

"I gather that the job hasn't been advertised yet. How are you going to explain coming to hear about the chance of a vacancy?"

"That's the bit I'm not sure about. I thought about saying that I had met Miss Hemming and that she mentioned having left Forrest and Creech, but it sounds a bit weak."

"It will be if this Miss Hemming denies all knowledge of you." Unable to stop himself, the reporter's eyes shifted to Midge's sticks which lay near where she sat. Midge followed the trajectory of his glance and flushed darkly. She opened her mouth to speak, but Palmer interrupted.

"My secretary's pretty trustworthy. If you say that she told you about Miss Hemming leaving, then I can fix things at this end."

"Yes," remarked Midge rather bitterly. "I am a bit too noticeable to make a decent investigator, aren't I?"

"Use it to your advantage," suggested the newspaperman mildly, dimly remembering the time when Geoffrey Carrington had feared that his niece would die of infantile paralysis. "Whoever's in charge at Forrest and Creech will have been badgered by reporters since Forrest died. He'll probably be deeply suspicious of all new employees, whether they are the typist, the office charwoman, or the man who comes to read the gas. If he looks on the surface and fails to realise that you might have hidden depths, that will make your investigations considerably easier."

Midge flashed him a smile which had nothing to do with the reference he had just written, but everything to do with the reporter's assumption that she could achieve things despite her withered leg and weak arm. She encountered too many people who clearly saw her as a useless specimen, unable even to fulfil so simple a role as being a proper niece to Mrs Carrington. She did not arrange the flowers; she could not be paraded round various drawing-rooms; and she would not be ultimately married off to some good-looking young man, preferably a Guards officer with a sizeable private income. To encounter a professional man who calmly stated that she could use her illness to deceive and confound her enemies was gratifyingly uplifting.

Mr Palmer rose and shook Midge's hand. "Good luck in your stalwart effort."

"Thank you. I shan't forget your help."

Midge knew that the next challenge was the hardest, that of trying to convince whoever was currently in charge at Forrest and Creech that she ought to be hired as a new typist. Fortunately, Dickie had managed to extract some useful information from Miss Burnham as to the inhabitants of the office. Hence Midge suspected that either Mr Wynne, the clerk, or Miss Hurst, the chief typist, would speak to her. Midge's heart was thumping uncomfortably as she slowly walked up Goose Lane and entered Romberg Street. As she reached Duke's Buildings, she would have given a large sum of money to turn tail and flee, but she forced herself to enter the dimly-lit hallway. She stared round for a moment, before spotting a door, beside which was screwed a brass plaque, which was badly in need of a good clean. Under the verdigris read the information, 'Forrest and Creech, Notaries at Law and Commissioners for Oaths'. Midge took a deep breath and knocked upon the door.

After a few moments, a shock-headed youth opened the door.

"Yes, Miss?"

"May I speak to Miss Hurst or Mr Wynne?"

"Why do you want to see them?" enquired the office-boy suspiciously.

"I have heard that there may be a vacancy for a typist," explained Midge politely.

The office-boy ran his eyes over Midge, wondering whether she might be another enterprising journalist trying to get a view of what some of the more sensational press had taken to calling the Scene of Violent Death. However, it was surely a bit unlikely at this late stage. Even the police had lost interest – they hadn't been back for days, which was a source of secret sorrow to young Davie, who had been showing off to all his friends about what he knew.

"What name shall I say?"

"Mi...," Midge coughed. "Mary Carew."

"Right you are, Miss. If you'd like to wait in here."

As Midge followed the boy into the dull corridor, she mentally kicked herself. A fat lot of use she would be if she fell at the first hurdle and gave her real name when she had been at such pains to arrange for references in the name of Mary Carew.

After a few minutes, a bell buzzed in the room near where Midge was waiting. A woman swiftly crossed the corridor and entered a room further up the passageway, banging the door behind her. Soon Midge caught the sound of raised voices. Checking fearfully in case anyone was watching, Midge sidled towards the noise of argument.

"It's all very well for you to say not to employ anyone new, Mr Wynne," complained a female voice with the hint of a country inflection, "but how am I expected to get all the work of the office done with two fewer members of staff?"

A male voice could be heard suggesting that there was less work to be done since Mr Forrest had died.

"You know fine well that's not true, Mr Wynne. If anything, there's more work to be done because we've had so many telephone enquiries to deal with and all those wretched reporters coming to the door with interminable questions."

Midge could not catch the response, but the female voice was sounding distinctly irritated.

"Perhaps the work will fall off soon, but what's to be done in the meantime. Do you think that telephones answer themselves? Here's Miss Peters working out her notice – and I'm not surprised after what you said to her – and Miss Hemming already left. That leaves me. Who's going to deal with the mail or the urgent telegrams if I'm busy taking shorthand from Mr Creech or trying to answer letters? It won't be you, that I do know! And what good is Davie when it comes to writing letters? Or reading them accurately, for that matter?"

"It's not safe to take on new people at the moment. How do we know whether she is a reporter or a police spy?"

"A police spy? Don't be ridiculous; the girl doesn't even look eighteen."

Midge mentally adjusted her age down to sixteen, for once blessing the fact that she looked younger and more vulnerable when she was tired.

"Anyway, the police don't employ cripples. Davie said that this girl was limping and used walking-sticks, so she can't be from the police."

There was another pause, before the woman added, "At least let me see whether she is able to type. If she is, we can employ her for a few months until Mr Creech decides what he wants to do."

The male voice grunted reluctant assent and Midge swiftly resumed her seat in anticipation of the descent of the woman, whom she presumed must be Miss Hurst.

When the door opened, the light fell upon a tall woman in her late forties or early fifties, who was dressed in a coat and jacket of severe cut and dull fabric. The older woman's salt and pepper hair was drawn back into a tight bun and her complexion was innocent of all aids to beauty. Midge blessed the fact that she had ignored Jenny's offer to raid her wardrobe anytime she wished. Anything Jenny possessed was far too well-cut to fit into an office run by this person.

In return, Miss Hurst ran her eyes over Midge approvingly. No trace of make-up, not even powder, and certainly none of that dreadful lipstick which girls seemed to adopt all the time these days.

"I am Miss Hurst and I gather that you want to work

for us as a typist. Where have you been employed before, Miss Carew?"

"I started with a Mr Carrington in Cambridge. He wanted typing done for a book which he is writing. When that finished I moved to London because I thought that there would be more jobs available. I've just finished working for Mr Palmer of the *Universal Record*."

"Why did you leave? Was your work not good enough?"

"Oh no," answered Midge softly, looking up at Miss Hurst with innocent grey eyes. "Mr Palmer types all of his newspaper reports himself, but he asked me to prepare some articles for a learned journal. They had to be typed in a certain way and he wanted a professional typist to do it for him. However, I've completed all the typing that he needs at the moment."

Miss Hurst bit back a smile on hearing this slip of a girl describe herself as a professional typist.

"Are you used to keeping office hours?" she demanded abruptly. "We work from eight thirty in the morning until five thirty at night. You will also work every other Saturday until one o'clock."

"I had to work late with Mr Carrington; he was rather absent-minded and never noticed how late it got." Having restored her confidence somewhat by this slanderous comment on her cousin, Midge found herself being quizzed on shorthand, before being asked to sit down at a typewriter and transcribe a letter.

Miss Hurst inspected her work carefully, before pronouncing it good enough.

"I shall take you to our clerk, Mr Wynne," she proclaimed. "He deals with the hiring of anyone in the office, so the decision as to whether to employ you will rest with him."

"Thank you, Miss Hurst."

Realising that she was over the first set of defences, Midge prayed for luck as she was ushered into the clerk's office. If only she were appointed, she might be of some use to Jenny and Mr Fletcher. Surely there must be something wrong at an office which feared police spies? But what if Wynne had seen her at the inquest? What if he recognised her?

Wynne's first words showed no sign that he had recognised Midge. "I gather that you are Mary Carew."

"Yes, sir," replied Midge, thinking that there was nothing to be lost by civility.

"What's wrong with your leg?"

Midge's face flamed. "I had infantile paralysis."

"So you always hobble about like that?"

Biting her lip, Midge nodded.

Wynne grunted. "Normally, part of a junior typist's job would include greeting clients and ushering them into to see Mr Creech, but obviously I can't let clients see you. Naturally, it follows from that that I cannot pay you a full wage. Do you understand?"

"Yes, Mr Wynne."

"How old are you?"

"I shall be seventeen in March."

Wynne grunted again, but this time his grunt concealed relief. If this girl was only sixteen – and she did not look as if she could be much older – then she could hardly be a police spy. She was probably too young to be one of those blasted reporters, either. Moreover, surely no reporter would have been so blind as to use another reporter to write a reference for them.

"I am prepared to take you on a week's trial, but if your work is not satisfactory, you will not be kept on."

"Thank you, Mr Wynne."

"Finally," added the clerk in impressive tones, "you may know that we had an unfortunate accident in the office. Under no circumstances are you to gossip about anything you see or hear at work. Is that clear?"

"Yes, Mr Wynne. I shan't gossip."

"Good. You may tell Miss Hurst that you are to start on Monday when Miss Peters leaves."

With that, Midge was dismissed.

Chapter Fifteen

When Midge left Duke's Buildings, she heaved a deep sigh of relief. However, remembering Arthur Palmer's warnings, she did not immediately hail a cab and set off back to Middle Temple. Instead, she slowly made her way to Romberg Street, where she waited patiently for an omnibus. She had found lodgings nearby several days ago in the vague idea that it would be helpful to have a bolt-hole that was not closely connected to either Mr Fletcher's house or his chambers. At that point, Midge had intended somehow scraping an acquaintance with someone – anyone – who worked in Duke's Buildings and who might be prepared to share their opinions of the dead man. Now that she had actually managed to land open access to Forrest's office it would be all the more important to conceal her identity.

As Midge slowly dragged herself along the road which led to her rather seedy lodgings, she found that she was picking out details that she would not normally notice. Puddles of rainwater stood dankly in shadows; slate roofs were dark and foreboding; the streets running off the main thoroughfare were narrow and the houses encroached upon each other like inimical, threatening beasts. A man stood on a corner, his grubby fawn mackintosh belted round him, a cigarette hanging loosely from his slack lips. Midge felt his eyes running over her and flushed, suddenly feeling very vulnerable. No-one knew that she was here; anyone could be lurking in these sunless streets.

Back in the rather more comfortable surroundings of Middle Temple, Jenny was also feeling ill-at-ease. Not only had Cottrell pointed out all the potential difficulties relating to the new evidence offered by Professor Schulmann, he had also taken the opportunity to remind her that the case against her father was bleak. As if this were not enough, he had finished up the discussion by reproving her for encouraging James to use his time and energy in inappropriate ways. After she returned from seeing Cottrell, Jenny hung around chambers, getting in everyone's way until Ronald pointed out that he had work which simply had to be addressed urgently. Jenny muttered crossly to herself, before taking herself off in a rage. When she returned home she was unreasonably offended that Midge was absent, and wandered around the drawing-room, angrily moving ornaments and books about. Then she felt inordinately guilty.

"Midge is giving up her vacation to keep me company. She's got work to do and she ought to be resting. I wasn't here this morning; why shouldn't she choose to go shopping?"

Nevertheless, despite Jenny's assumption that Midge must have gone shopping, she was growing concerned when her friend did not return until long after dusk. Once inside, Midge sank down by the fire and gave a deep sigh.

"I've got a job as a typist at Forrest and Creech. I'll be able to search for evidence that Forrest *was* blackmailing those refugees – or that he killed himself."

Jenny stared at Midge in amazement. At that point, Field entered, bearing a tray loaded with tea and sandwiches. Midge had had no lunch and gratefully seized upon the food while she gave Jenny further details. At the end, she warned Jenny that nothing might come of it.

"Don't forget, Forrest may have had enough time after he got back to his office to destroy any evidence of wrongdoing. It won't be easy to prove that he made up all those lies to have revenge upon your father."

Jenny was too delighted to hear any positive news to listen to caution.

"That'll show the others!" declared Jenny.

Midge looked up alertly. "What's up?"

Jenny pulled a face. "Staunton ticked the boys off; Cottrell ticked me off; even Ronald ticked me off."

"Why?" enquired Midge in some surprise. She had thought that Ronald liked Jenny.

Jenny scowled. "Cottrell warned me that it wouldn't help my father if we managed to antagonise the police while Staunton was annoyed about James investigating chemists' shops yesterday. He told him that 'his antics would bring the chambers into disrepute'. Then, when I was busy commiserating with James, Ronald – of all people – decided to support Mr Pompous Staunton."

"What did Ronald say?"

"He claimed that Staunton is the only senior person in the place and that Staunton wasn't the sort of man to approve of unorthodox methods of doing things."

"I suppose Ronald has worked with Staunton for longer than any of you," suggested Midge tentatively.

"He may have," snorted Jenny, "and Ronald may be correct that Staunton isn't trying to be deliberately unhelpful, but being the second most senior barrister in chambers doesn't given Staunton the right to tell James to grow up and stop making a fool of himself – especially when all James was trying to do was help my father."

Midge winced, but Jenny was not finished. "Nor does it give Staunton the right to tell Cottrell that I'm distracting the others. Distracting indeed! How would he like it if his rotten son were accused of murder? He made enough fuss last year when all the boy's tutor wanted to do was rusticate him."

Watching Jenny prowling angrily around the room, Midge was irresistibly reminded of her cat Bertie when he was annoyed. She suddenly wished that she were back at Brandon, curled up by the fire listening to Bertie purring. Reminding herself that Jenny's father was languishing in gaol, Midge forced her attention back onto what her friend was saying.

"I don't know whether it is a good thing that the police now know our idea. They oughtn't to have overlooked checking the chemists near Middle Temple in the first place, and they'll certainly find it a lot easier to look at the poison books than poor James did." Jenny bit her perfectly tinted nails nervously, before whispering, "But what if they do find that someone bought aconitine and they claim that that person was my father."

"Is that likely?" asked Midge. "It would be easy to prove that any signature in a poison book which purported to be his was a forgery, and surely it would be rather risky to pretend to be Mr Fletcher in – of all places – the area around Middle Temple? After all, he's pretty well known and his portrait is often in the newspapers."

"I suppose so," replied Jenny in unconvinced tones. "I thought that we'd achieved something when Cottrell admitted that the police hadn't investigated the lead properly, but now all I can see is the possible dangers."

"Did Cottrell have any fresh news?"

"No," sighed Jenny. "He said that, considering everything, Daddy was in good spirits, but I don't know how true that is. I can't visit Daddy at the moment, nor would Cottrell suggest any further lines of enquiry. All he did was rap my knuckles over James' arrest – albeit in the most gentlemanly manner possible – and warn me not to instigate any such undertakings again."

Jenny scowled in a manner which would have confirmed the elderly solicitor's opinion that Jenny was indeed what, in his young days, had been described as wilful. "I don't care. I think your plan is brilliant. But don't tell the others." She snorted mutinously. "I don't want to have to listen to inordinate lectures about breach of trust between employer and employee whilst you're enjoying

131

yourself digging through the effects of the late William Forrest."

A thought suddenly struck her. "Wynne gave evidence at the inquest, didn't he? What if he recognised you?"

"He wouldn't have taken me on if he had. Thank goodness you lent me that hat with the veil. I didn't look in the least bit like Mary Carew." Midge gave a slight frown. "Mind you, Wynne doesn't look in the least bit like you'd expect."

"What do you mean?"

"His voice is deep and commanding but he's nondescript-looking. You could easily mistake him for anyone in a crowd."

Jenny looked worried. "You mean there's nothing I could watch out for if he suddenly appeared in chambers asking about you?"

Midge thought for a moment. "He's got unusually light-blue eyes and wears good-quality clothes."

"That won't make him stand out in Middle Temple."

"He might come to ask something about Forrest, but I can't imagine that he'd ever connect me with you. If anyone – even James or Ronald – does ask about me, just say that I've gone back to Brandon. I don't want anyone to know that I'm still in London. They might wonder why I'd become invisible all of a sudden."

Chapter Sixteen

Later on, Midge was concerned to note her friend's appearance. Jenny looked white and strained, and appeared to be answering questions at random. Eventually, she admitted to having a filthy headache, but after several cups of tea she claimed to be feeling much better.

"Don't worry about me," she declared. "We need to think about you and to make sure that you look the part for your job. That means clothes. Let's go through what you have here and see what you need to get."

Since the girls had come away from Suffolk in a hurry, Midge did not have many clothes with her. Nevertheless, Jenny weeded these out rigorously, ruthlessly condemning one skirt as too well-cut, whilst a jersey was set aside as too scruffy.

"Does it really matter?" protested Midge, mildly offended as Jenny cast abjurations upon her attire.

"Of course it does," snapped Jenny. "Unless you can say that a previous employer passed you down a few of her clothes, there is no way that a girl of Mary Carew's class could have licitly acquired some of your things. Equally, no girl who wants to make her living would dare show up in an office wearing that jersey or this blouse."

"It's the jersey I wear when I'm grooming Bertie," explained Midge.

"It looks like it," muttered Jenny, as she pulled open the last of the drawers of the tallboy in Midge's room and lifted up a bundle of peach silk.

"Hey," objected Midge, "leave those alone."

"Just as well I'm here to vet this lot," declared Jenny. "I can't think of anything less suitable."

Midge glared at her, wondering why Jenny had suddenly turned all prim. "Why shouldn't I wear silk if I want to? No-one's going to see those."

133

"I'm delighted that Midge Carrington is allowing herself a few luxuries for a change," declared Jenny, "but this Mary Carew girl is only sixteen and not at all well off. She can't possibly afford that sort of frivolity." Jenny held up her hand as Midge continued to protest. "How do you know that someone won't check up on your lodgings? Anyway, if your landlady sees these, she'll throw you out for being immoral."

Midge turned brick red, before Jenny hastily explained. "I'm not saying that you are immoral, you goop. But I lay you ten to one in guineas that your landlady would think that you weren't just a typist if she saw those. After all, she's got the reputation of her own lodgings to think about."

"In that case," snorted Midge, "she could start by cleaning the front step properly."

"Oh, poor Midge! Is the rest of the house as bad?"

Midge nodded as she remembered the horrible bare room, with the iron bedstead and the stained patches on the wallpaper where the rain clearly came in. "Don't worry, Jenny. Given how little I'm being paid, it's just as well that I have got such cheap lodgings. They will fit the picture perfectly." She grimaced. "I dread to think how a real Mary Carew would survive on my wages."

"Never mind," declared Jenny fiercely, hating the fact that Midge was going to suffer on her behalf, "you shall simply wallow in luxury until Tuesday night."

With this noble aim in mind, Jenny insisted on Midge using scoopfuls of her most expensive bath salts before they changed for dinner. When Midge explained that she did not want to risk going to a restaurant just in case someone observed her, Jenny went down to the kitchen to give Mrs Field carte blanche.

"It's about time that you had some proper meals, Miss Jenny," remarked the housekeeper, who had known Jenny since she was a baby and was thus inclined to trespass into the realms of unrestricted free speech. "It won't do the master any good if you starve yourself into nothing."

Jenny passed her hand wearily across her brow. Mrs Field was undoubtedly speaking good sense, but she was increasingly finding that she had no inclination to eat anything at all. The housekeeper shot Jenny a worried look.

"I'll get Field to pour some sherry for you and Miss Carrington," she promised. "And what about a nice glass of burgundy with your meal? Your father would want you to dine properly."

"If they hang him, all his wine will go to the salerooms, so we may as well drink it," remarked Jenny bitterly, before wishing that she had kept her opinions to herself. Mrs Field looked stricken and her voice shook slightly as she remonstrated with her employer's daughter.

"Now then, Miss Jenny, that won't help Mr Fletcher." Hoping to distract Jenny, she asked, "Have you heard from Mr Mike or Mr Tom?"

"Tom can't leave Egypt, but Mike's hoping to come up next week to see Cottrell."

"Then I'd better prepare his room," suggested Mrs Field, before adding comfortingly, "You'll feel better when Mr Mike's here."

Jenny nodded politely, before turning to matters domestic.

During dinner, Jenny occupied herself by inventing a number of past histories for Midge's alternate persona, Mary Carew.

"I imagine her as a daughter of the Church who fell," she declared. "That will explain your nervous, worried expression."

"I don't look nervous," retorted Midge, offended.

"Ah, but you do. Or you will once you enter the

135

gloomy portals of Forrest and Creech. Hence you must have a possible explanation."

"How did I fall?"

"Might you have become passionately in love with the curate?" enquired Jenny. "I see a tall, handsome, worldly young man, whose devastating profile left you lovelorn and helpless in his grasp."

"What bilge have you been reading?" demanded Midge. "Anyway, our curate is suspected of being Low Church. I can't possibly envisage him indulging in worldly dalliance."

"That's because you lack imagination," Jenny riposted. "Either think of his homely appearance as being a Satanic ploy to encourage the village maidens to trust him, or pick on another good-looking man and think of him betraying the vicar's daughter with false promises of unwavering, undying love. Or," she suggested, becoming carried away with her theme, "you could have fallen passionately in love with the wicked Carrington of Trinity, only to be rewarded with betrayal followed by abandonment. These dons, my dear, are simply not to be trusted!"

Midge unsuccessfully attempted to fight down a blush. "Is that in my character of a daughter of the Church, or as a mere typist? Because I warn you, I gave the impression to Miss Hurst that John was about ninety. I said that he was frightfully absent-minded and was always keeping me late."

Jenny was momentarily distracted from her father's predicament. "I'd love to see John's face when he finds that out!"

"Actually," admitted Midge confidentially, "I think that he must be away at the moment, because I've had no response from my telegram."

"The one warning him that he had to write a good reference if asked?"

"Exactly. Either Forrest and Creech haven't contacted him or he isn't at Brandon, because he hasn't asked for any further explanation as to what's going on."

"Don't worry," advised Jenny, who could not bear the idea that something might go wrong with Midge's plan at the last moment. "If references are being sought, your Mr Palmer will have written a good one and the firm can hardly expect an absent-minded ninety-year-old to reply within a week."

"Quite," agreed Midge, before firmly directing the conversation onto safer topics. She had no desire to tell Jenny how hurt she had felt when John had not replied to her wire. It was only after some time that the possibility that John was away (rather than ignoring her in a time of need) had occurred to Midge.

Although Midge managed to keep Jenny occupied until the girls retired for the night, despair – and her headache – returned once Jenny had ensconced herself in bed.

'We have achieved nothing,' she thought. 'We haven't found where the poison came from; we don't know when or where it was administered; we don't even know whether it was directed at Forrest or was meant for someone else in chambers. If the defence can't supply answers to those questions then the jury is bound to side with the prosecution. Then Daddy will hang. I can't bear it. I can't bear it.'

Despite Jenny's repeating to herself that at least the defence might be able to use the evidence of Herr X and Mr Lipinski, it took her hours before she finally fell asleep. When she did so, it was to be tormented by confused nightmares in which defence counsel decided that they would no longer represent her father.

Jenny woke up with a whimper, before she realised that she was in her own bed, not in the Old Bailey. She switched on her bedside light and hunted round for her watch, then remembered that she had left it lying on her dressing-table. She slipped out of bed and tugged back the

137

curtains to see what sort of day it was. As she watched the grey light breaking across the black roofs she shivered, not from cold, chilly though the morning was. Instead, she shivered from fear. Dawn was the time when the sentence of death was executed; dawn was when men were made to mount a scaffold with their hands tied behind their backs; dawn was when the noose was carefully placed round their necks. And soon her father would face his own grim dawn, waiting for the hangman to release the trapdoor and pitch him down with his neck snapped and his life gone.

Soon after nine o'clock Jenny was summoned to the telephone by Field, who informed her that her father's solicitor was wishful of speaking to her. For a brief moment, Jenny dreamt that perhaps the case had been dropped, but Cottrell had no such glad tidings.

"Miss Fletcher? I thought that you ought to know that a date has been fixed for your father's trial. We have been warned that it will begin on January 11th. I have confirmed that Sir Everard will be free for the whole period of the trial and we expect that it will last between five to seven days."

"Have you..., does he..., what?" stammered Jenny, failing to sound in the least bit professional or competent. However, Cottrell was used to the bumblings of the ordinary layman and, while he gravely disapproved of becoming involved in police-court business, he recognised that even the most suitable of clients might occasionally become unstuck. Hence he was able to translate Jenny's request out of gibberish into English.

"Your father is aware of the date and is ready to put forward his defence of not guilty."

"Have the police said anything? Are they confident?"

"It would be most improper of the police to speak of the case now that it has gone to trial."

"Are you confident?" asked Jenny in a small voice,

aware that Cottrell disliked being asked such questions, but unable to stop herself. She heard the solicitor sigh and could imagine him sitting at his desk, rearranging the pencils testily.

"I do not pronounce on such matters; they are entirely in the hands of the jury. All I can say, Miss Fletcher, is that your father will make a good witness, inasmuch as it is his trade. However, the jury may discount some of what he says for precisely the same reason."

"May I see Sir Everard?"

"My dear Miss Fletcher, whatever for? I do assure you that your father's case is in the best possible hands. I may not sound overly sanguine, but that is because I do not wish to raise false hopes, not because I am not doing my utmost to help your father."

With Jenny's nightmare still fresh in her memory, she murmured something about wanting to make sure that Sir Everard presented all possible evidence.

A hint of amusement could be heard in the elderly solicitor's tones. "Lawyers – and those training to be lawyers – make the worst sort of client for a barrister, just as doctors make the worst patients. They always want to interfere and suggest how best to run things. The best way in which you can help your father, Miss Fletcher, is to allow Sir Everard to get on with his preparations and not to worry him with red herrings. He is a very experienced man who knows exactly what he is doing."

"Yes," acquiesced Jenny, miserably aware that Cottrell felt that she was a nuisance with her repeated insistence on intruding into the correct ordering of a murder trial.

After Cottrell bid her goodbye, Jenny stared aimlessly at the hand-piece of the telephone, until the irate voice of the exchange recalled her to a consciousness of where she was. Becoming aware that Field was probably lingering tactfully out of earshot, she called out that she would not want breakfast, before haring back to her bedroom. Closing the door behind her, she started to cry.

Half an hour later when Midge cautiously tapped on the door, Jenny was still crying, although she tried to pull herself together when Midge entered.

"What's up?"

"The date for the trial's set and Cottrell sounded incredibly pessimistic and he doesn't want me interfering. My father's going to be taken away and hanged by the neck until he is dead and I'm not doing anything useful. All I'm doing is annoying the police or people like Cottrell who might help him."

Since weeping and wailing was not much in Jenny's line, Midge felt rather out of her depth. She let Jenny run on a bit longer about how she was ruining other people's careers and getting them arrested. Then Midge asked practically, "How much sleep did you have last night?"

"Not a lot," admitted Jenny, rather shamefacedly. "Sorry, Midge, I can't think why I fell apart like that."

"I can. You can't stand inactivity and I can't think of a worst situation in which you are forced to be inactive."

Jenny sighed. "It's all so appallingly awful and I feel so impotent." She banged her hand down. "If I were in gaol, I'm sure Daddy would be doing more than I am, but even he told me not to try to investigate Forrest's antecedents. God knows what he'll say when he finds out what you're doing."

Midge bit back a remark that if she failed to find anything it wouldn't matter, but, judging by Jenny's expression, she had already thought of this for herself.

Jenny tried to shake herself out of her misery. "Oh well, I may not be able to do much, but at least I can go out and buy the odds and ends that you need."

"It's all right," argued Midge, who disliked being dependant upon others. "I'll do it."

"We can't go together in case you're seen with me and you ought to rest, not go shopping. Anyway, you don't even know where the suitable shops are."

"Do you?" enquired Midge. "I shouldn't have thought that Mary Carew would be able to shop where you go."

"One does saunter past other establishments occasionally," remarked Jenny, before forcing a grin at Midge. "Of course I know where cheaper shops are – where do you think I spent my so, so limited pocket-money when I was younger?"

Midge's recollection was that, far from being limited, Jenny had always had liberal amounts of pocket-money. However, she was prepared to admit that even the most lavish of parents was unlikely to have given their schoolgirl daughters the sort of allowance which would run to the eye-wateringly expensive silk and lace kimono which Jenny was wearing. So it was just possible that Jenny might indeed have some idea where less fashionable or frivolous articles were to be purchased. Moreover, if Jenny were as frustrated as she sounded, buying suitable clothes for poor Mary Carew might keep her occupied for a bit.

Hence that morning Midge rested in preparation for what she feared was going to be a very demanding task, while Jenny took herself off to do some whirlwind shopping with the aim of filling the gaps in Midge's wardrobe. Fortunately, the two were of similar build and size, although Midge groaned when she saw the hat which Jenny had deemed to be suitable for her adopted role.

"Really, Jenny, couldn't you have bought me something less like a dead rat?"

"My dear girl, I truly sympathise! It lacerated my spirit merely to try the ghastly object on, let alone purchase it. However, never let it be said that I put a sense of style before realism. You will look quite perfect as dear, innocent little Mary Carew in her first proper office job."

Midge, who was now staring at her reflection with a revolted expression, looked singularly unconsoled by this observation. Jenny laughed. "Honestly, Midge, I'll buy you any number of smart hats to make up for suffering this indignity." Her voice quivered as she added, "Just discover something which will help my father."

III

Allegretto ma non troppo

Chapter Seventeen

On Sunday afternoon, just after dusk, Midge emerged out of the house and into a waiting cab. Since Midge's story, should anyone ask, was that she had spent the days between gaining her new job and actually starting it back home in Cambridge, it had been decided that she would, in reality, make the journey from Liverpool Street Station to her lodgings.

"It will add verisimilitude if you can talk about a broken-down 'bus or dreadful queues," argued Jenny.

Midge had reluctantly agreed, but, by the time she had hung around in the cold waiting for an omnibus to appear, she began to see the value of Jenny's suggestion. She felt just as cold, wet and irritable as the fictional Mary Carew might, and there was certainly nothing to cause Mrs Smith, the landlady of Midge's new abode, the slightest suspicion that her new lodger was not what she claimed to be.

The next morning, Midge rose early. She wanted to make sure that she had everything ready for her entry into Forrest and Creech. As she pulled on the clothes Jenny had chosen for her, she thanked heaven that she hadn't taken off her coat during the interview.

'This skirt definitely looks cheaper than the one I was wearing that day.' She grinned. 'And thank goodness I wore my old coat by mistake in the rush of coming up to London. It certainly looks past its best.' She checked her appearance for a third time. 'Come on, Mary; off to work.'

When Midge arrived at the office, her main fear was that Wynne might have suddenly remembered seeing her at the inquest. However, the clerk was not present when she arrived. Instead, Davie, the office-boy, was busily opening up.

"So you got the job then?"

"Yes."

"Miss Hurst'll be pleased to have another typist. She's fed-up having to deal with all the secretarial work herself."

"Is it a very busy office?"

Davie appeared to think for a moment. "Yes, it's quite busy. What sort of office were you in before?"

"I worked for a journalist."

Davie blinked. "Cor, one of those reporters? I wouldn't half mind being one of them. Why did you stop?"

"It was only a temporary job."

"So you came here?" Davie grinned. "We've had all sorts of reporters round here – maybe including your previous boss. You know we've had a murder, don't you?"

Midge managed to sound scared. "My boss wrote about music, not crime. And Mr Wynne said I wasn't to talk about it. He said I'd lose my place if I did."

"I talk about it," declared Davie in a lordly manner, "and Wynne hasn't sacked me."

"But you've been here much longer than I have. They probably need to keep you."

Davie preened himself at this remark. "Started nearly five months ago, I did. So I know how everything's done."

Midge made a mental note to check the precise dates of when the extortion racket had begun. It sounded as if Davie had joined Forrest and Creech afterwards, but it would be as well to ask Professor Schulmann.

Davie glanced through a grimy window. "Here comes Miss Hurst. You'd better wait in the secretaries' room. She doesn't like people wasting time."

"Thank you."

Midge limped through to the room indicated by Davie.

She decided that she had better not sit down until Miss Hurst appeared, and she waited until the door opened.

Miss Hurst nodded approvingly. "You're nicely on time, Mary. I like punctuality in the office."

"Yes, Miss Hurst."

"Now, this will be your desk. In future, you can start your work when you come in. You can hang your coat and hat over there."

"Yes, Miss Hurst."

"Once you have done so, I have some letters for you to type. I want you to do them very carefully."

"I shall, Miss Hurst."

The secretary quickly hung up her own coat and hat before returning to her desk. Midge moved more slowly and could feel the older woman's eyes upon her. However, Miss Hurst made no remark until Midge had sat down, and then everything she said was in relation to the typing Midge had to do. Although Miss Hurst appeared to be treating her as a rather dim child, Midge was grateful that she was being given such clear instructions. Her supposed previous posts might explain away an unfamiliarity with office routine, but it would be disastrous if she made an error in the layout of her work.

Midge worked hard until eleven o'clock, at which point Miss Hurst informed her that one of her jobs was to make the tea.

"Davie can't be trusted to do it properly and sometimes he is out on errands. Miss Hemming always used to make it before."

Midge nodded and obediently followed the secretary to the small alcove which was devoted to a kettle, some crockery, and various tins and boxes.

Miss Hurst glanced at Midge's sticks. "Davie is meant to fill the kettle up first thing. Ask him to do so if he forgets. Now, Mr Wynne likes his tea weak, Mr Creech likes his tea strong, while I like mine at an ordinary strength. Here are the teapots and the tea-caddy. The milk and sugar are kept here. You will need to put sugar-bowls and milk on Mr Wynne and Mr Creech's trays. I take only milk."

"Yes, Miss Hurst."

"Davie likes strong tea with lots of sugar and milk, but you do not need to give him as much sugar as he wants. You may, of course, have what you prefer."

Wishing that she knew why Davie wasn't allowed such privileges, Midge nodded. "What about biscuits, Miss Hurst? Do I need to set out any?"

"Yes. Mr Creech's choice is kept in this tin; he has two. Mr Wynne's are here; he has three. Any uneaten biscuits must be returned to the correct tin. I do not have biscuits; Davie is allowed two." She ran her eyes over Midge's thin form. "You may have three if you wish."

"Thank you, Miss Hurst."

While the kettle was boiling, Midge thanked her stars that she regularly brewed up tea at Newnham. At home, Ellen did all that sort of thing. Midge suddenly felt uncomfortable. Surely Aunt Alice did not issue such strict instructions to her housekeeper – or count how many biscuits Ellen was allowed?

A command from Miss Hurst brought Midge swiftly back to the present. "Can you lift that kettle?"

Midge groaned internally. Surely she wasn't going to lose her chance of investigating Forrest's office just because she wasn't strong? "Yes, Miss Hurst. I make the tea at home."

The secretary watched her. "Wait!" she ordered, before disappearing. When she returned, she was carrying a wooden chair. "I imagine you make it sitting down."

"Thank you, Miss Hurst."

"I don't want any accidents with boiling water," stated

the secretary in severe tones. "We don't have time to waste on that sort of thing. Mr Creech isn't in today, so you can make the tea for Mr Wynne and I'll take it in to him. Then you can make the rest of the tea."

The rest of the morning past in a flurry of typing. By the end of it, Midge's right arm was aching. It had been weakened by polio and was protesting strongly at being made to work hard on a heavy machine. However, Midge tried to ignore the pain. The letters she had been typing that morning did not appear to have any bearing on the murder, but the very fact that she was able to read any of Forrest and Creech's correspondence filled her with delight. Surely she might come across something useful?

At lunch, Miss Hurst unbent sufficiently to give Midge instructions as to where there was a cheap restaurant nearby which catered for office-workers. The afternoon was devoted to more typing and making the afternoon tea. Miss Hurst was busy taking phone calls and Midge kept wondering what they were about. It would be absolutely sickening if something which might help Mr Fletcher was being discussed and she missed it.

Later that evening, as she sat on her narrow bed in the boarding-house, Midge tried to analyse what she had achieved.

'I've survived my first day without giving myself away. The question is, how do I search for evidence? I can't imagine that there's a neat file listing how much money Herr X paid over, but I can keep my eyes open. And maybe Davie noticed some strangers hanging around.' Midge's eyes lit up. It would be wonderful if she could supply evidence that Forrest had talked to someone after he had seen Mr Fletcher. Then she grimaced. The trouble was, how would she prove the identity of a mysterious stranger? Or that he had poisoned Forrest? The defence were bound to need more than a mere allegation.

Midge chewed her lip thoughtfully. 'The worst thing to prove is going to be suicide. If Forrest did kill himself and set out to take revenge on Mr Fletcher, he probably deliberately destroyed any paperwork relating to the refugees – even assuming it existed. Wynne has already testified that Forrest was nervous on the day of his death. I don't imagine he'll gossip with me, but I wonder if I could get Davie to tell me more? He seems quite keen to talk, and I don't suppose anyone normally gives him any encouragement to do so.' Midge tried to get more comfortable on the bed. 'I need to meet Creech. He's a partner, so he was in the best position to know about the refugees. He may even be continuing the extortion racket. If he is, perhaps he wanted all of the profits and polished off Forrest to do so.' Midge's momentary burst of excitement died down. 'The trouble with that theory, along with everything else, is how on earth do I prove it to the satisfaction of a jury? If only Forrest hadn't written that wretched letter.'

Chapter Eighteen

The following morning, Midge set off with more confidence than she had on the previous day. She hadn't made any horrendous mistakes yesterday to give herself away and her typing had been of an acceptable standard.

'I wish I knew what Jenny was doing,' she thought to herself, 'but I must forget that she exists. I'm not Midge Carrington; I'm Mary Carew. I don't know Jenny and I don't know Mr Fletcher.'

Today, Davie was whistling loudly as Midge entered the building. He stopped whistling to talk to her.

"You don't need to show up so early every day. Creech is never in before nine-thirty at the earliest."

"Miss Hurst said she liked punctuality."

"She doesn't expect you to be here at eight."

"I don't want to be late and I don't yet know how long the buses take."

Davie seemed interested in pursuing this theme. "Can't you walk properly, then? Do you always have to take a bus?"

Midge flushed. "Yes."

"What's wrong with you?"

"I had infantile paralysis."

"People die of that sometimes, don't they?"

"Yes."

"Cor! If you died, that'd be two deaths in the office."

With a great effort of will, Midge decided to continue talking to Davie. "I'd have been scared if I'd been here when Mr Forrest died."

"I wasn't scared," boasted Davie. "I don't scare easily."

"But weren't there police everywhere questioning everyone?"

"Yes, but they didn't scare me. Why should they?"

Midge attempted to look admiring. "Did you discover

the body?"

Davie's face dropped. "No. Mr Wynne found it in the evening. I'd left much earlier." He cheered up. "But it was exciting the next day. They checked everything for fingerprints and there was a man taking photographs. And there were loads of reporters. It was my job to stop them coming in. Mr Wynne was furious with them."

"Why was I furious?" demanded a third voice.

Davie swivelled round. "Good morning, sir. I was just telling Miss Carew how difficult it was to keep reporters away and how she mustn't talk to any of them."

"Is that so, Miss Carew?"

"Oh, yes, Mr Wynne. I do hope I don't have to deal with any. My mother wouldn't like my name to get into the papers."

Wynne grunted. "Small chance of that. But don't you go talking to anyone, either of you. And since you're here, Miss Carew, you'd better go and get ready. I've got an important letter to dictate."

Midge went inside, hoping that she had not overdone the innocent country-girl act. Davie departed singing 'Me and My Girl', in an apparent attempt to prove that he was not overawed by Wynne.

When Midge entered Wynne's office, the clerk was looking irritable. He curtly ordered Midge to sit down, and began to dictate a letter at top speed. Realising that she would never manage to take it all down correctly, Midge interrupted him.

"Please, sir, I can't go that quickly."

"Why not? I thought you knew shorthand. You said you did when I employed you."

"I do know shorthand, but I can't take dictation as quickly as that."

"Then you'd better improve if you want to stay here."

Despite this threat, Wynne slowed down. After he had finished, he leant over and took Midge's dictation pad. "Read it back to me."

Midge swallowed. What had she done to make Wynne suspicious? Had he recognised her? Her voice wavered as she began to read through the shorthand. At the end of it, Wynne gave a grunt.

"You appear to have taken it down correctly. I want it typed up immediately, so that it can catch the early post."

Midge retreated to the secretaries' office, where she found Miss Hurst already at her seat. The older woman looked up.

"Late on your second day, Mary? That's not a very good sign."

"I wasn't late, Miss Hurst. Mr Wynne told me to come and take dictation." Midge proferred her dictation pad. "He's told me to type it up immediately."

Miss Hurst bristled. "Has he indeed? Then I can inform you, Mary, that I decide the order in which things are typed. There is a great deal of outstanding correspondence to be typed – you managed very little of it yesterday."

Midge felt genuinely scared. If Miss Hurst thought that she wasn't getting through enough work and then Wynne complained about her shorthand, she'd get sacked before she'd discovered anything.

The secretary appeared to sense Midge's fear. "I do not hold you responsible for that." She snorted. "When you have more office experience, Mary, you will find that secretarial work involves much more than typing letters." She glanced out of the window. "Ah, here is Mr Creech. You had better take that document to Mr Wynne once you have finished typing it, and then you can get on with this pile of letters."

As she rose, Miss Hurst placed a large file on Midge's

desk. Once the secretary had left, Midge leafed through the file rapidly, before sighing. Honestly, what did she expect? She wasn't going to discover a convenient letter which said '*Dear Sir, re your outstanding extortion payments, we regret to inform you that unless you settle our account we shall have to report you to the police*'. She returned to her typing, concentrating fiercely. Something told her that, unless it was perfect, Wynne would make trouble.

Fifteen minutes later, she knocked on the door of Wynne's office and pushed the door open.

"What do you want?"

"You told me to type up this letter immediately, Mr Wynne. I've brought it for you to sign."

Just as Midge had suspected, Wynne inspected the letter carefully. "I suppose that will do." He fished in a drawer and produced some papers. "I want you to type answers to each of these – say that they will find a cheque enclosed to settle payment." As Midge hesitated, he sighed heavily. "Surely you can manage that?"

"Yes, sir, but Miss Hurst told me to get on with some outstanding correspondence."

"I think you'll find that I make the decisions round here, my girl. You do as you're told."

"Yes, Mr Wynne."

As Midge retreated, she found herself wondering whether this sort of squabbling was normal in Forrest and Creech or whether the recent death had made everyone much more tetchy. 'I wonder how Wynne got on with Forrest. I suppose Forrest was his employer, so he'd have to be a lot more polite to him than he is about Miss Hurst.' Midge suddenly pulled a face. 'And what on earth am I going to say if Miss Hurst comes back and I've gone against her instructions and typed up this stuff instead? But if I don't do it, Wynne will be furious and there's no point annoying him.'

As Midge rapidly placed another sheet of paper in the typewriter and rolled it up ready to start typing, she glanced at the first piece of correspondence and frowned. It seemed odd for a solicitor to be dealing with an account rendered for a silk umbrella. She looked at the next paper. It was a bill for twelve wing collars and eight shirt-fasteners, while the third was a bill for a suit at twelve guineas. For a moment she assumed that these must be accounts which Forrest had not paid before he had died. Then she saw that they were all made out to Leonard Wynne, Esq., and that the total cost came to over fourteen guineas.

"Surely that's rather a lot for a clerk to pay?" she muttered. Obviously, Wynne would be paid more than the miserable sum she was getting, but did he really earn enough to buy suits at twelve guineas? Or did he hope that a good-quality suit would last for much longer than a cheaper one? This was where she needed Jenny's advice – or James'. James looked as if he spent a fair amount on his clothes, but, presumably, he could afford it. Could Wynne? Midge's excitement rose. If Wynne couldn't afford those sorts of clothes on his wages, where was he getting the money to pay for them?

At that moment, Midge's cogitations were interrupted by Miss Hurst.

"Why are you staring into space?"

Midge jumped guiltily. "Sorry, Miss Hurst."

"Haven't you started those letters yet?"

"N... no, Miss Hurst."

The secretary came and looked over Midge's shoulder. "What are these?" she demanded.

"Mr Wynne asked me to type something for him."

"After what I said to you about getting on with the letters?"

Midge told herself that Mary would have been terrified.

153

"Mr Wynne *ordered* me to do it. He said..." Her voice trailed off artistically.

"And what did he say, Mary?"

"Please, Miss Hurst, he said that he made the decisions and I was to do as I was told."

"Indeed? Then I suggest that you finish those immediately, take them to Mr Wynne, and then get back to what you need to do."

Miss Hurst sat down at her own desk and began typing with savage vigour. It was typical of Wynne to ask Mary to undertake his private correspondence. Did he think it impressed his tailor to send in a typed letter rather than one written in ink? From what she'd seen of tradesmen, all that interested them was getting paid, not the letter which accompanied the account. She gave a snort. Wynne should think less about his appearance and more about his work. How could she type up the accounts when he hadn't made them out yet? No wonder Forrest had got fed up. Thank goodness Miss Hemming hadn't overheard that argument – she'd have told the police and then they'd have questioned everyone for even longer than they had. Not that the police cared about disrupting office routine or how Davie's head had been turned by the apparent glamour of criminal investigative work. At least he was settling down again – he wasn't the sort of office-boy she would choose to employ, but he was better than nothing, which was what Wynne had suggested last time she'd complained. Men! They thought they knew how to run things, but they had no idea at all.

Chapter Nineteen

The following morning, Jenny was moping at home when she received an urgent telephone call from John, who was both worried and annoyed.

"What the blazes is going on?" he demanded. "I've been away staying with friends and have only just received the most extraordinary telegram from Midge. I want to speak to her."

Jenny gulped, thankful that John couldn't see her face. "Midge isn't here at the moment," she faltered. "I'm afraid that you can't speak to her. And it might not be wise to discuss things over an open wire."

"Then I'll come and see you," threatened John. "I'm in London now, so don't leave. I'll be round within half an hour."

Jenny replaced the handset wondering what John was going to make of Midge's excursion into the world of a legal secretary. When the Lagonda pulled up, she was soon enlightened. Smouldering with rage, John demanded why she had encouraged Midge to start so reckless an enterprise.

"Can't you see that, at the very least, Midge could get into enormous trouble with the authorities at Cambridge? And if these people are crooks why are you sending Midge into the midst of them? Do you think you are the heroine of one of those detective stories that Midge used to read endlessly?"

Jenny looked at John contemptuously. "Of course I don't. But may I remind you," she continued in a voice of ice, "that my father is currently lying in Wandsworth and that if he is found guilty he will be hanged? Do you find it surprising that I'm prepared to accept Midge's help, even although she may run into danger? Can't you see? My father is in certain danger and no-one else is doing

155

anything about it. The police aren't, Cottrell can't, and you certainly aren't."

John had been about to hotly deny that it was any of his business to investigate a murder when he hear Jenny's voice waver.

"Look here," he said more soberly, "I know that it must be dreadfully difficult for you, but I'm worried about what Midge is doing. She's much too fragile to be living in cheap lodgings; you know how she hates the cold, and it makes her leg worse. And how could she, of all people, stand up to anyone who learned what she was up to? Even if they aren't crooks, they could still be devilishly angry with her."

Jenny stared at her hands, uncertain what to do. She could understand John's ire, but in many ways his anger was easier to deal with than his sombre statement of facts. She and Midge had discussed the possibility that Midge might run into danger, but seeing John's anxious face rammed home the message that she had sent one of her closest friends into potential danger.

'If something happens to Midge,' she breathed inwardly, 'I'll never be able to forgive myself. Never. But how could I forgive myself if I neglected any opportunity to help save my father? If only I could have gone, not Midge.'

The headache which seemed to be Jenny's constant companion began throbbing more incessantly than ever and she was only dimly aware that John was demanding Midge's address. Rousing herself with an enormous effort, she tried to reply.

"Please don't ask for it, John. Midge asked me to give it to no-one."

"Then I shall go round to Forrest and Creech and find Midge for myself."

"Don't," begged Jenny. "You'll give everything away if

you turn up there. Midge gave the impression that you were dreadfully old and absent-minded; they'll be terribly suspicious if you show up. And if you pretend to be someone else they'll wonder how Mary Carew got to know you. Please don't, John; you'll make everything much harder."

"I must see her. How do you suppose I can explain her absence over Christmas?" He snorted. "My mother told me that I was to invite you for a quiet Christmas – little did she know what you were up to."

Jenny made a swift calculation. "Midge said that she would try to telephone briefly tomorrow. Perhaps she might be able to come and see both of us in the evening after work. And, John…"

"Yes?"

"Might we meet somewhere other than this house? I'm worried that it might be watched."

"There's my father's flat," growled John, wondering whether Jenny was merely inventing excuses to put him off. "Just make sure that Midge shows up. I don't like what's going on and I want to speak to her."

"We will be there if she contacts me," promised Jenny, hoping that nothing would prevent Midge from doing so.

"Very well," agreed John in chilly tones. "But I'm not leaving London without making sure that she is safe."

Once John had left, Jenny took a headache powder and retired to her room. As she drew the curtains, she wished that she could retreat to her bed and stay cocooned from the world forever. She lay in the dark, desperate for her mind to stop racing, but unable to detach it from its chosen trajectory. What was happening to Midge? It was now Wednesday and she had heard nothing from her; not a letter, not a telegram, not even a scrawled note delivered by an errand-boy. And what on earth would she do if Midge did not contact her on the following day? John had been angry enough as it was; he would be incandescent with rage if he failed to see Midge. He might even invade the offices of Forrest and Creech.

Midge had agreed to try to telephone Jenny at lunchtime on Thursday, but she sat on a low wall soaking up the fitful winter sun for some time whilst she considered what – if anything – she had achieved. Not only was she still afraid that some unconscious mistake might expose her identity, but she was conscious of a dull aching misery which had nothing to do with the place of women in modern society but was all to do with her relationship with John. Why hadn't he tried to find out why she needed a reference? Was he still cross that she'd called him staid and boring? Why hadn't he contacted her? Throughout her speculations, Midge kept pushing away the utterly shaming thought that perhaps John had sensed her true feelings for him. No wonder he had no interest in providing the affectionate comfort and support which he had always given before; he must dread the embarrassment of meeting her again almost as much as she now did. Telling herself not to be a fool, Midge eventually dragged herself off to a telephone box sufficiently far away from the office that she would not be at risk of being seen by another member of Forrest and Creech.

"Are you all right?" demanded Jenny, her worried tones betraying that she had been panicking because Midge had not rung.

"Yes."

"Can we meet tonight?"

"Are you sure?"

"Yes. I need to see you."

"Have there been developments? I don't want to risk being seen at your house."

"I know. Could we meet at your uncle's flat?"

"What?" cried Midge in horror. "You haven't told him. Jenny, you promised!"

"No, of course I haven't. But John appeared and insisted on seeing you. When I couldn't produce you he threatened to turn up at the office."

A burst of pleasure coursed through Midge. So John did care after all!

"You'll have to tell John everything," urged Jenny, when Midge did not reply.

"Is John with you?"

"No, he's waiting at the flat, but I'll try to get there before you do."

Still nervous about being seen, Midge rang off, before returning to Forrest and Creech with new-found energy.

Later that evening, Jenny grimaced at her reflection in the looking-glass as she wondered how brunettes coped with their colouring. It would have been useful to have had the chance to reassure Midge that she would be taking pains to disguise her appearance somewhat, but doubtless Midge would manage. Jenny adjusted her wig for the fifth time, before snatching up the coat and bag that Mrs Field had lent her. After slipping out of the back entrance, Jenny set off in a loping gait most unlike her usual walk. Although there had been no repetition of mysterious cars attempting to follow her, Jenny was taking no chances. Once she was safely in a busy thoroughfare, she hailed a cab and ordered it to drive to Charing Cross as quickly as possible since she had a train to catch. After entering into the station, she made her way purposefully towards a stationary train before dropping swiftly behind a pile of luggage to tie up her shoelace. She then made her way out of the station and traced her way by a circuitous route through the maze of small streets off Fleet Street until she reached the block of flats where Midge's uncle kept an apartment for use when he was in town on business.

"What on earth?" asked John as he answered the door and took in Jenny's voice, apparently speaking from a stranger's body.

"I'm in disguise," replied Jenny. "Midge is nervous of being seen with me."

"I'm not surprised; you look ghastly."

Thinking that John's remarks, however rude, were preferable to his earlier complaints, Jenny refrained from argument. Hoping to distract him, she told John of the various events which had happened since she had left Brandon. John had been sardonically amused at the thought of one of Jenny's colleagues being arrested, but he was still concerned about the potential risks which Midge might be running. The news that another witness had been found to confirm that Forrest had been a blackmailer merely served to increase his fears. As John began pacing up and down the drawing room, it became clear that he was still as angry as he had been when Jenny had seen him last.

"I'm devilish glad that Midge has telephoned; this is a ridiculous situation and I want it to end today. Apart from anything else, she ought to be coming down to Brandon with me. My mother's bound to wonder what's up."

Watching John constantly glancing at his watch or looking down into the street, Jenny grimaced. No wonder John worried about Midge; he could never forgive himself for taking her to Greece where she had contracted polio.

Despite John's solicitude for his cousin's welfare, it was unfortunate that, when Midge finally entered, she giggled at the unexpected sight of Jenny in a brown wig. All sign of concern fled from John's face.

"Would you excuse us please, Jenny?" asked John stiffly.

Jenny had no difficulty reading the unmistakable signs of a man in the grip of extreme annoyance, but, equally, she had no intention of abandoning Midge to her cousin's wrath.

"Do go ahead," she urged sweetly.

John glared at her, before practically dragging Midge over to the window embrasure.

"What the devil do you think you are doing?" he demanded. "Of all the stupid, idiotic things that you have ever done this has to be the worst. Don't you realise how dangerous this could be? If you and Jenny are correct that there is something fishy about Forrest and Creech, you are running the very devil of a risk poking your nose around the office."

Midge looked at her cousin miserably; so John *was* still furious with her. Disappointment made her snap at him sharply. "I can't let concerns like that stop me when Jenny's father's in gaol."

"You dashed well ought to," urged John. "Don't you understand that, if you are caught, you could end up in an appalling mess?"

"If I were a man you wouldn't be telling me not to work for Forrest and Creech, you'd be congratulating me on my ingenuity. And I am aware of the risks, which is why I'm telling you what I'm doing."

"So that I can come and claim your corpse when you get hit over the head?" suggested John sarcastically.

"Precisely. At least, I've no intention of letting myself be murdered, but I'd like to know that you would do something if I suddenly disappeared."

"But…"

Midge overrode her cousin's protests. "I've got it all worked out," she informed him, not adding that she had intended to put her plan into operation much earlier. There was no point in letting John know how much she had hoped for his aid and assistance. "Part of my duties includes taking telegrams down to the post office. I'll wire you every day with what I'm doing. If you don't hear from me I want you to find out what's going on. It'd probably be best to check my lodgings first."

"Why don't you telegraph Jenny?"

"Don't be silly, John," sighed Midge. "I don't suppose that anyone will check up on what telegrams I send, but if they did, they'd soon be suspicious if I kept contacting Middle Temple or Mr Fletcher's home. You're much safer, particularly as I can use Greek to you. There's no-one in Forrest and Creech who looks as though they'll recognise a nice piece of Attic prose."

A reluctant grin crossed John's face. "Possibly not, especially when disguised in Roman letters."

Midge suddenly thought of something which might persuade John to agree. "If anyone sees that, they'll think that it's a code. And since one of my references came from a journalist, the obvious suspicion will be that I'm a journalist. No-one murders journalists – it risks much greater investigation!"

"Don't be too sure of yourself, Midge."

"No, Mr Carrington," replied Midge meekly.

"What the devil do you mean by calling me that?" expostulated John.

"It would be frightfully wrong of me to call an ex-employer by his first name," explained Midge patiently, but with a gleam of humour in her eyes. "It would be almost as wrong as you calling me Midge when my name is Mary Carew."

John hovered between annoyance and amusement. Eventually, he laughed. "All right, you win," he accepted. "However, since you're so keen on journalists, have you thought of how my father will react when he finds out that you are not pouring out womanly sympathy to Jenny and holding her hand, but are behaving like a low-grade private eye?"

Midge sighed and lowered her voice. "He'll be furious, but honestly, John, I am doing more for Jenny this way than any amount of sympathy. Sympathy isn't going to save Mr Fletcher."

John was rather afraid that even snooping around the office quarters of the dead man was not going to save Jenny's father. "Have you discovered anything?"

Midge frowned. "Only that Wynne seems to spend much more than I imagine a clerk earns."

Jenny looked up alertly. "How do you know?"

After explaining about the bills, Midge looked apologetically at Jenny. "It isn't necessarily a sign of something criminal. Wynne might have had a legacy which he had chosen to spend on luxuries."

"Or he could have won the money gambling," pointed out John.

"That's why I have to stay on at the office," declared Midge. "I need to search for more evidence."

John sighed irritably. "I don't want to quarrel any more, but one thing is certain – I'm not leaving you in some wretched boarding-house over Christmas." Seeing that Midge was disposed to argue about the necessity of keeping in character, he added cunningly, "It will look a lot more odd if you don't visit your family over Christmas and, in any case, Bertie is pining for you."

The idea of her devoted cat needing her brought a lump to Midge's throat. John could have no idea how much she was missing him. Realising that he was winning his argument with Midge, John turned to Jenny.

"My mother would like you to join us, Jenny. There won't be any other visitors."

"It's very kind of you," faltered Jenny, "but I don't know that I want to leave my father. I shan't be able to visit him, but I'd be so far away if he needed me."

Seeing the lost look on Jenny's face as she spoke of her father, Midge was determined to convince her friend to join her over Christmas.

"Please do, Jenny," she urged. "Aunt Alice will be far less likely to ask awkward questions about why I'm returning to Brandon on Christmas Eve. She'll think that I was keeping you company. Anyway, I've only got a few days' holiday, so you can be back in London soon."

"I'm more grateful than I can possibly say," stated Jenny.

Midge forced a smile. "Don't fuss, Jenny. We're not doing much."

"You're giving me hope," Jenny whispered, before leaving the room rapidly.

Chapter Twenty

On Saturday, Midge made her way nervously to the office. She knew that she would be told that day whether or not she would be kept on. It would be simply awful if she weren't. She glanced at Miss Hurst when the secretary arrived, but there was nothing in her expression to indicate what she thought. Instead, the secretary handed Midge a long letter, written in an untidy hand.

"You are to type that up and take it to Mr Creech when you are finished. You need to make two carbon copies of it."

"Yes, Miss Hurst."

The letter related, as far as Midge could see, to a singularly tedious property transaction. There was no apparent criminal significance to it, but it was hard to read what Creech had written. Eventually, Midge asked Miss Hurst for help.

"I can't make out what this phrase says."

Miss Hurst stared at it, turned the letter upside down, before turning it back up the correct way. "I think it says 'thereafter the charge will consist of £14 6s per annum', but I'm not certain about the figure. It could be £12 6s. You'd better check with Mr Creech. He wouldn't be at all happy if his client ended up losing money owing to a typing error."

Midge nodded, hoping that she looked scared, rather than pleased, at the idea of meeting the remaining partner of the firm. Clutching the offending letter, she made her way to Creech's room. When she got there, she heard raised voices. For a second, she wondered whether Creech was having an argument with Wynne, and then she realised that the men's voices were speaking in German. She translated rapidly.

"I am desperate. I tell you, desperate."

"You should not have come to this office."

At that moment, Wynne appeared.

"What are you doing here?" he snarled at Midge. "I've told you that you aren't to be seen by clients."

"I need to ask Mr Creech what something in his notes says."

"Why? Are you unable to read? Get back to your room and stop wasting time."

Shaken by the ferocity of the clerk's tone, Midge retreated. Miss Hurst looked up. "Well, Mary, was it £14 or £12?"

"I don't know," replied Midge limply. "Mr Creech was busy with a client and Mr Wynne told me to stop wasting time."

Miss Hurst looked at her sharply. The girl looked white and scared. Really, Wynne was a most unsuitable office manager. Anyone could see that Mary was inexperienced, and it was hardly her fault that Creech wrote illegibly. Wynne ought to be grateful that the girl was conscientious enough to try and type accurately. Miss Peters would have dashed off anything and then complained if she'd been rebuked for it.

"Start some of the other letters," she suggested. "When Mr Creech is free I'll take that letter in to him."

"Oh, thank you, Miss Hurst," replied Midge, only half acting. She didn't want another encounter with Wynne in the sort of mood he was in. He seemed perfectly capable of sacking her there and then.

Half an hour later, Midge was alone in the room. As a concession to Midge's disability, Miss Hurst had taken over the role of delivering the tea-trays, even if she had no intention of actually making the stuff. Midge was busily wondering whether Wynne would complain about her to the secretary when the door opened. Midge glanced up, expecting to see Miss Hurst, but instead it was the surviving partner of Forrest and Creech. In the few days that Midge had been at the firm, she had learned that Creech summoned the secretaries by a buzzer on Miss Hurst's desk. It hadn't rung, so why was Creech here? Midge glanced at him. His dark suit appeared no better cut than Wynne's, and his light-brown hair and moustache were in need of a trim. Did this confirm that Wynne was spending more than a clerk's income upon his clothes, or was Creech merely uninterested in his appearance?

Creech stepped forward, his lips stretched in a thin, tight smile which did not reach his eyes.

"Ah, Miss Carew, can you type this letter?"

"Yes, sir."

Midge glanced at the letter. It began '*Hochwürdigster Herr Bürgermeister Stellvertretender von Erlach...*' Midge froze. Why had Creech given a letter in German to her? He must be checking to see whether she had understood any of what she had overheard. What on earth should she do? Pulling herself together, she forced herself to behave as Mary Carew would have done. "Please, sir, I don't understand the words."

"They're German."

Conscious that Creech was watching her face, Midge tried desperately to show nothing more than honest concern. "But, Mr Creech, I don't know any German." She attempted to sound both apologetic and countrified. "I learned a bit of French in school and I had to learn some words of Latin for Mr Carrington, but I don't know any other languages."

"That's a pity, because it needs to be done in a hurry. Do the best you can." Creech placed the letter on Midge's desk and moved away to look out of the window.

Midge bent over her machine. She was sure that Creech was watching every move, but she had no intention of looking up at him. Instead, she began typing the urgent communication, but not at her normal speed, nor with both hands. Instead, she held one finger under the words as if she were tracing them out letter by letter. With her other hand, she typed slowly and carefully. Even when Creech departed, Midge maintained her pretence. Anyone who was listening behind the door would hear if she speeded up.

By the time that Midge had reached the final '*Mit vorzüglicher Hochachtung*', she had recovered herself somewhat. It was terrifying that Creech was suspicious of her, but surely it was significant? Why did it matter whether she knew German or not? And surely a normal employer would simply have asked her outright whether she knew any German? There must have been something odd about the conversation which she had overheard or Creech would not be behaving in this strange way. Midge cursed mentally. If only she had caught more of the conversation or had even seen who had been there. She could have then asked Professor Schulmann if he knew anyone of that description.

Meanwhile, Wynne had raised the question of Midge's future with Miss Hurst.

"Have you decided what to do about the girl?"

"I think that we should keep her. She's not very experienced, but she is willing and we'd find it difficult to pick up anyone good at short notice." Miss Hurst snorted, "In fact, on the wage we're paying her we'll be unlikely to get anyone at all."

"Is her typing accurate?"

"Yes; a little slow, but she seems to be increasing in speed."

Wynne frowned. "I had to tell her off for hanging around Mr Creech's office this morning."

"I hardly think that she was 'hanging around'," retorted Miss Hurst irritably. "She was out of the room for scarcely two minutes and you know how slowly she walks."

Wynne relaxed momentarily, before frowning as Miss Hurst added, "Why are you accusing her like that? You sound positively suspicious of the girl."

The clerk frowned. He had no intention of telling Miss Hurst all of his private thoughts. The less she knew the better. "I don't want clients seeing her. It doesn't set the right tone for the firm. But if you're sure that she isn't some nosey parker and that she is adequate, you can tell her that she may stay on until early spring when we shall review the situation."

"Very good, Mr Wynne. What about Davie?"

"What do you mean?"

"His appointment was meant to be temporary until we got someone better, but he's been here for nearly six months."

Wynne felt a burst of irritation rise within him. Annabel Hurst was far too inclined to interfere. "Davie's very cheap."

"I'm not surprised. His handwriting is appalling, he gets written instructions wrong, and he drops his aitches in front of clients."

"As I said, he's very cheap – half the cost of most youngsters."

"Price is not always the most important factor when employing staff."

"Would you like the cost of a better office-boy to come out of my pay-packet or yours?" enquired Wynne sarcastically. "Or perhaps you'd prefer to get rid of the Carew girl and do all the typing yourself."

With a distinct sniff, Miss Hurst turned round and left the room. That sort of silly remark merely indicated that Wynne had no idea how much work a secretary carried out in a day. It was just as well they did have Mary.

When Midge was told that she was to stay on at Forrest and Creech, she thanked Miss Hurst shyly, but there was no disguising her relief. The older woman attributed it to the natural pleasure any girl would have on keeping her job, unaware that Midge was gratefully reflecting that she would have longer to search for something which might help Mr Fletcher.

"We shall keep you into early spring at least," confirmed the chief typist, before asking in a burst of good humour, "Do you like springtime, or are you one of those people who prefers this crisp weather which we've been having recently?"

"I prefer spring," replied Midge politely. "I like to see primrosen opening their heads under the trees," she added helpfully.

Miss Hurst smiled to herself. There was no doubt that the new typist was indeed from the wide open lands to the east. No Londoner would use such old-fashioned words, but she herself could remember the village schoolmistress explaining that the correct plurals were primroses and houses, not primrosen and housen. She fell again to cogitating Mary Carew's background. Clever enough to get some education and lucky enough to have the money for a typing course, but why was she so shy of mentioning her family? The odd dialect words probably explained her origins – father a farm-labourer, mother perhaps with slightly higher aspirations. Had Mary struck them out of her life when she arrived in London, or had they disowned her? Miss Hurst frowned. Speculations about illegitimate children wouldn't get the letters to Spence, Barrow and Farmer typed and, in any case, the Carew girl looked far too young to be having children. Indeed, this morning Mary looked little more than a child herself, with the dark shadows under her eyes and wrinkled furrows on her brow.

At Forrest and Creech, the office staff were expected to work right up until one o'clock on Christmas Eve. Midge thought that the time would never pass, particularly when Wynne made her retype a page which he claimed was badly laid out. Eventually the clerk made a sour remark that Mr Creech had wanted her to have an extra ten shillings in her pay as a Christmas bonus.

"Oh, thank you, Mr Wynne," beamed Midge, certain that Mary Carew would have been grateful for such a gift.

"Thank Mr Creech, not me. And make sure you're back ready to start work on the 27th. We don't waste time in this office."

"No, Mr Wynne," replied Midge, reflecting that she would happily bet her extra ten shillings on the fact that the clerk had made her work twenty minutes extra into her holiday just to see how she would react.

Chapter Twenty-One

It had been agreed that Jenny would meet the cousins at Mr Carrington's flat, bringing both her own luggage and some of Midge's things which had been left at Mr Fletcher's house. When Midge arrived at the flat after a journey involving several changes by 'bus, just in case someone might be tailing her, she sighed with relief when she saw her uncle's Bentley drawn up on the pavement. John's Lagonda was fast, but she had no desire to drive to Suffolk in an open car.

"Try and get some sleep on the way down," urged John, after Midge had snatched a few sandwiches and declared herself ready to travel. "I don't want my mother quizzing me on why you look so tired."

Midge gratefully ensconced herself in rugs on the back seat. It occurred to her that Jenny looked as if she could do with some sleep, too, but her friend laughed off her concerns and insisted that she would keep John company in the front.

When the Bentley drew up at the sprawling farm-house, Mrs Carrington was waiting to greet them. She noticed Midge's pale face with concern, before reflecting that both girls looked as if they needed to be fattened up. However, Midge was distracted from all thoughts of investigations when she saw Bertie stalking across the hall, his tail raised high in greeting. She struggled to kneel down on the floor, before burying her face in his fur and whispering endearments in his ears.

"Midge is clearly engaged at the moment," laughed John. "Let me show you to your room, Jenny."

When Jenny strolled back downstairs, she was greeted with the information that Midge sent her apologies since she wanted to have a bath after the journey.

"That's all right," nodded Jenny, relieved that Midge

had remembered the plan to use a bath as an excuse to change out of her Mary Carew clothes and into something more suitable for Brandon and Midge Carrington. Midge had seemed dreadfully dreamy, as if she were living in a world of her own, and Jenny had worried about her giving the game away by appearing for tea in the wrong sort of clothes.

Midge, closely shadowed by Bertie, appeared as tea was served. Her aunt shot her a sharp look, wishing that she could cross-examine Jenny as to why Midge looked quite so worn-out.

'Midge looks positively sallow,' fretted Mrs Carrington to herself. 'You'd think she had been eating all the wrong sort of food, but the Fletchers have a good housekeeper.'

Midge sensed that her aunt was watching her, so she introduced a harmless topic. "Bertie nearly fell into the bath."

"Really, Midge," sighed Mrs Carrington. "In my young day we did not talk about baths at the tea-table."

"Did you talk about crinolines and fans instead?" enquired John mischievously. "Age is such a confusing thing. One of my wretched undergraduates asked me whether I had served in the war.

"Dons are all so stuffy and old," murmured Jenny. "I'm surprised that he only added ten or so years onto your age."

"Why was he asking you about the war?"

"Dearest Mama, he was trying to distract me from what he ought to have been discussing, viz. one long speech by Demosthenes."

"Just like Midge and her remarks on Bertie," suggested Mrs Carrington.

Since Midge was surreptitiously feeding her cat the ham from her sandwich as he lay on her lap, she was not pleased to be the focus of the conversation. Fortunately,

Mrs Carrington moved on to the arrangements for that evening. Jenny agreed to go to midnight mass with the others, although she decided that she would sweep all of her hair up under her fur hat and try to look as inconspicuous as possible. Midge, however, declared that the church would be too cold and that, if no-one objected violently, she would turn in. Since Midge's family were used to her needing more sleep than other people, no-one raised any objections, although Alice Carrington's eyes lingered on her niece's face for longer than Midge was entirely comfortable with.

Whilst Midge had fallen asleep with Bertie purring next to her, Jenny was observing the little village church with new eyes. John had told her that the vicar's wife was scatter-brained, but the flower-rota had clearly been properly organised. The austere grey stone was covered in holly, the blood-red berries standing out vividly against the waxy dark green leaves. Ivy rioted round the dark polished wood of the pew ends. Only the crusader's tomb in the side-chapel lay untouched, but he had enough decoration all year round – his armorial shield with its bright colours freshly restored, and the praying children by his side and his loyal hound at his feet. As the choir processed in, the choir-boys in crisply-laundered surplices and ruffs, Jenny reflected on how simple and straightforward everything looked: no murders, no suspicions, no treachery. Then she shook herself. Nothing was as it looked on the surface. A field might appear to be just a field of grain, but underneath it were worms and moles busily digging unnoticed. There might even be points of human activity – a tunnel, or a grave, or a coin horde hidden in fear during time of war, and its owner slaughtered and unable to retrieve it.

A solo treble launched into the first verse of 'Once in Royal David's City'. Jenny had heard some of the finest singers of the day perform at Covent Garden, but something about the innocent, sexless voice, so detached in its purity of form, pierced her to the heart. Was this to be the last Christmas that her father would be alive? Forcing herself to concentrate fiercely on singing the second verse with the rest of the congregation, Jenny scolded herself. It would be unbelievably shaming to cry in church – and not much recompense for the Carringtons' kindness to her.

Following tradition, various members of the congregation gave the readings. Jenny was distracted by the fact that General Whitlock stood to attention and addressed the church as if he were taking a parade. However, when it came to Mr Carrington, Jenny found little to entertain her. Midge's uncle had a good speaking voice, but how threatening he made the lesson sound. There was Herod deceptively sending out to find the anointed child, pretending that he only intended good, whereas he had murder in his heart. Now the organ was booming forth – was it Jenny's imagination that the lower notes sounded dark and menacing like Herod's command? And as the choir sang the first verse of 'The Holly and the Ivy', Jenny found herself wondering who was to bear the Forrest crown in *Rex v. Fletcher*. Did they have any chance of finding the real culprit?

On Christmas Day itself, Jenny crept into Midge's room shortly after Midge was stirring.

"I thought you wouldn't have managed to buy any gifts," she explained, as she stroked Bertie's head, "so I bought some for you to give. I hope you don't mind."

"Mind? I think you're frightfully organised – I hadn't thought of that at all."

Midge joined the rest of the family for morning coffee in the drawing room. Jenny was sitting next to Mrs Carrington, discussing curtain fabrics with her. The restrained good taste shown throughout the Brandon house made Jenny aware that her own home lacked a woman's touch. Mrs Field did her best, but there was a certain indefinable sense of incompleteness about the decorative scheme. Jenny sighed. Her only excursion into interior decoration had not gone well. In fact she blushed whenever she thought of the sulphur yellow walls which she had attempted to inflict upon those guests unlucky enough to stay in the smaller guest bedroom. Frocks, reflected Jenny, were much easier to manage, although she was currently struggling to care what she wore. Was this why Midge never seemed to make much effort? Was she too tired to care?

Suddenly realising that she had been neglecting her hostess and that Midge, who was curled up in a chair by the fire with Bertie, was too occupied to animate the conversation, Jenny snatched at a comment made by John several days earlier.

"Do explain to me, Mrs Carrington, something which John said."

"Of course, my dear," answered Alice, hoping that John had not been talking about the trial.

"What are the lunatic things which John claimed that Midge had committed in the past? I never heard that Midge was wild at home as well as at school."

"Do be quiet, Jenny," hissed Midge, who had no wish to have old faults raked over for her friend's delectation.

"Tomatoes," remarked Midge's aunt, reminiscently.

Midge blushed. "That was John's fault entirely."

"How? I thought that John was a paragon."

"He declared," remarked Midge, rousing herself enough to send a scowl in the direction of her cousin, "that girls were cowards; to wit, that he'd regularly gone scrumping for apples but he'd never encountered girls who did that sort of thing."

"And how old was John when he made this helpful and informative comparison?" enquired Jenny, fully aware that Midge had gone to live with her uncle when she was eleven and John an undergraduate at Cambridge.

"Nineteen."

"Men are very young for a long time," interposed Alice placidly. "I'm sure that you would give much better advice to a young cousin, Jenny; but, then, you are a woman."

"Do I take it, Mrs Carrington, that, following incitement by her cousin, Midge committed trespass and theft, before getting caught and being marched home in fetters, with penitence and fear writ large upon her brow?"

"The legal mind is so suspicious," murmured Midge, before her aunt could reply. "Apples weren't in season."

"But tomatoes were?"

"Yes, so I filched one and stuck it in John's egg-cup the next breakfast. And I didn't get caught. At least, not in the kitchen-garden."

"Not until poor Colonel Gregory's remarks on thieving vagabonds struck a chord in your uncle's mind and he decided to return to his early days as an investigative journalist," agreed Midge's aunt sympathetically.

"Living with a reporter when you have secrets to hide must be just as wearing as living with a barrister," commented Jenny, before her mouth twitched as she realised that she might not be living with one for much longer.

Chapter Twenty-Two

Despite such excursions into what Jenny insisted on calling Midge's Past, most of Jenny's thoughts were spent going over and over whether her father would have a future. No-one, therefore, was surprised that she went off with Midge and John to discuss matters in Midge's snuggery. John was determined to try and dissuade Midge from returning to Forrest and Creech and used every argument that he could think of. Nevertheless, Midge turned down all his entreaties to leave Duke's Buildings well alone.

"There's something odd going on and I intend to stay there until I have found out what." She quickly narrated how she had overheard the argument in German and how Wynne and Creech had reacted to her doing so.

Jenny frowned. "That's not enough to bring to court. Nor, unfortunately, is the fact that that visitor was desperate. It might have no connection with refugees – a man who was getting divorced might be desperate." She contemplated other possible leads. "What about the clients? Have any of them looked like refugees?"

"I'm not allowed to meet clients," admitted Midge in a tight, hard voice.

"Why ever not?"

"Wynne thinks that I'm not suitable in appearance."

Jenny was about to deny hotly that there was anything wrong with the clothes which Midge was wearing in her role as a hard-working typist when it suddenly occurred to her what Midge meant. An ugly flush of anger spread over her pretty face and from John's strangled exclamation it was clear that he was equally incensed.

"The only thing that was a little bit strange," added Midge, who was conscious that she had perhaps given away more than she meant to, "was that, when I stayed a few minutes late on Friday, Wynne was fussing round me trying to hurry me up out of the office. He told me that Mr Creech – that's the remaining partner – doesn't like people hanging around late because it means that he misses an express train home."

"Why?"

"Why what?"

"Why does Creech miss his train if you're finishing off typing?" demanded Jenny. "My father doesn't hang around at the close of day waiting to shut up shop; that's Thomson's job. Why is it different at Forrest and Creech?"

"I don't know," admitted Midge, "but that's what he said."

"I suppose solicitors aren't terribly grand," remarked Jenny, with the superiority which befitted a potential barrister. "But I still think it's a bit odd." Her eyes suddenly lit up. "Friday's pay-day. Maybe the extortion racket is still going on. Perhaps there are still people paying over half their pay-packet. That means there's another blackmailer."

"In that case," remarked Midge thoughtfully, "it might lead to another murder whilst your father is safely out of the way. Then no-one could doubt his innocence."

John was taken aback by his cousin's ruthlessness. "Steady on, Midge. Don't be so bloodthirsty."

Jenny had other concerns. "Who would take the risk of carrying out a murder when Forrest and Creech are already involved in one police investigation? Any death connected with that office will be looked at pretty carefully for some time to come." She sighed. "Cottrell has already warned me how difficult it may be to raise some of our speculations as evidence."

"Then we must get some evidence," stated Midge determinedly. "I'll try staying late on Friday again."

John frowned. "If there really is a murderer, it's simply not safe."

"Jenny's just pointed out that no-one would risk

causing another police investigation."

"No, Midge. I won't have you endangering yourself like that."

"I do wish you wouldn't turn down all my ideas," complained Midge in a mournful tone.

John relaxed at this sign that his cousin was giving way, but Jenny knew better. Midge might have complained, but she hadn't said anything about agreeing with John's edict; she was clearly going to carry on.

Midge changed the conversation. "I wish we could investigate the refugees. We can't be sure that they weren't involved."

John grimaced. "Considering the alternative of being sent back to Germany, I don't think that I'd hesitate too long before murdering a blackguard like Forrest."

Jenny nodded. "No, we mustn't neglect that possibility. I'll have another word with Professor Schulmann."

"Are you sure?" asked Midge hesitantly. "I mean, I know Professor Schulmann is a friend of your father, but, well..."

"What?"

"He must loathe what Forrest was doing, and he must have known that it would be very difficult to get enough witnesses to prosecute Forrest if Forrest called his bluff." Midge gave a nervous gulp. "Professor Schulmann knew when Forrest was going to see your father."

Jenny's eyes opened in astonishment. "Are you suggesting that he killed Forrest?"

"Not exactly. I just don't think we can afford to forget the possibility that he could have." Midge shrugged. "Forrest was an utter rotter – he certainly wouldn't listened have to a plea of 'Let my people go'."

Jenny looked sick. "But how could Professor Schulmann endanger his own friend?"

"Either," suggested John, "because he didn't realise

that your father would be accused or because he placed Forrest's death above all other considerations."

When the two girls returned to London, John made a further attempt to persuade Midge not to return to Forrest and Creech, but she refused point blank. For her part, Jenny had plans of her own. However, what she had not expected was to be confronted by her brother when she had hardly entered the house.

"Where have you been, Jenny?"

"Mrs Carrington invited me to stay in Suffolk."

Mike snorted. "I see. Father's lying in gaol and you went visiting. Don't you care about him?"

Jenny promptly fired up in anger. "Of course I do. I'm worried sick about him, but Mrs Carrington didn't want me to be on my own over Christmas."

"I suppose it doesn't matter if I was left alone?"

"I didn't know you were coming back. Why didn't you wire me?"

Mike scowled. The truth was that it had never occurred to him to do so, but he wasn't about to tell his little sister that. "I thought you might be glad of my support."

Jenny tried to pull herself together. Squabbling with her brother wasn't going to improve the situation, and her father would be pleased to see Mike. "Have you managed to visit Daddy?"

Mike shook his head. "They wouldn't let me in. I'm going to go into chambers tomorrow to speak to Thomson. Do you want to come in with me?"

Jenny murmured her agreement. All the time she had been in Suffolk she had had to fight down a haunting fear that something vital would crop up while she was away. At least Thomson could reassure her that it had not.

The following morning, Mike and Jenny went to chambers. Mike nodded distantly at James and Ronald, who were discussing business in the corridor. Then he turned to his sister.

"After I've spoken to Thomson, I'll go straight on to Cottrell's office. Don't you worry about things; I'll find out exactly what's happening and tell you later this evening."

Jenny stared at her brother in disbelief. "For God's sake, Mike, are you suggesting that I shouldn't discuss developments together with you and Thomson?"

"Please don't swear, Jenny. I know you're worried – so am I – but swearing does put chaps off a girl so quickly. As for Thomson, I do want to see him on my own. I don't think it's right for you to get involved in this sort of thing. Father would want me to protect you from it."

"I've spent the last fortnight 'getting involved in this sort of thing'," snapped Jenny. "And I'm frightfully sorry if talking to Thomson or Cottrell or the police for hours and hours isn't seemly, but don't forget that I'm training to be a lawyer and these are my chambers, too. What do you think I do in them? Discuss lace-making?"

"With that bounder Parry you probably could," grunted Mike. "He's far too dandified to be true. He'd be debagged and flung in the fountain if he turned up in the mess."

Jenny was so angry that she could hardly contain herself. "Then since you are so determined to speak to Thomson on your own, I shall take myself off to make the tea."

"All right," agreed Mike, thinking that this was a suitable activity, although one which he had dimly expected one of the typists to do.

"And after that," threatened Jenny, "you will find me discussing lace-making with Parry."

While Jenny stormed off to her own room, Mike shook his head. It was all very well Jenny getting angry, but she did not seem to grasp that normal chaps did not like this legal atmosphere, stuffed full of intellectuals. He had once made the mistake of trying to engage James in a conversation about rugger, but after James had apostatized it as a brutal game played by brutal men, Mike had been deeply thankful that he and his twin had finally persuaded their father not to force them into so soul-destroying an occupation as the law. A friend of his had gone into a bank and while old Stitters freely admitted that the work itself was of spectacular dullness – even worse than reading poetry – at least he seemed to have a whale of a time with racquets and rugger and fives. Doubtless, Mike mused complacently, the Middle Temple types entertained themselves with a genteel game of croquet when they wished to be excessively rowdy. No wonder they were so keen to let girls in – they were effeminate already. One simply could not imagine girls in the regiment; or, at least, not as actual officers. Naturally, there were one or two females smuggled in from the Bag of Nails on the odd occasions when a *fille de joie* was required, but those girls weren't, thank heavens, anyone's sisters.

While Mike was comforting himself with the thought that red-blooded men would soon show these acidulated types what was what on the rugger pitches, Jenny was pacing angrily back and forth in her room. She was very fond of James and saw no reason for Mike to sneer at him. After all, James was a fully-qualified barrister, whereas Mike had scraped into Sandhurst. And James had tried to help investigate the murder, which was more than Mike had done.

'All the twins ever do is laugh at me,' she snarled. 'And Mike's far worse than Tom. Tom may think I'm mad for wanting to become a barrister, but at least he doesn't keep telling me that nobody wants a bluestocking for a wife and that I'll be left on the shelf because a man would rather have a plain, amenable wife than a pretty, argumentative one.'

She suddenly suppressed a sob. 'And I *wasn't* abandoning Daddy by going to stay with Midge. I wanted to help.' A determined look came over her face. 'And I'm damned well going to follow up Midge's idea that Professor Schulmann needs to be tested. What's more, I think I know how to do it.'

She drew the telephone towards her and rang the Professor's number. He made no demur about seeing her nor, when she visited him an hour later, did he object to her suggestion that he let her speak to Herr X.

"That is a good idea, Miss Fletcher. I had been considering whether to ask you to do so."

Jenny sat up. "Why?"

Professor Schulmann smiled rather sadly. "My dear, your concern for your father is very touching. I have tried to persuade Herr X to agree to testify on your father's behalf, but he is reluctant to do so. Perhaps when he sees your grief and anxiety he will agree." He passed her a slip of card. "He is going by the name of Kinross at the moment. You can find him at this address. I shall contact him and ask him to be there at fourteen o'clock. I shall give you a letter of introduction."

Jenny was overwhelmed with gratitude. How could she have entertained suspicions of her father's friend? "Thank you, thank you."

Professor Schulmann patted her hand. "You must not thank me. I have done very little for your father and you must remember that Herr X may not agree to testify." He sighed. "The man has his reasons."

"If he doesn't, might I speak to Herr Lipinski?"

The professor frowned. "I am afraid not. Two nights ago he was knocked down in the street."

Jenny's eyes widened in horror. "Do you mean he was killed?"

"He is still alive, but he is very ill." Professor Schulmann looked gloomy. "I feel most guilty that I did not insist upon taking an affidavit from him when I had the chance. It would still have been open to attack by the prosecution, but it would have had legal force."

"Whereas your notes of what he told you do not?"

Professor Schulmann shrugged. "If Lipinski dies then we shall have a good case to introduce them as a record of the conversation, but I cannot be certain that the judge will let them be introduced."

"And the jury may regard them as an invention by the defence."

"Sadly, that is a possibility."

When two o'clock came, Jenny found herself in a run-down, shabby street in a poor area of the East End. She drew her fur coat tightly round her, feeling extremely conspicuous. It was obvious that she did not belong in these mean streets. As she knocked at the door, she suddenly wondered whether she had been incredibly stupid. If the Professor was a murderer, he might have decided to do away with her. Nobody knew where she was, nobody knew where she had been. She shook herself. Why would Professor Schulmann have decided to murder her just because she wanted to speak to one of the refugees? All he needed to have said was that Herr X had gone missing; that would have kept her away from Herr X without any danger of being hanged for murder.

At this moment, the door was opened to the limited extent of its chain.

"Yes?"

Jenny passed over the letter of introduction. "I have come to speak to Mr Kinross."

There was a pause. Then the chain was drawn back.

"Enter."

Jenny crossed the threshold nervously. The hallway was narrow and dim. She could not see properly. Then another door was opened, which shed light into the hall.

"Come into here."

After she had entered a living-room, furnished with shabby chairs and a chipped deal table, Jenny was able to see her host more clearly. Herr X was a thin, dark man with a narrow imperial beard. Lines of worry were stamped across his brow and he looked as scared as she felt. He indicated a worn chair.

"Please to sit here."

The two stared at each other for a moment. Then Jenny clearly her throat.

"Professor Schulmann said that you might be able to help me."

"Yes?"

"I am Mr Fletcher's daughter. Professor Schulmann asked my father to prevent Forrest from demanding money from refugees. My father tried to do as he was asked, with the result that the police think that my father killed Forrest. But they are wrong. It was just bad luck that Forrest visited my father on the day of his death."

"So why do you speak to me?"

"Because Forrest wrote a letter which said that my father was the blackmailer. It's not true. You know it isn't true. Please, Mr Kinross, help us. We need to show the court that my father was trying to help refugees. If you say that it was Forrest who was the extortioner, not my father, the jury will see that my father was not the murderer."

"Why should I help you? Why should I hand myself over to the authorities?"

"Because my father was trying to help you and others like you."

"And so I must return to Germany? Is that what you ask?"

"N... no." Jenny swallowed. She could understand the man's fears. "There is no justice in Germany now; that's why you fled. Do you want there to be no justice here, too? Do you want to see a man who tried to help you – and other Jews – hanged?" Suddenly, tears welled up in Jenny's eyes. "He's my father. I love him."

For the first time since the interview had begun, the man sounded uncertain. "You love him? And what of your mother? Does she love him?"

"She is dead. She died after I was born." Jenny looked beseechingly at her interlocutor. "Please, Herr Kinross. Please help me. You could save my father's life." She made a hopeless gesture with her hands. "I would not ask you if it were not essential. I cannot leave him to be accused of a shameful crime; I cannot see him die a shameful death. I must do everything I can to save him. No daughter would do otherwise."

"No daughter," repeated Herr X. "You think that a daughter would do anything to save her father?"

"Yes."

"The bond between a daughter and her father does not weaken as she grows up?"

Jenny shook her head wordlessly, fighting back her tears. She knew that it was weak to cry in front of the man she was trying to convince, but she could not help herself.

"If I testify, will you help me to stay in Britain?"

Jenny hesitated. She wanted to make wild guarantees that Herr X would be safe if he helped her, but she couldn't. It would be awful to make someone who had suffered so badly think that he was safe and then let him down. "I, and all of my legal friends, will do everything we can to support you. I wish that I could promise you more, but I cannot. I haven't the power to do more." Painfully aware of how little it was to offer, she added, "I hope that everyone will see that you should be rewarded for serving justice."

Herr X shrugged. "In the end, there is always cyanide."

Jenny exclaimed in protest, but part of her brain was telling her that this was a desperate man who spoke casually of poison. Was he the killer?

Herr X continued as if Jenny had not spoken. "I have more trust in you because you work with Herr Parry."

"You know James?"

"I met the honourable Herr in a discussion group. He is a sympathetic and high-minded individual."

"James?" repeated Jenny in incredulous tones. "James in a discussion group?"

Herr X gave a weary smile. "Why not? He is intelligent and interested in politics."

"I see. Yes, James is a sympathetic person."

"Very," agreed Herr X in heartfelt tones. "He said that the Herr Rechtsanwalt Fletcher was an honourable man. So I risk my life in your hands. I shall give witness."

"And you," whispered Jenny, "are an honourable man. I cannot thank you enough. You may help to save my father's life."

Chapter Twenty-Three

Whilst Jenny had retired from public view, not at home to visitors and unavailable to those who might seek her over the telephone wires, Midge was sitting in the lofty space of St Paul's listening to an organ recital and puzzling over something that she had read when typing up the morning's quota of documents.

'How can the estate of William Forrest only have around twelve pounds owed to it from unpaid debts? The invoice which I typed out this morning for Nathaniel Sampson, Esq. came to eight pounds and eleven shillings, and Spence, Barrow and Farmer have had their esteemed notice drawn to an unpaid account of nearly ten pounds? I know I was pretty dreadful at arithmetic at school, but even I can see that those two invoices alone are worth nineteen pounds and both of them were clearly marked as being work done by Forrest.'

Midge scratched her head as she tried to recollect how the other invoices which she had typed had been laid out.

'I'm sure that each invoice said which partner had done the work. Presumably that's to help accounting purposes and to ensure that the correct monies get credited to the correct man. So why is the estate not marked as being owed more money? It can't be that the money has already been paid or the firm wouldn't be sending out invoices. I suppose it might be that the income is divided in two and split between each partner, but that seems odd – how could they guarantee that each was working as hard as the other? Admittedly,' mused Midge, 'that invoice to Mr Craye was divided into two portions, according to which partner did the work, but surely that makes it even more unlikely that those other invoices for Forrest's individual work are meant to be split between him and Creech?'

Midge shivered. January was fast approaching and it

was being increasingly borne upon her that any hopes of a miracle resolution were over-optimistic in the extreme.

When Midge returned to her boarding-house that evening, she had made up her mind to look up the files of the accounts which she had typed, just in case both partners had been involved in the work for which the invoices had been sent out. However, she had no intention of hanging around after work again; instead, she decided to come into work early. She was strengthened in this view because Mr Wynne had looked meaningfully at his gold watch that morning when she had appeared at twenty-nine minutes past eight. At the time she had been irritated – she could not help it that the first 'bus had sailed past her, full to the brim with the result that she had had to wait for a later one.

The next morning, when her alarm clock shattered the cold, dark silence, Midge regretted her good intentions. Not only did she always dislike rising early, she hated getting up in the cold, and she could see her breath leaving her mouth in a white trail.

"Ugh," she remarked with a shiver, "it's colder than ever. Why am I doing this?"

A glance through the grubby panes of the window showed that frost had struck even in the narrow area at the back of the boarding-house. The rust on the railings was covered up by misty white lace and the solitary blackbird hunting for crumbs by the kitchen steps had puffed up its feathers in an attempt to keep warm.

"Ugh," repeated Midge. "I wonder if Mary Carew is allowed to make a practice of wearing two vests? Her coat certainly isn't warm enough for this sort of weather."

Midge had realised that, should someone burst in upon her, it would be vital to have an excuse ready for why she was looking through the files. She decided that the need to file the copies of the accounts which she had been typing the previous day would be a credible excuse so, with several copies lying to hand, she began to work her way systematically through the large filing-cabinets which were stored in a small alcove curtained off from the typists' room. The alcove was dark and it was necessary for Midge to turn on the light if she were to be able to see anything.

'Anyone who comes in will immediately know that someone's in here,' she reflected. 'The curtain makes hardly any noise. How will I get enough warning not to give myself away? I don't want someone standing there watching me for ages before I notice them.'

Twenty minutes later, Midge's caution was shown to be justified. Just as she was closing a drawer in one of the filing-cabinets, she heard a loud oath and Wynne, the clerk, fell, rather than walked, into the alcove.

"What the devil are you doing here?" he demanded abruptly with no thought for the politeness owed to a female.

"Oh, Mr Wynne, are you hurt?"

"It's no thanks to you that I'm not. What the blazes are you doing leaving your bag in the doorway for everyone to fall over?"

"I'm very sorry," began Midge, but the clerk waved away her apologies.

"What are you doing?"

Midge held out the account-copy which she was grasping in one hand. "Please, Mr Wynne, I need to file these."

The clerk snatched the sheet and glanced at it. "Why are you doing that now?"

Midge tried to look sheepish. "I ought to have filed them yesterday, but I forgot."

"Is that why you are in so early?" Wynne demanded in

a sharp voice.

"No, sir," replied Midge innocently. "I was nearly late yesterday because the 'bus was full and I didn't want to be late today, so I got an earlier 'bus." She giggled. "But I got an even earlier one than I'd intended, so I thought that I might as well get on with this whilst I waited for Miss Hurst to come in."

The clerk subjected her to a long look, glanced at the remaining account-copies, and then returned to the main room. Midge, who was watching him, saw him collect the various things that had fallen out of her bag when he had tripped over it.

"Ah, Miss Carew," he called.

Midge emerged from the side room. "Yes, Mr Wynne?"

"I think that you had better empty your bag so that we can check that nothing has been broken. Naturally, I shall pay for any damage, even although you should not have left your bag lying around in such a silly place."

'Glory, he's suspicious,' thought Midge. 'Thank goodness I don't have anything that might give me away.'

Midge obediently shook out the contents of her bag, taking care to make sure that her cotton handkerchief with 'Mary' tastefully embroidered in pink in the corner was prominently displayed the right way up. Wynne wrinkled up his nose at the sight of a magazine, the front cover of which showed a handsome young man who had his arms placed protectively round an adoring girl with a startlingly elaborate hairstyle. Then he picked up a half-empty bottle of cheap scent.

"I am glad that this is not broken," he said, before adding sternly, "but you are not to use this sort of thing here."

"No, sir," answered Midge sulkily.

"See that you don't."

"Yes, Mr Wynne."

The clerk gave her another glare, before moving across the room.

;If only he knew about Jenny's expensive bath-salts and the fact that I'm meant to be translating Aeschylus at the moment,' reflected Midge with a hidden grin.

The upshot of this early-morning interchange was that the clerk lay in wait to speak to Miss Hurst about Midge. However, this approach backfired. Miss Hurst believed that the female staff in the office came firmly under her jurisdiction and was annoyed with Wynne's remarks upon Midge's possession of scent.

"Since I have never seen Mary use any form of make-up, much less cheap scent," Miss Hurst remarked haughtily, "you will forgive me for stating that I see no reason why I ought to rebuke the girl for an offence which she has not committed." Seeing that the clerk was disposed to argue, Miss Hurst contemplated telling him that it was none of his business in the first place what the new typist had in her bag, but decided to exercise tact. "You'll have to excuse me, Mr Wynne, but I don't have time to talk about it at the moment. Mr Creech warned me that I would be needed to take shorthand first thing and here I am standing around, not having even taken off my coat."

Miss Hurst did indeed disappear off to the surviving partner's room, but Midge had no intention of spending any more time near the files. She worked diligently, not least because she was typing up more invoices, two of which seemed to suggest that the calculation of what was owed to the estate of William Forrest, deceased, was even more inaccurate than it had appeared on the previous day.

After Midge had made the tea and Miss Hurst had distributed it, the chief typist asked Midge what had happened to make Wynne cross. Midge, firmly in her role of a young and inexperienced typist fearing that she might be about to be unceremoniously sacked, spoke in a breathy, frightened voice.

"Please, Miss Hurst, Mr Wynne tripped over my bag and he was short with me about it."

"But he said something about you being in the side room, not in here."

"That's right, Miss Hurst," agreed Midge eagerly. "I needed to file the copies of these accounts which I've been doing, but I don't understand how to find the different files and you were that busy yesterday. I didn't like to disturb you when you were with Mr Creech. I was a bit early this morning and I thought I could maybe do them then. I've never learnt filing and Mr Wynne, he... well…" Midge's voice broke off artistically.

Miss Hurst sighed. Country-bred Mary Carew might not be that bright, but she seemed like a good worker and she never answered back, unlike pert Miss Peters, who had never been prepared to listen to advice from an older woman who had seen more of the world than she had. Mind you, with Wynne doing what, by all accounts, was nothing less than going through her bag, they'd be lucky to keep Mary for much longer. Miss Peters had left over less.

"I'll show you how the filing system works this afternoon," promised Miss Hurst.

"Oh, thank you, Miss Hurst," beamed Midge, thus confirming the chief typist's assessment of her as being willing but a little dim.

Chapter Twenty-Four

When Jenny left Herr X, she kept telling herself that she must not relax. It was all very well Herr X saying that he would give evidence, but he might change his mind. If he disappeared, there was nothing the defence could do about it. They didn't even have Lipinski as an alternative. She mustn't relax; she mustn't start to believe that her father would be miraculously saved.

The following day, while Midge was busy learning about filing, Jenny was busy making decisions. The first question was whether to tell Professor Schulmann what had transpired with Herr X. He could arrange for Herr X to swear an affidavit of his accusations against Forrest. On the other hand, if Schulmann had any connection with the murder – or knew which refugee had killed Forrest – he might also warn Herr X not to make an affidavit. Ultimately, it was probably safer to ask Cottrell to take such a statement. The second problem was much more troubling: the fact that James knew Herr X and had never mentioned him. Why had James hidden it up, even when they had all agreed how essential it was to track down refugees? And what was James doing attending a political discussion club? It sounded extremely unlike him.

Jenny bit her lip nervously. James wasn't a coward. If he feared being dragged into the investigation, it was because he had something to hide. And if that something was connected with Herr X, then that meant that James was connected with the murder. But how could he be? He and Ronald had given each other an alibi. Surely Ronald wasn't lying? Jenny was well aware that Ronald sometimes told Thomson that James had gone to check a fact in the law library when the real reason for James' absence was that he was sleeping off a late night. But Ronald must know that there was an enormous gulf between covering up for someone who didn't like getting up early and lying to the police in the midst of a murder investigation. To lie to the police would be madness. If the alibi were disproved, Ronald would come under immediate suspicion of having committed the crime.

Suddenly Jenny remembered the picture of Ronald shaking his watch and saying that it was playing up again. She felt sick. It couldn't be true. It simply couldn't be. James couldn't be a murderer. Jenny tried desperately to think straight. 'Daddy's able to approach his situation rationally. I must do the same,' she thought. 'If James doesn't have an alibi, I must consider him as a suspect, no matter how much I like him.' She grimaced. It was all very well liking James, but how well did she actually know him? She'd never suspected that he had political interests. What else didn't she know about him? After some thought, Jenny rang up James in chambers.

"Mike's driving me mad. Could I have dinner with you tonight?"

"Of course," replied James, mentally writing off his plans for the evening. Jenny sounded a bit worked up. It might be worth keeping an eye on her.

"Do you mind if I meet you in chambers?" Jenny gave an embarrassed cough. "Mike was cross about my going to stay with Midge over Christmas. If you pick me up from the house, he'll accuse me of enjoying myself when Daddy's in gaol. If I sneak out of the house, he won't realise that I've gone out to dinner."

"Of course," replied James for the second time. "Is seven all right?"

"Perfect. Thank you, James."

As James put the telephone down, he turned to Dickie, who had popped round for a chat.

"Sorry, old boy, I'm going to have to cancel tonight."

Dickie eyed him jealously. "That was Jenny, wasn't it?"

James looked at Dickie with interest. "Aha, an admirer!"

Dickie cast a look of deep loathing in James' direction. "You seem keen on her yourself."

"If you mean," drawled James, "do I want to smother her face with burning kisses of ardent young love, then, no, I am not 'keen on' Jenny in that sense. But she is an amusing dinner companion and she dresses superbly. Why should I not see the benefits in accompanying her occasionally? After all, she is the daughter of the head of chambers."

Dickie looked revolted. "You shouldn't speak of Jenny in that cynical way."

"Dear boy, you are so young."

"Yes, grandfather," retorted Dickie rudely. "Just make sure you don't get arrested again. Or maybe you don't mind since your head of chambers is safely in quod. What Sir Eustace would make of me being bailed I dread to think."

James ostentatiously untied the pink ribbon round a brief and studiously applied himself to the papers therein enclosed.

Although Jenny fully intended to tackle James in chambers, she turned up wearing evening dress as she did not want arouse his suspicions. When she entered his room, James was trying to finish some calculations.

"I'm sorry," said Jenny. "I've come too early."

James laughed. "It's all right; I'm just adding up my accounts." He glanced at his watch. "It's I who ought to apologise. I should have been changed by now. Will you excuse me?"

Jenny nodded and James left the room. He stuck his head round the door almost immediately afterwards. "Don't tell Thomson if you see him," he hissed

197

conspiratorially. "He disapproves of my changing in chambers; he thinks it's lowering the professional tone or something. I don't see why he can't understand that it enables me to get in an extra half-hour of work – assuming I'm working that is."

Jenny forced a grin. James sounded so very normal – just as flippant as usual. She looked at the mess of papers on his desk. Midge was busily looking through people's bills; why shouldn't she do the same? Thrusting aside the recognition that it was one thing to spy upon strangers and quite another to do so to friends, she lent over the desk and cautiously leafed through what was there. A curt letter from the Throgmorton Street branch of Lloyds suggested that James was overdrawn at his bank. The next couple of letters were bills from his tailor and a gentleman's outfitter. Then, at the bottom, came a letter from Mssrs East and Sword, Turf Accountants, which drew Mr Parry's esteemed attention to the fact that he owed the sum of £84 10s 6d and that they would be grateful if he could pay it before they were forced to take further measures, which might include obtaining a judgement against him. Jenny's eyes widened in shock. Under normal circumstances, she would have been very sorry for James, but her immediate response was one of suspicion.

"Does this mean anything?" she muttered to herself. "I wish I could ask Midge."

Ten minutes later, James returned, to find Jenny staring out of the window. Sweeping his papers into a drawer without looking at them, he locked the desk and turned to Jenny. "I'm sorry for the delay, but I'm all yours now. I thought we could dine at the Savoy. We can dance there or move on to the Devil's Disciple."

"Splendid," agreed Jenny, who wanted time to think about what she had seen and did not care where she went.

The Savoy was displaying its usual glittering

magnificence and both James and Jenny exchanged nods with acquaintances on various sides of the dining room. James examined the menu with care and, after they had chosen their meal, opened detailed negotiations with the wine-waiter. Jenny found herself staring at James. She knew perfectly well that a man could wear faultless evening dress and still be a murderer, but James looked just as he always did when he took her out for dinner, his sleek hair gleaming like the patent leather of his shoes and his grin breaking through his professional solemnity as he spoke. How and when did normality become twisted and destroyed? And how was she going to begin the conversation she had to have with him? When the meal was finished and Jenny had still not plucked up the courage to question James, she agreed to move on to the nightclub of James' choice, the curiously named Devil's Disciple.

"It's newer than the Four Hundred and the band are said to be excellent," declared James. "Apparently, the trumpeter only arrived on these shores last month and he's hot. It'll do you good to dance, particularly in that dress – it's new, isn't it?"

"Dear James, you always do notice that sort of thing, don't you?"

"Absolutely," agreed James, wondering what Jenny would think if she knew that he was busily contemplating whether loss of weight explained why the new and obviously expensive dress did not quite fit.

After they were seated at a minute table, squeezed into a space to the right of the dance-floor, some moments were devoted to the important question of what to drink. James was firmly of the opinion that the eponymous Devil's Disciple was the best thing which the bartender made, whereas Jenny opted for the intriguingly named Baboon's Tears. The first cocktails were swiftly succeeded by a second round, since James claimed that another

Despondent Simian would give Jenny a better chance to work out its component parts. It was while Jenny was considering this point that James insinuated a question about where Midge was. Jenny stuck to her prepared response.

"She's in Suffolk."

Something about Jenny's voice alerted James' suspicions. "I say, Jenny, are you up to something?"

Feeling decidedly underhand, Jenny attempted to look James straight in the eyes.

"No, James," she replied as innocently as she could.

James laughed softly. "I suppose your father took a very conventional line on lying when you were younger. What a pity; it has damaged your natural ability."

Realising that if she were going to tackle James she had better do so soon, Jenny summoned up her courage. "I had a very enlightening conversation with someone today."

James looked up from lighting his cigarette. "In relation to the case?"

"Exactly." Jenny swallowed. "What would you say if I told you that I had discovered someone in chambers who did not have an alibi for when the tea was made?"

"I'd be surprised. The police went into things pretty thoroughly."

"And if that person knew one of the blackmailed refugees?"

"Have you traced more of them?"

"No. I've been talking to one of them."

"One of the Herren X und Lipinski?"

Jenny nodded.

"And what did they say?"

"Herr X – or Kinross – said that he knew you rather well."

James was shocked out of his customary suave manner. "What?"

"Indeed. You met him in a political club; you were sympathetic; he trusted you."

"I don't know anyone called Kinross."

"But you're a member of a political club, are you not?"

"Well, yes, but..."

"And you met Kinross there?"

"There was no-one of that name."

"He knew yours. Doubtless he would recognise you if he saw you."

"That's not much of an identification."

"I was thinking more of him picking you out of a group of men." James started to protest, but Jenny carried on. "When you knew that we were searching for refugees, why didn't you say that you knew some?"

"Because I didn't know that the people I met at that particular place were refugees."

"Indeed. Did you not notice his accent?"

"As you won't tell me who is making this accusation, I can't tell you. But there are quite a lot of types in the East End who have Russian accents, you know. It doesn't make them all refugees."

"His accent is German."

"There are plenty of men who were born in this country who possess Germanic accents – possibly because they speak Yiddish at home. How was I expected to connect this man with the refugee racket?"

"Perhaps because you are a barrister and, supposedly, trained to make logical connections."

"And maybe it's because you're only a pupil that you are making illogical deductions."

Jenny ignored this insult. "You don't have an alibi. Ronald's watch doesn't work properly. There is no proof that you weren't lacing the tea with poison."

James was struggling to remain calm. "Honestly, Jenny, don't be ridiculous."

"The police have made out a case against my father on less evidence. He had never met any of the refugees – Professor Schulmann said so, and so did Herr X. But you had met one of them and you were 'very sympathetic'. Daddy was supposed to have managed to add poison to Forrest's tea when Forrest was in the room. Your alibi doesn't stand, so you could easily have added poison in the pantry – without anyone watching you."

"Do you really think that I'd risk poisoning your father?"

"There was no risk of that if you added poison to the sugar. You know that he doesn't take sugar in his tea."

"What motive could I possibly have? I wouldn't kill a man just because he was an extortioner."

"No? Then perhaps you were offered a consideration to do it." Jenny reached inside her evening bag and drew out a letter. "You're overdrawn, you owe money, and you're being dunned for £85."

"Where the blazes did you get that?"

"You left it lying around on your desk."

"Possibly because it never occurred to me that you would be so ill-bred as to poke and pry amongst my private letters."

"Your father isn't being accused of murder."

"Which makes it acceptable to accuse me of being a hired assassin? Ignoring any moral issues, do you really think that I'd risk my neck for £85?"

"More like £210 from what I could see," snapped Jenny. "In any case, it isn't the total which matters, it's the consequences of what would happen if you didn't pay. The Inns of Court don't take kindly to barristers being county-courted or made bankrupt."

James lit another cigarette with a shaking hand. "Look here, Jenny, calm down and listen to me. Yes, I owe money – mostly because I lent some to a friend who was in a hole.

Yes, I may have met Herr X, but I had no idea who he was – he didn't trust me with his real name. But that does not mean that I killed Forrest. Apart from anything else, where did I get the poison and why would I have been fool enough to help your investigation by going round asking for aconitine in chemist's shops?"

"You could have avoided the one you bought it from."

"I tell you I never bought any. And I had other ways of raising the dibs than laying myself open to blackmail by murdering for money. Long before there was any risk of being county-courted, I'd have told your father and asked for help."

"Why hadn't you already?"

"Because I would much prefer that my Head of Chambers regarded me as a competent member of the Bar rather than an irresponsible idiot," growled James. "If I want embarrassing conversations, I can talk to his daughter."

Jenny ignored this thrust. "My father strongly disapproves of gambling and you know it. You thought it was hilarious when he ordered Dickie not to discuss racing with Charlie because he didn't want Charlie to succumb to bad influences."

James shrugged. "I imagine I would have survived whatever cutting summary of my character he chose to read me."

"He might not have stopped at lecturing you."

James stared at Jenny. "What on earth do you mean?"

"What if he had found out and he decided to throw you out of chambers?"

"For running up a debt?"

"For being threatened with being county-courted."

"Don't be silly, Jenny; your father wouldn't have over-reacted like that. I wasn't county-courted, and I wouldn't have been. So there was no question of bringing the profession into disrepute. Thus it follows that I wouldn't have killed to raise the money to avoid being thrown out of chambers."

"My father nearly threw you out of chambers once before."

"How the devil do you know anything about that?"

"I heard him say something."

"Then you heard a dashed sight too much – and it was years ago, anyway."

Jenny shrugged mutinously. "I don't care."

"I suppose I'm being old-fashioned in assuming that friendship would prevent an accusation of murder being flung at me?" James glanced at Jenny's expression and his anger partially evaporated. "Honestly, old girl, be logical. That letter from Forrest is the worst point against your father, but it has no connection with me."

"That letter could be coincidence – Herr X didn't know that Professor Schulmann had asked my father to tackle Forrest. And maybe you weren't so sanguine earlier."

"That's easy enough to check. Ask your father what he'd have done if I really had been county-courted. Or have you got some other idea in your mind? Do you think that I've been burning to get my revenge for the last three years and suddenly decided to polish him off? I was only too grateful that it was him I'd been appearing with, not Staunton."

Jenny could not conceal her surprise. James rolled his eyeballs. "What on earth did you think I'd done, Jenny? Forge papers? Embezzle money? Bash a client over the head? I did what nineteen out of twenty young idiots do when they're worried about something. I had far too much to drink, with the result that when I appeared in court the next day I felt like death and could hardly string a sentence together. I'd have lost the case for our client if your father's other case hadn't ended early. He appeared in court just in time to save things." James gave an unexpected grin. "I can't say that I exactly enjoyed the interview which followed our victory, but I don't hold that against your father. I deserved everything which he said, and I was dashed lucky he stuck to caustic words rather than resorting to action."

Jenny made an unconvinced sound.

"I mean it, Jenny. He'd have been entirely justified in throwing me out of chambers for unprofessional conduct. Or he could have told Thomson the truth, rather than pretending that I'd had an attack of nerves."

"You don't have any."

"I had 'em all right that evening." James' grin widened. "I hope I didn't spend the following few months looking like a penitent sinner, but I probably did. However, the point is that I felt relief and gratitude, not hatred. And it is precisely because of how your father handled that situation that I know I could have approached him over money worries. If you don't believe me, ask yourself whether your father would have let you train with a man who's as unscrupulous as you seem to think I am."

When Jenny did not reply, James sighed again. "I know it's hard on you, Jenny, but it's not a very good idea to keep accusing people of being mixed up in this. You need to be professional about it, just as you would if you were appearing in court."

"But this isn't a client; it's my father. He's going to be hanged. I know it. And I can't do anything to save him."

"Getting yourself killed isn't going to help. What's to stop my having poisoned your cocktail – or strangling you in the taxi on the way home?"

Jenny turned white. James gave a humourless laugh. "Have you just realised how silly it is to make accusations directly to a putative murderer? Good. Perhaps that will stop you taking such dreadful risks in future."

Jenny managed to nod. James wondered if he had made his point sufficiently clear. "Of course I'm not going to strangle you – or do anything else to you. But I don't want to be forced to explain to your father why you've been murdered."

Chapter Twenty-Five

Jenny spent much of the night unsure whether she had been horribly unkind to a good friend, or whether she had stupidly warned a murderer that he was under suspicion. In the circumstances, it was unfortunate that she was scheduled to visit Wandsworth that morning. Looking at the haggard reflection which greeted her in the mirror, Jenny was tempted to cancel her appointment but she knew that her father would worry if she did so. Instead, she drew her make-up towards her, hoping to disguise the fact that she had spent most of the preceding hours in tears. That this effort was not entirely successful was made clear by her father's concerned greeting when Jenny was shown into the interview cell.

"Are you all right, Jenny? You mustn't worry about me."

Jenny nodded, conscious that a warder was watching her every move and hoping that it was true that they did not eavesdrop on conversations.

Mr Fletcher was unconvinced by Jenny's reassurances. "You look thinner."

Jenny airily dismissed this statement. "James took me out for dinner last night which explains my slightly distrait manner."

Looking at the suspiciously heavy make-up around Jenny's eyes, Mr Fletcher wondered how he would react if he actually believed that his daughter was out enjoying herself for half the night whilst he lay in the shadow of the noose. However, he did not have long and there were other matters which he needed to pursue.

"I may reserve judgement on that. More to the point, what's this that Mike said about you trying to do some private investigation of your own? I thought I told you not to."

Jenny cursed her brother under her breath, wondering how many cats he had let out of the bag.

"Yes, but one or two ideas occurred to me."

The K.C. eyed his daughter a trifle grimly. "You aren't poking your nose into Forrest's past life, are you?"

Jenny shook her head, consoling herself that she was not under oath and that, technically, Midge was poking her nose around, not she.

"Well, don't. Dubious men have dubious friends and I don't want anything happening to you. Parry will doubtless dine out for years on the story of how he was arrested, but if you are found – for example – on enclosed premises with nothing to account for your presence, Forrest's associates would have no hesitation in pursuing the highest penalty possible just to keep you out of their hair."

Having hopefully disposed of any further inventive ideas which might occur to his daughter, Fletcher continued. "Although I fully appreciate the motive underlying certain recent actions, neither you nor the others in chambers can take the law into your own hands. Moreover, I don't want you to get into the habit of using your appearance to persuade men to undertake things for you." In a murmur, he added, "Your mother was beautiful, too."

Since her father hardly ever mentioned his dead wife, Jenny diagnosed despondency. As she was trying to think of something to say, Fletcher shot Jenny a suspicious glance.

"I don't want you badgering Everard either; he knows what he's doing."

"I haven't badgered anyone," protested Jenny hotly.

"Cottrell seemed to think…"

"Cottrell seems to think that I should be sitting at home sewing embroidery whilst Mike pops in occasionally to cheer up the little woman."

"I don't think that you are being entirely fair to Cottrell," remarked Fletcher. "Apparently Staunton thinks that you are a bad influence on the younger men."

Jenny blushed, wondering again whether she had been dreadfully unfair to James. "Daddy, is James absolutely reliable?"

"As far as I know, he is completely reliable. Why?"

"Did you once threaten to throw him out of chambers?"

"Did he tell you that?"

Jenny fidgeted. "Only under pressure. I..., well, I sort of misunderstood something."

Fletcher's eyebrows rose. "Indeed? What, precisely?"

Reluctantly, Jenny narrated the events of the previous evening. Fletcher suppressed a groan. "Possessing an alibi for the time at which the tea was made does not imply guilt. Nor does the lack of an alibi. After all, my defence rests on the supposition that the crime was committed by someone outside my chambers who is blackmailing refugees. Does that sound like Parry to you?"

"No. But I was thinking about different motives last night."

"Then let me reassure you that I have no intention of requesting Parry – or anyone else – to leave my chambers. If he had come to me with his money worries, I should indeed have subjected him to a homily regarding the conduct appropriate to a member of the Bar. However, I would also have lent him the necessary money – and taken steps to ensure that he had so much work to do that he had no time to get into further mischief."

"Oh."

"You might tell him that I do not intend to take notice of what reached my ears unofficially. You may also tell him that I authorise Thomson to lend him such funds as he needs from the chambers accounts – I'd prefer not to put anything in writing at the moment, just in case the prison authorities become as suspicious as you were."

"You really do trust James, then?"

"Most definitely. In fact, I trusted him enough to have had him in for a consultation along with Cottrell yesterday afternoon."

Jenny's face revealed her surprise. "Why didn't he tell me that? I wanted to believe him. I would have if he had told me."

"He didn't tell you because I ordered him not to." The barrister grimaced as he recalled the bleak tone of the conversation. "I thought that it would upset you."

"Oh." There was a pause. "I've been beastly unfair to James, haven't I?"

Fletcher tried to reassure his daughter. "Parry will forgive you, my dear. He knows that you are worried."

"He was awfully decent to me last night," admitted Jenny. "I thought he'd never want to speak to me again, but he took me home. And he came out here with me." She swallowed. "I just wish I could do something useful. I don't want to be a decorative ornament, which is what Mike seems to think I ought to be."

Even as he was pointing out that her visits to him were useful, it occurred to Patrick Fletcher that it would be a very good idea to change his will. If he were hanged, Jenny would need a guardian until she came of age, but his sons no longer seemed suitable. He had long ago realised – and regretted – that the twins took their tone from the heartier, unreflective elements around them, whether at school or in the mess. Jenny needed a different attitude from her guardians. Perhaps he might persuade Everard to join Cottrell in that challenging undertaking. Was not one of Everard's daughters attempting to stand for Parliament, of all occupations? Perhaps that would give him insight into Jenny's determination to pursue a career.

The warder coughed discreetly.

"You'd better be going now," warned Fletcher, wishing that he could spend longer with Jenny. He had a nasty suspicion that she was more in need of reassurance and comfort than he was. If he were hanged it would all be over in a few months, but for her the misery and humiliation and despair would last for years. Thank God there was enough money to save her from outright want.

While Jenny was talking to her father, James had been telling Ronald and Dickie about Jenny's accusations. Ronald was appalled at what James told him, but Dickie, who had wandered in casually, appeared amused.

"What are a few accusations between friends," he enquired expansively. "Jenny's opened the field up quite a bit. If you don't have an alibi, nor does Thornley. What's your secret shame, old man?"

"Possibly that I've got an application before the Master in two hours and I'd rather like to prepare for it," retorted Ronald.

Dickie was not to be put off. "We now know all about Parry, but what about the rest. La Jenkins? Thomson?"

James took a hand in the conversation. "Ethel's evidence rules La Jenkins out."

"That still leaves Thomson and Staunton."

"I've been doing a little digging around. At the key time, Thomson was having a long conversation with Wontners. And since he telephoned them, I imagine it would be very easy to check the telephone records. In fact, I wager that our Inspector Groves has already done so."

"How do you know about Thomson?" asked Ronald curiously.

"I enquired. I thought it might be useful to have it established."

"In case Jenny made any more of her helpful

suggestions?"

"How swift you are, Thornley. One might even think that a future in the law awaited you."

"Aha!" declared Dickie in high delight. "That leaves Staunton. His motive must clearly be to encompass Fletcher's death in the hope of inheriting all of his cases. Fat chance – Fletcher's a far better silk than he can ever hope to be."

The door, which was partially ajar, opened wider. "Indeed?"

The three men spun round. There, in the doorway, stood Staunton.

"I was attracted by the unseemly noise coming from this room. I intended to ask you to moderate your voices; I did not expect to walk into an accusation of murder."

"It wasn't," protested Dickie.

"It sounded remarkably like one to me – complete, it would appear, down to motive. How fortunate for me that I wished to ensure a civilised calm within chambers. Otherwise I should not have gained this exceedingly enlightening insight into the hitherto unsuspected opinions which are held by the members of Sir Eustace Leadbetter's chambers."

Although by convention even the most junior barrister might address the most senior by his surname, Dickie sought to assuage Staunton's anger by using the utmost formality.

"I beg your pardon, sir; I can assure you, sir, that I was merely attempting to find an example which was so unlikely as to be laughable."

"If you do not mean such comments then I would suggest that, until you acquire a rather more adequate command of the laws of slander than you currently appear to possess, you do not say anything at all in relation to serious legal matters. No chambers can afford to pay out over unnecessary slander actions." Staunton turned to Ronald. "Thornley, when your visitor has left, I wish to speak to you."

With that, the barrister stalked off.

Dickie glanced at the others apologetically. "Sorry about that."

James lit a cigarette. "I know your set doesn't do much crime, but it's always a good idea to consider alibis in this sort of affair. Staunton was in at Marylebone Magistrates Court until ten past three on the day of the murder."

Dickie sounded rather sulky. "Ethel left the pantry for a few minutes at around half past."

James coughed. "And do you imagine that Staunton could magically appear within twenty minutes, even if he had run from Marylebone?"

A trace of a grin crossed Dickie's face at the thought of the plump barrister running. "No. I don't. As I said, fat chance." He shrugged. "And fat chance that Staunton won't complain to Leadbetter. What a life!" With that, he lounged off.

James watch Dickie leave with a certain malicious amusement. "That'll teach him to laugh at poor old Jenny."

Ronald glanced at James. "Don't you mind her accusations?"

James grinned tolerantly. "I didn't find them extraordinarily amusing, but at least she constructed a damned good case against me – much better than Purcell did against Staunton." He blew a smoke ring. "Frankly, I had a nasty feeling that, if that letter hadn't been sent by Forrest, our friend the police inspector might have decided to clap the gyves upon my wrists instead of Fletcher's." James' expression grew serious. "You know, old boy, I rather wonder whether Jenny has started to think that her father did it after all."

Ronald looked distinctly surprised. "Why?"

James lit another cigarette. "Obviously, the claims about Fletcher blackmailing Forrest are rot. But there's a different possibility. Fletcher must have known that how hard it would be to prove that Forrest was extorting money. Those refugees won't give witness in court – they'll lose their right to stay here if they do. Furthermore, even if Forrest did pledge good behaviour, what was to prevent him from restarting his trade in a few months?"

"So Fletcher decided to polish Forrest off and stop the whole process for good?"

"Precisely." James shrugged. "I can't honestly say that I believe it myself, but would you be surprised if the poor kid's tormenting herself with doubts?"

Ronald frowned. "I suppose not. She's had life pretty easy until now, which isn't much of a training for withstanding knocks."

"Perhaps not. But she's certainly finding life hard at the moment; I'd bear that in mind if she says anything silly."

Ronald snorted. "She can't say anything sillier than our helpful colleague from next door. And now I'll have to listen to Staunton's complaints."

"Well, for God's sake, calm him down," urged James. "If Staunton walks out of chambers the press will get hold of it and dress it up to look as if he left because he discovered something criminal going on here. That won't help Fletcher's chances – or ours."

Chapter Twenty-Six

On Friday morning, Midge was unexpectedly accosted by a stranger as she made her way up the steps of Duke's Buildings.

"Please, do you work at Forrest and Creech?"

Midge stared at the speaker in amazement. Surely she had heard him before? There was a gravelly undertone which was identical to the voice she had heard quarrelling in German with Creech.

The unknown repeated his question. "Do you work at Forrest and Creech?"

"Y... yes."

"I wish to speak to Mr Wynne."

Glancing at his clothes, which appeared to be of a continental cut, Midge's excitement grew. Was this one of the refugees? Had she finally discovered a real clue?

"Please come in. I shall show you into the waiting-room. May I take your name?"

"Tell Mr Wynne that his collector is here."

Wondering what on earth he meant, Midge nodded. Once the visitor was in the waiting-room, Midge stood in the corridor, deep in thought. Clearly, the man was disinclined to give his name – was that suspicious? Or was he a debt-collector who did not want to state outright that Wynne owed money? Perhaps he realised that Wynne might get sacked if the news crept out; an unemployed man was unlikely to be able to repay debts.

Suddenly, Davie appeared. "Wotcher, Miss Carew."

"Is Mr Wynne in yet?"

"No."

Midge thought that the real Mary Carew would probably refer to the stranger, so she had better do so too. "There's a visitor for him."

Davie grinned. "The man who came up the steps with

215

you?"

Unaware that Davie had seen her, and shocked by how easily he might have caught her out in a lie, Midge nodded. "Yes. He spoke to me."

"Better watch out for fireworks, then."

"I don't understand."

Davie grinned even wider. "Want to put a shilling on it?"

"I don't bet."

"That's coz you'd lose. Here comes Wynne."

The clerk stalked up the outer stairs. When he entered the corridor he glared at Midge and Davie. "What are you two doing out here, gossiping and wasting time."

"Sorry, sir; Miss Carew was asking me what to do with your visitor."

Wynne sighed impatiently. "Good grief, girl; don't you know anything? Put him in the waiting-room and offer him tea."

"I've done that already, Mr Wynne," murmured Midge. "He's only just come in."

Wynne handed his coat and hat to Davie. "Hang those up and I'll deal with this visitor." He glanced at his watch. "I can't think why Vintners and Talisman are sending their office-boy round at this time. They know that the draft isn't promised before luncheon." With that he stalked off, not listening to Midge's protest that the visitor didn't look like an office-boy.

Almost immediately after he opened the door of the waiting-room, Wynne let out a roar of rage.

"What are you doing here? I've told you not to come back here. Get out."

Midge couldn't make out the other man's words. Then Wynne's voice came again. "Creech has told you not to come here any more. Clear out and stay out."

The mysterious stranger emerged, gesticulating with his

hands. "They ask me is it really finished."

"How many times have I to tell you, yes! I don't intend to talk to you or them again. Now go away."

Watched by Midge and Davie, the stranger left. When he had gone, Wynne turned to them.

"Why are you still here? You can't be expected to be paid if you don't work properly. Standing around in a corridor isn't working."

Midge attempted to sound scared. "I'm sorry, I..."

Davie interrupted her feeble answer. "I thought you might be needing me, sir. Just like you did before."

Wynne glared at him. "Don't be cheeky or I'll box your ears."

Davie walked off jauntily, leaving Wynne with Midge.

"Why were you talking to that man?"

"He spoke to me in the street. He wanted to come in."

"Well, you're never to let him in again, do you hear? He's a madman."

Midge let her eyes widen. "Is he dangerous?"

"Not if you don't speak to him."

Midge shivered. "I won't."

When Midge was making tea later on, she took the opportunity to speak to Davie. Although she had no desire to rouse anyone's suspicions, she thought that it would have been odd if Mary hadn't shown some interest in the scene which she had observed.

Glancing round to check that no-one was in earshot, she asked, "What happened this morning? How did you know Mr Wynne would be so angry?"

Davie puffed up his chest. "I know a lot, I do."

Midge made herself nod admiringly. "You do."

"Is it worth a shilling to tell you? That's what I bet you."

Midge looked unhappy. "I've got my rent to pay," she

whispered. "And you heard Mr Wynne threatening to dock my wages."

"Old skinflint, he is," declared Davie.

"He said that man was mad. What if he comes round again?"

"He won't," replied Davie, reflecting sadly that that was a nice little earner gone. It wasn't going to be easy getting another like it. "He used to come round late every Friday night to see Wynne. Then he stopped a few weeks ago. And you heard Wynne. Would you come back after that?"

Midge shook her head, hoping that her disappointment was not showing. It was absolutely sickening. If the stranger was one of the refugees there was going to be no chance of getting someone to follow him and find out where he lived or who he was. Her best lead had gone.

Chapter Twenty-Seven

When Saturday came, Jenny arrived at Mr Carrington's flat rather early. John gave her tea and updated her as to the little detail that Midge had been able to wire him.

"There's clearly something to do with the accounts that's caught her eye."

"Accounts?" repeated Jenny in perplexity. "We're trying to investigate a murder, not look into whether the costs add up. What did she say, exactly?"

"Not much, don't forget that she was reporting in a short telegram."

"Yes, but what did she say?"

John unfolded the telegram. "Literally translated, we arrive at the following: it is necessary for the people and the dead thing – or perhaps, dead man – to call for a scrutiny of the accounts having been rendered by the hellenotamias to the people."

"What?" exclaimed Jenny inelegantly.

"Rather poor prose composition, I agree, and her use of 'hellenotamias' is infelicitous in this context," remarked John.

"But what does it mean?" demanded Jenny, who was uninterested in any infelicities in prose style. "What is a helleno-thing?"

"Treasurer of the Greeks," John explained. "There were several who basically looked after the money raised by the Athenian Empire. However, they could be subjected to various scrutinies – as indeed could other officials." As Jenny glared at it him, it occurred to John that, at this moment, she was unlikely to relish a learned disquisition on the subject of how the Athenian democracy tried to ensure that proper returns were submitted by all officials with access to public money. "I think Midge must mean that there's something wrong with some of the accounts in the office," he added hurriedly.

"How can a dead man call for a scrutiny?" snapped Jenny. "Midge should have used English, it would all be much clearer."

"Possibly," John agreed soberly, "but there's no chance that anyone in Forrest and Creech could understand that wire. As for the dead man, do you think that there could be something wrong with Forrest's accounts? You're the lawyer; what might that mean?"

Jenny shrugged. "Thomson deals with all of my father's accounts. I've no idea, unless Creech is trying to perpetrate a fraud by taking any money owed to Forrest – that might explain the reference to the dead man."

"Or perhaps the clerk, Wynne, is carrying out the fraud."

"Maybe they tried it earlier," suggested Jenny excitedly. "If Forrest caught them stealing his money, he'd want revenge. Maybe they killed him to stop him from talking."

"That would depend on how far back any peculiarities in the accounts date," cautioned John. "Don't assume that Midge has found a solution – it may be that she merely spotted something strange. That wire came on Wednesday; she may have discovered later that there was nothing in her idea."

Jenny paced about waiting for her friend to arrive. When Midge finally entered the flat, Jenny had to restrain herself. Clearly, Midge needed sustenance before she was quizzed as to what had been happening. However, Midge waved away this consideration and, as the three were consuming lunch, she began by telling them what had happened on the previous morning.

"I think the stranger was a refugee."

"Can you be sure of that?" queried John.

Midge shook her head in irritation. "No, I can't, but think about the evidence. He speaks German, his clothes aren't English, and there's obviously something odd going on." She gave a frustrated snarl. "Even Davie knows more about it than I do."

Jenny screwed up her face in thought. "It sounds as if whatever was going on has finished for good. Presumably, it's rather hard to run some sort of crooked operation now that the police are interested in the office."

"Ye-es," agreed Midge slowly. "Davie said that the stranger used to visit every Friday until a few weeks ago. That would tie in with someone paying over most of their wages in extortion. And the police investigation would explain why he stopped coming."

"Wynne clearly knew who the visitor was," argued Jenny. "That suggests that Wynne is the extortionist. But if you're right and the stranger spoke to Creech, doesn't that mean that Creech is also involved? After all, Creech ordered him not to come round again."

"Perhaps Creech believed Wynne's tale that the man was mad," pointed out Midge. "If so, he would naturally order him out."

"In German?" asked Jenny, before sighing. "The trouble is, we want to interpret this as implying that they're all up to their necks in the refugee racket – and thus the murder – but we need something which stands up in court." She rapidly explained what Herr X had told her. "Even if Herr X does give evidence, it's just his word against the letter. There's no proof. And if Lipinski dies, it will be all too easy for the prosecution to allege that we're inventing what he said." She looked at Midge appealingly. "What was it you discovered in the accounts? Was it of any use?"

Midge felt guilty. She knew perfectly well that Jenny was hoping that she had discovered something which would prove Mr Fletcher's innocence beyond doubt, but what she'd found so far was much too nebulous for that.

"If only I'd stayed late on one of the previous Fridays I might have been able to discover what was going on."

John frowned. "I'm glad that you didn't. You don't want to be caught alone in the office after dark by two desperate men."

Midge gulped. The thought was a frightening one. She forced herself to concentrate upon explaining the oddities between the accounts which she had been making out and the amount that appeared to be owed to the estate of William Forrest.

"Sounds like straightforward theft to me," grunted John. "Taking a bit of a risk, though. It would require knowledge of only a couple of those transactions to blow the lid on what was going on."

"I checked back in some of the accounts," stated Midge, "and the link between Forrest and Creech and the various clients all seem to be quite well-established, some of them going back several years." She paused. "One thing did strike me as a bit odd. The sums on the last invoices were all much larger than in any of the earlier accounts. In fact, there was one which was meant to be overdue, but I couldn't find any traces of earlier invoices in the files."

"Maybe they get put elsewhere after a few months," suggested John. "Or maybe unpaid accounts aren't put in the files until they are settled."

Midge apologised. "I wasn't able to look through all the files properly and it's difficult to find excuses to look at them when anyone else is around."

Jenny was silent whilst the two cousins began wrangling about whether Midge should have used 'Treasurer of the Greeks' or 'steward' to refer to Wynne. Suddenly she exclaimed, "Tax!"

"Tax?"

"Yes," nodded Jenny eagerly. "Look, if these accounts go back several years, and if they're all frightfully small and unimportant except for the very last invoices, they'd be absolutely perfect for a tax fraud."

Seeing two blank faces staring at her in bemusement, Jenny reflected that presumably technical legal points were as bizarre to classicists as the finer points of Athenian public administration were to her. Patiently she tried to explain what she meant.

"Every business has to pay tax, and that tax is calculated on the amount of money which has been earned by that company. Obviously the Revenue does not necessarily believe every estimate of how much tax is owed. Hence it is necessary for companies to keep books which demonstrate that what they claim they earned in the tax year is indeed what they earned. All right so far?"

"Yes."

"Well, this is where the fraud can come in. It is possible to lower your tax liability by fraudulently claiming that your business has had fewer or less valuable transactions than in reality. If you claim that you made ten pounds on a transaction, rather than a hundred, then you have reduced your tax liability by ninety per cent. Multiply that over several transactions and you can save a great deal of money."

"How do you disguise the fraud?" asked Midge with a frown. "After all, invoices have to be sent out to get the correct money paid back, even if someone later claims to have been paid much less."

"It depends partly on the size of the business, but in a medium-sized one like Forrest and Creech I'd expect there to be two sets of books – company and private."

"The company set available to any stray Revenue officials and the private ones which represent the actual amount of trade?" suggested John intelligently.

"Exactly," agreed Jenny, before groaning. "The trouble is, while I know the principle of that sort of fraud, I don't really know how to go about proving it. Would you mind if I sounded Dickie out very carefully? I could pretend that I was trying to read up on it."

"But Dickie isn't a tax barrister," pointed out Midge in some surprise. "He said that it was as dull as ditchwater."

"I know that," exclaimed Jenny in irritation, "but he knows a lot more than I do. And if he doesn't have the right answer, he'll either look it up or he'll ask one of his friends who does know."

John had other concerns. "I'm not very happy about you speaking to this chap. What happens if he starts speculating about why you are suddenly interested in tax fraud a few days after Christmas? He must know that there's only one thing that you're concerned about at the moment. Once he dismisses the possibility of tax evasion at your father's chambers. there is only one other firm which you might be thinking about – Forrest and Creech. From there it's a simple step to discovering that Midge is working under a false name."

Jenny looked rather appalled at this summary of events. "Dickie wouldn't give anything away," she protested. "And he can't be involved in the murder because he didn't visit our chambers that day."

"Perhaps not," commented John grimly. "But what if he is seen hanging around Duke's Buildings or – even worse – attempting to speak to Midge? How long do you think that Midge would last after that?" He turned to his cousin. "Are you absolutely sure that you haven't aroused anybody's suspicions?"

"Wynne doesn't like me," admitted Midge, relating how the clerk had searched her handbag.

John frowned. He had not been happy when Midge had started on this hazardous enterprise, and he was even less happy with the revelation that Midge might be working for a business which broke the law. "What about Creech?"

Suspecting that John would react badly to the tale of how Creech had tested whether she knew German, Midge attempted to put things in the best possible light. "I gather he was rarely in the office before Forrest died and I don't do much typing for him." Seeing that her cousin looked unconvinced, Midge played her trump card. "Miss Hurst is the person in charge of lesser mortals like me and I think that she's sorry for me." Midge grinned at John. "She's from Ely, so she's used to slightly dim creatures from Cambridge. She certainly spent ages patiently explaining the joys of the office filing-system to me. From what she let slip, Miss Peters, my immediate predecessor, didn't treat her with enough deference so I'm currently so respectful that I can't recognise myself at all."

"I'm not surprised," remarked Jenny frankly. "I can't imagine you being restrained and demure."

"Ah," Midge declared, "that's because I've talked myself into the role. If I can't get to sleep at night, I lie awake concocting Mary Carew's previous experiences. She's a very timid creature and very respectful of her elders and betters."

"Definitely not like you, then," Jenny retorted, adding before Midge had the chance to speak. "Nor me, either. I don't know how you manage to restrain yourself when that Wynne creature was searching your bag."

"I told myself that here was the opportunity to display those frightful handkerchiefs which you insisted on me having." Midge grew serious. "Actually, there was something else that I noticed in the files. Tucked away at the back of one drawer were several files which seemed to be empty. The only reason that I opened them was that I thought it was a bit silly to keep the spare files in the most inconvenient place. When I opened the last one just in case there were any letters in it, I found a number of headings."

"And?"

"Well, it was full of names like Yannonov, Rubenstein and Goldberg."

"Forrest might have had a lot of business in the East End," suggested Jenny.

"Yes," admitted Midge, "but these people don't appear to have proper files with addresses or letters or anything to suggest what their business actually is. Nor is there any evidence that they've called round and seen either of the partners. It was just a list of names."

"Without anything more," commented Jenny gloomily, "I don't see how we can tie those names into the case."

John rose. "Let me make some coffee," he suggested, thinking that a change of topic was in order.

Jenny fidgeted until John had gone into the tiny kitchenette. Her father's warnings about the possibility of Forrest's associates using the full panoply of the law to seek vengeance should they discover her working against them had worried her when he raised them. Now that Midge appeared to be on the cusp of a meaningful discovery, Jenny was again struck by fear in case her friend might end up in difficulties.

"I say, Midge, you will be careful, won't you?" she urged. "You're already living under an alias; don't get spotted doing anything else suspicious."

"Surely it's not a criminal offence to give a false name?"

"No-o-o, but using an alias would hardly help if you were accused of something else. Think what the police might make of it."

"I'm not going to be accused of anything," maintained Midge. "Anyway, the police haven't shown any interest in the office. Miss Hurst said that all they did was question people – they hardly looked anywhere except in Forrest's own room, though they did take papers from it." She glanced at Jenny. "You'd better be careful with Professor

Schulmann, too."

Jenny shrugged. "I shall, but do you genuinely think that he might be a danger?"

Midge shook her head slowly. "No, not really. We now know of two crimes taking place connected with Forrest and Creech – extortion and fraud."

"The fraud isn't certain," Jenny admitted reluctantly.

"True, but what other explanation can there be for those invoices? And think about who knew what was going on. The refugees certainly knew about the extortion, but how could they have become involved in the tax fraud? And the same goes for your father. Don't you think it's most likely that someone who knew about both crimes carried out the third?"

Jenny looked at her friend edgily. "That means that you're sharing an office with a murderer. Please, Midge, you must be careful."

"I know." Midge glanced apprehensively round to check that John wasn't listening. If he'd heard that particular comment from Jenny he'd be bound to try to forbid her from returning. "I'm being very careful." She frowned in thought. "What I'd like to know is why did Wynne discover the body so quickly? What was he doing hanging around so late at night."

Jenny tried to recollect what had been said at the inquest. "He stated that Forrest told him that he was feeling a bit odd and would deal with things in an hour of so. Wynne waited for a bit until he decided that he really had to get home."

"I know that you would delay things if your boss told you that he needed you to wait while he completed something urgent, but it's not natural to hang around work for so long." Midge gave a brief grin. "I certainly haven't spotted anyone else staying on 'til practically nine o'clock – certainly not young Mary Carew."

Jenny grimaced. "If Wynne hadn't found the body that night, it would have been a lot harder for the police doctor to suggest a time of death – or when Forrest was poisoned. Then the case against Daddy would have been much weaker."

Midge nodded in agreement. "Yes. It's all a bit too convenient for the prosecution. But how do we prove otherwise?"

Chapter Twenty-Eight

Although Midge had insisted upon returning to her lodgings on Saturday evening, Jenny had been unable to take her mind off the idea of her friend being waylaid and murdered. Mike had not improved matters on Sunday by lecturing her about not antagonising the police by going over ground which they had already covered. Although Mike was passing on a warning from Cottrell, and although Jenny knew that Mike had already had the same discussion with their father, she still found it intensely annoying to be treated like the small sister she once had been. She managed to preserve a diplomatic silence for most of this disquisition, but when Mike concluded by criticising their father, Jenny lost her temper.

"I can't imagine what the gov'nor's being doing letting you get so out of hand," grumbled Mike. "It's all the same with girls; give them an inch and they take an ell. He should never have let you start playing around as a lawyer; now you think that you know everything and won't listen to advice."

"Daddy is not letting me play around," snorted Jenny. "If you must know he's incredibly demanding and he certainly doesn't encourage me in the view that I know everything. Most of the time he's bitingly sarcastic because I've neglected some small detail in legislation or because I can't remember the correct precedent."

"The correct precedent for dealing with crime is to leave it to the properly regulated authorities."

"The police," snapped Jenny, "are the properly regulated authorities and they arrested Daddy."

"Yes, well..., that wasn't exactly what I meant."

"What did you mean?"

"Oh, stop cross-examining me, Jenny. I'm worried about the gov'nor too, but can't you understand that you can't take the law into your own hands? I don't want to see you in the dock as well as Father."

"You're not going to. I haven't done anything, and I haven't achieved anything."

Mike reminded himself that his sister was in need of masculine support. She certainly couldn't get it from the junior barristers in chambers and their father wasn't in a position to give it. That left him to do the best he could. "Cheer up, Jenny," he stated awkwardly. He glanced at his watch. "Look, I've got to get back to Salisbury. I should have left earlier. But don't forget, let me know if you need me. I'll look after you."

"Of course. Thank you, Mike."

While Jenny was wandering around the house, wishing that Mrs Field would stop sighing heavily every time Mr Fletcher was mentioned, James was doing some thinking of his own. 'If no-one makes any attempt to occupy Jenny,' he decided, 'she may end up coming out with further unhelpful accusations.' He shrugged. 'It must be pretty grim being stuck alone in that barrack of a house watching time tick by. Maybe that's half the reason why she went for me. But I don't think I'll invite her out to a nightclub. There's far too much loose talk about the Fletcher case; she'd be vilely upset if she overheard anything.' He grinned. 'A concert will do – they don't let drunks into the audience, whatever rules apply to the orchestra.'

Jenny had been both surprised and relieved when James rang up with his invitation to come to the Albert Hall that evening. She had no real desire to go to a concert, but she feared that James would think that she was still suspicious of him if she refused. And it would fill up the time.

Whilst James had no expectation that the performance of Russian music would be enlivened by such excitements as a drunken horn-player or an intoxicated conductor, equally he had not expected Jenny to begin to sob silently in the middle of the Tchaikovsky symphony. James, like most Englishmen, had considerable objection to being publicly associated with such embarrassingly open displays of emotion.

'Damn it all,' he writhed as he hurriedly passed Jenny his silk handkerchief, 'It's not as if they're playing the Fifth Symphony. How can she weep at the First?'

Jenny was intensely apologetic at the interval.

"I can't think what came over me," she began, but James waved her apologies away. Romantic composers were perhaps not the best entertainment to offer someone living under considerable strain – maybe he ought to have stuck to a jazz-band after all.

"What you need is a drink. Knowing how beastly hot it gets in here, I ordered some white wine for us in advance."

"Thank you."

Once they had reached the bar, Jenny waited at the outer edge of the crowd as James threaded his way through to where the drinks were served. As she stood there, mindlessly watching the figures weave backwards and forwards, she suddenly heard her name. When she turned round, to her displeasure she noticed a young married woman of her acquaintance. Stephanie Reynolds was, in Jenny's view, irritating and cloying. Jenny could just about summon up the necessary politeness to listen to a dissertation on the joys of married life, but she could not bear it whenever Stephanie began to quiz coyly whether Jenny, too, had a particular man in her sights. Tonight, however, Mrs Reynolds ignored the strains of harmonious love and instead clasped Jenny to her bosom.

"My dear, how unutterably ghastly it all must be for you."

"Evening, Stephanie," murmured Jenny, adeptly

231

removing herself and hoping that not everyone in the vicinity had heard her.

"I simply could not believe it when I read in the papers what had happened. I wanted to rush round as quickly as possible to be at your side but dear Hugo said not and, as you know, I do think that it is so important to listen to one's life-partner."

"Quite, Stephanie."

"And now I find you here, at a concert of all things." A little tinkling laugh fell from Mrs Reynolds' lips as she added, "Of course, I'm delighted to see you, but just a *leetle* surprised. I'm sure that I should not want to go out enjoying myself if dear Hugo lay in gaol. But perhaps you don't think that your bond with your father is to be compared to the life's bond with one's mate?"

Listening to this insincere gush, Jenny realised two things: first, that Stephanie Reynolds actively disliked her, and, secondly, that everyone nearby was listening in while trying to appear as if they were not.

"Is dear Hugo here tonight?" asked Jenny with interest. "I thought that I had read in the papers that he was at Antibes?"

As the particular paragraph to which Jenny was referring had mentioned that the captivating Miss Dolly Treadgold had been seen enjoying a short holiday from the stage in the company of, among others, Mr Hugo Reynolds, the noted financier, it was not surprising that Stephanie Reynolds looked as if she wanted to bite Jenny.

"He was in Antibes," she said with heavy emphasis, before adding in so low an undertone that Jenny was uncertain whether she had heard correctly, "and he isn't in gaol."

Fortunately, at this point James reappeared. He took in the situation at a glance, ignored Stephanie Reynolds' expression of avid curiosity, and led Jenny off, announcing as he did so that he'd prefer that Jenny didn't speak to chorus-girls. The look on Stephanie's face – and the hastily-suppressed amusement of the rest of her party – made Jenny give a tiny giggle, despite the circumstances.

"You shouldn't have said that," she murmured. "Stephanie'll be furious."

"Serves her right," declared James robustly. "If she makes that sort of remark, she deserves that sort of riposte, although it's hardly fair to chorus-girls to be compared to her. Very decent lot, some of 'em."

"Did you hear what she said?"

"No, but I saw your expression." James handed Jenny her glass. "Not that you really needed learned counsel's backing. You appeared to be standing up for yourself quite nicely." He grinned at Jenny supportively. "You're probably the only one of her acquaintances who's dared comment on her roving husband. Such training will be very useful for when you have to listen to judges making unkind remarks from the Bench."

Jenny's face twitched and James cursed as he realised how tactless his comment had been.

"Were you good at learning vocabulary at school?" he demanded, determined that he would somehow distract Jenny from her preoccupations. After all, that was mostly why he had invited her out that evening.

"It varied. Why?"

"Because I have been observing my next door neighbour, who appears to be a very earnest young man with badly-cut hair and a red tie."

"Do you mean the one who stood on my foot and didn't apologise?" asked Jenny.

"Good grief, woman, do you still hold to such conventional expressions of cultural behaviour? Surely you should realise that between two workers there is no need to apologise."

"Don't be silly, James; you can't accuse the poor man of being a Bolshevik on the grounds of needing a haircut."

"I can," declared James smugly, "and I do. Currently, you have given the impression of being an enemy of the people with your reactionary petty-bourgeois responses to the backward-looking music of the first half. Do you want to share Tukhachevsky's fate when this chap is given command of the People's Commissariat of Enlightenment?"

"Where does my ability to learn vocabulary come into it?" pursued Jenny, ignoring the lesser matters of the alleged treachery of a former Red Army hero and sticking firmly to the personal.

"I intend to conduct a very intense discussion about 'new musical forms', 'interpretative modal ideas' and 'objectivist principles'. I might even make reference to Avraamov's Symphony for Factory Whistles. I expect you to show the correct understanding of these terms."

This frivolity brought a brief smile to Jenny's face. "Have I committed ideological errors? But, Comrade Parry, a true son of the Soviet would have immediately understood that my grief was caused by my consideration of the plight of the serfs under the imperialist oppression which has been thrown off for good as we now march forward into the light of freedom under the banner of Comrade Stalin."

James winked at her. The thin young man had reappeared in the midst of her speech and was actually apologising to her for trying to reach his place. Jenny, despite her current fears, still looked very attractive and James suspected that the young man's suddenly rediscovered manners had more to do with her smile than with her use of the word Comrade. Nevertheless, it was clear that the stranger was itching to join in their discussion on the importance of ridding Soviet music of all traces of class-enemy character and the need to avoid the trap of allowing formalism to creep into any music, particularly the symphony.

Jenny tentatively suggested that the symphonic form itself, with its emphasis on careful positioning of different categories of instrument, harked back to the court orchestras of great noblemen, such as the Esterhazys and, as such, was riddled with tendencies which could only undermine the chances of writing the true Workers' Symphony.

"Should we not experiment with new sounds more representative of the workers?" suggested the stranger, who appeared worried by Jenny's revolutionary desire to abolish the symphony altogether. "Factory whistles, after all, have been used to considerable effect."

Jenny now fully justified James' belief that she could pick up new ideas swiftly. "Quite; we ought to be listening to Avraamov, not Czarist reactionary works. However, an alternative to new instruments would be to rearrange the orchestra altogether. Why should the first violins be placed nearest to the audience? Why not experiment and have one trombone and two piccolos in the centre and depose the conductor? Exile him to where the double-basses currently are!"

James murmured something about the need for an orchestra to sound balanced, but Jenny snorted. "Any dissonance which results from a truly collectivised orchestra would represent the struggles of the workers to free themselves from the demands of the kulaks and... and outdated modalities of control."

Conscious that she had shot her bolt with this splendid idea, Jenny sank into the background as James became embroiled in an argument as to what one Beltov had said against the Narodniks, and what the sainted Vladimir Ilyich of blessed memory had said about all of them. Materialism and Empirio-Criticism definitely was not in her line at all, even if James sounded rather worryingly well-informed about the whole matter.

Chapter Twenty-Nine

While Jenny was grateful to James for his attempt to take her mind off things, she found it almost impossible to maintain an appearance of equanimity as the date for the trial grew closer and closer. All she could think about was whether Midge had discovered anything new. For her part, Midge was also conscious that there was hardly any time left. She was exasperated that she had discovered so little which could be presented in court, but she was also worried about how tired she was getting. Although there had been points at Cambridge when she had wondered whether she would cope, at least she had not faced the additional strain of thinking that one of her fellow-students was a murderer who might turn upon her if they suspected that she was trying to track them down.

"What if we've got it horribly wrong?" she muttered as she lay in bed on Tuesday night. "It's all very well arguing that the tax fraud makes it likely that the murderer was someone from Forrest and Creech, but it doesn't prove it. If there isn't actually any connection between the office and Forrest's death, then all I've achieved is to raise Jenny's hopes unnecessarily."

Midge lay shivering under the inadequate blankets, listening to the pain in her leg. Whilst most people might think of pain in terms of sense or touch, Midge thought of her constant companion as an orchestra. It was bad enough when the strings played swooping semi-quavers of urgent throbbing, but when the oboe proclaimed its keening obligato melody over the lower lines, she was left sick with pain piled on pain. It was possible to force herself to carry on during the day, but lying in the enfolding night it was far harder for Midge to divert her thoughts away from the ravenous ache which gnawed at her leg and arm like an animal. Resisting the temptation to shift position in bed, Midge compelled herself to think logically.

'If I haven't enough evidence, then I need to find more. Wynne's got far too much money for an ordinary clerk, so he must be involved in either the extortion or the tax fraud. But I need to investigate Creech. The question is, how?'

Midge moved incautiously and winced as an explosion of pain rocketed through her leg.

"Damn," she swore softly, "damn, damn, damn!"

Eventually Midge drifted off, only to wake up the next morning grey and drained. Fighting through waves of fatigue, she washed and pulled on what she hoped was a suitable outfit for work.

As Midge made her way into Duke's Buildings, she tried to force herself to look more alert, but the effort was not entirely successful. Miss Hurst shot Midge a sharp look as she greeted her. The girl did not look the type for dissipation, but you could never tell. Then the reflection that country-bred Mary Carew had never had a proper office job before supplied an alternative explanation for the girl's appearance. Nevertheless, Miss Hurst kept a careful eye on Midge until she was sent off to prepare the tea.

There appeared to be an enormous amount of work to get through that morning, and Midge, who was tired from her bad night, struggled to keep up. By lunchtime, she had not yet completed typing out a detailed memorandum and Miss Hurst, who appeared to be in a bad mood, greeted this failure impatiently.

"Really, Mary, you ought to have got that completed before."

"Yes, Miss Hurst."

"It's just as well that Mr Creech isn't in today. There's nothing that makes him more annoyed than work not being completed on time." The secretary frowned at

Midge. "I hope that you're not slacking because you've been told that you're being kept on. There's no room in this office for that sort of girl."

"Oh no, Miss Hurst," replied Midge, sounding upset. "It's just that I didn't want to make mistakes. Mr Wynne told me that it was very important not to get anything wrong."

The older woman scanned Midge's face, but saw nothing other than honest concern.

"Very well, but you must not go for lunch until you have completed it and Davie has returned from taking it round to Fairbanks. I don't want the office left unattended."

"Yes, Miss Hurst."

Midge continued typing diligently until Miss Hurst left. Then she paused to consider the position. Creech wasn't in; Wynne and Miss Hurst had gone out for lunch. That left Davie, who was to run an errand after she had finished the memorandum. Midge glanced at her watch. It was half-past twelve. It would take around fifteen minutes to finish typing the document. Wynne and Miss Hurst normally took around an hour over lunch, so wouldn't be back before half-past one. If Davie took half an hour to run the errand, that would leave her with nearly thirty minutes in which to search Creech's office – more if she finished the document quickly. She turned back to her typing with renewed vigour.

Twenty minutes later, Midge was alone. She was more than a little annoyed that it had taken her nearly ten minutes to persuade Davie to deliver the document. He hadn't wanted to go out into the rain, and it was only by Midge pointing out that she would get no lunch at all unless he set off and returned before one-thirty that he eventually gave way, grumbling all the time about the unreasonableness of her request.

Praying that Creech had not left his door locked, Midge cautiously set off to raid her employer's office. She did not know precisely what to look for, not least because she suspected that any compromising documents would probably be kept in Creech's home. She could understand that Wynne might not want to undermine appearances by keeping financial documents in his lodgings where – if Mrs Dickens was a guide – they might be read by an inquisitive landlady. But that consideration would not apply to a solicitor with his own home. Nevertheless, Midge kept looking.

Most of the documents on Creech's desk seemed to be straightforward legal transactions undertaken by the firm: property transactions, wills, queries about inheritances. Midge sighed. None of those appeared to have any bearing upon either tax fraud or extortion and time was passing rapidly. It would be disastrous if she were discovered where she had no business. She thought that Davie would take his time, just to make her suffer for sending him out in the rain, but she could not rely upon it.

After she finished going through the papers on the desk, Midge thought for a moment. There was no chance that she would be able to break into the safe and, in any case, the police had already seen inside it. She rattled the drawers of the desk again in frustration. Why did they have to be locked? Then a distant memory of a detective-story occurred to her. She bit her lip. She would be extremely vulnerable if someone walked in while she was lying on the ground. But it was silly not to act just because she was frightened of being caught in such an exposed position. She would be almost as vulnerable standing up – it wouldn't require much effort to overpower her and batter in her skull; Creech's marble inkstand would achieve that easily enough.

Telling herself not to be a coward, Midge lowered

herself down to the ground and stared up at the underside of the desk. There was nothing underneath the main body of the desk, but surely there was something on the bottom of the lowest drawer? About to reach out for it, Midge suddenly remembered the existence of fingerprints. She squirmed under the desk and looked at the slip of paper which was pinned there. It showed two sets of numbers – a short one and a longer one. Hastily Midge copied them down, before using tweezers to see if there was anything on the other side. There wasn't. Ensuring that everything looked as it had done before she had intervened, Midge removed herself from underneath the desk and then stood up.

"I'd better smudge the handles of the desk with the back of my wrist," she muttered. "If anyone was suspicious enough to look for fingerprints they'd wonder why the handles were clean. But smudged handles might just mean that Creech had closed them when he was wearing gloves."

Having done this, Midge retreated, intending to memorise the numbers and then destroy her note. There was still twenty minutes before Miss Hurst or Mr Wynne were due to return, but Davie might come in at any moment.

Five minutes later, Miss Hurst returned. She raised her eyebrows at the sight of Midge typing.

"Have you still not completed that memorandum, Mary?"

Midge sounded nervous. "Davie's gone to deliver it. I thought I'd better try to catch up with the typing while he was out." She picked up a handwritten letter. "This isn't the memorandum, Miss Hurst."

The secretary looked at it. "No, it isn't. I'm glad to see that you are working hard." She glanced at the clock. "And since Davie clearly isn't going to be back in time to let you go out for lunch, it's just as well that I brought you something."

Midge was genuinely surprised. "For me, Miss Hurst?"

"We can't have you eating nothing. And you'd better eat it before Mr Wynne comes back – he doesn't approve of food being consumed in the office."

As Midge hastily ate a cheese sandwich, two points occurred to her. First, that Miss Hurst must have deliberately returned early to ensure that she had the chance to have some lunch. Secondly, it was terrifying how easily she could have been caught if she had carried on searching for only a few minutes longer. She shivered. If that had happened, Miss Hurst would have been giving her the sack, not a cheese sandwich. Or the secretary would have called the police. Either way, the attempt to spy on Forrest and Creech would have been well and truly exposed. Quite what the result would have had upon Mr Fletcher's defence, Midge did not like to contemplate.

Chapter Thirty

Midge had alternate Saturdays off, so was able to go to her uncle's flat late on Friday evening. Midge had told her landlady that she was going to visit a cousin in south London and would be spending the night there. Mrs Dickens had accepted this, thinking that Mary was homesick – the girl hardly exchanged a word with anyone else in the house, not that that was necessarily a bad thing when you thought how that Flossie and Ethel were always gassing away, fit to try anyone's patience.

Midge looked very tired when she made her way up the stairs to the flat, but her first action when John opened the door was to grab a pencil and scribble something down. Then she turned to John, too concerned with what she had discovered to waste her time worrying about matters of the heart.

"Have you got the drawings?"

"Yes, not that I could make head nor tail of them."

"Thank goodness. I was terrified that they would get lost or intercepted. I'm sorry to be mysterious, but would you mind giving me a few minutes to reconstruct something?"

"Of course not. I'll get you some sherry."

When Jenny arrived half an hour later, Midge was reclining on the sofa with her eyes shut. Jenny shot an anxious glance at her, but Midge opened her eyes at her and smiled.

"Now that you've come, I'll explain what I've been doing." She picked up the paper which she had been working on. "First of all, I found a number hidden under Creech's desk." She showed Jenny it. "Do you think that could be a bank account?"

Jenny looked interested. "Yes. We might be able to trace it if it were. And even if it isn't a bank account, surely

243

those numbers refer to something fishy? Why else would anyone hide them?"

Midge nodded. "That's what I thought." She frowned. "The only problem is that it may not be connected with the murder. It might be that Creech has been siphoning off money from clients' accounts."

"And keeps the stolen money in a secret account with a false name," suggested John. "Ye-es, I can see that might happen, but surely it was a bit stupid to hide the details under a desk? If the police suspected embezzlement, they'd have found it."

"They didn't find it when they were looking for evidence of murder. Maybe that was because they concentrated upon Forrest's room. Or maybe Creech replaced it after they had gone."

Jenny frowned. "Why doesn't he keep it openly among his own papers?"

"Maybe he doesn't trust his colleagues." Midge sounded excited. "Look here, Jenny, what if this was originally Forrest's account? If Forrest had stashed away a lot of his profits from the extortion racket, Creech might have decided to do him in and steal the money. It isn't his own account, which is why he's terrified of forgetting the numbers. He wouldn't stand up to scrutiny if he did forget the details, because he can't be certain what name and address Forrest gave."

"Or," suggested Jenny, "maybe he and Wynne are both in the extortion racket together and he doesn't want Wynne to know that he's been creaming off more than his fair share." She snarled in frustration. "This is just like everything else. We can speculate. We can suggest malpractice. But we can't prove that anyone is a murderer."

Midge sighed. Jenny's assessment sounded all too accurate. "I still haven't found any proof, but I think that we may be finally onto something with the refugee business. Look at this list."

"Fis[cher] – 935787," read Jenny obediently. "Lip[inski] – Little – 936927; Yan[nonov] – Farmer – 936821; Gold[berg?] – MacFarlane - 937263; Rub[enstein] – Robertson – 937445. There are lots of these. What do they mean, Midge?"

John grabbed the paper. "You mentioned some of those names last week, didn't you?"

"Yes," nodded Midge, "but they were on a different list. I've found another list with more names." She corrected herself. "Actually, the second list showed a shortened form of one name and then another name next to it."

"So, for example, you've restored 'Rub' as meaning Rubenstein?" queried John, who was used to the concept of reconstructing otherwise meaningless Latin inscriptions from only a few letters.

"Exactly. I wouldn't have paid any attention to this list except that I saw Lip and Yan and it reminded me of Lipinski and Yannonov."

"And the second name?" questioned Jenny.

"I think," declared Midge, suddenly worrying that she was wrong and that she had raised Jenny's hopes for nothing, "I think that they may stand for an alias. If I'm right then the numbers may be those on their false naturalisation papers."

Jenny was waving her arms around excitedly. "And we can check! We can ask Professor Schulmann whether Lipinski's papers have 936-whatever on them." She paused, a flaw having suddenly occurred to her. "The Professor never referred to him as Little," she pointed out in a small voice.

"Possibly not," agreed John, "but it surely can't be coincidence that Lipinski's name is on this list. How many people are there in London called Lipinski? Anyway, he

245

might well use his real name with the Professor – he had nothing to fear from him."

"More to the point," Midge argued, "he'd be much more likely to use his real name than his false one. If his papers are in the name of Little, no-one who wanted to trace him would achieve much searching for a Mr Lipinski."

"Why does Fischer not have another name next to it?"

"I don't know," stated Midge, who had puzzled over this question herself. "The only thing I can think of is that he became Fisher, spelled the English way. Or maybe they weren't using aliases at that point – his was the first name on the list and all the numbers get higher as you go down the roll."

"How on earth did you find this?" demanded John.

Midge grinned. "The silly thing is, I wasn't actually looking for it. I couldn't find my eraser, so I looked in the drawer of the desk which Miss Peters used. There was a sheet of blotting paper with these names and numbers scribbled on it. I nearly didn't pay any attention to it because I was in a hurry to get something finished."

"Did you steal it?" asked Jenny.

"No fear! After Wynne searched my bag I've become very cautious about having anything in the least bit suspicious in it. I drew little drawings and posted them out to John each lunchtime. After all, what could be suspicious about a doodle of a field? – even if the blades of grass do represent numbers."

"Clever!" applauded Jenny, before frowning in concentration. "Do you think that this Miss Peters was in on it?"

"I doubt it. I think that whoever is running this show supposed that no-one would pay any attention to an old scribbled piece of paper in an empty desk. And it would be on ready access to add to as need be. There were several names on the other side that I haven't managed to read yet."

"Why not?"

"Because, Jenny," explained Midge patiently, "I don't want to be seen turning the paper upside down or to put it back the wrong way. Also, there's a limit on the number of times that I can risk being seen near someone else's desk – even if she has left."

"You've run a devil of a risk as it is," snapped John, who was distinctly worried about this discovery, with all that it suggested. "I think it's time that we took this evidence to the police."

"The police?" echoed Midge in stupefaction. "But we want the defence to have this, not the police."

To Midge's surprise, it was Jenny who overrode her, not John. Jenny had been doing a lot of thinking over the previous week, particularly in relation to the realities of what evidence would be admissible, and what would be easily challenged.

"We don't need to approach the police immediately, but we certainly need to pass this on to Cottrell and Denys, who may then choose to contact the police." She attempted to explain her reasoning. "First of all, the trial starts next week. Sir Everard will need enough warning if he is to use this. Secondly, he may decide that there isn't quite enough evidence to be convincing. In that case, he may tip off the police and get them to raid the entire place." Jenny pulled a face. "I don't think that the evidence is strong enough – it would be easy for the prosecution to suggest that we planted it."

"Would a police raid help us?" asked Midge in unconvinced tones.

"I hope so. You've got enough to suggest some sort of fraud. That would give the police a pretext for searching every filing-cabinet, bookcase, desk and drawer in the building. If they happened to turn up evidence of refugee-running so much the better."

"Don't forget, Midge," added her cousin, "the police would be bound to pass over what they found to the defence. They could hardly pretend that nothing was happening when the defence tipped them off in the first place."

"Especially not if I'm there to witness any raid," agreed Midge. "I'd love to see that beast Wynne carted off in a Black Maria."

"Vengeful little thing, aren't you? However, you won't be there."

"Of course I shall. How do we know that the police will raid the place on Monday? They may keep it under observation before they took any action. If I don't turn up for work as usual, it might scare off the murderer."

"And we don't yet know who that is," commented Jenny soberly. "We can throw any amount of mud around about how dubious the firm is and how it may have criminal antecedents. However, throwing mud won't actually prove that Forrest wasn't killed by my father. We don't know where the poison was bought, how it was administered, or who administered it. We don't even know why Forrest had to die. For all we know someone may have wanted to kill my father – it may have been pure chance that Forrest drank the poisoned cup. And don't forget that we somehow have to explain away those wretched letters which Forrest wrote."

This accurate and realistic summary cast a temporary gloom on the trio. Midge tentatively suggested that, with so much doubt cast over Forrest, perhaps the jury might give Mr Fletcher the benefit of the doubt.

"That will mean that he goes through life knowing that everyone he meets thinks that he was lucky to get off," remarked Jenny bitterly. "How do you think that my father will like that? – his career in ruins, cut by society and feeling that he is a millstone round my neck because nobody will employ me or want to marry the daughter of a gaolbird who escaped the noose by inches."

John judged this to be the correct moment to go and open the wine, leaving Midge to cheer Jenny up as best she could. Once Jenny had recovered herself somewhat, John telephoned for dinner to be sent up. The restaurant attached to the block of flats produced sound, if unexciting, food, and John was determined that Midge have some decent meals over the weekend. Midge had said nothing to him about the inadequate and badly-cooked provisions which faced her in her lodgings, but John had guessed that boarding-house fare was unlikely to be good or attractively presented.

After dinner, John promised to run Jenny home, leaving Midge curled up by the fire. Half-asleep, Midge heard the car doors slam and then the motor start. She wriggled round into a more comfortable position, blessing the fact that the room was dark, lit only by the flickering flames in the grate.

"It's so lovely to be warm and safe," she breathed in a thin wisp of a voice, before closing her eyes.

Minutes passed. Suddenly, there was sound of a key being inserted into the lock of the outer door. Sitting bolt upright in terror, Midge heard the door swing open cautiously. Midge licked her lips, which had suddenly gone dry. She had not really believed that somebody might trail her to the flat. Now she did. She was alone in the flat. And John had said that the owners of the next-door flat were away on holiday. There was no-one who would come if she screamed. She was on her own.

A few minutes later, Midge heard the sound of stealthy footsteps approaching the door to the drawing-room. She forced herself to stay calm as the door slowly opened. She could dimly perceive a dark figure on the shadows of the threshold.

"Don't move, or I'll smash your head in," she ordered.

"What the devil?"

"John?" gasped Midge in relief.

"Yes, of course it's I. What's going on?"

Midge made no reply, fearing that her voice would tremble if she spoke. Instead, she put the poker back where it belonged, before sinking down onto the sofa in relief.

"I suddenly didn't like the idea of leaving you here alone," explained John, "so I pushed Jenny into a taxi and came back. I'm sorry if you got a shock, but I thought that you might have fallen asleep – that's why I didn't barge in noisily."

Midge murmured something meaningless, but her cousin had a question which he wanted answered.

"I know that I must have startled you, but do you normally attempt to attack everyone who comes to visit?"

Despite – or perhaps because of – John's semi-humorous tone, Midge promptly burst into tears.

"Come on, Midge," he cajoled. "Tell me, is it so bad?"

Hearing the affection in John's voice, Midge winced. How wonderful it would be to lie back against John's broad chest and leave everything up to him. He would protect her from the world and she would not have to keep struggling, fearing failure and discovery at every minute. But she knew that she could not give in to the siren voice which bid her cease her efforts.

"What's up?" urged John, thinking that Midge must still be reacting to the shock of believing that he was a burglar.

As John put his arm round Midge protectively, her determination to keep showing a brave face to the world fell away.

"Oh John, it's awful," she wailed. "I'm so tired and it's so ghastly at work. Every time Wynne enters the room, he watches me with a horrible sneering look in his eyes. Even Davie decided to walk part of the way home with me today – I'm sure he was testing me. I feel as if I have to think through every move before I make it in case I somehow give myself away. The only time I'm not scared is when I'm too exhausted to care any more."

"Are you able to rest at all when you leave the office?" asked John, who had noticed for himself how wan and worn-out Midge had been looking since she started living under her false identity.

Midge gave a hollow laugh. "When the pipes aren't gurgling and banging, the two girls who share the room along the corridor are talking. The walls are paper thin and I can hear everything they say. I suppose it's good for copy but I have to be so careful whenever I have meals with them. They think that I'm stuck-up because I hardly speak; they don't realise that I'm scared of being spotted as a fraud." Midge paused. "But the worst of it, John, is that I sometimes feel that I'm actually turning into Mary Carew. I can't risk awakening suspicions, so I have to be Mary in ever fibre of my existence. I know I'm lucky. I know that if I hadn't had good fortune, I'd be Mary in reality – no father to pay for my education; no aunt to spoil me; no uncle to persuade Newnham that my stupid leg won't affect my degree." She sniffed inelegantly. "But pretending to be Mary makes me feel as if I'm fated to turn into her. I feel so cut-off and alone."

"You don't have to carry on," John pointed out gently. "No-one would blame you if you stopped. I wouldn't and Jenny wouldn't. And, from what she's said, her father certainly wouldn't."

"But I would," replied Midge unanswerably. "How could I live with myself if Jenny's father were hanged, and

I'd given up at Forrest and Creech just because I hated being cold and tired and living in a third-rate lodging-house?"

"And frightened," added John. "Don't forget the fact that you may be in danger."

"If I were a man you wouldn't be encouraging me to give up; you'd be despising me for being an unutterable coward."

"Soldiers sometimes retreat."

"For tactical reasons," replied the daughter of a colonel, "or if they've been defeated in battle. But this would be neither. This would be desertion in the face of the enemy."

John had been unaware of quite how much a strain Midge had been finding her double-life. He had worked out that she was in considerable pain from her leg – even if that was something he knew Midge would prefer not to discuss – and he could guess that trying to search for evidence in an unfriendly atmosphere must be nerve-wracking. However, the psychological demands of living perpetually as another person had not occurred to him. Was that why Midge had appeared to look in perplexity at the array of cutlery at dinner? Was she re-emerging into her own world and finding it foreign to her?

"Feeling fear isn't necessarily a sign of cowardice," pointed out John, reverting to an earlier point. "I can tell you, I felt dashed well terrified when you threatened me and, in my defence, I'd claim that to be a perfectly sensible reaction."

A wavering smile crossed Midge's face. "I don't think that you're a coward. I'm trying to stop myself from being one." She glowered momentarily. "Sometimes it's stupid, little things which make me most of all want to run away."

"Such as?"

Midge hastily searched round for an alternative to the

fact that she was being underpaid because she walked with a stick and was thus deemed unsuitable to meet clients.

"My landlady Mrs Dickens keeps telling me that I don't look fit for work."

"She's probably only trying to be kind."

"I know. And I feel sorry for her; I really do. She's got a rotten life, struggling to keep body and soul together, with no-one to help her. But I'm sure she's been searching my room – some of my things were in the wrong place."

"These women are all nosy-parkers," declared John firmly. "She's probably just poking about – she isn't an emissary of Forrest and Creech."

"How can you be so sure?"

"She'd think it dashed odd if your employers tried to spy on you and she'd talk about it. No malefactor would take that kind of risk. In any case, you won't be there for much longer. Don't forget that the Cambridge term restarts very soon."

"Cambridge?" repeated Midge with the air of someone referring to an exotic mirage at the other end of the world.

"Yes. You'll have to be in Newnham when term starts."

"But... but..."

"Don't be silly, Midge. You worked hard to get into Cambridge and you can't possibly give it up. You've done very well with what you've discovered so far; there probably isn't much else left to find and, even if there is, you can leave it up to the police to search for it."

Midge looked unconvinced by this argument, but she was too tired to protest further. Moreover, the reflection that she had collapsed into tears in front of John left her wanting to flee his presence, comforting though it had been.

"Don't bother about things tonight," John advised her. "You go to bed and get a proper rest – I'll stay on guard."

Midge forced a smile at this remark, before retreating. Once she had left, John spent some time pacing backwards and forwards.

"This can't go on," he decided. "Midge looks exhausted. As Jenny said, we're no further forward in discovering who murdered Forrest. All we've done is stirred up a lot of mud from the bottom of a particularly murky pond. Is Midge really achieving anything other than ruining her health?"

Chapter Thirty-One

John's lucubrations led to him sending an urgent wire late that night. The upshot of his telegram was that while Midge was still asleep Geoffrey Carrington appeared, looking distinctly unimpressed at being dragged up to London on unexplained grounds. His temper was not improved by his son's explanation of why he had requested his presence.

"I'd like to wring Palmer's neck and, whilst I'm at it, I could wring yours too. What were you doing letting Midge get involved in this escapade?

"Well, sir," remarked John mildly, "she didn't show much sign of stopping when I tried to dissuade her. At least I saw her once a week and had some chance of keeping an eye on her – if I'd attempted to forbid her from taking the job all that would have happened is that I'd never have seen her."

Geoffrey Carrington glared at his son. "I did wonder why you suddenly wanted to go up to town on a weekly basis."

John laughed. "Honestly, Father, what else could I do? Midge has already pointed out that if she'd been a man we'd all be congratulating her on having got a foot in the door of the suspect firm."

"You needn't tell Midge," admitted Geoffrey, "but Sutton made several attempts to get some inside details. He couldn't even get an interview out of them, let alone slip a secretary in."

"At least it shows that Midge wasn't so far off track in what she was doing," John pointed out, before sighing. "You know, I think that we'd better get used to women invading our realms. When the war comes, they'll be doing a lot more than a bit of undercover investigative work."

"Midge isn't any woman."

"Are you going to tell her that?" enquired John. "I know she's frail, you know she's frail, but she's damned if she'll give in just because she's frail. It must be bad enough dragging your way round Cambridge like some worn-out wraith whilst all your colleagues are sailing gaily by on bicycles on their way to punting or balls. How inadequate would she feel if she backed out of what she and Jenny appear to think is the sole chance of saving Jenny's father's life?"

"Your mother thought that Midge seemed very disinclined to talk about Cambridge – do you think that we have done the wrong thing by letting her go up?"

John shrugged. "The experiment had to be made and at least she's young enough to repeat a year if necessary."

"That's why she didn't stay on at school to sit for a scholarship," agreed Mr Carrington before adding, "You do realise that if the defence decide that they want to pursue this idea of tax evasion, they may call Midge as a witness? Everything will then come out – how will Newnham react to the fact that one of their undergraduates spent the Christmas vacation working as a typist under an assumed name?"

"I hope that the authorities can be persuaded to see that Midge was acting to uphold justice. That, certainly, will be the line which I shall take – that is if the Principal of Newnham is prepared to listen to a wet-behind-the-ears don like me."

Mr Carrington laughed. "Scared of a lady-don? Really, John, I thought that you had more courage."

"The old ones with beady eyes terrify me," admitted John frankly. "They make me feel like a small boy who's been caught stealing jam. I have the greatest respect for Midge going to supervisions on a regular basis with them."

Although John was fairly certain that his father had been restored to a better humour, Midge was not to know this when she emerged from her bed after ten o'clock. She limped into the sitting-room, rubbing her eyes sleepily and with John's dressing-gown swamping her thin body. She froze in mid-yawn as she perceived Mr Carrington watching her with sardonic amusement.

"Uncle Geoffrey?" she stammered in horror, guessing that John must have told his father everything. Her fears were confirmed by his greeting.

"Miss Carew, I believe?" As Midge continued to gape at him as if she had never seen him before in her life, he sighed. "Really, Midge, what on earth do you think you're doing?"

"If I were one of your reporters, you wouldn't be asking that," countered Midge.

"If you were one of my reporters, I'd give you the worst rocket of your life for having gone so far ahead without telling me what you were doing." A slight tremor twisted Mr Carrington's lips. "Then I'd congratulate you for showing such resourcefulness and initiative. I might even suggest a bonus in your pay-packet." He frowned. "However, given that you are my niece, rather than a journalist…"

Midge eyed him uncertainly. She somehow doubted that her uncle would listen to any argument about the new roles now available for women. Moreover, whilst she fully intended to stick to her resolve to return to work on Monday whatever her uncle said, she had no desire to listen to a long lecture on irresponsibility, danger, or the opposing demands of Cambridge.

Geoffrey Carrington nearly laughed out loud at Midge's expression before contenting himself with telling her that, while he personally might be glad to get rid of her, he had no wish to explain to his brother why Midge had been knocked on the head and carted off to a police mortuary.

Midge risked a grin, assuming correctly that her uncle

would hardly make that sort of joke if he were as annoyed as she had first feared.

Geoffrey glanced at his watch. "You know, I should have expected to have heard from the defence team by now. Surely they must see how important it is that someone gets Midge's evidence from her own lips?"

"Maybe Jenny hasn't managed to get in touch with Cottrell yet," suggested John. "I don't suppose that she'd attempt to beard Denys in his own house."

Midge muttered, "That's what you think," *sotto voce*, but both men ignored her.

Minutes passed in desultory conversation before the telephone bell suddenly shrilled. "That'll be news of Cottrell," declared John as he leant over to answer it.

A loud squawking could be heard and John's eyebrows snapped together.

"Don't worry, I'll be there as soon as I can, Jenny," he promised.

"Cottrell," hissed Midge. "Ask her about Cottrell."

"Oh, yes; have you told our friends? No, not about this, but about what we discussed last night? What did they say? Good. Don't move; I'll be there immediately."

"What's up?"

"There's a problem at the Fletchers' house," declared John briefly. "I'm going round right away."

"What is it?" demanded Midge. "Is Jenny all right? Is it her father?"

"Don't know," grunted John as he went out into the hall to collect his coat and hat. "I'm not sure when I'll be back."

"What about Cottrell?" shouted Geoffrey, seeing that his son was about to disappear.

"Jenny managed to speak to him this morning. He said he needed to discuss matters with Denys, but that they'd probably come round here before lunch. Jenny gave them the address. Look, I must go now."

With that, John was off. What seemed like seconds later, the Lagonda could be heard driving at speed down the quiet road.

'Oho,' thought Mr Carrington, 'blows the wind in that quarter?'

Midge watched John's rushed departure with mixed feelings. On the one hand she was desperately worried that something had happened to Jenny. On the other, she had been conscious of a sudden shock when she observed John's response to Jenny's panicky call. Moreover, this was the first time that her friend had not turned to her for help. However, Midge did not have long in which to muse upon what a stab in the heart felt like; shortly afterwards the doorbell rang and Geoffrey ushered Cottrell and Sir Everard Denys into the room. Midge inspected the famous barrister with interest. She had expected someone tall and slim, like Jenny's father, or elegant and sophisticated, like James. Instead, she saw a short, tubby man with untidy hair and the air of having got dressed in a hurry.

"Is Miss Fletcher here?" enquired Cottrell.

"No," replied Midge, uncertain what had happened and, in any case, unsure how much Jenny would want her father's solicitor to learn.

"No matter," commented Denys. "It is your evidence which we need to go over." He turned to Geoffrey. "As you will know, Carrington, I should not normally talk directly to a witness before the trial starts, but there is not time for Cottrell to question Miss Carrington, refer her evidence back to me and then seek any further necessary clarification. I trust, therefore, that you will forgive this breach in legal etiquette."

Geoffrey nodded. "I quite understand. Neither of us has any intention of talking about your visit other than with my son and Miss Fletcher, both of whom know much more than I do about my niece's evidence."

It soon became apparent that the barrister had spoken correctly about how long he needed with his surprise new witness. Midge was taken aback by the level of detail Sir Everard seemed to demand, and how every point was examined minutely. A chance remark from Midge that she feared that Creech was suspicious of her led to a careful analysis of the fact that Creech had asked her to type a letter in German. After asking exactly what Creech had said, Denys wanted to know what his tone was like when he spoke.

Midge wrinkled her brow. "It seemed fairly neutral, but I thought that he was observing me quite closely."

"Why did you think that?"

"He kept watching my face. He didn't look at the paper, even when he laid it down on my desk."

"What did you reply to him? Use your own words as far as you are able to recollect them."

"I said, 'But, Mr Creech, I don't know any German. I learned a little bit of French at school and I had to learn some Latin words for Mr Carrington, but I don't know anything else.'"

The listening men noticed how Midge's accent and manner seemed to change when she quoted her speech as Mary Carew.

'That could be awkward when we get her in the witness box,' reflected Denys. 'If prosecution counsel notices, then he'd be a fool if he doesn't suggest that she is rather a calculating creature. That'd be a shame, because I suspect she isn't.' He ran his eyes over Midge. 'Looks exhausted. I wonder how far she'll stand up to cross-examination?' Putting this thought aside for the moment, Denys suddenly snapped out a question in German. Midge answered in the same language, and learned counsel frowned. With war coming, it would presumably be useful to have as many German-speakers as possible, but it could be devilish unfortunate if the prosecution decided to demonstrate that Midge regularly lied to her employers, even if she had done so for the best of motives.

The barrister patiently took Midge through every aspect of her life and work at Forrest and Creech. By one o'clock, Midge was looking more and more tired, but Sir Everard still had many questions to ask. Eventually, Mr Carrington, with one eye on Midge's weary face, proposed a break for lunch. Sir Everard reluctantly agreed, but requested that he might continue his questioning afterwards. Geoffrey made an excuse to get Midge out of the room. She disappeared gratefully to lie down in the guest bedroom, while Geoffrey returned to the main room.

"I hope you don't think that I'm being inhospitable," he began, "but do you really have to cross-examine my niece this afternoon as well as this morning? You can see for yourself that she looks exhausted. She had infantile paralysis as a child and she tires very easily. Working at this wretched job has drained her dreadfully."

Cottrell, who considered Midge a most surprising friend for mercurial, metropolitan Jenny, nodded sympathetically. Denys, however, shook his head.

"We could easily take the rest of her evidence tomorrow, but I want to see how well she will cope with the physical strain of being a witness. If we call her – and, from what she has told us, it will be important that we do – she will have to speak for some time to give her evidence. More to the point, prosecuting counsel will set out to destroy her credibility. If your niece can be portrayed as a fantasist and a liar, the damage to their case will be lessened."

"Sir Reginald Hilliard is appearing for the Crown," averred Cottrell. "He is particularly good at suggesting that witnesses are unreliable."

"How long will Midge be on the witness-stand?" demanded Mr Carrington.

"At least two hours," returned Sir Everard. "Is she strong enough to cope? She will have to stay alert because Hilliard lays cunning traps. Most witnesses never see them, and those who avoid one nearly always discover that they later walk into a second trap."

Geoffrey Carrington frowned. He had no desire to see Midge suffer in the witness-box. Moreover, as a journalist, he was all too aware that her evidence would be widely reported in the newspapers. Midge had become much more reserved since her illness and he worried what effect public notoriety would have on her.

"Is there anything that can be done to avoid her giving evidence?"

"That is very unlikely," stated Sir Everard implacably. Although he would be sorry to see the girl suffer for trying to help her friend, his client's interests had to come first. Patrick Fletcher's chances would improve if Forrest could be shown to be a crook and a tax evader.

"Then what can we do to help her?" demanded Geoffrey

"Naturally, learned counsel are not allowed to coach their witnesses," commented Denys with a slight smile, "but Miss Carrington appears to be an intelligent woman. Moreover, from what Cottrell tells me, young Miss Fletcher has a number of, ah, legally-minded friends who are eager to help her."

Hubert Cottrell nodded emphatically. He had observed with disapproval the enthusiastic aid of Parry *et al*. The sort of help which Sir Everard was carefully refraining from articulating was much more suitable than looking at poison books in respectable apothecaries' shops.

"I see your point," agreed Mr Carrington. If those

young men in Fletcher's chambers practised their cross-examination technique on Midge, she would be much better prepared to stand up to Sir Reginald Hilliard. Not for nothing was Hilliard noted for destroying witnesses with the ferocious good-humour of a tiger presented with a lame antelope.

Thus it was that Midge, after a short lunch snatched as she lay in bed, returned to face further detailed examination. As she sat there, attempting to deal with Sir Everard's forensic probing, Midge reminded herself that campaigns were fought in all sorts of ways. She had felt that her lodgings and her office equated to mud and shell holes, but facing up to Sir Everard was like being targeted by a sniper: you knew that he would eventually get you – the question was when and where.

When the barrister finally decided that he had extracted all the information from Midge that she could give, he turned to Geoffrey.

"I gather that you stand *in loco parentis* to Miss Carrington. I should like your agreement to her returning to Forrest and Creech on Monday."

Midge was distinctly aggrieved by this remark, suggesting as it did that she had no voice in the matter.

"I've already said that I'm going back on Monday," she pointed out, but the three men ignored this protest.

"I can see that you fear alerting anyone in the firm to the possibility that my niece is not what she appears to be," Geoffrey responded slowly, "but surely Midge could send a telegram saying that she was ill? At the worst, they'd only thinking that she was taking an unauthorised holiday."

"Then they would sack her immediately she returned," argued Cottrell, certain that such conduct would not be tolerated in his office.

"Exactly," agreed Sir Everard. "Moreover, I should imagine that any unexpected behaviour will attract

263

considerably more attention in the run-up to the trial than it would during normal conditions."

Midge again attempted to assert her independence. "Short of physically dragging me back to Suffolk, you can't stop me from turning up to work."

Mr Carrington had no intention of carrying on a debate about the emancipation of women in front of one of the most respected barristers of the day, but the glare he shot Midge made his feelings on the subject abundantly clear.

"Do you intend to inform the police of your suspicions?" he asked Sir Everard.

Denys frowned. "The problem is timing," he admitted. "Obviously, we shall have to inform them eventually – we can't connive at tax fraud, if that's what's been going on. Nevertheless, I don't want the police to know too early. If they have time to investigate our charges in detail, they may be able to show that fraud was the limit of Forrest's criminality. The worst thing for the defence would be if we raised the possibility that the firm supplied refugees with false papers for the purpose of extorting money from them, only to discover that the prosecution could defeat our claims. That's why I'd rather leave telling the police for at least another week and certainly not let them suspect anything before the defence open their case."

"That means that you want my niece to remain working in an office which may well harbour a murderer."

"Yes; every day she remains will help us."

"It's too dangerous," argued Mr Carrington, before turning to his niece. "I'm sorry, Midge, but I'm not prepared to let you risk your life in this way."

Midge scowled. "Would you say that if I were a man? You would let a male reporter do what I'm doing. You'd be pleased with his initiative."

Sir Everard, who was blessed with a sense of humour, conjured up the picture of a male reporter, with a badly-shaved chin and dressed in a skirt and stockings, pretending to be a typist. However, Midge's mention of reporters suggested a possible way out of the impasse.

"I say, Carrington, what if you put some of your enterprising young cubs on to shadowing Miss Carrington. Surely she would be safe if there was always someone watching her? You wouldn't have to fear suspicious traffic accidents or abductions if she had a bodyguard."

Geoffrey was about to refuse, when Midge asked him for a few words in private. Thinking that this was better than airing their disagreements in public, Mr Carrington followed her out into the hall.

"Look, Uncle Geoffrey, I know that you're worried about me running into danger, and I do appreciate your concern, but I'm not a little girl. I'm well aware of the potential risks and I'm happy to accept them."

"You may be," snorted her uncle, "but I am not."

"How else can I help Jenny?" pleaded Midge, before adding in a low, bitter voice. "It's not as if I can follow suspects or even investigate tearooms. But I *can* do this."

Mr Carrington, who had fully intended telling his niece in no uncertain terms first, that she would be returning to Brandon and, secondly, what he thought about her arguing with him in front of strangers, suddenly changed his mind. He remembered John's words about how inadequate Midge's disability must leave her feeling; if he were to refuse Midge's request, would Midge be left with the impression that she was substandard and second-rate?

"You are just as stubborn as your father," he commented unflatteringly. "Doubtless you will be delighted to drink poison in your tea on Monday."

"Dear Uncle Geoffrey, thank you," purred Midge, before promising, "I shan't drink any tea or eat any food in the office.

"And how do you intend to explain that?"

Midge laughed. "I'll pretend that I'm on some sort of strange diet, just like those that Mrs Gregory follows. Aunt Alice told me that it was important to keep up to date with the village gossip, but I never thought that that particular piece of information would come in useful."

"You," declared Mr Carrington, with a glare at his niece which did not entirely hide the beginnings of a smile, "are a cursed little nuisance and I cannot imagine how your long-suffering aunt has put up with you for so many years."

Chapter Thirty-Two

Shortly after it was agreed that Midge would be returning to Forrest and Creech on Monday morning, the legal representatives departed. Midge attempted to telephone Jenny, but there was no reply. Concerned as to what might have gone wrong, Midge was eager to go round to her friend's house immediately, but Mr Carrington vetoed the scheme.

"You look exhausted and it won't do you any good to hare round London on a wild goose-chase. Jenny will telephone when she is able to and, in any case, she has John with her. Go and get some rest whilst you can."

Recognising that this was sensible advice, Midge took herself off to bed. Her brain was so full of all the questions which Sir Everard had asked her that it took her some time to drift off to sleep.

'If Sir Everard thinks that my evidence is important, then I've done some good,' she thought with relief. 'I have helped Mr Fletcher and I'm not a hopeless failure who gets in the way of everyone else's efforts.'

As Midge was relaxing properly for the first time in weeks, Jenny was facing more complicated emotions. When John arrived, Jenny had checked through the letter-flap that John was indeed who he said he was. This was startling enough, but, when Jenny opened the heavy front door, John was shocked by the ravaged expression on Jenny's face.

"Jenny, what's happened?"

For an answer, Jenny led him into the morning-room.

"Please take them away, John; please, please, please."

As Jenny's voice ascended higher and higher, John turned to stare in astonishment at two children who stood as still as statues on the Aubusson carpet.

267

"Who are you?" he demanded.

The children remained motionless, watching him with dark, frightened eyes.

John turned back to Jenny, who had her hands held over her eyes as if to avert some hideous sight.

"Jenny, what's wrong? They're little children."

Jenny began to shake. "Take them away, take them away."

Realising that Jenny was practically hysterical, John strode across the room, wrenched the top off a decanter, poured a large helping of brandy into a heavy crystal tumbler, before returning to Jenny and thrusting it into her hand.

"Drink that," he commanded.

Some of the colour came back into Jenny's face after the first gulp, but John made her drain half the glass, before conducting her to the nearest chair.

"That's my father's Napoleon brandy," observed Jenny, rather irrelevantly. "He'd have a fit."

"You can drink the rest of it in a minute," retorted John, thinking that it was Jenny, not her father, who was having fits. "Now, tell me what's going on."

Jenny tried to pull herself together. "Sorry, John. I can't think what happened to me. Field's gone to take a suit to Wandsworth and Mrs Field needed to do some shopping. I'd telephoned Cottrell and when the doorbell rang I thought that it might be you or Cottrell. But I found those two instead."

"Who are they?"

"I don't know. They asked for my father. I said that he wasn't here and that they had better leave, but the older one pushed past me, pulling the other one in behind her. They've been standing like that ever since." Jenny shivered. "Standing like ghosts and staring and staring at me."

John's experienced eye suggested that perhaps Mr

Fletcher's cognac was starting to take effect, but he could see that, even without the benefit of alcoholic stimulant, the two children were decidedly unnerving, standing motionless and alien in Mr Fletcher's drawing-room. Moreover, it was certainly true that they had a fixed, unwinking stare.

Leaving Jenny for the moment, John returned to the centre of the room. Seen closer up, the children appeared rather uncared for. The older girl looked around eleven whilst the younger one was maybe five or six. John knelt down on one knee on the carpet.

"Hello, I'm John. What's your name?"

The little girl stared at him fixedly, but the older girl spoke for the first time.

"Mr Fletcher. Where is he?"

John regarded the child with interest. Was it his imagination or did she speak with a distinct German accent. The 'w' of 'where' sounded much more like a 'v' than the soft 'w' which a native English-speaker would say. Regular holidays in Austria had resulted in John speaking fluent German, so he repeated his words in that language. There was no doubt that both children understood him, although it was somewhat disconcerting that the younger one immediately burst into tears.

"Oh God," groaned John. What a time for Jenny to be out of action. Running his hands through his hair, he suggested to the older girl that she take her sister to the bathroom and wash her face.

"Perhaps you'd like some food or chocolate after that?" he offered, before asking Jenny where the bathroom was. When he had shown the children upstairs, he ran back down to Jenny.

"They're German," he explained. "Perhaps they are refugees."

Jenny was about to declare that she could not care less

whether the girls were refugees or sea-monsters, when it struck her that presumably they were as much victims of circumstances as her father was.

"What are we going to do?" she asked in an exhausted voice which suggested how much strain she was under.

"Find out if they have any relatives in this country," declared John. "Then ask them why they want to see your father." He paused. "You do realise that they may be Jewish and know no-one in London?"

There had been a refugee girl at school with Jenny and an image of how Esther must have felt when she arrived on British shores, unsure where her parents were, flickered through Jenny's mind. Her mouth twisted. "Poor little beasts." She laughed hollowly. "God knows what they'll have made of my exhibition, but try to reassure them that they'll be safe here." Then her face clouded over. "How are they going to react to the fact that my father's in gaol? They'll be bound to think that he's been taken by the secret police."

"Let's deal with one thing at a time," suggested John sensibly. "They may be frightened to tell us anything, but perhaps Professor Schulmann might help us. If the worst comes to the worst, I could always take them to my mother."

At this point, Jenny burst into tears and tried to thank John. As John put his arms round her, the thought occurred to Jenny that it was – to say the least – rather bad form to sob your heart out in the embrace of your best friend's cousin's when you knew that your best friend was in love with the said cousin.

John let Jenny cry for around five minutes. Then the children reappeared, looking cleaner, but still as wary as wild animals.

"Sit up, Jenny," he said gently. "Do you think that you could help me to get the children to the kitchen? They may need food."

Jenny sat up, wishing that she did not have to. The world was a peculiarly threatening place at the moment and John's comfort had given a few moments of safety. She stood up and listened to John trying to persuade the children to follow him down to the kitchen. However, when they saw the stairs which led down to the kitchen and scullery, the younger girl tugged at her sister's hand and retreated hurriedly backwards.

"She must think it's a trap to get her locked up," suggested Jenny. "Tell her that I'll go down and unlock the back door. Maybe that will help."

Since a cold draught soon filtered up the stairs, it was obvious that there was indeed a door down below. The older girl muttered urgently to her sister and, while the little girl stayed upstairs, she went downstairs and, after shooing Jenny away from the back door, called for her sister to join her. When both children were in the kitchen, John asked one of them to push the back door nearly closed, so that the place would not get too cold. After carefully extracting the key, the older girl did so.

"What about food?" asked John.

"I'll look in the pantry," offered Jenny. "There may be some milk in the refrigerator."

She soon returned bearing some cutlery and plates, as well as bread and cheese. She placed these on the kitchen table, before fishing out a milk bottle. The little girl stretched out her hand for the milk, but her sister rebuked her in a burst of harsh German.

"Dear heavens above," swore John. "She's only eleven and she thinks the milk may be drugged."

Jenny bit her lip as she saw the strain on the face of the older child. Then she turned on the kitchen tap, before filling four glasses in full view of the children. She placed them on the table.

"Tell her to choose two and then to watch us drinking the remaining two. When she sees that we're not frightened of it maybe she'll drink it too."

John did so, observing the indecision on the older child's face. She knew her sister was thirsty, but could she trust water drawn from a tap? Eventually she decided that she might, for she allowed her sister to drink half the glass. Jenny then fetched a selection of tins from the pantry. Hunger glistened in the eyes of the little girl and she whispered urgently to her sister. Reluctantly, the older child studied the pictures on the tins before selecting one of corned beef and another of pears. However, she pointed at both Jenny and John, making it clear that she expected both of them to share this strange meal. Jenny disliked corned beef at the best of times, but gave in, merely remarking to John that this was not her idea of an elegant luncheon party. John grunted his agreement.

The four were in the middle of this strange meal when Mrs Field arrived. The children started up in fright, but the housekeeper spoke to them in soothing tones. When John said that he thought that they did not speak much English, she was unperturbed.

"Poor little mites; I'd like to know who's abandoned them like this. I'd give him a piece of my mind!" Then she turned to Jenny. "What are you going to do with them, Miss Fletcher?"

At the use of Jenny's surname, the older girl stared at her.

"Flet-chair?" she repeatedly. "Is Flet-chair?"

Jenny nodded, before summoning up her exceedingly limited knowledge of German. "Herr Fletcher – mein vater. Fraulein Fletcher – ich."

The girl licked her lips, darting her eyes from Jenny to John.

"Go and find some proof," urged John. "Have you got

your passport?"

"Yes," nodded Jenny and raced off, to return shortly with both her and her father's passports. The older girl picked up the heavy gold-stamped passports and turned to the description. She appeared to be reading it carefully for she kept looking up at Jenny to check whether she did indeed have blonde hair, blue eyes and was of slim build. By the end of her scrutiny, she appeared to have relaxed a fraction.

"What that little one needs is a bath and a nap," declared Mrs Field. When this was translated, the older girl cast a swift look at her sister, before nodding uncertainly. However, something about the housekeeper's manner seemed to reassure her, for she went upstairs with Mrs Field, leading her sister by one hand.

"God Almighty," declared John when they were left alone, "I have no idea what is going on, but I'm not surprised that you found it all a bit much."

Jenny blushed at the reminder of her unimpressive collapse. Then she stabbed the rough top of the kitchen table with her fork.

"You know, John, I never really understood why having polio had such an effect on Midge's outlook. I mean, she was always very individualistic before it and quite happy to follow her own course, whether or not it was the popular choice."

"She still is," interjected John. "You won't find Midge following a mob."

"I know," agreed Jenny, "but she never cared what people thought before. When she came back to school, she was so grey and lost and defensive. She hated everyone staring and discussing her."

John reflected sadly that Midge still appeared grey and lost when she was tired, but Jenny was not finished.

"No wonder she became more reserved and reclusive."

Jenny shuddered. "It's so hateful knowing that people are staring at you, pointing you out to their neighbours and talking about you."

"Has that been happening to you?"

"Oh yes; I'm quite notorious, it seems," declared Jenny, attempting to sound matter-of-fact, but merely sounding bitterly unhappy. "Every time I go anywhere, heads turn to stare. Or people suddenly find a reason to move away. A few try to be tactful, but can't think of anything to say to me. In fact, I'm thinking of charging an entrance fee – like they have in circuses for freak shows. It might help to pay Cottrell's fees."

John growled angrily at the thought of people shunning Jenny in her time of need. "At least those chaps in chambers appear to be trying to support you," he pointed out.

"Yes," agreed Jenny wearily. "But I've got to the stage that I wonder whether, for example, Ronald sent me flowers because he wants to cheer me up or because he hopes that my father will reward him for his loyalty if he is acquitted. Or, indeed, whether he's the murderer and wants to keep close to me so that he can find out what all my plans are to help my father. I've even started to think that Cottrell might not be on Daddy's side."

"Don't assume that everyone is against you," advised John. "I'm not." He added as an after-thought, "And nor is Midge."

"And I ought not to have dragged you away from her," commented Jenny guiltily, thinking that that statement was applicable on several levels of meaning.

"Now that you have," remarked John, who was feeling guilty that he had abandoned Midge with hardly a word of explanation, "let's try and work out what to do next. Presumably Professor Schulmann is the best place to start. We've got to find out who those children are and why they turned up here."

Chapter Thirty-Three

Whilst John and Jenny were attempting to deal with the two unexpected visitors, Geoffrey Carrington had also been busy. Like all newspapers, the *Universal Record* maintained a staff of crime reporters and Mr Carrington knew David Sutton, the chief crime correspondent, well. Hence Sutton was prepared to come round to the flat in response to a guarded invitation. His trust was rewarded when Geoffrey informed him that he had an inside source planted in Forrest and Creech.

"How the blazes did you manage that? I sent two bright girls round to try and get a typist's job when one of theirs stormed out in a huff."

"It's my niece," admitted Carrington, before going on to explain that he wanted Sutton to arrange protection for her.

Sutton whistled at the news. "You know, old boy, much though I'd like to have a scoop, you may want to consider whether you should encourage your niece's journalistic ambitions to that extent."

"She hasn't got any journalistic ambitions that I know of," remarked Geoffrey. "She was at school with Fletcher's daughter and she cooked up this idea to try and help the defence, not to acquire a scoop. In fact, the less she gets mentioned by the press the happier I'll be."

"The younger generation!" commented Sutton with a grin. "I'm glad I'm single and don't have to worry about independent-minded young women. I'm not saying that they're not useful at times, but they have absolutely no respect for tradition or how things are done."

Geoffrey gave a grim laugh. "Midge was a bit more than independent-minded as a girl; she was wild!" As he spoke it occurred to him that perhaps he had got so used to trying to protect and shield Midge from the effects of her polio that he had forgotten that her underlying character remained the same, despite the fact that she could no longer walk properly. Any other girl of her age would be exploring new freedoms and experiences – was it so surprising that Midge had taken on this bold approach to Jenny's troubles?

Sutton recalled him to where he was. "Do you want round-the-clock observation?"

"Yes. The closer we get to the trial the greater the potential risk. I don't want some crook thinking that the best way to prevent inconvenient evidence from being given at trial is to arrange a gas-leak in Midge's lodgings."

Sutton scribbled a note on his reporter's pad. "It shouldn't be too difficult to place someone in the boarding-house. And since the trial's coming up fairly soon, we ought to be able to justify the manpower. Fortunately things are fairly quiet at the moment and it's going to be the trial of the year, so our much-respected editor oughtn't to jib too much about costs." He glanced at Carrington. "We will get an exclusive interview out of this after the trial, won't we?"

Geoffrey raised his hands in a gesture of frustration. "I don't really want it for her, but there will probably be less speculation about Midge if one paper has an exclusive." He frowned. "But I don't want any comments about her appearance. Not unless you want to end up reporting on your own violent end."

The crime reporter laughed at this threat, but all the time he was trying to catch a dim memory. Hadn't something gone wrong with the girl? Wasn't there a time three or four years earlier when Carrington went on no foreign trips, despite being a diplomatic correspondent? It was only when Geoffrey ushered Midge into the room so that Sutton could see exactly who was to be protected that a blinding flash illuminated the reporter's brain. Of course, this thin wraith of a girl who limped and looked so washed out had had infantile paralysis and the talk at the time had been that Carrington was waiting for her to die. No wonder Carrington wanted her to be guarded, but how the devil had she managed to achieve something that had utterly defeated his own trained and experienced team?

Although Sutton gained no real answer to this particular question, by seven o'clock he had arrived at a clear plan of campaign. Midge was to return to the boarding-house the following evening, when she would be shadowed by a reporter but, in the meantime, Sutton suggested that it was best if she stay immured in the flat.

"There's no point risking being seen at Fletcher's place," he pointed out.

"I wish I could go and find out what's happening," sighed Midge, accepting the inevitable. She was just too distinctive to smuggle herself in unseen if there was anyone watching Jenny's home. Moreover, John had made a cautious telephone call to say that no-one was in any danger, but that an unexpected problem had turned up which was being dealt with. As Sutton said, there was no point taking unnecessary risks and destroying Midge's carefully-created false identity.

Midge did not give Sutton any details of precisely what she had been investigating at Forrest and Creech, but she did request him to look into Miss Hemming and Miss Peters, the two secretaries who had worked at the firm. The reporter was used to people guarding potential scoops and he was quite happy to take on this additional job. He was also pleased when Geoffrey Carrington invited him to stay for dinner. It would give him the chance to study Midge more, and it was easy to entertain her with tales of the gory, unexpected or plain bizarre crimes which he had reported upon.

When John had suggested that Professor Schulmann might help with the two unknown German children, Jenny had nearly started crying again out of relief that she would be rid of them. Jenny was by no means unkind or unimaginative, but she had reached the stage of mental exhaustion when she was utterly unable to cope with the unexpected. She was trying to prepare herself for the sight of her father in the dock; she was worrying about Midge's safety; and she knew – and was furious – that she had been called as a witness by the prosecution. Two little refugees with whom she could hardly communicate on her own were one demand too many.

When Jenny managed to contact Professor Schulmann's residence, he sounded very surprised, before promising to come round immediately. John was relieved to hear the news. "Schulmann'll know what to do with them," he told Jenny, before muttering to himself, "Dash it all, I can't keep talking about 'them'." He turned to the children and asked them their names.

"Franzisca," announced the older girl definitely, before glaring at her sister, who seemed disposed to argue. "And she, she is Olga."

"Yes, I am Olga," agreed the little girl obediently.

Neither John nor Jenny was in the slightest bit convinced that the girls' names were, indeed, Franzisca and Olga, but, as John reflected, if it helped to make them feel that little bit safer, who was he to demand the truth? After explaining to the children that a friend of Miss Fletcher's, a Jewish professor of law, was coming to see them, John shot a worried glance at Jenny. "You must try and get some rest before the trial begins."

Jenny passed her hand wearily over her brow. "I know. Cottrell told me that Sir Reginald Hilliard is leading for the prosecution and I daren't take risks with him." Then she noticed that 'Olga' had strayed near the window. "Don't!"

she ordered urgently, as she dragged the child away. Olga gave a tiny whimper of fear, which broke off almost as soon as it was uttered. Jenny tried to put her arms round her in comfort, but Olga struggled, and backed away. Jenny looked sick. "I'm sorry; I didn't mean to scare you." Then, realising the pointlessness of trying to explain when Olga did not understand English, she turned to John. "Please tell them that I didn't mean to be unkind. It's just that anyone outside may be a journalist or a policeman, and they mustn't go near the windows for any reason whatsoever."

Looking at Jenny's face, translucent with exhaustion, the blue veins showing through her pallid skin, John attempted to reassure the children that Jenny was not unwelcoming, she was just extremely tired.

In response, Olga rattled off a burst of harsh German. "What did she say?" demanded Jenny. Then, when John looked unhappy at the idea of translating, Jenny again demanded to know what had been said.

"She said," replied John very uncomfortably, " 'My mother was very tired too. Then they shot her. Will they shoot you?' "

"No, but they're going to hang my father," replied Jenny bitterly, before realising guiltily that this was not the sort of thing to tell small children – and fugitives from Nazi Germany at that.

Franzisca drew herself up very straight and asked John whether their presence was endangering him and the woman on the sofa. If so, they would leave at once.

John ran his hands through his hair. It was about time he joined the Territorials if the world had reached the stage in which eleven-year-olds were forced to offer to swap safety for perdition. A hasty, but admittedly slightly confused, explanation left Franzisca with the impression that Mr Fletcher was being tried for political reasons, but that Jenny would be spared. However, the main thing was that John had convinced Franzisca that she would be safe for the next few days.

Unsurprisingly, John did not choose to discuss these events with his father over an open telephone line, nor did he think that it was advisable to leave the house until some solution had been discovered as to what to do with the children. It was with considerable relief, therefore, that he greeted the appearance of Professor Schulmann shortly after seven o'clock. Whilst Jenny went to fetch the children, John rapidly filled in what had happened. Jenny reappeared shortly afterwards, carrying Olga, who was three-parts asleep. At a signal from the Professor, John and Jenny left him to speak to the children on his own. Jenny was inclined to be offended on John's behalf, but he merely gave a rueful grin.

"It's a better security if I don't overhear their real names. For all you know, they could be Herr Goebbels' brats."

"In that case, we could lock them up in their own barbed-wire camp," declared Jenny vengefully, before sighing. "Actually, I think I'd find that difficult, even if they were his spawn. It's hardly their fault whoever their parents are. And surely Frau Goebbels was on the cinema news a few weeks ago – I don't suppose she's been shot."

John laughed. "Imagine the propaganda value if we could prove that the so-beloved propaganda minister was a bigamist or that these poor little beasts were his illegitimate offspring. You'd be welcoming journalists to report that."

Although John did his best to keep Jenny distracted, he was conscious of the strain of waiting for Professor Schulmann to finish his conversation. Naturally, the eminent jurist must have plenty of demands on his time, but Jenny, too, was facing pretty horrendous demands. Neither John nor Jenny articulated their secret hope that the children would be found somewhere more suitable to stay. However, Jenny's relief when Professor Schulmann announced that he thought that he might have a solution was palpable.

"I know that your father's trial begins on Wednesday," he added apologetically, "but do you think that you could keep the children tonight?"

"Of course," responded Jenny. "I'd hardly throw them out into the cold!"

"I must ask one other favour," explained Professor Schulmann. "As you must have gathered, these children are refugees. It would simplify matters enormously if I could have a guarantor who is prepared to sign a legal document which states that he or she will be liable for the children's upkeep. It would be unlikely," he added hastily, "that you actually would be put to such a cost, but such a document will help to ensure that they are allowed to stay in this country."

Jenny bit her lip. "I'm too young, aren't I? I'd have to be twenty-one."

"I'm quite happy to sign, sir," interrupted John before Jenny could work herself up. "Apart from anything else, I can prove an income."

"Thank you, Mr Carrington," replied the Professor, with an odd little bow. "Would you be able to come with me to sign the necessary preliminary documents?"

"Of course, sir."

"They will be all right, won't they?" asked Jenny anxiously. "If you can't find anyone… It's just it's all so sudden and the trial…"

Professor Schulmann caught a note of guilt in Jenny's voice. "My dear Miss Fletcher, I am deeply grateful to you and Mr Carrington for what you have done already. Most people would have called the police and, as you know, the girls have every reason to fear the police."

Jenny winced, but the Professor was not finished. "I do

not fully understand why the children were sent to this address, but there are certain coincidences which I do not like."

Chapter Thirty-Four

When John and Professor Schulmann left, Jenny felt very alone. She wished that she had not insisted earlier that the Fields go out that night, but at that point she had not expected John to leave her. Moreover, Jenny was all too conscious that, since her father's arrest, the Fields had refused to take their normal time off. Tonight had seen the ideal opportunity to give them something of a break. She ought not to be selfish about it. And Franzisca had been very good helping with her little sister. Jenny gave a rueful grin. Boarding-school might have taught her how to order around the younger ones, but it certainly hadn't shown her how to bathe or feed a five-year-old.

"They're easier when they're a bit older," she muttered to herself. "Less inclined to drop egg everywhere, for a start."

As she wondered how long it would be before John returned, Jenny was surprised to hear a brisk knock on the door. It didn't sound like John. It sounded much more authoritarian. For a moment, Jenny hesitated. Then she shook herself. What had she to fear? She wasn't living in Germany. It was probably Cottrell or Sir Everard. Hoping that it was the latter, she made her way to the front door and opened it as far as the latch allowed. There, on the doorstep, his arm raised to knock again, stood Inspector Groves. Jenny's heart sank.

"Good evening, Miss Fletcher."

Terrified that he had come to tell her that her father had died in Wandsworth, Jenny undid the latch and opened the door.

Groves entered into the hall and followed Jenny into her father's study.

"Perhaps you might be good enough to help me, Miss Fletcher."

"Yes?"

"I should like to speak to the children."

Jenny turned very white. Even had the Professor not warned her that he was worried, she would have been scared by the implication that the police were watching the house.

"What do you mean?"

"Really, Miss Fletcher. Do you deny that you have two children on the premises? Two refugee children?"

"I fail to understand why you are asking me such questions."

"I want to see them and to talk to them."

"Indeed?"

"Yes, Miss Fletcher."

Unconsciously mimicking her father, Jenny gave a dry cough. "Assuming for the moment that there are two such juveniles within the house, may I ask for your authorisation to interview them?"

"Miss Fletcher, you are doing neither yourself nor your father any good. You merely leave me with the impression that you have something to hide."

"Do you have a warrant for my arrest as well?" enquired Jenny with interest. "It sounds very much as if you are threatening me."

"What I am doing is requesting to speak to the two girls who were observed entering this house this morning."

Jenny glared at him. "Have you any children, Inspector?"

"Yes. A boy."

"And how old is he?"

Despite himself, a proud smile spread over Groves' face. "Albert is nine."

"I see. How would you like Albert to be dragged off in the middle of the night and questioned? You wouldn't, would you? Then think whether you'd like him dragged off by the police of a foreign country." Jenny shot Groves a disgusted glance. "They're defenceless little girls with no-one to protect them. Would you be proud of arresting them?"

"I'm not going to arrest them. I merely want to talk to them."

Jenny snorted contemptuously. "You won't go anywhere near them without a warrant and, even if you get one, it will only take me saying 'Polizei' to make them stay mum."

"So you do admit that you have them here?"

"Dear me, Inspector, don't you understand the legal concept of 'without prejudice'? I thought I had made it quite clear that I was talking hypothetically. And if we aren't talking hypothetically, my answer is this: show me your warrant and then we can discuss things."

"It is unfortunate that you are adopting this attitude, Miss Fletcher. I had hoped that someone who is training to be a lawyer would have understood the importance of helping the police in their enquiries."

When Jenny made no response, Groves picked up his hat. "Very well, Miss Fletcher, I must bid you goodnight."

After Jenny had shown the Inspector out, she latched and bolted the door, before sinking back against it. She was conscious that she was shaking, but all she could think about was that she had annoyed the police. 'If I'd handed the children over, Groves might have helped Daddy,' she thought. 'He might have softened his evidence against him. Nothing would have happened to the girls. They wouldn't have been sent back to Germany. Why on earth didn't I hand them over?'

Two hours later, John and Professor Schulmann returned. Jenny swiftly explained what had happened.

"I didn't know what else to do other than to refuse to

let Groves question them," she ended. "If he does come back with a warrant, I'll have to let him talk to them. But I don't know why he was so eager to speak to them – surely they can't know anything of importance?"

The Professor looked very worried. "My dear, I'm afraid that it is not what they know which is important, but who they are."

Jenny stared at him, comprehension slowly dawning. "You mean...?"

"I mean that they are the daughters of Herr Elsner – the man you called Herr X."

Jenny tried very hard to stay professional. "In that case, the prosecution can allege that Herr X invented his story in return for our help to keep his children in this country. They'll say that when I went to see him we cooked up the plan together."

"I am afraid so," agreed Professor Schulmann.

"That claim will sound even more believable now that John has agreed to guarantee their upkeep."

"Yes."

"And," continued Jenny, "since Groves knows that the children are here, there is no chance that the prosecution won't learn of their presence."

Professor Schulmann nodded.

Jenny stared at him sightlessly. Everything that Midge had discovered would now be called a fabrication. All the evidence she had so painstakingly acquired was worthless. Even the numbers, which had seemed such clear proof that the false naturalisation papers had been supplied by someone at Forrest and Creech, could now be set aside. It would be all too easy for the prosecution to claim that those numbers from Midge's list which actually appeared on the false papers had simply been supplied by Herr X. The rest would be untraceable – and thus equally suspect.

A solitary tear welled up in Jenny's eye. "I've sacrificed

my father's defence for two children I've never seen before in my life," she whispered.

The two men said nothing.

While it did Midge the world of good physically to have decent food and to be able to sleep without fearing that someone might suddenly burst into her room, there were drawbacks to Midge's short return to her own world. For two days she had thrown off Mary Carew's persona, particularly under the pressure of Sir Everard's cross-examination, when she had had to keep all her wits about her. The short freedom to be herself made it all the more difficult for Midge to force herself to become Mary again. Although returning to her seedy lodgings ought to have helped Midge to re-enter her false identity, in fact she rebelled against it, noting with revulsion the dirt and the everlasting smell of overcooked cabbage. Similarly, when on the following morning Wynne snapped at her, Midge did not apologise and look terrified as she normally did; instead she glared at his retreating back, her jaw jutting out and her face suddenly looking older and more authoritative. Despite Midge's earlier confidence that Miss Hurst had not the slightest suspicion that she was not whom she claimed to be, the secretary directed a few thoughtful looks at Midge. Eventually she spoke.

"Was your sister pleased to see you, Mary? You seem a little distracted this morning."

'Immortal gods, she thinks something's up,' Midge realised with horror. Summoning all her reserves, she invented a suitable excuse for her demeanour.

"It was my cousin I was visiting. She be a terrible cook and I was up half the night with stomach-ache."

"Well, you mustn't let it affect your work. And it won't do to be short with Mr Wynne; it's not acceptable."

"No, Miss Hurst. I'm very sorry, Miss Hurst," gabbled

Midge, trying to work out whether saying 'I be very sorry' would be normal if she had spent the weekend talking to another country cousin, or whether it would be over-egging the pudding.

Stomach-ache provided Midge an excuse for not partaking of tea and biscuits and when she went out for lunch, she noticed that there was a youth lounging around, a cheap gasper hanging from his mouth. Midge passed him without a word, but a warm flame burned inside her. The youth was no unemployed man seeking work; he was already on the pay-roll of the *Universal Record*. Nevertheless, despite this cheering sight, Midge was genuinely scared.

'I'm sure Miss Hurst was suspicious. She asked about my sister, but I told her on Friday that I was going to stay with my cousin. What did I do wrong? Was it because I was cross with Wynne's filthy manners?' Midge gulped, forgetting for a moment how intensely aggravating she found the way the clerk's eyes always seemed to travel up and down her bad leg, constantly reminding her – without saying a word – that she was second-class material and taken on as a charity-case. 'What will happen if I didn't convince Hurst that I had stomach-ache? Oh God!'

Midge decided that she had to stop thinking as Midge and to think as Mary Carew might. Hence she returned to the office having obviously spent most of her lunch-break in tears. The upright, determined stance at her desk, which had unconsciously alerted Miss Hurst to something odd about Mary that morning, had given way to slumped shoulders and a tendency to sniff. Finally, Mary made no attempt to meet anyone's eye, not even that of Davie, who wanted her to help him add up the stamp-money. Eventually, Miss Hurst grew irritated by the new typist's retreat into misery.

"What's wrong, you silly girl? Have you sent off the wrong letters?"

"No, Miss Hurst."

"Then what is it?"

"Please, Miss Hurst, I don't want to lose my place here."

The typist sighed. Mary really was very young after all. "Just because I told you off this morning doesn't mean that you'll get your notice."

Midge sniffed. "Mr Wynne glared at me when I came back."

Miss Hurst resisted the temptation to say that Mr Wynne glared at everyone. Being a man, he was allowed to get away with manners which would get a typist sacked on the spot. "Mr Wynne has to give evidence in an important trial this week."

Midge stared at her with wide-open eyes. "Ooh, Miss Hurst, has he? I'd be that scared standing up in front of everybody."

"I don't suppose it will worry Mr Wynne," commented Miss Hurst dryly.

"Will you have to give evidence, too?" asked Midge in admiring tones.

"Yes, so you may have to man the office for part of the day."

A flicker of excitement crossed Midge's brain, but she forced herself to react as inexperienced, nervous Mary Carew.

"Will I have to answer the telephone?" she asked, biting her lip in a frightened manner.

"Of course you will," replied Miss Hurst briskly. "In fact, if you're going to become a proper secretary, it's about time you learned a decent telephone manner. You won't get on if you can't do everything in an office."

Midge nodded ingratiatingly. "I know, Miss Hurst. I want to work up to a better job so I can send money back home," She clapped her hand to her mouth and sniffed again. "So sorry, Miss Hurst. I don't mean I want to leave; it's just that I want to be sending money back to my dad. There's the others to think about, you see."

Miss Hurst privately considered that Mary was on about the lowest wage you could offer to anyone who could actually type. Little wonder she wanted to earn more, whether that forced her to leave or not. "Do you have many brothers and sisters?" asked the secretary in politely-uninterested tones.

Midge had not spent hours imagining her putative background for nothing. "Four brothers and two sisters," she replied eagerly. "Joe's nearest to me in age and he be working on the farm, but wages is so low now there's nothing to spare, even with Matthew joining him this year. Ezekiel's next – he be wanting to join the army when he's older. Then there's Clara and Aggie, but Jemmy be the baby." A fond, dreamy expression crossed Midge's face. "Jemmy's my favourite, but he's that naughty."

Miss Hurst had no interest in Mary's little brother, but she did hope that Mary would manage to answer the telephone in a manner more suited to a London office. It was odd how thinking about your home strengthened your native accent, but it certainly was not appropriate to Forrest and Creech. Mind you, it was interesting that her guess about Mary's farm labourer father had been correct. Mary was just a touch vulgar, but as long as she did not talk about her family she would probably pass muster.

Chapter Thirty-Five

Unsurprisingly, Midge slept badly that night. She felt as if she had been walking unsuspectingly along a goat-track and that suddenly the path had broken off, ending abruptly in a precipitous drop onto jagged rocks far below. She was unsure whether she was still on the path or slowly rotating in the air waiting for the horrible thud which would announce the end. Even the thought of the silent reporters watching over her safety, one after another like tutelary spirits, failed to reassure her. Although she had been frightened before, the sudden shock that day had been even more disturbing because she had finally relaxed at her uncle's flat, where she had been warm and secure.

'I must not relax for a moment,' Midge determined. 'It's all because I enjoyed myself talking to Mr Sutton and Uncle Geoffrey. If I hadn't, I'd still have been playing at Mary Carew and it wouldn't have gone wrong today.'

When Midge appeared at work the next morning, she looked more like her usual weary self. Since Midge looked younger than her age when tired, this was all to the good for lulling anyone's suspicions that she was older than she claimed. However, no-one could have prepared her for the appalling shock which she received when a tall man walked into the office.

"I've finished talking to Mr Wynne," the visitor announced, "so, if you aren't too busy, Miss Hurst, I'd be very grateful if you could spare me a few moments."

Midge bent her head over her typewriter, wishing that she could somehow make herself invisible. What was Inspector Groves doing in the office? Had Cottrell decided to tell him what they knew? But Sir Everard had argued that it would be deleterious to the defence case to involve the police too soon. So why was he here?

Whilst Midge was panicking that if Groves recognised

her he might give her identity away, the inspector was puzzling over her familiar face.

'Where have I seen that girl before?' he pondered at the same time as making polite conversation with Miss Hurst. 'I'm sure I've seen her before. Where?'

Meanwhile Miss Hurst, who had shown the inspector in to see Mr Wynne and thus knew that he merely wanted to go over her statement for the trial, had no intention of allowing Midge to overhear her discussion. There was nothing secret about it and her evidence was bound to be reported in the papers, but she had a sense of what was fitting, and talking to a policeman in front of junior typists was definitely not suitable for a woman of her seniority.

"Mary, go and make tea for Inspector Groves," she commanded, intending to get rid of the girl for a few minutes. "You can send Davie along with it." Miss Hurst was somewhat surprised to see Midge edge out of the room almost as if she did not want the inspector to see her. Remembering Midge's comments about her family, the typist wondered if some of them had got into trouble for poaching. Mind you, girls of Mary's class tended to be nervous in the presence of the police, whether they had reason to be or not. She dismissed the Carew girl from her mind, but Groves did not. Immediately he had noticed Midge's sticks he remembered exactly where he had seen her before. But why was Miss Fletcher's friend masquerading as a typist?

Midge could hardly believe her luck when Inspector Groves did not denounce her as an impostor. Instead, he merely thanked her courteously for making his cup of tea. Nevertheless, Midge was desperate for her lunch hour to arrive so that she might send a wire to Jenny warning her that Groves might remember who she was. However, events appeared to conspire against Midge. First, Miss

Hurst informed her that she was to have only thirty minutes that day since Mr Creech was eager to tackle as much work as possible, as he had no idea how long he would be delayed at the trial on the following day. Then, when Midge was dismissed late to her lunch, Wynne seized the pile of telegrams which she was clutching.

"I have to send a wire of my own," he stated with a smile which revealed his yellow teeth, like a wolf's fangs. "I am sure that I can relieve you of an extra burden, Miss Carew."

"Thank you, Mr Wynne," replied Midge politely, whilst inwardly cursing the clerk for removing her ostensible reason for going to the post office. Clearly it would be dangerous for her to be observed by Wynne sending her own wire in case it aroused his suspicions.

Taking a sharp turn off the main road, Midge made her way to a telephone box which she had noticed previously. Hastily digging out some coppers, she dialled the chambers of Sir Everard Denys. When his clerk answered, he sounded very disinclined to put Midge through to the barrister.

"Please," begged Midge. "It's terribly important. It's about the Fletcher case and he told me to telephone him."

For a moment, Midge thought that the clerk was going to refuse, but he put through the connection.

"Sir Everard?"

"Speaking."

"It's Midge Carrington. I've got two urgent pieces of news."

"Indeed?"

Reminding herself that she must avoid using names on the telephone where possible, Midge attempted to explain. "The inspector came to where I work this morning. He saw me."

"Did he recognise you?"

"He must have done."

"That is unfortunate. What is the second piece of news?"

"I don't understand how the letter we're so worried about was posted by its author."

At the other end of the telephone the barrister frowned. "Presumably it caught the six o'clock post."

Midge tried to explain coherently without mentioning that Forrest's letter denouncing Fletcher had been sent to Scotland Yard. "But it can't have done. There wasn't time for him to write it. We leave at half-past five. And, in any case, the letter arrived at its destination on the following morning. That means it caught a later post, not the six o'clock post."

"Why is that a difficulty?"

"The writer went to his room when he got back. He never left it. He can't have posted the letter. The man who found him said that he had to get help to break down the door. That was confirmed by his helper, which means that the second man can't have posted it either. So who did?"

"Are you sure that the writer couldn't have written it earlier and given it to the office-boy to post? If the boy forgot, then he might have posted it later that night."

Midge scowled. She thought that Davie was perfectly capable of lying about it, if only to put himself in the limelight. But she still didn't see how Forrest could have written a long letter between his return from Mr Fletcher's chambers and when Davie went off duty. She said so. "The writer got back just before five o'clock and I can't imagine he wrote the letter quickly without bothering to check it. It was important and must have taken time to write."

"And he was meant to be feeling ill," agreed Denys. "It sounds like a locked-room mystery. The press'll love it; the jury will be flummoxed by it."

"Will it be useful?"

"We'll have to call a lot of witnesses to establish each point," warned the barrister, "but anything which helps to cast doubt is of use." He coughed. "I'm glad that you telephoned. Yesterday a man telephoned my client's work, claiming that you had applied for a position within his firm. He described you, as well as giving a certain name."

Midge's voice shook. "Are you sure?"

"Yes. He spoke to the clerk. He wanted to know whether you had worked there."

"What did the clerk say?"

"He denied all knowledge of you. I gather he thought that the man was a journalist to begin with, since the business in question has been pestered by them. It was only when the man described you that he grew suspicious."

"Do you know who it was?"

"I am afraid not, but I suggest that you are very careful indeed. It may well be that the man comes from the authorities. Quite why he is so keen to trace you is unclear, but I want you to say nothing whatsoever if you are approached by anyone like that."

"Yes."

"You may ask for me, but otherwise you must say nothing at all, no matter what is said to you. I am not yet ready to pass certain things on to the other side. Can you manage that?"

"Yes," replied Midge, hoping that she did not sound as scared as she felt. Why had Groves been asking questions at Mr Fletcher's chambers? And if it wasn't Groves, who was it?

IV

Allegro vivace

Chapter Thirty-Six

Trials at the Old Bailey tend to attract attention, but even the experienced journalists who had gathered to report on what seemed set to become the trial of the year were taken aback by the number of smartly-dressed men and women thronging round the entrance to the courtroom. One enterprising reporter decided to fill in time by ascertaining why people had chosen to observe this particular trial.

"I know the accused," exclaimed one shrill voice, belonging to a woman with raven-black hair, startlingly red lips and no eyebrows to speak of. "Well," she added, "I don't really know *him*, but I know his daughter and I always thought that there was something odd about her. They do say that insanity runs in families. It makes me shiver to think that I have sat next to her at dinner."

"But such a thrill, my dear," consoled her friend, who was wearing a tiny pillar-box hat, bedecked with a long osprey-feather. "I do envy you. Imagine being able to say that you have sat next to a murderess."

"The daughter of a murderer," suggested the reporter, who was rather keener on accuracy than either of the society women.

"Look! That's her!" exclaimed the first woman, forgetting her grammar in her excitement.

"Do you think that she'll have to give evidence?" asked her friend eagerly. "Do you think that she'll burst into tears?"

"Maybe her father will confess when he sees her in court," suggested the raven-haired female. "Wouldn't it be dramatic?"

Despite the hopeful speculations of the sightseeing public, Mr Fletcher showed no inclination to confess to murder when he was led into the dock. Standing very upright, almost as if on parade, he declared his name in a carrying voice, before answering emphatically that he was not guilty. A ripple of excitement sped round the onlookers gathered in the wooden-panelled courtroom, but the glare of the eminent and learned judge, Mr Justice Hawkroyd, served to quieten the crowd.

Of the amateur detectives, only Ronald and James were present in court. Although they were not representing anyone, as barristers they had the privilege of sitting in the area reserved for observing counsel. Witnesses who had not yet given evidence were forbidden from watching proceedings, so Jenny was sitting miserably in a waiting-room. John was in Cambridge, attempting to explain Midge's absence, while Midge herself was sticking doggedly to her typewriter at Forrest and Creech, hoping upon hope that she might make a last-minute discovery.

Sir Reginald Hilliard rose to open the case for the crown, his white wig contrasting with his black silk gown and the dark surroundings of the courtroom. He carefully set out the reasons why the police had decided that the accused was guilty, and he missed no opportunity to underline how disgraceful it was for a King's Counsel to betray the very laws which he had sworn to uphold. In particular, Sir Reginald made the most of the dead man's final epistle. "In this letter William Forrest speaks of Patrick Fletcher's threats; he speaks of Patrick Fletcher's intention to blackmail him; he speaks of fearing Patrick Fletcher. This, ladies and gentlemen of the jury, is what William Forrest spoke of in his letter; but by the time the police received the letter, William Forrest could speak no more. It is the prosecution's case that, in this letter, Mr

Forrest named his own killer."

After this dramatic opening, Sir Reginald started to lay out the evidence against Fletcher. Much of this had already been raised at the inquest but here, in the full trial, the defence was able to cross-examine the witnesses in detail. Sir Everard waived the opportunity to question Forrest's second cousin, who swore that the body which he had viewed in the police mortuary was indeed that of William Anthony Forrest, solicitor. Although Sir Everard saw little sign of grief on the un-ravaged countenance of the dead man's closest relative, there was little point in antagonising the jury by appearing to be heartless.

The second witness, however, attracted more attention. Police Constable Roberts carefully related how a man 'whose name I subsequently ascertained to be Leonard Wynne' had accosted him with the words 'Officer, I've found a body.' Further questioning from Sir Reginald extracted the information that he and the clerk of Forrest and Creech had broken down the door and discovered 'the corpse of a man whose name I subsequently ascertained to be William Anthony Forrest.'

Hilliard sat down triumphantly, as if suggesting to the jury that this discovery of the corpse in his own office was a crucial fact. Sir Everard rose in his place, pushed his wig back into position and stared at the constable somewhat owlishly.

"Tell me, constable, is it the case that you actually burst through the door into the deceased's office?"

"Yes, sir," replied Roberts stolidly. His sergeant had warned him that the defence would try to trip him up and make him contradict his evidence. Saying as little as possible seemed like a good tactic until he saw what the advocate was aiming at.

"So the door was definitely locked when you entered."

"Yes, sir."

"Might it not have been the case that it was merely blocked by the body lying against it?"

"No," declared the constable, pleased that he could prove this famous barrister wrong. "The body was lying by the desk. It couldn't have blocked the door – it was too far away. And I saw it when I squinted through the keyhole. I couldn't have done that if it had been slumped up against the door."

Counsel for the defence hesitated momentarily. He very much wanted to know where the key to the door had been discovered, but had no desire to alert the prosecution's suspicions as to why he was pursuing this line of enquiry. In the end, he asked in a rather frosty tone, "Was it really necessary to break the door down? You may have destroyed valuable evidence by bursting into the room."

Constable Roberts sensed disapproval and reacted accordingly. "I don't see what else I could have done, sir, since the key was found in the deceased's pocket."

Sir Everard concealed his pleasure at this reply. There was no way now in which the prosecution could claim that the key had been left in the keyhole. That would help when it came to raising Miss Carrington's query as to how Forrest's accusation against Fletcher had reached a letter-box.

Wynne's evidence confirmed Constable Roberts' regarding the discovery of the body and how they had been forced to break down the door. The rest of Wynne's testimony was identical to what he had said during the inquest, although he did remark that Forrest seldom took any refreshment during the afternoon. Unwilling to dwell on a point which suggested how lucky Fletcher had been to be able to poison Forrest, prosecution counsel chose to focus upon the fact that Forrest had said that he was feeling unwell when he reached Duke's Buildings.

When it came to the cross-examination by the defence, Sir Everard gave the task to his junior counsel, Wolsey, in the hope that this might suggest that the defence had little interest in the organisation and activities of Forrest and Creech. According to instructions, Wolsey asked a number of harmless questions while staying strictly clear of anything concerning refugees, false papers or blackmail.

Some of the more experienced trial-watchers were starting to wonder whether Sir Everard Denys was ever going to start to attack the prosecution case. They had not come to watch his junior ask straightforward questions; they wanted thrills and the cut and thrust of cross-examination for which Denys was widely renowned in legal circles. However, they did not have long to wait. Following the rather dull evidence from Alexander Creech, which mainly confirmed the information given by Wynne, Dr Brook, the police pathologist, was summoned to the witness stand. He started by summarising his qualifications and experience, before repeating the evidence which he had given at the inquest regarding the characteristics of aconitine poisoning. He also repeated his belief that Forrest must have ingested the fatal dose around three to four hours before his death.

"Could you estimate what time that might be?" asked Hilliard.

"Naturally, I cannot be precise, but taking into account the contents of the stomach, I would estimate that the deceased ingested the aconitine between three and five o'clock in the afternoon."

"The prosecution will be offering evidence that between three and four o'clock the deceased was in the accused's chambers and that, during this period of time, he was served a cup of tea by the accused. We suggest that the most likely explanation for the death of William Forrest is that he was poisoned in Patrick Fletcher's chambers by

Patrick Fletcher."

Sir Everard rose in his place, ignoring Sir Reginald's smug smile of triumph. Rather than immediately following up the possibility that Forrest had been poisoned after he left Fletcher's chambers, not whilst he was in chambers, counsel for the defence began to ask about stomach contents. Translated into layman's language, the pathologist explained that Forrest had clearly eaten a substantial lunch, probably accompanied by one or two glasses of wine.

"Can you be sure that the traces of alcohol which you found are associated with wine, rather than – say – beer or whisky?"

Sir Reginald appeared to be deeply amused by this question, leaning over to whisper something into his junior's ear. Junior counsel was seen to grin, but Sir Everard was waiting.

"I cannot be certain as to the precise type of alcohol ingested," answered Dr Brook pleasantly, "but I can be sure that alcohol was ingested. As there are only traces left, I have every reason to assume that the alcohol was consumed a good few hours before death. Lunch seems a likely time and wine is more probable at lunchtime than whisky. Naturally, this is, to a degree, speculation on my part but I gather that Mr Wynne could give you more guidance on Mr Forrest's preferences."

Nothing on Sir Everard's face suggested that this reply was a disappointment, or that he had cherished a hope of suggesting that Forrest had returned to his own office and tossed off a glass of whisky after the strain of his interview with Fletcher, unaware that it was poisoned. Instead, he turned to other liquids.

"You say that there was evidence of tea in the deceased's stomach and bladder. Could you tell the court whether he appeared to take milk with his tea?"

"There was little evidence of anything which suggested that he had drunk milk. I should suggest that the deceased only added a dash to his tea, but it might be best to confirm this supposition by asking one of his colleagues."

Junior counsel could be seen sniggering at this suggestion, but Sir Everard maintained an air of calm.

"Was there much liquid in the stomach contents?" he enquired.

Dr Brook frowned. "Do you mean, did I measure the precise amount?"

"Yes," agreed Denys, who had asked the question merely to probe whether every detail had been checked. He had few expectations that he could suggest that the autopsy had not been carried out properly: Brook was a cautious old devil and there was little chance that he had not measured and tested everything which could be measured and tested.

"The precise amount was around 250cc. Naturally, some of this liquid was originally food which was in the process of being digested."

"So, how much might you attribute to having derived from the tea which the dead man had drunk?"

"Perhaps in the region of 150-180cc."

Sir Everard smiled at the jury as he admitted ignorance. "I confess that I find this sort of scientific measurement very difficult to visualise. Could you perhaps tell us approximately how much 150cc is when translated into the ordinary, homely cup of tea?"

The assembled press laughed at this shaft, whilst several members of the jury looked distinctly relieved that the eminent doctor would be forced to speak in a language which they could understand.

"At a very rough approximation," sniffed the pathologist with contempt for the deeply unscientific and humdrum measurement of an uncalibrated cup, "and I

303

must emphasise that this is only a very rough equivalent, it would appear that the deceased had drunk a cup of tea."

Sir Everard frowned. Surely there was something odd here. He sought elucidation. "Are you saying that the deceased had drunk a cup of tea or that there was the equivalent of a cup of tea in his stomach?"

"Naturally he must have drunk a cup for that amount to appear in his stomach and bladder," retorted the pathologist.

"Indeed. But let me clarify my question. Was there the equivalent of a cup of tea in the deceased's stomach and other organs?"

"Yes."

"And you are suggesting that this tea may have been used as a vehicle for conveying the fatal dose of aconitine which killed him?"

There was a hushed silence in court. Why was counsel for the defence emphasising the very fact which demonstrated that Fletcher had had the means and opportunity to kill Forrest?

"That sort of conjecture is for the police to make," declared Brook. "What I am stating is that the deceased was poisoned by aconitine and that he had tea in his stomach contents. These are facts which can be – and have been – scientifically tested to ascertain their truth."

"You have very properly refrained from spinning conjecture," purred Sir Everard, "but I wish to put a point to you which, as a doctor, you are well-suited to answer. Since the prosecution has agreed that Mr Fletcher offered the deceased tea at around three thirty, and since you estimate Forrest's time of death as between six o'clock and eight o'clock, would you not be surprised that the deceased still retained in his body the tea which he had drunk at least two and a half hours earlier."

Without waiting for Brook to reply, Denys turned to

the jury. "I apologise for discussing this sort of thing in front of ladies, but I ask you whether it is normal for a man to drink a full cup of tea and not to have, ah, relieved himself for nearly three or possibly five hours after he drank it. I would suggest that most people would micturate within the hour after drinking a full cup of tea."

Several members of the jury blushed as they realised what learned counsel was suggesting, but thoughtful frowns on some of the reporters indicated that they had grasped Sir Everard's point. Was it really likely that Forrest had drunk tea at half-past three and still had it in his system at six, or seven, or eight o'clock? The beer-swillers amongst the journalists, who were used to the problems of digesting large quantities of liquid, doubted it strongly, while even those of more temperate persuasion looked interested. Meanwhile, the pathologist was attempting to suggest a solution.

"The deceased may have had certain medical idiosyncrasies of the bladder."

"Idiosyncracies," repeated Sir Everard, in a tone of heavy contempt. "I am a plain man, Dr Brook, and, like most plain men, I prefer a simple solution. Is it not much more likely that, instead of Forrest having some unexplained and hitherto unnoticed idiosyncrasy which enabled him to tolerate tea swilling around his body for hours on end, the tea which you found was drunk much later? To put it in straightforward language, I suggest that Forrest drank another cup of tea much later than three thirty."

Since the pathologist seemed unwilling to reply, counsel for the defence reiterated his question.

"Is it not perfectly plausible that Forrest may have drunk one cup of tea at Mr Fletcher's chambers and another cup later?"

Forced to respond, Dr Brook was heard to agree, in

tones of deep unease, that this suggestion was possible.

"Could he have drunk this second cup at five o'clock?"

"We have not yet proved that there was a second cup."

"But you have accepted that it might exist. I repeat my question. Could Forrest have drunk a second cup of tea at five o'clock?"

"Yes."

"At six o'clock?"

"It would depend on whether he was still alive."

"My dear fellow," retorted Denys with ferocious good humour, "I am not suggesting that a dead man got up and made himself a cup of tea. Let us keep out of the world of fantasy and remain in our own. Were Forrest alive at six o'clock, could the tea which you found in his stomach have been ingested then?"

"Yes."

"At six fifteen?"

"Yes."

"At six thirty?"

"Yes."

Having managed to force the reluctant pathologist to admit this much, Sir Everard drew his gown round him, intimated that he had no other questions of the witness, and sat down.

Chapter Thirty-Seven

On the following day, the prosecution started by calling a handwriting expert who provided a great deal of technical evidence to prove that Forrest had indeed written the letter which accused Patrick Fletcher of attempted blackmail. Since the defence case was that the letter was a tissue of lies, whether or not it had been written by Forrest, Sir Everard did not make heavy work of cross-examination. Nor did he devote much time to the typewriting expert who demonstrated that an inexpert typist had typed the copies of the other letters using at most three fingers. However, the barrister was much more on the offensive when it came to dealing with Detective Inspector Groves.

The inspector was used to giving evidence at trials and he required little guidance from the prosecution as he set out the various actions he had taken once called in to investigate Forrest's death. He explained how the receipt of Forrest's letter had raised suspicions that Patrick Fletcher was guilty of pre-meditated murder, and related how he had searched Fletcher's chambers and home, as well as questioning all who had been present in chambers on the fateful day. He further narrated how, after careful searching, he had discovered a copy of letters apparently from Forrest to Fletcher hidden inside a secret drawer in Forrest's desk.

As defence counsel rose to question Groves, most of the watchers in the public gallery felt that the prosecution had drawn together a compelling case. Naturally, the series of letters was lethal, but the inspector had hinted that Fletcher had not been disposed to co-operate with the investigation, once it was obvious that he was under suspicion. Moreover, Groves had emphasised how there had been no chance of interference with the corpse after its discovery. This, coupled with the fact that the medical evidence showed that Forrest had not stopped off in a pub for a quick – but poisoned – drink on the way back to his office, caused whispered speculation as to whether the eminent barrister would hang.

"They'll let him off on appeal," suggested one thin man, who was nervously biting his fingernails. "He's one of them; lawyers always stick together."

"No, they won't," countered his neighbour. "No Home Secretary could dare take the risk. He'll swing within three weeks of conviction, no doubt of that."

Sir Everard was well aware that public opinion was moving against his client. The newspapers had spread themselves over the previous day's events and, although nearly all the evidence against Fletcher was circumstantial, Sir Everard knew that Forrest's letters would be seen as damning by the jury. Hence he was determined to suggest that the police had leapt too eagerly at the lure of Forrest's final letter and had ignored all other possible explanations. The barrister's first attack focussed on the police search of Fletcher's chambers.

"Were you specifically looking for aconitine?"

"Not at that point," admitted Groves. "We did not know what poison had been used until the autopsy."

"Were you even sure that poison had been used?"

"We had every reason to suspect that it had been. The appearance of the corpse suggested an unnatural death."

"But you could not have been certain that poison was the cause of this death?"

"We had every reason to suspect that it was the cause," repeated the Inspector. "The police doctor told us to treat the death as suspicious. He thought that poison was involved."

"So, you were searching various premises with the belief that William Forrest might have died from unnatural causes, but you were uncertain whether you were looking for arsenic, belladonna or monkshood. Surely that must have made it difficult to know whether you were looking for a phial of poison or a packet of garden weedkiller?"

"We started by impounding various items from the pantry in which the tea was made."

"Yes," agreed Denys slowly. "Of course, these various items were tested, were they not?"

"Yes," agreed Groves, who knew as well as counsel for the defence did that no traces of aconitine had been found in them. Nevertheless, Sir Everard rammed home this point.

"We are grateful for your thoroughness. Perhaps you can confirm that no trace of aconitine was found in the tea-caddy?"

"No."

"Nor in the bag of sugar?"

"No."

"Nor in the milk-bottle?"

"No."

Groves started to explain that the tea-pot, sugar-basin and milk-jug had been washed up before the police reached the building, but Sir Everard had changed tack.

"Now, you have told the court how you and your officers searched Mr Fletcher's chambers. Perhaps you can tell us whether you found any aconitine in his room."

"No," admitted Groves, "but he could have thrown it away."

"That is speculation," rebuked the barrister. "Did you find aconitine in the typists' room?"

"No."

At this point the judge intervened. "Is there any need for this witness to keep repeating what he has already said in answer to questions from prosecuting counsel?"

"M'lord, I wish to establish without doubt that no trace of aconitine was found in Mr Fletcher's chambers."

"I realise that, but must we go through the building room by room?"

"I feel that there are some rooms which are particularly important to discuss."

Mr Justice Hawkroyd frowned. He wished to allow the defence latitude, but he did not want unnecessary repetition. "Perhaps you might concentrate on those rooms," he suggested.

Sir Everard bowed. "As your lordship pleases." Then he turned on Groves like a duellist seeking a mortal blow, not a flesh wound.

"There are two rooms on the top floor; did you search those?"

No trace of emotion could be seen on the inspector's face as he admitted that he had not.

"Why not?"

"I gathered that they were unused."

"I see," remarked Denys with a heavy frown. "So you were prepared to call a man a murderer, but you were not ready to take the basic precaution of searching the entire building in which he was supposed to have carried out his crime?"

"It was obvious that the accused could have thrown away whatever container he had used to hold the aconitine," argued Groves rather sulkily. It had only been some time after Fletcher's arrest that he had learned from his sergeant that the top floor of chambers had been ignored. True, his team had been badly understaffed that day, but he had desperately hoped that no-one would discover the oversight. Now it had been displayed in public.

"Did you show similar carelessness when searching my client's place of residence?" asked Denys, well aware that the house had been subjected to minute scrutiny.

"We searched every room for poison."

310

"But you found none?"

"Again, it could have been thrown away."

"But you found none?"

"No."

"And have you found any evidence that Mr Fletcher had bought any aconitine recently?"

"No, although he may have used a false name to purchase it."

"But you have no evidence of him doing so?"

"Not at present."

"Then I put it to you that there is absolutely no evidence that Mr Fletcher bought aconitine; there is no evidence that he took aconitine into his chambers; and there is no evidence that he made any use of aconitine once there. You searched his house and found no poison; you searched his room in chambers and you found no poison; those other parts of his chambers which you searched also produced no poison. Any comments on poison are pure speculation, unsubstantiated by the slightest evidence which connects Mr Fletcher to the purchase or possession of aconitine."

"He probably kept the poison on him and then disposed of the container later," reiterated Groves.

"But, Inspector, you are here to give evidence as to facts, not speculation."

With that, Sir Everard dismissed the witness. Geoffrey Carrington, who was watching from the press benches, felt that Denys had made the best of a bad hand but the jury did not look convinced by his arguments. No matter what the defence argued on other points, if they could not explain away Forrest's letters they were sunk.

The prosecution now dealt with the typists from Fletcher's chambers, eliciting the information that neither of them had made the appointment for Forrest to see

Fletcher. Miss Ellis was also examined regarding her arrangements with the tea. She was clearly in a combative mood, not helped – as she explained afterwards – by the similarity between prosecuting counsel and her first employer, who had been a sarcastic old beast who enjoyed humiliating a girl. Hence when Sir Reginald asked her whether she had prepared the tea-tray, she snorted.

"Yes I did, and I didn't put poison in the tea or the biscuits."

"No-one is suggesting that you did, Miss Ellis," pointed out the judge. "Please answer Sir Reginald's questions without making unnecessary comments."

Counsel repeated his question. "Did you put the cups out and made the tea, and so forth?"

Ethel glared at him. How would he like to have to stand in the witness-box and admit to doing demeaning things like carrying around tea-trays, for all the world like some overworked skivvy?

"I laid out the cups and put the kettle on."

"And did you leave the tray alone at any point?"

"I didn't stand over it while the kettle was boiling," Ethel snapped tartly. "I have plenty of things to do without watching kettles."

"Once the kettle had boiled, did you make the tea?"

"Yes."

"What did you do after that?"

In a voice of one goaded to extreme irritation, Ethel explained that she took it along the corridor, knocked on Mr Fletcher's door and brought the tray into his room.

"Did you leave the tray at any point between when you made the tea and when you brought it into the accused's room?"

"No."

"How did the accused react when you brought it in?"

"Mr Fletcher said 'thank you' as he always does, him

being a gentleman unlike some people."

There was no doubt in several listeners' minds that the secretary did not consider Sir Reginald Hilliard, K.C., to be anything approximating to a gentleman, but counsel was not to be distracted by this lowering insight into his character.

"And did the accused seem to you to be in normal spirits? Or did he appear worried?"

"Mr Fletcher didn't appear to be about to murder someone, if that's what you mean. And I don't believe that he did it, whatever you say."

"Please control yourself, Miss Ellis," insisted the judge, with a warning frown.

The secretary subsided.

Sir Everard used his cross-examination to confirm delicately that there would have been opportunity for someone to gain access to the tea-things before Miss Ellis made the tea. Then, feeling that the typist's loyalty had been made clear to the jury, he allowed her to retire from the witness box.

Although Arthur Thomson was equally loyal to his employer, he was more discreet in his approach to giving evidence. When pressed, he confirmed the fact that it was very unusual for Fletcher to make his own appointments, and he also admitted that the barrister had given no indication that this was a professional consultation by Forrest. There had been, for example, no sign that Forrest was to be charged a fee.

Thomson's reluctance to make these statements had been reasonably well-disguised, but when it came to questions about Fletcher's income it was clear to everyone that Thomson did not wish to answer. The clerk was fully aware that the admission that his arraigned employer enjoyed an income many times greater than most of the jury earned – or could possibly earn – might turn that self-same jury against him. After being forced to admit that Fletcher had earned well over twelve thousand guineas the previous year, Thomson was then asked whether this was a normal figure for his employer to make.

"I believe that Mr Asquith used to make ten thousand guineas before the War, and Sir Rufus Isaacs twenty thousand."

Sir Reginald glared at the clerk. "I did not ask, Mr Thomson, for a comparison between the late Prime Minister and the accused. I asked whether Fletcher normally earned a figure in the region of twelve thousand guineas per annum."

"I cannot say exactly what *Mr* Fletcher earned," replied Thomson, with a heavy emphasis on his employer's title. "I cannot speculate regarding years past without proper access to my account books."

Sir Reginald was happy to end his questioning on this note; the main thing was that the jury had Fletcher's wealth rammed down their throats. His next witness might help to explain why Fletcher needed still more money and why he leapt at the chance of blackmailing Forrest. Thus, much to the rage of several people present, the clerk of court demanded the presence of the next witness for the prosecution.

"Call Miss Fletcher."

Chapter Thirty-Eight

Since Jenny was a witness, even if called much against her will, she had not been allowed to observe the proceedings either that morning or the previous day. Hence, as she made her way towards the witness stand to be sworn in, she faced for the first time the sight of her father sitting in the dock, for all the world as if he were a common felon. Biting her lip and desperately trying not to show any emotion, she had turned to mount the steps into the witness box when she saw the black cap lying on the desk in front of the judge. Jenny had taken considerable time over her make-up that morning, keen to ensure that she did not look too white and worried. However, despite cosmetic aids to beauty, she blanched at the brutal reminder that murder was a capital offence. If the jury did not believe her father, he could be dead within a month.

Hilliard had calculated that the jury might not like the apparent disparity in age and experience if he were to examine the accused's daughter. Therefore it was not he but his junior counsel, Edwin Drage, who rose to lead Jenny through her evidence. The prosecution were well aware that their next witness was, to all intents and purposes, a hostile witness, but there was little chance that the defence would call her. Hence they had taken the risk of summoning her themselves.

After preliminary questions regarding her age, residence and occupation, Drage turned to the fact that Jenny, as a fledgling barrister, would naturally have discussed her father's upcoming trial with her father.

"I should be concerned for my father whether I was training to be a barrister or not," returned Jenny uncompromisingly.

"Indeed. But presumably you discussed the trial."

"Yes."

"And what did your father say?"

Sir Everard contemplated objecting to this line of questioning, but young Miss Fletcher appeared to have herself well in hand and he could not imagine Fletcher himself having said anything damning.

"He said that he put his trust in the jury system."

"Anything more specific than that?"

"Not exactly," hedged Jenny, hoping that Drage would take the lure. The next question showed that he had – hook, line and sinker.

"I should like you to repeat to the court what else the accused said about this trial."

"He said that you would try to give me a hard time because you didn't like women witnesses." Jenny paused, before adding, "Oh, and he told me not to argue with the judge because Mr Justice Hawkroyd was extremely fair."

Keen observers afterwards claimed that a tremor passed across the learned judge's mouth at this statement. However, there was no doubt that Drage flushed beneath his wig. "So there was no suggestion that you might, shall we say, interpret evidence in a certain way, a way which would be more favourable to Mr Fletcher than any normal person would take it?"

"Certainly not! My father is a man of honour; he does not lie, nor would he ask me to do so."

Jenny's blunt speaking appeared to discompose Drage, who turned to discuss finances. He led off with a sarcastic remark regarding how expensive clothes were these days.

"Oh, absolutely," agreed Jenny. "That's why I never throw anything away. For example, I've had this suit for two years and this hat is remodelled from last year. I can save a lot of money by doing that sort of thing."

Jenny seemed disposed to carry on chatting about hats for the rest of the day, but Drage felt that his cannon-shot had turned into a squib. He dropped back onto the safer topic of how much Jenny had for her allowance. Jenny was quite open about it.

"My father gives me five hundred pounds a year. Of course, half of that comes from my mother's money. She died shortly after I was born and left all of her money in trust for me." Jenny fingered her pearls. "My jewellery is hers as well."

Sir Everard was purring quietly into his papers. Fletcher's daughter was undoubtedly a clever specimen; immediately she had been warned that the Crown would claim a financial motive for the murder, she had grasped that she might be deemed a cause of pecuniary demand. To avoid that pitfall was useful, but to have managed at the same time to suggest that she was a frugal, unhappy, motherless thing was a particularly fine achievement. Even Fletcher admitted that his daughter had a taste for expensive raiment and Sir Everard himself had seen the girl glittering at a legal dinner in diamond clips and a bracelet to match. Whether those particular trinkets had also been left to her by her mother was a moot point, but Sir Everard rather doubted it. And since Sir Everard's own daughters had repeatedly informed him that, during times of crisis, a girl simply had to boost her confidence by purchasing and wearing the newest of new hats, learned counsel could only admire young Miss Fletcher's willingness to do what she could to help her father's case. If the worst came to the worst, the silk reflected, he might well take the girl into his own chambers; she had brains as well as beauty.

Drage, meanwhile, was still determined to extract some sort of concession from Jenny that her father spent a lot of money on her. One of the key problems which the prosecution faced was why a wealthy, successful barrister should run the risk of engaging in actions which would destroy him professionally if even a hint of a suspicion as to what he was doing were to leak out. Hence it was imperative to suggest that Fletcher spent too much money and had got himself into trouble financially. An extravagant daughter would be one explanation.

"Does your father give you presents?"

"Naturally."

"What was the last one which he gave you?"

Jenny smiled sweetly. "It was a commentary on the Tax Act."

Sir Everard failed to disguise a snort of laughter, but Drage ploughed on.

"And the present before that?"

"Does taking me to a recital of Handel count as a present?" asked Jenny in return.

"Yes," agreed Drage, thinking that Patrick Fletcher must be damned dull to live with. His own sister would have been appalled to be dragged off to listen to a series of caterwauling contraltos. Contemplating what Edwina had managed to coax out of their father inspired his next series of questions.

"Does your father buy you hats?"

"No," replied Jenny in shocked tones. A female barrister might have guessed that Jenny was contemplating what disastrous purchases might result if Mr Fletcher were let loose in a hat shop, but Drage thought that Jenny meant that her father never provided the money for such purchases.

"Does your father make you presents of money?"

"My father says that I must live within my allowance."

"So he does not make you gifts of money?"

"No," agreed Jenny, thinking that, technically, paying off her account at the dressmakers when she had got into a hole did not count as a gift. A loan of money, accompanied by a caustic lecture on improvidence and the dangers of running into debt, was not the same as a gift, even if Jenny did not really think that she would be made to repay that loan.

"Does he buy you jewellery?"

"Occasionally on my birthday."

"What did he give you last time?"

Jenny frowned in recollection. "It was either a pair of earrings or a small brooch."

Neither of these sounded excessively extravagant, but Drage made one last effort.

"So, your father has not recently given you any jewellery except on your birthday?"

"No."

Patrick Fletcher, sitting motionless and impassive in the dock, as he had sat for hour after hour, was impressed with Jenny's ability to stick to the letter of the question, rather than the spirit. Technically, she was quite correct. Technically, she had won an expensive pair of diamond clips in a wager. And, since she had, in the first instance, bought them herself there would not be – thank God – any trace of their purchase in his own accounts to cast doubt on her tale.

"Now, Miss Fletcher, naturally you must be worried about this case."

"Yes."

"And naturally you must have spoken to some of your father's friends?"

"A few."

"Was a Professor Schulmann one of those friends?"

"Yes. He believes in my father's innocence."

"And have you met a Herr Elsner, known to you as Mr Kinross?"

Trying to show no emotion, Jenny agreed. "Yes."

"In fact, his children stayed at your house, did they not?"

"For one night."

"For one night. I see."

319

Jenny braced herself for more and harder questions, and was incredulous when Drage indicated that he was finished. She was unaware that the prosecution had decided to do no more than establish her knowledge of Herr X and his children. As they saw it, there was no point in pressing Jenny in relation to fabricated evidence; she would merely deny it and there was always a danger that the jury might believe her fervent denials. Much better to keep the real attack for Herr Elsner himself.

With Drage finished, Sir Everard popped up to ask some questions for the defence. He swiftly drew out the information that Mr Fletcher spent most evenings at home working or listening to music, but that he sometimes went out to legal dinners or to the opera.

"Would you say Mr Fletcher was careless with money or improvident?"

"No."

"Does he approve of gambling?"

"No."

"Does he approve of extravagance?"

"No," replied Jenny, trying to keep all trace of feeling out of her voice. If anyone were extravagant it was she.

"Has your father shown any signs of worry or concern recently?"

"No."

"Did your father appear to be perfectly normal in the days leading up to the murder?"

"Yes."

"Finally, as the person who knows him best, do you think that your father is guilty of this hideous crime?"

Much to her embarrassment, Jenny started to cry. Digging in her handbag, she found her handkerchief and blew her nose violently.

"No. I don't believe any of the accusations against him.

Why would he blackmail Forrest? If he needed more money he could take on more cases. And since he wouldn't have blackmailed Forrest, there would have been no need to murder him. My father is an innocent man."

Jenny faced no more questions and was able to make her way to a seat next to Thomson, who looked with concern at her white face and hoped that she was not going to faint. Sir Everard, too, had noticed Jenny's pallor, but he cynically reflected that if the girl passed out it would do no harm with the jury. In fact, he was distinctly pleased that she had cried. He knew that Miss Fletcher had been wound up as taut as a coiled spring, but it was more than likely that some of the jury would have considered her self-control an indication that she was too hard-boiled by half.

Whilst Jenny had managed to preserve both her temper and her self-control under questioning, her brother Mike failed to do either. His army uniform disposed the jury in Mike's favour, but Hilliard soon dragged out of him the fact that his father had several times paid his gambling debts. A tall abstemious-looking man in the jury could be seen to frown at this point and Mike's blustering response that 'dash it all, of course a man plays cards in the mess' did not appear to endear him further to that particular jury-member.

"Naturally, you might well play cards amongst your brother officers," purred Hilliard, "but does each one of those officers play for high stakes?"

"You can't call ten pounds a game high stakes," protested Mike.

"Many families earn less than ten pounds a week," pointed out prosecuting counsel.

"Yes, well, quite."

"Would you care to clarify what you mean by that?"

"Err, nothing, really."

"Do you mean that you consider ten pounds to be nothing?"

"Not exactly," replied Mike, who did.

"Or do you mean that you do not care about those who are less fortunate than yourself?"

Sir Everard protested at this line of questioning and, to his considerable relief, Mr Justice Hawkroyd upheld his protest. However, it was clear that damage had been done. Sir Everard did what he could do to dispel the picture which the prosecution had created of a rather arrogant, spendthrift young man, but even Mike's fervent asseveration of his father's honesty did not seem to go down especially well with the jury.

Although Denys was glad that Mike's twin brother was still in Alexandria, so had not been called to provide similarly disastrous evidence, the barrister was unhappy that the judge, after a swift glance at the clock, decided to halt proceedings after Mike's evidence. It was always unfortunate if the jury were left to mull negative evidence overnight, and Mike had certainly counteracted any positive image which Jenny had left of the Fletcher family. Dickie, who had exercised his right as a member of the Bar to attend the court, was fuming.

"Damned idiot," he muttered to Ronald, who was sitting next to him. "Why couldn't he have kept his mouth shut? He couldn't spot even the most blatant of snares."

"No wonder he wants to transfer to the Air Force," agreed Ronald. "Presumably large pits for the careless to blunder into are a bit more obvious from ten thousand feet."

Dickie sniggered, before sobering up as he caught sight of Jenny. She looked as if someone were removing her entrails without anaesthetic as she watched her father being escorted down into the cells by a pair of warders.

"I hope to blazes that the defence have got something

up their sleeve. The jury looks like a hanging one so far."

Chapter Thirty-Nine

At Forrest and Creech, the strain was beginning to tell on Midge. The newspaper reports of Mr Fletcher's trial suggested that things were not going well and she was growing more and more frightened. Why had someone rung up chambers asking whether she had worked there? And who had rung up? If it had been someone from Scotland Yard, why hadn't he gone round to chambers to question Thomson and the typists about her? Surely a policeman would know that there was no chance of picking up a guilty change of expression on the telephone? And if it wasn't a policeman, who was it? It was all very well trying to reassure herself that it was one of the journalists who was meant to be guarding her, but what if it wasn't? Sir Everard had said that the enquirer had been a man, which seemed to rule out Davie, whose voice was not fully adult. That left Wynne or Creech. The idea of being under suspicion at work was so horrible that Midge forced herself back into considering what Inspector Groves was up to.

'Is he playing cat-and-mouse with me?' she worried. 'What if he questions me and raises further suspicions about who I am? What if he comes into the office again and denounces me?'

On Wednesday, Midge felt particularly alone and insecure. She knew that those on the side of the defence would be at the trial all day. Jenny's friends would be with her in the courtroom; even Midge's uncle would be observing the trial. There was no-one who could be reached in an emergency. Nevertheless, Midge was determined to go in to work. With Wynne and Miss Hurst called as witnesses, this was her best chance to search the office properly. However, things did not work out as planned. The first problem was that Davie the office-boy seemed disposed to hang around in the typists' room.

"What you doing, working as hard as that when no-one's about?" he complained.

"Miss Hurst told me to complete these documents."

Davie rolled his eyes. The Carew girl wasn't exactly anything to boast about, not with that gammy leg, but he'd never thought that she was this dim. "Just 'cos she told you to do it doesn't mean you have to. Wynne told me to do things, but I'm not pushing myself am I?"

"But I ought to," murmured Midge, firmly in her role as nervous Mary.

"Is that what you were taught at school?" scoffed Davie. "I've heard you with Wynne – 'Yes, sir; no, sir; three bags full, sir'. You want to be a free spirit, Miss Carew, not go begging round your elders and betters."

Midge decided that even Mary might resent this sort of comment. "I bet you were made to say 'Yes, sir' and 'No, sir' at school."

"You'd lose your bet then. Never been registered by the state, I haven't." Davie noticed the junior typist's surprise and preened himself. "I'm independent, that's what I am."

Midge could think of some other words to describe Davie. Fortunately, Davie did not realise this. He slicked back his oily hair, adjusted his virulent tie, and offered to fetch some cigarettes.

"Old Creech keeps them for clients; he never notices if one or two go missing. So I've got some in my drawer."

"No, you mustn't. Miss Hurst would smell the smoke."

"You are dull. How are we going to pass the time then? And I can't keep calling you Miss Carew. Not when I'm as close to you as this."

Midge glared at Davie with some asperity. It was bad enough him having talking to her in this personal manner, but much worse was the fact that if he were not there, she might finally have the chance to search the previous secretary's desk thoroughly in peace and quiet. "I'm meant to be typing a letter for Mr Creech," she declared. "I really can't talk to you at the same time."

Davie stepped back, surprised by the patrician iciness which had unconsciously crept into Midge's voice. "You won't exactly attract the boys, will you?" he scoffed. "Don't you know you need to encourage a chap, not reject him?"

Desperately trying to remember that she was Mary Carew, Midge stopped herself from pointing out that she did not want to encourage chaps who didn't wash properly. Instead, she bent her head down over her typewriter. Davie lurched round behind her and planked an oily, wet kiss on her ear.

"There, you can't say I don't know what to do with a girl," he announced and stalked off.

An uncontrollable shudder ran through Midge, but it was not entirely the result of Davie's unwanted attentions. It had suddenly occurred to her how easily Davie could have been holding a paperweight in his hand and smashed it down on her skull. There was only Creech in the building and by the time anyone found her she would be stone dead. Midge was fighting down the temptation to grab her bag and flee the firm forever when the buzzer on her desk went. With a wistful glance at the outside world far away through the window, she picked up her dictation pad and pencil and made her way to Mr Creech's room.

When she entered, Creech tapped his watch meaningfully.

"Where is my tea, Miss Carew?"

"I'm sorry, Mr Creech. I didn't realise that it was time."

"Then hurry up and bring it."

Midge made her way to the alcove and carefully laid out the requisite number of biscuits. As the kettle boiled,

Davie appeared. Midge glanced at him uncertainly. It was unfortunate that they had had an argument just when she needed someone to carry the tea-tray up the corridor. Creech was obviously in a bad mood and she strongly suspected that he would complain if she brought him his refreshments section by section.

"Will you take this tray to Mr Creech, please, Davie? I'll make your tea whilst you're taking it."

"Why should I take the tray? That's not my job."

"Don't be unfair," protested Midge. "You know Miss Hurst takes the tea-trays for me. Surely you could carry it to Mr Creech just this once?"

Davie laughed irritatingly. "If you'd been a bit less stuck-up, I might have."

Realising that the office-boy must have resented being told off, Midge sighed. "Please, Davie."

"No."

"But Mr Creech is in a bad mood. Do you want me to get sacked for not giving him his tea?"

"It wouldn't bother me."

"All right then. I'll bring Mr Creech just a cup and I'll tell him why."

Davie scowled. "Girls are such tell-tales. But it's as well you weren't here when Forrest was alive. You'd have had to run back and forward with his tea, sticks or no sticks. And he had toast and jam along with it every afternoon. How would you have coped then? He wouldn't have let you think yourself too important to make the tea, I can tell you."

"I make the tea every day," pointed out Midge irritably. "So obviously I don't think that I'm too important to do so."

"Yes, you do. And you aren't half as important as you think you are."

About to make a curt retort, Midge reminded herself

that she was there to gather information, not quarrel with Davie. "I don't like making toast over a gas fire. I'm scared it catches fire."

This admission of female cowardice restored Davie's pride somewhat. "I suppose I'd've had to do it for you," he remarked with lordly tolerance. "I sometimes did it for Miss Hemming. I s'pose she was scared, too." He glanced at the tray. "I'll take that if you mind the office for me for a bit at lunch."

Midge pretended to be reluctant. "I don't want to end up with no lunch again."

"Wynne told me that the office wasn't to be left unmanned. So if I go out, you have to stay."

"Why can't you go at your usual time? Why do you have to go during my break?"

"Coz the man I want to meet can't do earlier, see? And he can't come round here; Wynne would make a fuss."

"What if Wynne comes back and you're not there?"

Davie looked uncomfortable at this idea. "He won't. And if he does, you can tell him that I'm taking a letter round." He picked up the tray. "That'll keep him quiet."

After he had had his tea, Creech kept Midge busy taking dictation until well after one o'clock.

"I'm afraid I've delayed you," he remarked as he stood up. "Take some extra time over lunch if you want."

"Thank you, sir," replied Midge politely.

"Just make sure that you get that last document typed up by four o'clock; it's urgent."

"Of course, sir."

Midge retreated to the typists' room, while she waited to see if Creech would leave. Soon she saw him striding along the pavement. After swiftly checking that Davie was, indeed, absent, Midge made her way to Wynne's room. This was her best – quite possibly her only – chance to search it, since the clerk rarely appeared to leave his room. Praying that the room would not be locked, Midge gently tried the door. It opened. Midge inserted herself and pushed the door to, before glancing rapidly round. She had no specific plan, but, as she looked about her, a shaft of sunlight illuminated the gloomy room. Midge frowned. There was a long row of box-files along the top of the bookcase. That was only to be expected in a solicitor's office, but why was one of the files much less dusty than the others? Had it been consulted recently, or was there some more sinister explanation?

Midge could not quite reach the file, so she used one of her sticks to hook it towards her. Then, leaning against the bookcase so that she did not lose her balance, she pulled the box-file down and opened it. Her heart sank momentarily as she saw a pile of papers. She knew quite well that no-one would have been stupid enough to keep any unused aconitine, but it would be wonderful to have proved that the poison which killed Forrest had been available in his own office. She scowled angrily at the papers. What use to the defence was a long series of draft instructions about a will? If it covered criminal activity then it must be couched in code and there was no chance that she could crack it over her lunch. She flicked through the file, cursing the difficulty of lifting papers using a handkerchief. Then, suddenly, the papers parted to reveal the familiar dark blue and gold cover of a passport. Telling herself firmly that it might belong to the testator, Midge opened the passport. An oddly familiar face stared up at her, but for a moment she did not recognise it. Then she blinked in shock. Surely that was Wynne? But why was he wearing a beard? And why was he calling himself Trant?

It was at this moment that the sun chose to disappear. Midge moved closer towards the window, only for her eyes to widen in horror at the sight of Creech returning to the office. She mustn't get caught in Wynne's room; it would wreck everything. Hurriedly, she thrust the papers back and tried to manoeuvre the box-file into position. Then she snatched up the passport and hastened as quickly as possible back to the typists' room. She stared round, wondering where on earth to hide the passport. It was madness to have taken it, but, surely, at last she had found some cast-iron evidence. And without the passport, Wynne would find it much harder to flee the country. But she had to hide it or she would be sacked – or worse. Her bag wasn't safe; Wynne had searched it and Creech might do the same. The drawers of the desk were equally obvious. Her eyes alighted upon her typewriter. In a moment, she had forced up the heavy machine and thrust the passport underneath. She was in the process of innocently typing when the door opened.

"What are you doing here? I thought I told you to go out to lunch."

Midge looked up, forcing herself to appear as normal as possible. "I wanted to type this letter."

Creech advanced into the room. "It's just as well I came back or I wouldn't have found you doing this sort of thing." His smile appeared to twist. "I forgot my gloves. They're clearly useful for more than their usual purpose."

As he advanced into the room, Midge grew sick with fear. Creech was going to strangle her. He didn't want to leave any fingerprints in the room; that was why he was putting on his gloves. Midge tried to rise, but Creech was now so close that Midge was able to do little more than shrink back. The solicitor gave her a puzzled frown.

"You don't need to look so startled. I merely wanted to see what you were typing."

"I'm so sorry, Mr Creech," whispered Midge, wondering whether she had made a mistake about his intentions. "I didn't have breakfast this morning and I suddenly felt faint."

"You didn't have any tea, either. Surely you aren't banting – you're thin enough already."

Midge blushed at this personal comment, but it gave her an idea. "My cousin said that it might help my leg if I didn't eat meat and if I avoided tea."

Almost imperceptibly, Creech relaxed. That explanation sounded idiotic enough to be true – there was no telling what quackery one woman would suggest to another.

"If that sort of diet makes you faint at work you will have to stop following it," he warned sternly. "We don't have time to waste with stupid fainting-fits. And I told you that letter doesn't have to be ready until four o'clock, so there was no need to miss your lunch on that account, either."

"No, Mr Creech; sorry, Mr Creech. I was just worried that I wouldn't get it done in time if something else cropped up."

Creech sighed and walked off, thinking as he did so how wrong Wynne had been about Mary. She certainly didn't pose any sort of a threat. Wynne probably didn't realise that Mary's conscientiousness and timidity arose from fear of losing her job – it couldn't be easy for a crippled girl to compete for jobs when everyone assumed that she'd be ill and unreliable. Creech pushed aside the problems faced by Mary and turned back to his own. He thought that he'd better keep the office going for a few more months. Then he would sell the name and move to another part of the country altogether. That was the safest thing. The police interest was bound to die down and no-one would be surprised if he decided that a change of scene would do him good.

Chapter Forty

After Creech left, Midge could feel herself shaking with reaction. More than anything else, she wanted to put her head down on her desk and sob uncontrollably.

'I can't go on,' she thought. 'I can't. I can't. And I've still got to get rid of that passport. I should never have taken it. I should have left it where it was and told the police.' She swallowed. It was just as dangerous to leave the passport underneath her typewriter as it was to walk out the office with it – particularly since it was smothered with her fingerprints. Nevertheless, it required considerable determination to retrieve the passport, place it in an envelope and then put it in her bag.

As Midge forced herself to walk along the dimly-lit corridor, she was waiting for Creech to summon her into his office. She could hardly refuse to obey. But what would happen afterwards?

'If only I can get out of here without being searched,' she prayed. 'I can't be forced to open my bag if I'm outside amongst other people. All Creech could do is to call the police. And I'd rather be arrested than murdered.'

Once outside, Midge forced herself to stay alert. Until she was on the bustling main streets she was not safe. She was concentrating so hard on trying to pick up the sounds of someone following her that she did not notice Davie coming towards her until the office-boy accosted her.

"You said you'd wait until I came back," he remarked accusingly.

Midge stared at him for a moment. She'd forgotten all about Davie in her desire to get out. "Yes, but Mr Creech was there, so the office isn't being left unmanned."

Davie looked scared. "Did you tell him I was out?"

"No."

"Err, you won't, will you?"

"What do you take me for?"

"A pal. Thanks, Miss Carew."

With that, Davie rushed off. Midge stared after him for a moment, before continuing towards the post office. 'That's my alibi,' she thought with relief. 'He's obviously frightened that he'll get into a row for having sneaked out. It didn't sound as if the man he was meeting was any too respectable, either. So if Davie claims he was in the office, I couldn't have been searching Wynne's room without him seeing me. Thank goodness for that.'

After Midge had posted the passport to John, she felt somewhat more safe, although it still required a great effort of will to return to Duke's Buildings. Even the most closely-argued propositions that no-one would dare kill her when there were only two people in the office did not entirely convince her. After all, if Creech or Davie were to hang for her murder it would not be much consolation to her. However, when she re-entered the office, she discovered that Miss Hurst had returned only a few minutes earlier.

"You are very late," she snapped at Midge.

"Mr Creech kept me late. He told me to take the time at the end of the lunch-hour."

Miss Hurst snorted. "I don't suppose that he thought that people might have been trying to ring up since two o'clock."

"I'm very sorry," faltered Midge, wondering what had happened to make the typist so cross.

"Well, now that you are here, we need to make a start." The secretary proceeded to rattle off a series of instructions which left Midge wondering whether she would be expected to work all night. Miss Hurst then searched through some notes on her desk. "I thought so," she sighed. "Mary, can you look up the telephone number for

A. E. Webster in the directory. I need to cancel his appointment with Mr Creech."

Midge obediently lifted up the heavy directory which was stored on a shelf next to her desk, and began mechanically leafing through the end pages. She was busily running her finger down the appropriate column when she suddenly noticed a faint dot next to Z. N. Weaver, chemist, of Barnet, almost as if a pencil mark had been rubbed out. She paused. No-one had yet come forward to say where the aconitine had been bought. Barnet was a long way from Holborn. No-one in the office lived in North London. Why would a north London apothecary have a central London solicitor? There must be plenty of solicitors in Barnet or Hampstead.

"Haven't you found it yet?" demanded an irritated voice.

Midge forced herself to think what Mary might do. Somehow she found Webster's entry and managed to gasp out, "I don't know what the 'Reg' bit before the number means."

"It's short for Regent," explained Miss Hurst, reflecting that there were problems with country girls who lacked metropolitan knowledge. "Now tell me the number."

Midge complied and then returned to her typing. 'I haven't seen anything,' she told herself. 'I must forget all about it until I get out of here. And I mustn't make mistakes.'

Quite how Midge managed to continue acting as if she had nothing on her mind she never afterwards knew. Partly it was because she was so exhausted with strain that the easiest thing was to stare fixedly at the sheet of paper in front of her and to forget that anything else existed. To forget that Midge Carrington was meant to be in Cambridge; to forget that Jenny's father was on trial; and not even to think about Bertie because the thought of his warm purr would make her cry and there was nothing in the conveyancing document which she was typing to make anyone weep – unless it was with boredom. Focussing exclusively on her work with such fierce concentration attracted a pleased glance from Miss Hurst. Mary might be a little dim at moments, but at least she worked and didn't want to chatter all the time like Miss Peters, who had been quite capable of missing out a whole line in a document because she was trying to tell you about the new hat she had seen in the Army and Navy Stores.

Fortunately, when it reached half-past five, Miss Hurst seemed to think that enough work had been covered for them both to leave as normal. Midge had not dared to prepare a note to pass to the lurking newspaperman, who appeared to be attempting to save the souls of Romberg Street by marching up and down wearing a placard which warned passers-by to repent or be damned. Since Miss Hurst soon overtook Midge, the reporter began by approaching her with an appeal to consider her sins.
"Do go away!" she snapped angrily. "This is the second time today that you have accosted me."
This rejoinder helped to explain why the typist had been in a bad mood when she returned to the office after lunch, but Midge hoped that the reporter had not aroused Miss Hurst's suspicions. When the secretary glanced back a few minutes later, Midge was even more edgy, but the placard-wearing zealot was no novice. He had ignored Midge entirely and was in the process of asking a prosperous-looking gentleman his views on the ease with which rich men entered heaven. Apparently unconcerned by a request that he go to the devil, the reporter offered a badly-printed tract to several office workers, before finally making his way towards Midge.
"Any news?" began the journalist, before breaking into

a lament that Midge had apparently not heard of one of the lesser-known prophets of the Old Testament.

"I really don't want your tract," declared Midge firmly, realising that someone else must be approaching, but unwilling to abandon all chance of passing on her news. "I've plenty of information I could read if I want to. And I don't wish to learn about Old Testament prophets."

Since Midge's comment about having plenty of information was fairly obvious, the reporter allowed himself to drop back away from her to engage another pedestrian on the fraught subject of the Book of Revelations. No matter how much he seemed to be working his way randomly through the early-evening crowds, he always kept behind Midge. Suddenly, he darted up an alleyway and then reappeared, looking much more respectable without his sandwich-board, and now wearing a hat and gloves, which he had kept hidden under the boards. He already knew where Midge lived, so he avoided leaping onto the same 'bus. Instead he raced ahead through several back-street short-cuts, so that he could intercept Midge before she turned into Paradise Street, where her lodgings were.

Pointing at the grimy street-name, the reporter appeared to be asking for directions. Judging by the way in which she was pointing backwards, Midge also appeared to be telling him where to go. In reality, she was hastily passing on the information about Z. N. Weaver, as well as explaining that Wynne appeared to possess a false passport. In response, the reporter drew out an envelope and stabbed at it with his finger. However, this was no map; instead, it was a written instruction asking her to report back on Wynne's demeanour.

"He wasn't there today," replied Midge, with a sinking heart. Part of her had hoped that, with the discovery of a chemist's address, she was rid of Forrest and Creech forever. However, clearly this request must be important or such meticulous planning would not have been involved.

The reporter raised his hat. "Thank you, Miss. I'll follow your instructions and try not to get lost."

Midge smiled at him, but inside herself she was hoping that it would not be she who would lose her way in the tangled labyrinth of Forrest and Creech.

Chapter Forty-One

The next morning saw Midge unable to contemplate breakfast. She had once seen a violin-string tightened so far that it snapped, the long end lashing out uncontrollably and malevolently, whilst the short end disappeared among the instrument pegs. The uncontained violence had given her a fright at the time, but she now felt that she was wound up as tightly as that string had been before it broke. Despite her exhaustion, she had had great difficulty in falling asleep the previous evening and she had woken up several times in the grip of formless, shifting nightmares, where the one recurrent theme was a sense of being hunted, unable to escape from her pursuers.

'I mustn't start imagining things again today,' she told herself sternly. 'I was frightfully silly yesterday. I must be rational and sensible. Jenny has to give evidence; I bet she won't break down and cry – and she's got much more to worry about than I do.'

This reflection served to force Midge inside Duke's Buildings, but the reporter's instructions that she was to observe Wynne's demeanour were answered sooner than she expected. She had not even taken off her rather worn coat when the clerk pounced on her.

"A word in my room," he demanded.

Midge followed him in trepidation.

"Were you in here yesterday?"

So, thought Midge, trying to ignore her pounding heart, suspicion had finally fallen on her. It would not require much acting to sound like frightened little Mary.

"No, Mr Wynne, I wasn't."

"Really?" asked the clerk with an unpleasant smirk.

"No," protested Midge.

"Then what did you do yesterday?"

Midge wrinkled her forehead. "I was with Mr Creech

until around half-past one. Then I went out for lunch. When I came back, Miss Hurst was there and I only left our room to make tea."

Wynne looked momentarily deflated, before returning to the attack. "What about before Mr Creech sent for you? You were alone then."

On the point of complaining that, far from being alone, she had been pestered by that oleaginous little rat, Davie, Midge suddenly realised that her choice of vocabulary and her underlying complaint would hardly do. Hastily, she substituted something more suitable to Mary's position. She sniffed artistically.

"I'm very sorry, Mr Wynne, but I couldn't stop him from coming in. I *told* him that I needed to get on with some work, but he wouldn't listen."

Wynne raised his eyebrows abruptly. Flirting with the new typist sounded most unlike Creech. And surely all clients had been put off to different days. "Who is 'he'?"

"Davie," mumbled Midge, in embarrassed tones.

"Very well, Miss Carew," glared the clerk, before adding menacingly, "but if I find that you have been lying to me…"

"Oh no, sir," gasped Midge, before escaping. Fortunately, Miss Hurst appeared to have been delayed, so Midge had the chance to recover herself. One part of her was pointing out that practically everything she had ever said to Wynne was a lie, whilst another part was busily trying to work out whether the clerk had spotted that his passport was missing. If he had, did that mean that he had been contemplating flight? Or had something completely different roused his ire?

After such a dramatic start to the day, Midge was nervous as to what else she would face. However, apart from Wynne's bad temper, everything seemed to go as normal. True, she was still filled with the dread of being discovered, but the very fact that the office had more people in it than on the previous day made her less afraid that someone might attempt to hit her on the head or force-feed her aconitine. Moreover, she consoled herself that she could soon leave for good. After all, once the defence opened its case, no-one would expect her to stay on. Nevertheless, despite these thoughts, Midge could not help feeling guiltily relieved when the end of the day came. She had observed nothing useful, but at least she could sneak back to her lodgings, place her spindly chair with its back under her door-handle, and lie down and sleep. Relief at escaping from Duke's Buildings soon gave way to weary pain as she alighted from her 'bus and began to plod slowly towards Paradise Street. An Austin car was parked on her side of the road, but she paid it no notice until one of the doors opened and a man of around forty accosted her.

"Miss Carew? I am a police officer and I want to have a word with you."

Midge stopped dead and began to back away. She was about to be abducted. Where was the reporter that Sutton had sworn would be there to protect her?

The man read Midge's terrified expression as guilt.

"Oh no you don't," he warned. "Either you come quietly or I'll arrest you."

Midge was continuing to back away when the driver of the car emerged smartly, cut off her retreat and practically lifted her into the back seat. The doors were locked and the car whirled off, weaving its way rapidly in and out of the London traffic. Midge tried to keep her eyes open for landmarks, but she did not know London well and had no idea of where she was going. All she could think of was that she would be tortured and shot, or possibly sandbagged and flung in the Thames. As the car slowed down, she tried unobtrusively to open the door next to her, reasoning that she had more chance with the traffic than she did with abductors who did not even bother to hide their faces – she had read enough books to know that that meant that they intended to kill her. However, the man sitting alongside her was too quick for Midge. Grabbing her arm, he held onto it as the Austin swung into an entrance.

"What's the point of trying to escape right by the Yard?" he chided. "We'd have caught you in no time. Or you'd have ended up under the wheels of a lorry."

"The Yard?" repeated Midge in bemusement.

"Yes. Inspector Groves wants a word with you."

Suddenly realising that there were a number of uniformed policeman going briskly about their business, Midge began to laugh uncontrollably.

"That's enough of that," ordered the plain-clothes detective, thinking that he could hardly shake a girl who could not walk properly, and uncertain how else to deal with her.

Midge had no intention of explaining why she was laughing, but she did accept with gratitude the opportunity to splash some cold water on her face before she went upstairs to Groves' office. It gave her the chance to pull herself together, but she was unaware that it also gave the driver the opportunity to slip upstairs and inform the inspector that they had not been followed.

Groves rose to greet Midge as she was ushered into his office. He waited until she was seated before speaking.

"Well, Miss Carew, or do you prefer Miss Carrington?"

Midge stared at him, unsure how to reply. Clearly he had not been fooled by her change of name at Forrest and Creech, but why had it taken him so long to question her? And – more importantly – how far could she refuse to answer his questions? Sir Everard Denys had emphasised how vital it was that she did not tell the police anything at all. If she were to give way under interrogation, then she would be presenting the prosecution with the very evidence which the defence hoped to spring on them at the trial.

Groves repeated his question. Midge continued to stare at him. The terror of thinking that she had been abducted, coming on top of the cumulative fears of the previous weeks, meant that she was so tired that she could hardly think. Indeed, she found it difficult, at that moment, to remember who she was meant to be. Meanwhile, the inspector was beginning to get annoyed. He had had an arduous session in the witness box and now it looked as if he were to be faced with an uncooperative creature who would delay him still further that evening.

"Surely you can hardly think that it will help matters to deny either your real name or your alias when I have been introduced to you under both?" he remarked pointedly.

The slight touch of sarcasm in Groves' voice broke through Midge's exhaustion. 'Damn him,' she thought, 'I shan't just deny my name; I'll deny him any conversation. That way I shan't have to think about anything at all.'

Normally, Midge made considerable efforts to ensure that she did not allow herself to dwell on the gnawing agony which was her constant companion – if she did so it would all too easily overwhelm her. Nonetheless, that evening she took the deliberate decision to stop fighting and to retreat into the pain which could blot out everything else. Like a ship setting sail at the dead of night, Midge cast off her moorings and allowed herself to drift on an uncharted sea of pain, floating wherever the black waves sent her.

Unsurprisingly, Groves was considerably taken aback by the sight of a witness who seemed to have suddenly removed herself mentally from the room. He tried asking questions loudly and he tried asking questions softly, but she responded to neither. She even ignored long silences, which, in the inspector's experience, most people felt compelled to fill. If she had started rocking backwards and forwards or muttering to herself he would have known what to think, but this girl did neither. She merely stared straight ahead of her with eyes that looked like hooded pebbles and which had about as much expression in them.

Finally, in a desperate attempt to provoke some reaction from this mere slip of a girl, Groves went outside the room and remained there for some time, hoping that she might try to have a look at the file lying on the desk. If she did that, he would know that she had been acting. But Midge made no move, not even after fifteen minutes. The streak of caution which had expanded after her weeks at Forrest and Creech warned Midge to stay where she was. Moreover, somewhere amongst the waves of pain crashing round her was a recognition that she was amongst policemen and, whilst there, no-one would strike her with paperweights or poison her with aconitine. Therefore, as long as she did not actually fall asleep, she could let herself drift as close to unconsciousness as she liked.

Groves spent another hour trying to get Midge to talk but, at the end of it, he summoned the police doctor, who took one look at her and said that she was unfit for questioning.

"How soon could she be questioned?"

The doctor shrugged. "It depends. Certainly not tonight. What's she in for?"

"Witness."

"Then let her go home," commanded the police doctor, in a tone of some surprise that Groves had not done so already.

Groves sighed. He was not a cruel man and he had no interest in tormenting someone who looked as if she would fall over if you blew on her. "It's the Fletcher case," he explained. "I don't have time to waste. And, if it comes to that, I don't even know where the girl's home is."

Resisting the temptation to remark that discovering things was what policemen were for, the doctor bid a jovial goodbye and took himself off. Groves thought for a few moments. He could hardly charge the girl with obstructing the police, and she certainly did not look well enough to be held in a cell overnight. But if he let her go, she would tell the defence anything important long before he got another chance to question her. He shrugged, then pulled the telephone towards him, wishing that Miss Carrington did not possess such an unmanning stare – almost as if she was one of the blind Fates that he had read about at school.

"May I speak to Miss Fletcher? It is Inspector Groves."

The butler asked him to hold the line and Groves could hear a murmured colloquy at the other end. Then a man's voice spoke.

"This is Ronald Thornley. I am one of Miss Fletcher's colleagues."

Groves remembered the tall barrister. "Well, Mr Thornley, I have Miss Carrington here and she seems rather ill, so I thought it best that she went back to stay with Miss Fletcher, rather than wherever she's been staying at the moment."

"You say she is ill. Why is she at Scotland Yard? Has she been attacked?"

"No, no. Two of my men picked her up on her way from work. I've had her examined by the police doctor; he thinks it is exhaustion."

"I shall be round immediately."

When Ronald put down the receiver, he frowned, before heading back to the drawing-room, where Jenny was talking to James. John had not yet returned from Cambridge and James had executed a smart manoeuvre to get rid of Dickie.

"What's up?" asked Jenny wearily. "Was it another of those wretched reporters?"

"No. It was Groves. He wants me to go round to the Yard and collect Midge. What on earth is she doing in London? I thought she'd gone back home. And what's this about her working?"

"Midge? Oh my God, she's dead and it's all my fault."

Rather than rebuking Jenny for swearing, as Mike had done, Ronald grinned sympathetically at her. "Don't be an idiot; I'm not an undertaker. Groves pulled her in for questioning, but she's exhausted, hence his request for help from you."

"She got a job at Forrest and Creech to help me," stated Jenny. "And now I've made her ill." She broke off, conscious that she was perilously close to tears. One of her articles of faith was that once you allowed a man to start feeling superior to you, he never stopped. If she were to howl all over Ronald, he would never take her seriously again.

"Midge must have had nerves of steel to do that," remarked Ronald admiringly. "I'll go and fetch her."

Chapter Forty-Two

When Ronald arrived at the Yard, he asked directions to Groves' room from a suspicious constable. There he found the inspector who appeared harassed.

"I don't know why you lawyers have to meddle with things."

"I was not, in fact, a party to Miss Carrington's activities," returned Ronald mildly, "but you have my sympathy."

Groves grunted. Even if Thornley were not involved, he would bet his shirt that young Miss Fletcher knew exactly what had been taking place. However, he was relieved to see that the barrister's voice appeared to have roused Miss Carrington.

"Come on, Midge," coaxed Ronald. "I'll get a taxi and take you back to Jenny's."

"I'll send you round in a police car with a constable," offered Groves, before adding, "I'm not trying to follow you to discover where you go; I'm trying to make sure that nothing happens on your way there."

"Thank you," replied Ronald, who had indeed suspected the inspector's motives. Nonetheless, by the time they were driving through the dark streets, he was glad that the stolid constable was with them. If nothing else, the man was more experienced at discerning whether they were being tailed or not. However, as they met nothing more exciting than a cyclist riding without lights, Ronald was free of that particular worry when the police-car drew up outside Mr Fletcher's imposing house. After being thanked by Ronald, the constable drove off, although Ronald was unaware that the man had no intentions of driving more than a few streets away. Groves had ordered him to keep watch on the house to see whether anyone visited the Fletcher residence after Midge returned.

Jenny seized upon Midge's arrival with guilty relief. She felt dreadful that Midge looked so exhausted, but at least she had not caused Midge's death.

"Come and have some soup by the fire," she commanded. "You look frozen."

Midge did not want to eat, but she allowed herself to be led into the drawing-room, where James was shocked to see her grey, drawn expression. However, Midge brushed away any startled questions about her health.

"Did my message get through?"

"What message?"

"The one about the chemist's shop. Was my idea correct?"

Jenny stretched out her hands in apologetic confusion. "Midge, I've no idea what you're talking about."

Midge looked as if she were ready to pass out. "I sent a message via a journalist yesterday. There was a dot next to a chemist's name in the office directory. I wondered if it might be important – no-one in the office lives in Barnet and I couldn't imagine why any one of them might visit a chemist up in North London. And I warned the journalist that Wynne has a false passport."

James, who had been treated to a remorseful apology from Jenny whilst Ronald collected Midge, managed to make sense of Midge's stumbling explanation and he tried to reassure her. "There's no reason why we would have been told about your message. Either it will have gone straight to Sir Everard or your journalist friend Sutton will have investigated it further. Cottrell will be able to tell us what happened."

"Did Cottrell know what you were doing?" demanded Ronald.

"Yes. And Sir Everard did."

"In that case, we need to tell Cottrell and Denys that you have left the office."

Midge could be heard whispering that she would go back if it would help.

"Certainly not," forbade Jenny. "You look all in."

Ronald and James agreed and Midge gave up. She was too tired to argue; moreover, she was conscious of a deep relief that she could finally escape from the strain of living a double life. Mary Carew would be no more.

It was agreed that Ronald would attempt to get in touch with either Denys or Cottrell, whilst Midge lay down for a bit.

"There's no point you telling your story twice," declared Ronald sensibly. "If Sir Everard is free he'll be bound to want to quiz you and you'll be more help if you're not exhausted."

"Exactly," agreed Jenny, despite being desperate to discover the latest details. She went upstairs with Midge, noticing with concern how slowly Midge was walking. She could never forgive herself if she had made Midge more ill, but – equally – she could never forgive herself if she had neglected any chance to save her father.

"Do you want a bath?" she asked abruptly, trying to disguise her distress.

Midge shook her head. "I just want to sleep and sleep and sleep."

"You shall do so," declared Jenny fiercely as she threw an extra eiderdown onto Midge's bed. "And you shall be warm. Whoever heard of sleeping under only three blankets in the middle of winter?"

Midge gave a weak grin then, as reaction began to sink in, she burst into hopeless sobs. Jenny put her arms round her and begged her not to cry, but Midge seemed unable to stop. Just as Jenny was becoming seriously worried, Midge hiccoughed and tried to pull herself together.

"I'm sorry; that was very feeble of me."

"Don't apologise," urged Jenny, trying to think of

something which might make her friend laugh. "At least you're in the privacy of a house – I burst into tears listening to Tchaikovsky in the Albert Hall *and* I was with James."

Midge gave a damp smile. "That doesn't sound much like you." She sighed, "I cried on John, but at least I'd threatened him with a poker first."

"O wicked, lawless Midge," Jenny remarked. "Has no-one enlightened you as to the principles of the Offences against the Person Act, 1861?"

"I thought that John was a burglar or an abductor," protested Midge.

"You don't have to worry about burglars here. Nothing shall disturb you until Cottrell or Sir Everard turns up."

Despite Jenny's hope that Ronald would quickly be able to inform counsel for the defence that there had been developments, it was nearly two hours later before Cottrell appeared. On the other hand, it meant that Midge was more coherent, following a short sleep. She swiftly explained what had occurred since she had been cross-examined by Sir Everard.

"We did receive the information regarding this chemist," stated the solicitor, "and I understand that one of Sutton's reporters is following it up. Nevertheless, you must understand that it is very speculative. Furthermore, I gather that the reporters could discover nothing unusual about the antecedents of either of the previous typists at Forrest and Creech." He sighed. As a lawyer, he viewed Miss Carrington's activities with disapproval, but, he consoled himself, at least there seemed no chance of a man of law becoming arrested in this particular investigation.

James looked sympathetically at Midge. If he had spent days pretending to be a typist, he would prefer to have his evidence greeted with more enthusiasm. However, Cottrell was not finished.

"You do realise that the very fact that you were working at Forrest and Creech will enable the prosecution to claim that perhaps it was you who created all these suspicious-looking pieces of paper?"

"I didn't," protested Midge. "Moreover, I could hardly make up evidence of a tax fraud. I don't understand tax, and I know what I saw on the invoices."

"I do not necessarily doubt your word, but you need to be aware that you will face considerable opposition in attempting to convince others." Cottrell gave a small, tight smile. "Indeed, the more accurate your evidence is as a reflection of the practices of that particular firm, the more likely that you will be subjected to a barrage of hostile comments both from Sir Reginald Hilliard and from those members of the firm who are recalled to give further evidence. You will be, ah, Actaeon torn apart by hounds."

As an uplifting statement, this assessment of Midge's possible fate when she reached the witness-box was felt by most of those present to have been a notable failure. However, at least Cottrell agreed that Midge could not return to Forrest and Creech. He then begged the favour of speaking to Miss Fletcher alone.

"Cheer up, Midge," said Ronald, rather awkwardly. "Solicitors love telling people bad news."

"Exactly," agreed James. "That's why we're barristers. Cheerful, helpful types like us would never develop the gravitas which Cottrell wears like a heavy ulster, even in the height of summer."

"I *don't* lie," protested Midge, "and I think it's dashed rude of him to disbelieve me. Anyway, Actaeon was torn apart by his own hounds and I'm blowed if Wynne belongs to me in any shape or form."

James grinned. "True, but you didn't listen closely enough to Cottrell. He very carefully said that he did not necessarily doubt your word." James became serious again. "Actually, Cottrell's quite right to warn you that you'll be savaged by the prosecution; they're not going to take at all kindly to some girl turning up and trying to spoil their case for them."

"That's where we come in," added Ronald. "Obviously, Denys – or even Jenny – can't coach you in what to say, but there's nothing to stop me or James or Dickie from cross-examining you. Most people only ever give evidence once in their lives so they are easy meat for predatory, carnivorous barristers who hunt their prey year after year."

"This way we can turn you from a waddling duck into something harder to catch," remarked James, before biting his lip as he realised that his analogy had been distinctly infelicitous. "Err, what are you going to do about your lodgings?"

Ronald realised that James was trying to change the subject and backed him up. "We should send a wire tonight – you don't want your landlady to alert the police about a missing lodger."

"I don't suppose that she'd bother."

"Nevertheless, we ought to and, whilst we're about it, we can draft something to send to Forrest and Creech."

Neither task took especially long. Then Jenny returned, looking upset.

"Lipinski's recovered consciousness."

"Surely that's a good thing?" queried Midge.

"Yes, but he may not recover sufficiently to give evidence." Jenny shrugged. "He's adamant that someone pushed him into the path of the car."

James' eyebrows rose. "You mean he is alleging that someone tried to kill him?"

Jenny nodded. "Exactly. I should have been more suspicious at the time of his accident, but I didn't think about attempted murder." She shrugged. "And his

351

description of the man is very weak. He noticed a beard and that was it."

"A beard?" repeated Midge. "Wynne's picture in his false passport had a beard."

"That doesn't mean that Wynne was the man who attacked Lipinski," warned Ronald. "Someone could have been paid to carry it out – and they may not have intended for him to die. It might have been a warning not to talk."

"Or," remarked James, "it could have been a random attack by a complete stranger. That said, it does sound infernally suspicious."

Midge was watching Jenny. "What else is up? Cottrell told you something else, didn't he?"

"Yes." After briefly explaining to Midge what had happened when the two little girls had turned up, Jenny attempted to sound professional. "Herr Elsner – that's Herr X's real name – has spoken to Professor Schulmann. Elsner was questioned by the police – which we guessed from the fact that the prosecution asked me if I'd met him. It is quite clear that the police think that I've bought his testimony."

"Do you mean to say," demanded Midge, "that because these kids turned up on your doorstep and – in the middle of all that is going on – you had the decency to take pity on them and to ensure that they will not be returned to their homeland, the prosecution can allege that this was done out of cold-blooded calculation?"

"Yes."

"So they think that John's a perjurer, too?"

Jenny shrugged. "From what Herr X said, the police think that John didn't realise what I was up to."

"Or," interjected Ronald, "they think that he did, but they don't think that they can prove it."

"If they're going to think that sort of thing about John, then I'm dashed glad that I didn't give Groves any information," stated Midge heatedly.

"Quite," agreed James. "We need to keep everything we can right up our sleeve. Wynne's false passport could be useful. Juries don't like people with double lives."

"Wynne was awfully angry this morning," warned Midge. "If he knows it's gone, he may take fright and flee."

"That would be no bad thing," commented James judicially. "Flight tends to be interpreted as evidence of guilt."

Jenny looked up hopefully. "Maybe we should encourage him to flee."

"I shouldn't do that until Denys wants it," cautioned Ronald. "He may be able to achieve more by recalling Wynne to the witness-box and asking him to explain some of the things Midge has discovered."

"All right," promised Jenny with a sigh. "But how are we going to prove that he's the murderer?"

"It's not certain that he is," Midge pointed out. "It might have been Creech."

Ronald frowned. "Don't go so fast, Midge. I know that the firm appears exceedingly dubious, but the murderer must have known where both Lipinski and Herr X were living. Otherwise, the murderer would not have been able to arrange an attack on Lipinski or realise that Herr X's daughters had arrived here. Don't forget that Lipinski made a one-off payment and must have dropped all connections with Forrest and Creech as soon as possible."

Jenny looked up in horror. "Ronald, you're not suggesting that it was Professor Schulmann after all? He knows far more about the refugees than anyone else."

Ronald shook his head. "It doesn't seem very likely, not least because I can't see why he would wish to undermine Herr X's evidence, even if he was the murderer. But you have to consider all possibilities."

Midge suddenly remembered the telephone call to Mr

353

Fletcher's chambers. "Sir Everard said that a man rang up Thomson asking whether I'd ever worked there. Professor Schulmann can't have been behind that. He knows perfectly well that I'm Jenny's friend and he's seen me, so he'd have recognised a description of me without needing to try to check my identity with Thomson."

Jenny relaxed. "Thank goodness for that. And thank goodness you're out of that office." She frowned. "Creech and Wynne are the only men in the firm, aren't they?"

"Yes, now that Forrest is dead," agreed Midge. "Obviously, it can't have been Miss Hurst who rang up and I don't think that anyone would describe Davie's voice as being a man's. He sounds far too young." She shrugged. "And if Lipinski said that it was a man who pushed him under that bus then it can't have been Davie. Even if he had put on a false beard, he's nowhere like fully grown."

"That's all very well," argued James, "but what would Creech or Wynne's motive be for killing Forrest? Assuming that they were in the refugee racket, surely they must have known that it would be disastrous to have the police conducting a murder investigation on their premises?"

"Ye-es," agreed Midge. "But what if one of them lost their temper?"

Jenny looked unconvinced. "You might hit someone over the head during a furious argument, but poisoning is different. You'd have to purchase aconitine in advance – and, it appears, without being the purchase being traced."

Midge shrugged. "Maybe they quarrelled over the share of the loot. Wynne seems very avaricious. Or maybe Forrest got cold feet."

Ronald was still pursuing the question of who had seen Herr X's daughters. "I don't quite see how Wynne – who would have been at work when the girls turned up on Saturday – knew that they were here. He had to be certain that they were in order to make an allegation of collusion sound probable."

Midge shrugged. "Maybe someone was watching this house. After all, the children said that they'd received a message to come here. Why shouldn't the crook know where his victims are living? In any case, I wasn't in the office on Saturday – Wynne might have taken the day off. Or perhaps it was Creech. Or perhaps that stranger who came to the office speaking German was reporting where they lived."

"That's speculative."

"I know it is, Ronald," retorted Midge, "but someone could have been keeping tabs on those girls. It wouldn't require much organisation to then lurk outside here to see if they did turn up – or to follow them when they left wherever they've been living."

Jenny nodded. "And it was only a few hours later that Professor Schulmann arrived. If the watcher recognised him and saw John go off with him, he might have guessed what was happening." She shivered. It was horrible thinking about crooks lying in wait outside her home. "I don't mean that they'd assume that John had signed papers for their upkeep. I mean that there was enough contact between me and Herr X to be able to allege that I'd bought his evidence." She tried desperately to be fair. "I know that Herr X must have felt that he had to tell the police everything, but it's disastrous that he's admitted seeing me and wanting to help my father. I don't think that Wynne's false passport is enough to defeat that and Forrest's accusation from beyond the grave."

355

Chapter Forty-Three

After the case had been discussed from several angles, Ronald, with one eye on Midge's weary state, offered to drive her to her uncle's flat. Jenny looked blankly at the barrister.

"Surely Midge doesn't need to go out again?"

Ronald sighed; Jenny was reacting like a layman. "I shouldn't be suggesting another journey unless it was important. The prosecution are bound to suggest that you and Midge cooked up her evidence together. If she stays with you tonight, they can argue that every word she makes in the witness-box is based on a fabricated story."

Jenny bit her lip. "I'm sorry, Midge; I ought to have thought of that before."

"Parry, will you come with me in case of accidents?"

James nodded, while Jenny went to the telephone to warn Mr Carrington.

The next day, Ronald's caution was seen to have unexpected benefits. The first of these was that Field could quite honestly deny all knowledge of Miss Carrington's whereabouts when Groves appeared at nine o'clock, ready to question Midge. Moreover, since Jenny had already set off to the Old Bailey, it was distinctly difficult for Groves to find out from her where her friend now was. By the time that Cottrell had advised an argumentative Jenny that she could not obstruct Groves in the execution of his duty, Geoffrey Carrington had already summoned the staff doctor of the *Universal Record* to examine Midge. Dr Beatty had had no hesitation in declaring that Miss Carrington was unfit for questioning until at least Monday. Groves had been disposed to argue, at which point Carrington had smiled sardonically.

"Such dedication to duty is most admirable, Inspector, but I think that you may be unaware that Dr Beatty writes a column under the by-line Hippocrates."

Groves stared at the reporter in some surprise.

"I gather," remarked Carrington, as if to the air, "that Hippocrates has planned a series of articles upon the subject of medical ignorance in the great institutions of the land. I am unsure how your superiors would respond were they to learn that Hippocrates has hastily added the Yard to his list of targets. Apparently Dr Beatty thinks that the unfortunate misinterpretation of the McNaughton rules which occurred in the Daniels case has considerable scope for further comment."

Scowling, Groves gave way. He knew perfectly well that his Chief Inspector would have his guts for garters were the Daniels case to be splashed across the papers again. After all, Chief Inspector Adams had come close to losing his job over the affair and, somehow, he believed that Adams would learn why Hippocrates had chosen to rake up the issue at this juncture.

"I shall consult with my superiors," he threatened, knowing that Carrington would guess that this was a harmless gesture.

"Of course, Inspector," smiled Carrington. "I should expect no less. And, naturally, when Dr Beatty certifies that my niece is sufficiently robust to be able to help you, we shall let you know."

Conscious that he had lost a trick, but consoling himself that the girl probably was genuinely unfit, Groves returned to the Yard. Meanwhile, in the Old Bailey, Ronald, James and Jenny were listening to Sir Reginald at his most orotund. The K.C. was spinning out the uninteresting evidence of two detective constables who had never expected to be called, since all they had to say was that they had questioned many chemists, but had failed to find any evidence of the purchase of aconitine. Several people had begun to fidget while the second constable confirmed in considerable detail the evidence of the first. However, as a slip of paper was passed to Hilliard, he drew his questioning to a close with almost unseemly haste, before turning to the judge.

"M'lord, late last night the prosecution was informed by the police of a development which is of considerable significance. May I beg your indulgence to recall a witness?"

There was an excited rustle in the court. Had the aconitine been found?

"Is the witness present?"

"Yes; he has just arrived."

Jenny, who was watching from the well of the court, was so relieved that she was not going to be recalled to be questioned about the refugee children that, for a moment, she did not take in the implication of the fact that Wynne was the witness who had been summoned so hastily. When she did, her first thought was thankfulness that Midge had not returned to Forrest and Creech that morning. Her second was concern as to what the clerk had to say.

After Wynne was reminded that he was still on oath, Sir Reginald asked him to outline how staff obtained employment at Forrest and Creech.

"When we have a vacancy, which is not often, we normally advertise."

"And have you had any vacancies recently?"

"Yes; two of our typists were upset by Mr Forrest's death and felt that they did not want to work in the same building where someone had died."

The clerk's sniff as he concluded his sentence made abundantly clear his views on such feminine foibles. However, Sir Reginald was more interested in the latest recruit to the firm, rather than old employees.

"Have you recently employed a new member of staff?"

Sir Everard rose to protest. The knowledge that Wynne

had become suspicious of Midge had forced him to contact the police the previous evening. If he hadn't, it would have left Wynne a free hand to destroy any evidence of fraud. This way, the police might just discover something – although from Hilliard's demeanour it didn't sound as if he had any doubts about Wynne's veracity. However, despite the fact that he had been the one who had effectively broken Midge's cover, Sir Everard had no desire to let Midge be attacked before she had given evidence. "Surely, m'lord, there can be no relevance in discussing secretaries who joined Forrest and Creech *after* Forrest's death."

"Is there a purpose to your questioning, Sir Reginald?"

"Very much so, m'lord; this witness will help to show that the allegations of one of the defence witnesses are both inaccurate and untrustworthy."

Mr Justice Hawkroyd frowned. He was unhappy about this attempt to damage as yet unnamed witnesses before they had had the chance to say anything but, equally, he could see that it would be difficult to recall Wynne in the middle of the defence case.

"Very well, you may proceed."

Sir Reginald bowed, before turning back to Wynne.

"Perhaps you might tell the court about your new member of staff and how you came to employ her."

"She called herself Mary Carew and she appeared before Christmas, claiming to have heard about a vacancy in the office. Our chief typist gave her a trial and we kept her on as we were very short-staffed."

"Did you follow up her references?"

"Yes. One was from the music correspondent at the *Universal Record* and the other one was supposed to come from some university professor in Cambridge."

John, who had just returned from that august seat of learning, winced despite his overriding concerns for Midge. Somehow he felt that he would not be allowed to forget using his college's name in this most inappropriate manner. Meanwhile, the crime correspondents had turned as one to glare at the representative of the *Universal Record*, whom they considered to have pulled off a fast one.

"So, Miss Carew's recruitment was irregular?" asked Hilliard, recalling the court's attention to matters under discussion.

"Yes. If it had not been for Christmas we should not have taken her on and I very much wish that we had not," Wynne declared bitterly.

"Why do you say that?"

"She proved to be most unsatisfactory; in fact, I understand that Carew was not even her real name, so her references must have been forged."

Sir Everard protested at these statements, but the judge, scenting something peculiar in the air, chose to give Wynne his head. He proved to be vengeful in the extreme.

"She was a very fanciful sort of girl, always dramatising herself. She even claimed that the office-boy tried to flirt with her." The clerk allowed himself a dry cough. "That, if I may say so, would be a most unlikely scenario."

Since few of those present had yet set eyes on Midge, Wynne's final aside had little effect except to prepare them for a girl of outstanding ugliness. However, Wolsey, Denys' junior defence counsel, bristled. He had thought that a girl who sent coded messages in Greek sounded pretty odd, but making cheap jibes about a girl's lameness was distinctly below the belt.

"You say that she was fanciful," continued Hilliard. "Was there any other reason why you found her unsatisfactory?"

"She was always poking around where she had no business to be. I had already decided that she must be replaced and, when I discovered that she had been in my room whilst I was giving evidence, I took the decision that today would be her last day at the firm."

"Did she know that?"

"Oh yes," snapped Wynne. "I made it abundantly clear to her. That must be why she's come forward with this pack of lies."

"Doubtless we shall hear Miss Carew's or, I should say, Miss Carrington's remarkable statements from her own lips," commented Hilliard. He bowed politely towards Denys, with nothing in his manner to indicate that he had spent most of the previous evening fulminating about how the defence had attempted to outwit him. If Groves hadn't had the sense to speak to the clerk about the false typist, and if Wynne hadn't believed Groves' information and co-operated with him, then the prosecution case would have been dealt a nasty blow.

As Sir Everard rose, he was cursing the mischance that had allowed Wynne to paint Midge in such unflattering colours before she had any opportunity to tell her story. He turned his attention to attacking the clerk without giving away too much of Midge's story.

"You said in your evidence that Miss Carew 'claimed' to have heard about a vacancy in the office, but is it not the case that you actually had two vacancies for typists in your office?"

Wynne glared at defence counsel, wondering how much he knew. "She did claim it," he maintained stubbornly. "She isn't a proper typist."

"That doesn't mean that she was wrong in her understanding that you had a vacancy," pointed out Denys. "How many typists had left in the month before Miss Carew's employment?"

"Two," growled Wynne sulkily.

"So, when you state that Miss Carew 'claimed' that there was a vacancy, she was, in fact, entirely accurate." When Wynne did not respond, Sir Everard's mouth snapped like a rat-trap. "Was there, or was there not, a vacancy for a typist in your office?"

"There was."

"Why did the other typists leave?"

"They were upset about Mr Forrest having died on the premises."

"So, Miss Peters did not leave because you were offensive to her?"

"No," protested the clerk, but his denial sounded less convincing than his other statements.

"And was Miss Hemming perfectly happy there?"

"So far as I was aware."

"Doubtless we shall be able to gain corroboration from her as to her state of perpetual bliss whilst she worked at Forrest and Creech," remarked counsel smoothly, ignoring a warning glance from Mr Justice Hawkroyd. "Now, turning to other matters, you have stated that this young lady wasn't a proper typist. If this is the case, perhaps you might enlighten us as to how she managed to type your firm's letters for nearly a month."

Several hastily-suppressed guffaws indicated that not everyone was ready to believe that Midge had been as much a fraud as Wynne had attempted to suggest.

"Matters of typing are left to Miss Hurst," blustered the clerk, before recalling something. "However, there have been times when I had to make Miss Carew retype documents which were done badly."

"And when was the last of these times?"

"I can't remember," growled Wynne angrily. "I told you, Miss Hurst deals with most of it."

"However, given that your new typist began on a week's trial, she cannot have done too badly if you continued to employ her."

"We were very short-staffed at the time."

"So naturally you were also advertising for an

experienced typist at the same time?"

"I believe that we were looking for one," agreed Wynne.

"Can you produce copies of your advertisements or letters to secretarial agencies?"

"I should have to check Miss Hurst's files."

"Come, come, Mr Wynne. You are the only clerk in a small firm; you must know whether such letters or advertisements were placed. Apart from anything else, you would have had to authorise any disbursements connected with such advertisements."

"I cannot recollect whether we have any copies of letters," stated the clerk firmly, before adding. "However, I can tell you this: that girl is a most untrustworthy specimen. She probably lies to be noticed – a pathological type."

"Perhaps you would care to tell the court what your medical qualifications are," snapped Sir Everard. "And if you have none, you ought to confine your statements to matters which fall under your remit. After all, on those matters which you, as a clerk, ought to know about, your claims seem to be unable to be proved. Doubtless there is some explanation for this – whether that is because of your incapacity or because they never happened."

On this unsatisfactory note, Denys sat down, mentally awarding Hilliard full marks for his method of undermining the defence star witness.

V

Presto

Chapter Forty-Four

Sir Reginald Hilliard was well aware of the effects of his bombshell. He was tempted to drag proceedings out until the end of the day, but in the end he concluded the prosecution case at around three o'clock, calculating that this gave Denys just enough time to start the defence, but not enough time to undo any of the consequences of Wynne's testimony. If Denys were forced to open his case, it would give the prosecution the opportunity during the weekend to mull over the line which the defence intended to take.

Sir Everard knew exactly what Hilliard intended and he was also abundantly aware of the dangers of the jury spending two days wondering what lies the mysterious Miss Carew was going to spin. In some respects, the K.C. wished that he had confronted Wynne with the false passport, but the risk had been too great. If Wynne had denied it outright, there was a strong chance that the jury might have believed him. It wasn't as if the photograph, with its attendant beard covering most of the face, resembled Wynne especially closely. A denial would, in turn, have undermined Miss Carrington's story of false passports being issued. Nonetheless, Sir Everard thought it safe to refer in oblique terms to his belief that the dead man's firm was not a typical solicitor's office.

"The prosecution has made great play regarding the letter which Forrest is alleged to have sent to Scotland Yard. They have taken you through it line by line with a handwriting specialist; they have even had a fingerprint analyst tell you how traces were found of Forrest's fingerprints. However, our case is not that Forrest did not write this letter. Indeed, we are happy to accept the evidence of all these scientific specialists. But, although Forrest may have written the letter, that does not prove that what he wrote was the truth. To put it bluntly, we maintain that what Forrest wrote was a pack of lies.

"Moreover, you have already heard for yourselves significant errors in the police investigation. They were so sure that Mr Fletcher – a distinguished man with an honourable record of service in the law – had done this deed that they did not bother to search his chambers properly. What else and where else have the police failed to search? Certainly, they appear to have utterly failed to consider the possibility that – if the poison were indeed introduced in the defendant's chambers – perhaps Patrick Fletcher himself was the target. After all, he is a well-known prosecutor with plenty of enemies amongst the criminal fraternity, and it is not unknown for prosecutors to suffer unwarranted attention after such trials."

The jury listened stolidly to this, but several of the reporters were amused.

"Think Hilliard's quaking in his boots?" asked one.

"It's a ploy to remind the jury that until this moment Fletcher's been on the side of the angels," snorted his neighbour cynically.

"Better pray there are no criminals on the jury, then," added the first. "What odds'll you give me on the man in the brown suit?"

With one eye on the clock, Denys turned to the ludicrous allegations that Fletcher was in debt and desperate for money.

"My learned friend is regarded as being one of the most painstaking and able advocates currently practising," he declared, glaring at Hilliard as if daring him to disagree.

"As his daughter has pointed out, were he in need of money, he would merely have to accept a few more briefs – there is certainly no shortage of solicitors who wish to brief him. Moreover, the defence will be calling Mr Fletcher's bank manager to prove that he was in no financial difficulties whatsoever and that all of his financial transactions are extremely straightforward."

Sir Everard managed to talk for another twenty minutes without mentioning Midge once. However, when Mr Justice Hawkroyd indicated that it was time for the court to rise, Denys took advantage of the chance to closet himself in consultation with Fletcher. Rapidly outlining what had been taking place outside the court, he turned to his old friend.

"What do you think, Patrick? I had planned to begin with Schulmann and the refugees' evidence before I brought in Miss Carrington. Now I wonder whether the best thing is to get her into the box before she can be questioned by the police."

"Surely they will learn of most of the information from Cottrell?"

"Yes, but not every detail. Also, I don't want those insidious remarks of Wynne preying on the jury's mind for too long. The longer they go unchallenged, the greater the chance that the jury will utterly disbelieve everything Miss Carrington says."

Fletcher grimaced. "That man Wynne must be a malevolent scoundrel. I've known the girl for years and never seen any signs of her being a liar, pathological or otherwise. Nor can I imagine why she would be so stupid as to start dramatising herself in a place she believes to house a poisoner." He sighed as Denys began to speak. "I know, Everard, my word on that point is less than naught; murderers will say anything."

"It all depends on how she stands up to cross-examination," fretted Sir Everard. "I'd not intended to call her before Tuesday – that would have given her a bit more time to rest."

"She can't do much worse than my son," grunted Fletcher. "Damned young idiot couldn't even spot a tank-trap like that question about high stakes. Jenny's the only one with any brains."

Assuming correctly that Fletcher was referring to his own offspring and not the entire body of witnesses, Denys gave a brief smile. "Let's hope her friend has brains too."

True to his word, Ronald organised the junior barristers into a relay of expert interrogators. Indeed, conscious that there was little time and that Hilliard was a ferocious cross-examiner, Ronald sent Dickie round to question Midge on Friday afternoon. He wanted to observe events in court himself and felt that Dickie would be of more use helping Midge than in the Old Bailey. Although Dickie felt sorry for Midge, his professional training took over and he soon treated her to a battery of disbelieving snorts or repeated questions. Midge was left wondering whether she would ever be able to stand up to Hilliard, but when James and Ronald appeared on Saturday, Midge was determined not to make some of the mistakes which she had made on the previous day. Since her uncle had warned her about Wynne's claim that she was a pathological liar who sought attention by making up wild stories, Midge was also on her guard about sounding pleased with herself. However, as she explained to Ronald, this was relatively straightforward as she still felt that she had not uncovered as much as she might have done.

"Don't worry about that," argued Ronald. "The defence wouldn't have half as much a chance of persuading the jury if you hadn't been able to stir up all the mud at Forrest and Creech."

Nevertheless, despite this and similar remarks, Midge felt exceedingly nervous when she waited to be summoned on Monday morning. Being interviewed for her place at Newnham had been distinctly nerve-wracking, but no-one's life had depended on her performing well. Moreover, she had not been expected to perform in front of a packed court, knowing that the reporters were busily scribbling down every word she said, ready to be picked over, digested, and spat out for half the country to read the next day. When she limped up to the witness-box, she felt the eyes of the entire court on her. Nor did the sight of Jenny's white face or the judge's scarlet robes reassure her – they only confirmed the danger Mr Fletcher was in. Swallowing with difficulty, Midge managed to swear in a shaky voice to tell the truth, the whole truth, and nothing but the truth.

Sir Everard observed Midge with some concern. Damn it, the girl looked white enough to pass out, which wouldn't do much to convince the jury that she was telling the truth. After requesting that Miss Carrington be allowed to give her evidence sitting down, the K.C. began to take her through her statement. Since this included details of the organisation of Forrest and Creech as well as an explanation of how she found various notes and files which aroused her suspicions, there was a lot for Midge to say. At one point, counsel for the Crown seemed disposed to argue the validity of discussing naturalisation papers and whether or not Forrest and Creech was guilty of supplying false ones. Sir Everard was not to be deflected.

"We shall, of course, be introducing further evidence to substantiate our claims that the deceased was guilty of extorting money from hapless refugees who fell into his clutches. However, we felt that it would be easiest for the jury to understand these points if we called Miss Carrington first, since she can provide an overall narrative of events."

Having thus suggested to all listening that he had always intended to call Midge as his first witness, Sir Everard returned to the question of the invoices which had seemed to be at odds with the accounts. Finally, he asked Midge to explain to the court why she had undertaken her hazardous enterprise. When Midge had first answered this for Ronald, he had pointed out that stating that Jenny had asked her to help sounded as if neither of them had had any confidence in Mr Fletcher's innocence. Hence Midge now gave a much more robust answer.

"I have known Mr Fletcher since I was twelve and I never doubted his innocence. Since we knew that Forrest was actually extorting money from refugees, rather than helping them, Miss Fletcher and I thought that it would be worthwhile investigating Forrest's business. No-one knew who I was, but Jenny's picture had been in the papers. So, in the end, I went, not Miss Fletcher."

This final remark pleased Sir Everard. Far from suggesting that Miss Carrington wanted notoriety, it implied that Fletcher's daughter was practically on the point of knocking on the door of Forrest and Creech when her friend reluctantly stepped in. After a complimentary remark about her devotion to justice, defence counsel indicated to Hilliard that the witness was now his.

Midge watched Sir Reginald rise, with a sheaf of papers in his hands. Her palms were clammy and she could feel her heart racing.

'I mustn't be sick,' she thought. 'And I mustn't sound panicky. Just pretend he's Ronald in a bad mood. Or that he's James being sarcastic.'

Meanwhile, Sir Reginald had decided to begin by adopting a fatherly tone with this surprise witness. You could never tell how juries responded to young women and there was no point needlessly antagonising them by attacking the witness too early.

"Naturally, you will have talked this trial over with your friend, Miss Fletcher. Perhaps you can tell us how much you discussed things with her?"

"Miss Fletcher was staying with me when she learned that her father had been arrested," replied Midge cautiously.

"So presumably you returned to London together and planned your attempt to get a job at Mr Forrest's firm?"

"Not exactly."

"What do you mean by that?"

"I applied for the job before telling her what I had done."

"So it was all on your initiative that this occurred?"

"No," disagreed Midge, well aware that she had already said that she and Jenny believed that Forrest and Creech was a suspect organisation. "Jenny – that is, Miss Fletcher – made the original statement that she wished that it was possible to have someone take a job inside Forrest and Creech."

"And when was it that she made this statement?" asked Hilliard in a voice of deep disbelief.

"It was shortly after Mr Fletcher was arrested." Midge smiled at him. "There were several other people present when she said it."

Deciding that there was no point pursuing this particular hare any longer, Sir Reginald turned to another theme – that of Midge living a lie and deceiving her employer.

"When you applied for this post, did you apply under your own name?"

"No. I have already explained that my uncle is a well-known reporter and I thought that someone might recognise my name and wonder if I was a reporter."

"So you wanted to avoid anyone suspecting that you were a reporter?"

"Yes."

"In other words, you wanted to pretend to your employers at Forrest and Creech that you were an honest, hard-working typist?"

Midge defied the temptation to say that she would hardly have presented herself in the guise of a dishonest, lazy typist.

"Naturally. And, whilst I was there, I did work hard."

"But did it not occur to you that when, for your own reasons, you gained employment at Forrest and Creech, you were lying to your employer? Did you not care that you were breaking your employer's trust in you?"

"Oh yes, we did worry about that."

"We?" pounced the barrister.

Midge smiled at him peaceably. "Obviously, Jenny – that is, Miss Fletcher – and I discussed what I would be doing and she talked with considerable concern about any possible breach of trust between employee and employer."

Jenny fought down an unexpected laugh. She did indeed remember that conversation, but, as she recollected things, her concern had been at the prospect of having to listen to Ronald lecturing her about breach of trust. However, as long as she was not recalled for questioning, Midge appeared to have taken the sting out of Sir Reginald's question.

John, who was in court to provide moral support for his cousin, was less sanguine. 'How long will Midge get away with playing the innocent?' he worried. 'When will Hilliard wake up and remember that she is a Cambridge undergraduate?'

It seemed that learned counsel was reading John's thoughts, for he changed tack almost immediately.

"You speak of discussing matters with Miss Fletcher. Presumably you were in considerable contact with her as you passed on your latest exciting adventures?"

"No."

"No? Come, come, Miss Carrington, are you really telling the court that, after a day spent prying into your employer's affairs, you did not go racing round to Miss Fletcher to report your extravagant speculations?"

"Yes."

"So what did you do in the evenings? Did you, perhaps, see one of Miss Fletcher's colleagues in the evenings?"

"No."

"Let me check that I have this quite correct: you are a young lady of eighteen – although you told your employer that you were sixteen."

Midge resisted the desire to point out that she hadn't been on oath and that Forrest and Creech were a bunch of crooks. Instead, she stuck firmly to the question.

"Yes, I am eighteen."

"And you really expect the court to believe that you, at eighteen, and in the middle of these most strange and exciting events, did not seek out companions to share your evenings? Companions with whom you would, quite naturally, talk over the events of your working day?"

"I did not go out in the evenings – I was too tired."

"Really? A girl of your age was exhausted by an office job. I find that most strange."

"Yes," declared Midge firmly. "I don't suppose you have any idea how tiring it is to be a secretary, especially when you aren't used to it."

"Look at the jury," hissed Geoffrey. John obediently turned his head and saw what his father meant. One of the older women on it was nodding emphatically. Was she a typist? Could Midge have convinced her?

Sir Reginald was still on the attack, determined to ram home the picture of a liar and a fantasist who refused to admit that she had cooked up her story with the aid of others.

"Miss Carrington, you have given the impression that you are indeed that very innocent creature, Mary Carew, whom you played to perfection in the offices of Forrest and Creech. However, you will forgive me if I doubt that this picture is entirely accurate. Aren't you in fact a very cunning and determined young lady who will stick at nothing to achieve her aim? You are an undergraduate at Cambridge, so you can hardly be stupid. Doubtless were we to visit you in your rooms at Newnham we would discover a much more vibrant and stylish woman. After all, aren't we all supposed to accept that women undergraduates are very sophisticated creatures these days, as much busily enjoying themselves drinking cocktails or on the dance floor as they are swotting earnestly in libraries? Or do you, Miss Carrington, claim that you are so tied up adding to intellectual understanding that you have no time for such socialising as might lead to a greater knowledge of the world than you currently appear to possess?"

'Damn him,' thought Midge. 'How dare he sneer at me?' Suddenly a vision of Arthur Palmer advising her to take advantage of people's preconceptions of her polio-status rose before her.

"I don't go out much," she maintained, staring at the advocate straight between the eyes, daring him to disbelieve her. Then, forcing herself to appear calm, she turned to the jury. "The thing is, I had infantile paralysis when I was younger and my leg still hurts. I can't go dancing in the evenings and I get tired easily."

Jenny was raging with anger over the interchange. She knew how much that admission cost Midge; Midge, who hated people to be constantly asking questions about her bad leg and why she walked with sticks. However, Sir Everard, who privately thought that Midge had overdone her projection of limpid innocence in the earlier part of her evidence, gave her full marks for her last statement. A swift sideways glance at the jury confirmed his opinion – personal attacks on witnesses were damnably treacherous things, and the jury hadn't liked that final stab of Hilliard's.

On the other hand, Sir Reginald was not to be put off. "May I put it to you, Miss Carrington, that you are young and that you might naturally become caught up in the excitement of the case. Are you certain that you were not motivated by a desire to have the limelight? Did you not wish to tell your story to an aghast audience who would listen to your intrepid exploits in awe?"

"I did not wish for that."

"You yourself have said that you don't go out much because you had infantile paralysis and you have to walk with a stick. Might you not see this case as an opportunity, perhaps, to play up to the gallery a little? It would be perfectly understandable if you wanted attention, given your peculiar circumstances."

"I do not want attention," snapped Midge, her voice shaking with suppressed anger at prosecuting counsel's insinuations. "And I certainly wouldn't choose a courtroom in which to 'play up to the gallery'. I leave that to you."

There was a stunned silence in court, broken only by a few sniggers from where the press were gathered. The judge regarded Midge thoughtfully. In his personal capacity, he considered that Hilliard had asked for that last remark and more, but, in his position as a judge, he had to maintain order within the courtroom.

"I take it, Miss Carrington, that what you meant to say was that learned counsel are the most appropriate people to make long speeches in a courtroom, speeches which may include some elements of emotion within them."

"Yes, my lord," agreed Midge, regretting that her annoyance at prosecuting counsel's suggestion that she was a show-off and a glory-hunter had led her to losing her temper, but grateful that the judge had let her off so lightly.

Chapter Forty-Five

After Midge's contemptuous rejoinder to his attack on her, counsel for the prosecution grew angry. He had heard the laughter from the reporters and he knew the exchange would feature in the evening papers. No-one – far less a barrister of Sir Reginald's standing – would look forward to reading that some girl had turned his accusation of showing-off back upon him. As Dickie had told Jenny, on the rare occasions when Sir Reginald indulged in the passion of anger in court, he invariably sought to destroy whomsoever stood in his way. He did so now. Question after question poured from him, all intended to trip Midge up and to make her say something which contradicted previous evidence. Midge stuck stolidly to her story, deeply thankful for the time that Ronald had spent in mock cross-examination of her. Eventually, Sir Reginald moved from attack on facts to attack on character. In particular, he seemed determined to paint her as a treacherous viper who had invented her evidence with the help of Jenny.

"Miss Fletcher is training for the law; doubtless you must have discussed what evidence you would give today?"

"Oh no," Midge shook her head. "Oh no, Sir Reginald. Mr Fletcher's colleagues told me that two witnesses couldn't possibly discuss their evidence together."

"So, despite the fact that you and Miss Fletcher are close friends, you managed to spend the entire weekend avoiding the subject of the trial?"

"Yes. I was warned that you'd try to suggest that we were cooking up evidence if she, in her natural distress, talked about the trial. So I stayed with my uncle, not Miss Fletcher."

"'Cooking up evidence'," repeated the judge in distasteful tones.

"Sorry, my lord; I should have said colluding to

fabricate evidence."

It is uncertain whether Sir Reginald would have let Midge's statement go if he had known that 'Mr Fletcher's colleagues' (a phrase which made them sound extremely learned and experienced) were none other than two very junior barristers. However, he did not pursue the issue, preferring to drive home the idea that all the evidence from Forrest and Creech was the result of collusion by other means.

"Presumably Miss Fletcher must have been of great help when you were discovering this so-called evidence regarding tax fraud?"

Midge sensed danger and asked Sir Reginald for clarification. He snorted in disgust.

"Are you telling me, Miss Carrington, that you don't understand a straightforward question?"

"I don't understand what you are implying."

"Then let me make myself clear. Did Miss Fletcher guide you as to what documents to search for?"

"No. When I told her that I was confused by accounts which could not possibly balance, she suggested that perhaps there was a tax fraud, but by that time I had already seen the documents which had raised my suspicions." Midge paused momentarily. "Given that I was typing them, I could hardly overlook them."

"Yes," drawled Sir Reginald. "You were indeed typing some of these documents whose details apparently drew your attention. However, you will forgive me for suggesting that you are not the best person to interpret such documents. You are not, I imagine, a qualified accountant. Nor are you a proper typist – surely it would be easy for you to imagine that some things which you saw were rather more important than they were in reality?"

"No; I know what I saw."

"Perhaps then you might explain how it is that, when

377

Inspector Groves returned to the office where you claim to have seen these mysterious accounts, he found nothing to substantiate your claims?"

"It would be easy to burn anything suspicious."

"I see," replied Hilliard heavily. "So, all we have is your word – and only your word – for the fact that these strange invoices and accounts did not tally. Let us now turn to the supposedly peculiar names which attracted your attention. Might it not be the case that, having discussed some of the details of the defence case with Miss Fletcher, you decided to distract the police by leaving a helpful list of distinctive names which you could claim were refugees?"

"Are you suggesting that I planted evidence?" suggested Midge hotly.

"I am asking you if you did. Why are you so reluctant to reply?"

"I'm not in the slightest bit to reluctant to reply. My reply is very clear. At no point did I plant evidence. At no point did I invent any."

"But you seem to have invented an entire life for yourself, did you not, Miss Carrington – or should I say Miss Carew?"

"There is a distinct difference," argued Midge, hoping that the jury would agree with her.

"Doubtless you can distinguish between different types of invention," responded Hilliard smoothly. "You appear to be remarkably adept at it, considering your age."

Sir Everard rose half-way but prosecuting counsel moved swiftly on. "We have already heard you state that you were very tired by your arduous job as a typist. Perhaps you could tell us how, when you were so very exhausted, you managed to remember these names which you claim to have seen in the course of your duties? Presumably you did not dare to smuggle out letters since – as you claim – you feared that your bag might be searched."

"Mr Wynne searched my bag once," declared Midge firmly. "So you are quite correct, I couldn't possibly risk trying to take a list out with me when I left. So I drew tiny pictures to remind me of names and numbers."

"You drew pictures," repeated Hilliard, in tones of great incredulity. "I have seen these pictures which purportedly represent names, and I may say that I see no proof that they do indeed show names. Let us take, for example, Herbert Little. Can this scrappy drawing of a crescent and two stars really represent him?"

"Yes," nodded Midge. "The two stars stand for February and the crescent represents night."

"But," interrupted Sir Reginald, "we are referring to a man named Little, not Knight, or Dark, or even Moon."

There was scattered laughter at learned counsel's sarcastic tones, but Midge was not finished.

"Well, for me, night means owls, and one owl is Athena noctua."

Sir Reginald was no ornithologist and he was forced to seek clarification.

"Athena noctua is the zoological name for the Little Owl," explained Midge.

This time there were a few suppressed sniggers against Sir Reginald, but he ploughed on.

"And what does fbach stand for?"

"Robertson." Midge turned to the judge. "Does your lordship wish me to explain?"

Hawkroyd nodded, rather intrigued by this interchange, which was rather different from the usual arguments about intestines or a witness' previous criminal record.

"f stands for filius, the Latin for son, while bah is short for Bahadur."

'Bobs,' thought the judge, quicker than Sir Reginald to catch the reference to the military hero.

"Lord Roberts' nickname was Bobs Bahadur,"

379

explained Midge, for the benefit of those who had not grown up in an army cantonment.

"What did the 'c' stand for?" enquired the judge.

"Nothing, my lord. It struck me that I could explain away Bach – the composer – a bit more easily than random letters."

Sir Reginald turned with a sneer towards the witness. "Do you really mean to tell the court that you managed to invent this code before you even knew what sort of names you would need to hide? What use is a code which the police, for example, could not use in evidence?"

"But," Midge maintained reasonably, "it wasn't meant to be a code; it was merely a mnemonic to make sure that I didn't forget anything. No-one else needed to understand how I worked them out."

Learned counsel looked unconvinced. With a crafty smile, he turned to Midge. "Now, Miss Carrington, you have stated that you made these little notes shortly after you saw the names. Presumably you would not have had much time to think of how to disguise the names."

"No," agreed Midge cautiously.

"Perhaps you might care to take part in an experiment. How long, for example, would it take you to come up with a drawing which represented Sir Everard Denys?"

Midge frowned thoughtfully for a moment, whilst the court waited in silent anticipation. Jenny was digging her nails into her hands. If Midge were to fail this test, Sir Reginald would pour scorn on her claims to have noted down the names of the important files. That would lead to the jury distrusting her word on more important issues.

"I'd draw a cake," Midge declared.

"A cake?" Sir Reginald's tone was a marvel of ridicule and disdain.

"Yes."

"Perhaps you might care to enlighten the court as to

how you arrived at this interesting representation of m'learned friend."

"It's easy," Midge announced happily. "Saint-Denis is a royalist church in Paris – I might have gone for a church spire and a fleur de lys, but that would be too obvious. But Louis XVI's remains were buried in Saint-Denis; Louis was married to Marie Antoinette and she said 'let them eat cake'."

"Ingenious," muttered Ronald, appreciating Midge's somewhat warped logic. "But will the jury believe it?"

Sir Reginald was not to be defeated by one lucky solution. "And, with his lordship's permission, how would you remember his name?"

Mr Justice Hawkroyd looked as interested as the rest of the court to see what cryptogram might illustrate his distinguished nomenclature.

"Well, I'd have to avoid any talons or eagles because that might raise people's suspicions," explained Midge. "I'd probably drop the 'h' off the name, which would leave me with 'awk' which sounds like the bird auk. I've got a painting of a guillemot – guillemots are auks – so I'd do a tiny seascape with a gap where the guillemot ought to be. As for the –royd bit, I'd either draw a crown for 'roi' – king – or, if I thought that was a bit easy to guess, I'd do laurel leaves for an emperor. Or," she added, sensing that Sir Reginald did not like this fluent series of inventions and determined to demonstrate that she genuinely could have created such mnemonics quickly and under strain, "I'd draw Admiral Tirpitz's forked beard to remind me of naval power and *King* Wilhelm's expansion of the navy."

"I'm sure the court will be interested in such inventive possibilities," suggested Sir Reginald with heavy irony. "Of course, they may find it rather harder to re-interpret such contorted drawings several hours later."

"Possibly," argued Midge, unmoved, "but that's the

way my brain works. In any case, I knew that they stood for names which I had read earlier in the day – that makes it a lot easier for me to remember than anyone else."

It was no part of counsel for the prosecution's job to admire defence witnesses, but Sir Reginald Hilliard found himself respecting Midge against his will. Unless the jury decided that she was too clever by half, they would be bound to believe that she had indeed been able to obtain the information which she claimed to have smuggled out of Forrest and Creech. That would raise their suspicions that there had been something odd about the firm. Sir Reginald glanced discreetly at his watch. Miss Carrington had been in the witness box for nearly three hours. He had set out to destroy her and had not managed it – to continue to attack her would soon become counter-productive. He contented himself with a few straightforward questions regarding Midge's use of a false name and identity to achieve her ends, and then sat down.

Counsel for the defence rose in Hilliard's stead. Sir Everard could see that Midge was looking increasingly exhausted, but he was determined to allowing Midge to restate some facts in a much less hostile atmosphere.

"Thank you for your patience in explaining complicated matters to the court, Miss Carrington," he began with a small bow. "I shall not delay you much longer. Can you confirm that you discovered all your information within the confines of Forrest and Creech?"

"Yes."

"Can you confirm that you discovered accounts and invoices which you believed did not make sense when taken together?"

"Yes."

"Can you confirm that you discovered two lists of names, one set of which had lists of foreign names, English names and numbers?"

"Yes."

"You discovered the number of a bank account hidden under a desk in Alexander Creech's room?"

"Yes."

"You discovered a passport in the clerk Wynne's room?"

"Yes."

"Finally, counsel for the prosecution has suggested that you were motivated by a desire for notoriety. It seems that he believes that you wanted everyone to think that you were brave in working at Forrest and Creech. I ask you, Miss Carrington, do you think that you were brave?"

"No."

"Can you tell the court why you do not think this?"

"I was scared all the time."

"Why is that?"

This possible question had been the cause of much friction between the junior barristers. James had argued hotly that Midge ought to point out that she knew that she would have no chance if someone attacked her. Midge had felt uncomfortable with such an obvious plea for sympathy. She did not like references to her leg and for her to force it upon the attention of the jury seemed not quite straight. Dickie had suggested that she talk about her concern for Jenny and Mr Fletcher, while Ronald had offered the idea of the need to serve abstract justice. All these suggestions flitted through Midge's mind, but in the end she stated quite simply,

"I was scared because I could never forget that someone had already been murdered there."

There was a small, still hush in the courtroom as Midge's words conjured up the fear which she had felt. And, as Sir Everard indicated that he was finished with her, every eye in the court watched Midge as she limped painfully and slowly from the witness-box.

Chapter Forty-Six

After the high excitement of Midge's evidence, the comments of Mr Fletcher's bank manager were considered to be a devilishly dry affair. However, Midge was not there to hear him outline how the accused lived well within his means and did not appear to have any unexplained sources of income. Immediately Midge had finished her evidence, John bundled her out of the courtroom and into his car. At that point he insisted on her downing a decent amount of brandy from his hip-flask, before he speedily drove her back to Mr Carrington's flat. Once there, John carried her up the stairs, ignoring Midge's faint protest that she could walk. Much to her surprise, Mrs Carrington was waiting inside.

"What are you doing here, Aunt Alice?"

"I had no intention of hanging around at Brandon, waiting to discover what had happened. But I don't want to hear about it now – you look like you need a rest."

Midge nodded gratefully. Apart from seeking reassurance from John that she had performed reasonably well, she had not discussed the trial on the way back and she had no desire to go over the details now. The brandy had momentarily taken the grey look from her face, but she was so tired that she had started to shiver.

With Midge safely out of the way, John was able to tell Mrs Carrington what had taken place. Alice winced at the description of Hilliard's attack on her niece and seemed disposed to argue with John that prosecuting counsel had only been doing his job.

"Surely he could see that Midge is frail? Why didn't he take pity on her?"

John frowned. "I know that Midge is weak physically, but there's nothing wrong with her brain. The way in which she could think up those bizarre mnemonics demonstrated that all right." He gave an embarrassed laugh. "I tried to think how I'd disguise various names, but I couldn't come up with anything half as ingenious as she did."

"It sounds like a peculiarly demanding parlour game," agreed his mother. "But, more to the point, do you think that she was believed?"

"I don't know; I hope so."

"And how did you get on in Cambridge?" pursued Mrs Carrington.

John winced. "I told Father that female dons make me feel like a small boy caught stealing jam. Well, the Principal of Newnham made me feel like a small boy who had dared to deny that he'd stolen jam, even although he was caught in the pantry, with jam on his collar and fingers."

"You never stole jam," interjected his mother, offended at such a thought.

"That's as may be," replied John with feeling, "but Miss Lytton appears to have mistaken her profession – she could cross-examine just as well as Sir Reginald Hilliard, K.C."

"And?"

"The upshot is that, since Midge was summoned to be a witness, she cannot be held responsible for missing the first week of term, but she can be expected to have done her vacation reading and is expected to return to all her lectures and supervisions immediately the trial ends."

"But Midge is exhausted!" protested Mrs Carrington. "She looked positively ill when she came in."

"She looked worse as she left the Old Bailey," grunted John. He flung up his hands. "I'll help her as much as I can, but a lot will depend on how her supervisors react. In fact, I thought I saw one of them tucked away at the back of the courtroom." He laughed bitterly. "Miss Harlington's specialist field is Greek forensic oratory, so I hope she enjoyed herself."

Meanwhile, as Midge's cousin and aunt discussed whether she still had a future at Cambridge and as Midge herself slept the sleep of the dead, in the dock Mr Fletcher's feelings were momentarily raised. Could there be a glimpse of hope? Might Midge's evidence help sow doubt in the jury's minds that Forrest was not the innocent victim which he had been painted to be? Fletcher firmly suppressed these fledgling hopes. It was too dangerous to be optimistic – the jury would probably dismiss Midge's evidence as the deluded ravings of an over-imaginative bluestocking. Moreover, even although the evidence about a possible tax fraud sounded eminently believable, it was not necessarily enough to save him, not least because it would take some time for the police to trace the original invoices and compare them with the accounts at Forrest and Creech.

During the lunch-interval, Jenny succumbed to fears similar to those besieging her father. She hid them up as best she could, but she could not help remembering that there were very few days left in the trial; Midge had seemed to be an essential part of the defence case – what if she had not convinced the jury?

The afternoon session was taken up by the evidence of the refugee racket. Sir Everard, who was determined to ram home Professor Schulmann's credentials, began by reading out a long list of Schulmann's qualifications, before asking Schulmann about each individual qualification. This took some time and James, who was exercising his right as a member of the Bar to be present, reflected that if the jurors had been listening properly they ought to be wondering why Schulmann wasn't trying the case instead of Hawkroyd.

After he had fully set out Schulmann's legal experience,

Sir Everard asked the Professor what he knew about how money had been extorted from refugees. Schulmann carefully repeated the evidence which he had laid before Fletcher, explaining how there were a number of refugees who had bought false documents and were then blackmailed into regularly handing over money. Since this fitted in very well with Midge's evidence, Sir Everard was happy to let the Professor tell the story in his own way. At the end of the recital, the barrister turned to him.

"Finally, Professor Schulmann, could you explain why you approached Mr Fletcher for help in this matter? After all, with your legal experience, you know a great number of lawyers. Why did you ask my client to help you?"

"It is because Mr Fletcher possesses a reputation for scrupulous honesty and fairness that I approached him. The matter was very sensitive and I needed a man of great integrity."

"So, knowing him to be scrupulously honest and fair, do you believe the accusations which have been made against him?"

"Certainly not. I told him about the extortion which was being practised. Mr Fletcher spoke to Forrest because I asked him to."

"Thank you very much."

Hilliard rose to cross-examine.

"You are a friend of the accused?"

"That is so."

"And, naturally, you wish to help your friend?"

"I wish to help a man whom I believe to be innocent of the charge made against him."

"But, surely, the fact that you are his friend must make you more inclined to believe the protestations of the accused?"

"I believe him, because I know him to be a man most honourable and just." Professor Schulmann made a quaint little bow. "Indeed, it is precisely owing to my great esteem for Mr Fletcher's scrupulous honesty and fairness that we are friends." His eyes drifted over to where Jenny was sitting. "And it is my esteem for Mr Fletcher which has given me the honour to be introduced to Miss Fletcher, who is also devoting herself to the pursuit of justice."

Sensing that Schulmann was going to carry on repeating how much he respected the accused, Hilliard moved onto the subject of the refugees.

"You stated that a number of refugees were caught up in this so-called plot to extort money. How many of them have actually spoken to you about it?"

"Three."

"And did each of them claim to have suffered extortion?"

"No, one of them knew what was happening to his friend and alerted me to the problems. He was not himself being blackmailed."

"I see. This plot, with its wide ramifications, can only produce two apparent witnesses to extortion."

"The others are scared to come forward. They fear being sent back to Germany."

"Or perhaps the 'others' do not exist, any more than this plot exists."

"That is not so."

"Then let us turn to one witness who has come forward – Herr Elsner. He has two children, has he not?"

"Yes."

"And you visited the children at the house of the accused?"

"Yes."

"They stayed the night there?"

"Yes – because I asked Miss Fletcher to let them stay. You must understand, Sir Reginald, that they are young and easily frightened."

"You asked Miss Fletcher to help you. I see. Did you also ask Herr Elsner to help you?"

"I was trying to help him."

"Let me make myself quite clear, Professor Schulmann. Did you ask Herr Elsner to support your story that Forrest, the murder victim, had been extorting money from refugees?"

"I asked Herr Elsner to testify as to what he knew about Forrest. I did not ask him to make anything up."

"That was before Miss Fletcher came to the aid of his children?"

"Yes, but at no point did I ask or persuade Herr Elsner to supply an untrue version of events. And I categorically deny that Mr Fletcher asked me to arrange any false testimony. Mr Fletcher became involved with the refugees only because I approached him for help in dealing with Forrest. Mr Fletcher did not ask me."

Although Sir Everard used his re-examination to get Professor Schulmann to repeat his belief in Fletcher's probity, Jenny felt sick as she listened. It was clear what the prosecution were alleging, and she suspected that the jury agreed. After all, what had the defence to offer as an alternative?

Herr X was the next witness. Again, he set out testimony that far from extorting money from him, the accused had been doing his best to help him. However, when Hilliard rose to cross-examine him, it soon became apparent that prosecuting counsel intended to handle him more severely than Professor Schulmann.

"Currently, Herr Elsner, you have the status of a refugee?"

"Yes, Sir Reginald."

"But that status was granted on the basis of false papers?"

"Yes."

"So your status as a refugee may be revoked by the government?"

"Yes."

"And you have two children? Two little girls?"

"Yes."

"And how old are they?"

"Five and ten years old."

"Naturally, as a father, you must love them?"

"I love them very much."

"And you have told us very eloquently about what happened to their mother in Germany. You will forgive me for asking this, but their mother's death must mean that you are even more concerned that your two little girls stay in this country?"

"Yes."

"I am sure that the entire courtroom has sympathy for you and understands your fears. However, may I put it to you that you must have worried about the fact that you did not have a genuine right to remain in Britain? After all, if you did not have genuine refugee status, nor did your children."

"That is so."

"And you would, therefore, be very eager to ensure that they had the chance to gain genuine refugee status?"

"Yes."

"Because you love them and want them to be safe?"

"Yes."

"And in the last few days, have you received a guarantee that your children will be looked after by a British citizen if necessary?"

"Yes."

"And this guarantee applies even if you are no longer in this country?"

"Yes."

Hilliard turned to the judge. "M'lord, my final questions relate to a few points of fact in relation to where this witness's daughters have been recently. This witness was not actually present when the events took place, but he knows of them. Hence, with your lordship's permission, I should like to put my points to this witness." He sketched a bow in the direction of the defence, "Of course, if m'learned friend objects to a father answering for his daughters, I am happy to call the elder of the two children as a witness. It would not take her long to tell the court the details I seek, but I should prefer not to put the child through that sort of experience."

Hawkroyd glanced at the defence silk. "Sir Everard?"

Hiding his annoyance, Sir Everard indicated his acquiescence. "If it is a matter of two or three questions of fact, I do not object."

"Very well, Sir Reginald, you may proceed."

Hilliard bowed. "Thank you, m'lord." Then he turned back to the witness. "Herr Elsner, your daughters recently left where they had previously been living, did they not?"

"Yes."

"And they spent a night at the house of the accused?"

"Yes, but I did not know about it until afterwards. I was away. And they are not there now."

"But they spent a night there, after the trial had begun?"

"Yes."

"Finally, can you confirm that it is a Mr Carrington who has agreed to provide upkeep for your two little girls if necessary?"

"Yes."

Hilliard turned towards the jury. "You may have recognised the surname as being the same as that of Miss Carrington, who gave evidence earlier. Mr and Miss Carrington are cousins. And, like Miss Carrington, Mr

Carrington is a friend of Miss Fletcher." He turned back to the witness. "Thank you, Herr Elsner, for your evidence."

Elsner bowed and left.

The next defence witness was an elderly, bent man, who walked to the witness-box with considerable difficulty. After hearing Denys' explanation that the witness had recently been in a very bad accident, Mr Justice Hawkroyd readily gave permission that the witness might give his evidence while sitting down.

"You are Nathaniel Leon Lipinski?" began Denys.

"Yes."

"You are by nationality German?"

"I was. But I am a Jew, thus Germans say that I am not German."

"So you understand injustice?"

"Yes."

"And you fled to this country to escape injustice?"

"Yes."

"Because of the conditions within Germany, you were unable to come here legally?"

"Yes."

"So you were forced to come here without genuine papers?"

"Yes."

"But once you got here, you wished to acquire the right to stay here?"

"I did not want to go back. I knew that I would be killed. I was given the name of a man who would help me. He was Forrest – the man whom they say was murdered."

"Presumably, Forrest did not help you out of the goodness of his heart?"

"He asked for four hundred pounds."

"And did you give him it?"

"Yes. I had some property in France. I sold it."

Lipinski made a gesture with his hands. "When you have a choice between dying or living, wealth no longer seems important."

"Why did you not stay in France?"

"I know what happened in 1870 and in 1914. A line on a map will not keep Hitler out of France."

"So you came here to be safe?"

"That is so. And I am safe. I am grateful that this country believes in justice."

"You are highly educated, are you not? You have a degree?"

"I had the honour to study at Gottingen University."

"So you are not a stupid man, Mr Lipinski. But you must know that admitting to having bought false papers means that you may be sent back to Germany. Why have you come to this courtroom today to admit that you bought false papers from Forrest?"

"I know I may be sent back. And then I shall die. But this is a free country. It is not ruled by murderers. So I must serve justice in this, a just country." The old man shook his head, as if in disbelief. "Do I not know where injustice ends? My son is dead. My country, the country for which I fought as a loyal German, killed my son as a poisonous animal. Would I stand back and let this man be killed, too, when I knew that the accusations against him were untrue?"

In the silence which followed this statement, Jenny heard one of the jurors sob. For a moment her hopes rose; then she saw Sir Reginald get to his feet.

"Now, Herr Lipinski, you have clearly suffered considerably. However, you understand, do you not, that as part of our system of justice I must ask you some questions?"

"Yes. And I shall answer them."

"Very well. You say that you were told to hand over

four hundred pounds in order to gain false papers, do you not?"

"Yes."

"And you were not troubled again by demands for money?"

"No."

"Herr Elsner has claimed that he was made to pay a regular weekly sum. That did not happen to you?"

"No."

"And Herr Elsner has claimed that others were made to pay a regular weekly sum. So your case appears very different, does it not?"

"Perhaps."

"Indeed. Now, to turn to your own emotions, you obviously have sympathy for the accused; have you any sympathy for the dead man at the heart of this case?"

Lipinski hesitated and Sir Reginald pounced. "Do I take it that you have no sympathy for Forrest, even although he was murdered?"

"He threatened to send people back to be murdered if they did not pay him."

"I shall repeat my question. Did you have any sympathy for him?"

"No. How could I when I learned what he was doing?"

"You disapproved of it?"

"Of course."

"Did you think that he ought to be punished for it?"

Lipinski shrugged. "I could do nothing. To have reported him would have endangered people."

"Had it been possible to punish him without endangering anyone you would have been pleased?"

"I should have thought that justice had been done."

"So you would sympathise with whoever punished him?"

Lipinski suddenly scented a trap. "Not if they broke the

law to do so."

"The tragic death of your son must incline you even more towards wishing to punish those who have made refugees suffer, must it not?"

"You are implying that I have made up my evidence. You are suggesting that I want to help this man, the Herr Advokat, because I approve of the death of Forrest."

"I am implying nothing. I am merely asking questions. Do you wish those who have preyed upon refugees to be punished?"

"Yes, I do. Forrest was cruel and greedy. He did not care that people were desperate and fearful of death. He, too, deserved to suffer. But I would not create more injustice to see him suffer. As for my son..." Lipinski's voice broke. "As for my son, he is dead. He died through injustice. I thought that there was justice here. But this man is accused of something he did not do. He did not take money from me; he tried to help me. If he is convicted, then there is no longer any justice to be found in Europe."

Chapter Forty-Seven

After the proceedings halted for the day, Ronald came with Jenny to visit Midge. James had had to go back to chambers after lunch to prepare for a case in which he was appearing and, when Jenny saw how weary and drawn Midge looked, she was glad that there was one fewer person present to overwhelm Midge.

"Did I do all right this morning?" Midge asked Ronald hesitantly. John had tried to be reassuring, but he was not a barrister.

"Yes. You gave your evidence clearly; the jury ought to have had no difficulty following what you said and what you discovered."

Midge twisted her hands uncomfortably. "I wish I hadn't said that I was frightened. People will be bound to think that I was behaving inconsistently – one moment panicking and the next moment hunting around for peculiarities in the accounts."

"Rot," disagreed Ronald. "They'll be much more likely to believe you because you admitted to a human failing."

"It would have been very odd if you hadn't been frightened," pointed out Jenny.

"Why did Sir Reginald have to sneer about the invoices?" demanded Midge, before growling, "I don't see how not going to dances means that I'm a complete idiot who couldn't recognise crookery when it was rammed under my eyes to type."

"He was so busy trying to get in snide remarks about Newnham girls that he never stopped to think that you're reading Classics," declared John soothingly. "He probably doesn't know how steeped you are in lascivious emperors, treacherous counsellors and vengeful kings. Most witnesses aren't – unless they work for the Diplomatic Service. It gives you an unnatural advantage in spotting devilment."

Midge laughed ruefully. "Oh well, at least Hilliard didn't accuse me of being a woman of the night and the offspring of slaves foisted upon the citizenry as one of them."

"But," teased John, "if we carry on that Demosthenic vein, we must note that you more-or-less accused one of the leading K.C.s of the day of being a self-important ape."

"Don't remind me," begged Midge. "Honestly, Jenny, I'm really sorry about that, but I couldn't bear him suggesting that I made up my evidence so that I could show off in court."

"He was trying to make you lose your temper."

"I know, and I did. I hope I haven't harmed the case."

"I shouldn't think so," stated Ronald, thinking that there was no point Midge getting into a state about what was done and finished. "After all, you made him lose his temper too, and that harmed his case. Rancour never goes down well with a jury. They'll discount any good points he made because he was so obviously out to get you."

"He certainly won't get a good write-up in the *Universal Record*," stated John with repressed heat. Geoffrey Carrington had looked as if he wanted to strangle Sir Reginald during his sarcastic asides about Midge's life at Cambridge. John had no doubt that, without exerting undue influence, his father would ensure that in at least one paper Midge's evidence – rather than the personal exchanges between Sir Reginald and her – would be reported fairly.

"What happened this afternoon?" asked Midge.

"Professor Schulmann seemed credible," answered Jenny hesitantly. "Hilliard didn't try to browbeat him, but Herr X got pretty roughly handled." She winced. "Hilliard never actually accused him of perjury, but by the time he'd pointed out that the children spent the night at our house and that John has guaranteed their upkeep, it was obvious

397

what everyone must think. He even pointed out that John was your cousin."

"Ouch."

"Exactly." Jenny shrugged. "I suppose we knew what would happen, but it was pretty beastly all the same." She pulled a face. "If Herr X is sent back to Germany I'll never forgive myself, but what else could we do other than call him?"

"Don't forget," pointed out John gently, "that he could have disappeared if he'd wanted to. He must have decided it was worth the risk to testify."

"Precisely," agreed Ronald. "As for Lipinski, I don't think he cares what happens to him."

Midge glanced up in surprise. "He gave evidence? I thought he was terribly ill."

"He looked pretty ghastly," stated Jenny, "but he sounded very sincere. I hope..." Her voice tailed off.

"What was said about the attack upon him?" demanded Midge.

Ronald shook his head. "Nothing. Denys' junior counsel told me afterwards that Denys thought that it was far too dangerous to bring it up."

Midge sounded puzzled. "Why?"

"Because it would have been all too easy for Hilliard to suggest that Lipinski's sufferings had turned his brain. If he'd painted a picture of Lipinski thinking that everything was a conspiracy against him, how much credence would the jury have given to Lipinski's evidence?"

"That's not fair," protested Midge.

"But it so easily could be true," remarked Ronald soberly. "Honestly, Midge, you get some pretty queer types in the Old Bailey. You're too decent to know what can go on."

Midge blushed at this unexpected compliment. "I suppose if he'd talked about being attacked by a man with a beard, the jury might even have suspected poor Herr X of having been involved." She sighed. "I do wish that Sir Everard had let me talk about the dot by the chemist's name in the directory. It might have helped."

Ronald shook his head. "It was too much of a risk. I gather that Sutton sent some journalists up to check on Mr Z. Weaver and he denied all knowledge of aconitine. Imagine what would have happened if we'd raised the subject in court and we hadn't then called dear Zacharias. The prosecution could have poured scorn on all our other suggestions and said that they were just as untrue as our attempt to hound an inoffensive chemist into admitting to selling deadly poison when he can't even manage to sell toothpowder to the good citizens of Barnet."

Accepting that Ronald had a much better grasp of legal tactics than she did, Midge moved onto something which had been puzzling her.

"It said in the paper that Wynne stated that Forrest hardly ever took tea in the afternoon. Did he actually say that?"

Ronald nodded. "Yes."

Midge frowned. "Then he's lying. Davie told me that Forrest was always drinking tea, and that he liked toast and jam with it in the afternoon."

"Maybe Davie's lying," pointed out Jenny.

"But why?" argued Midge. "We were having an argument at the time." She sounded embarrassed. "I know he was trying to make a point about my leg, but I can't imagine he'd invent a detail like that."

"By God," declared Ronald forcefully, "I'd like to get my hands on the little brute."

Jenny was concentrating on this new evidence, rather than Davie's ill manners. "Presumably Wynne wanted to rule out the idea that Forrest was poisoned at his office. Does that mean that he's definitely the murderer?"

"Not necessarily," pointed out Midge. "I know it's horribly suspicious, but it's not proof." She sighed irritably. "The trouble is, even if we call Davie to give evidence, he's perfectly capable of lying – and that will just give Hilliard more opportunity to say that I'm a fantasist."

Jenny sat up. "Wynne has lied and Davie might lie, but what about the typists who left? Remember that one of them sounded as if she hadn't much enjoyed life at Forrest and Creech. Why would she lie to help out Wynne?"

Midge frowned. "Miss Hemming might lie because she's afraid of being accused of having poisoned Forrest. She was the person who made all the tea before I came." She gulped. "Or she might lie because she actually did kill Forrest. We've completely neglected her."

"All the more reason for asking her about Forrest's tea habits," declared Jenny. "If she agrees with Davie, then we'll have proof that Wynne's a liar. And if she agrees with Wynne, then we need to pay much more attention to her – or to Davie."

"Yes," agreed Ronald. "I certainly think that we should investigate the matter. It's certainly not enough on its own to overset the prosecution case, but it's a suggestive point."

"More than suggestive, surely?" demanded Jenny. "We'd finally have proof that Forrest could have been poisoned in his office and it will lessen Wynne's attacks on Midge if he's shown to have lied."

"Wynne will claim that he didn't know that Forrest took tea and toast in the afternoon," pointed out Midge gloomily.

"That would be unfortunate for him," remarked Ronald dryly. "He's already sworn on oath that he did know. Well spotted, Midge."

Chapter Forty-Eight

The next morning dawned dark and cold, with a bitter wind slicing through the wet streets and bringing slashing rain in its wake. Under normal circumstances, Midge would have turned over and gone back to sleep, but she had an idea she wanted to put into practice. Meanwhile, in her own home, Jenny was already pacing around her room, frightened as to what the day would bring. Sir Everard had warned Jenny the previous evening that he would begin by calling Mr Fletcher to give evidence.

"It won't be easy for you to sit there and listen to Hilliard cross-examining your father," he pointed out, "but I need you to be there, demonstrating your belief in him."

"Of course I shall be there," declared Jenny, before adding with a brave attempt at a smile, "and I shan't object whatever Hilliard says."

"Is your brother going to be present?"

"No."

"That may be no bad thing."

The suspicion of a blush mounted Jenny's cheeks. She knew that the barrister must have a low opinion of how her brother had performed. Nevertheless, she had no intention of telling Sir Everard that she had warned Mike that he had not helped the case and that it might be better if the jury did not see him again.

Despite Jenny's determination not to show any emotion, she found it extremely difficult to contain herself as her father stepped forward to give his evidence. Patrick Fletcher was an austere, distinguished-looking man with fine features, but his daughter could discern new lines on his face and the strain about his eyes. She consoled herself that no-one on the jury would know that he looked any different from usual, and forced herself to concentrate on what was being said. Denys began by asking Fletcher to answer again the grave charge which lay against him.

"Are you guilty of this crime?"

"No," replied Fletcher firmly.

"Were you guilty of attempting to blackmail William Forrest?"

"No."

"What is the true explanation of the allegations contained in the dead man's letter?"

Fletcher instinctively tried to hitch his gown up round his shoulders, before realising that he was the witness, not the advocate. Despite this momentary mistake, his voice was clear as he addressed the jury. "Each allegation is wrong. Far from Forrest approaching me to seek advice and then falling foul of a wicked blackmailer, Forrest was a man of distinctly dubious antecedents who used his contacts with vulnerable refugees to attempt to bleed them dry.

"Let me take the allegations in turn. First, he did not seek me out; I summoned him to answer the extremely serious accusations which Professor Schulmann had passed on to me. Secondly, Forrest had no interest in protecting the innocent as he alleged. He did not supply false papers to Herr Elsner out of compassion; he supplied them so that he might later demand money with menaces. Thirdly, the demand which I made of Forrest was not that he give me money – I should have scorned to touch it – but that he desist from his despicable extortion. Finally, the only warning which I issued was that I should do my best to collect enough evidence to prosecute Forrest and send him to gaol for persecuting the victims of tyranny and oppression."

"So would you say that Forrest's letter was a distortion of the truth?"

"It was a pack of out and out lies."

"And the other letters discovered after his death, which

purported to be copies of letters to you?"

"Another pack of lies, invented to make Forrest's spurious claims sound more convincing."

Denys took Fletcher through various other points, including his finances and that he had at no point ever purchased aconitine or any other poison. All this took some time, but eventually it was the turn of Hilliard to attempt to undermine the good impression which Fletcher had created. Sir Reginald, who had often seen the advocate in action in court, had no intention of underestimating Fletcher's ability and he had decided to use that very ability to the prosecution's advantage. If he could emphasise the fact that Fletcher was utterly at home in the Old Bailey, then the jury would be less inclined to trust the accused's apparently open and decent manner. However, Hilliard's first question showed no indication of this plan.

"Did you dislike William Forrest?"

Fletcher had no desire to hide behind mealy-mouthed half-truths, even if they might have been temporarily successful.

"I thought the man a bloodsucking parasite."

"That is very emotive language, but, of course, you are a very experienced courtroom performer."

Listening anxiously, Jenny suppressed a groan. Even the choice of the word 'performer' suggested that her father was acting out a lie and could manipulate his hearers at will.

"I can assure you that this is positively my first appearance as a witness."

Hilliard allowed a dry smile to break out. "That answer rather demonstrates what I meant, Mr Fletcher. You are a very experienced practitioner in court, although – naturally – as a barrister in the past, not as the accused."

Fletcher waited.

"Do you not agree?" demanded Hilliard.

"I am sorry; I was not aware that you had asked me a question."

"I had, so please answer it."

"Of course," replied Fletcher courteously. "I am indeed experienced – I believe that I was called to the Bar five years after you were yourself, Sir Reginald."

Despite the circumstances, Ronald smiled. His head of chambers had delicately reminded the court that not only was counsel for the prosecution more experienced, but that he had even been knighted for his services to the legal profession.

"Let us now turn to your children and the expenses which you bear because of them."

"Two of my children, sir," returned Fletcher coldly, "are currently in the Army serving their country, and my third child is studying law, with the aim of serving Justice. Not one of them makes demands which my income cannot withstand, and not one of them is a criminal."

Although Hilliard considered that the jury were unlikely to believe the alleged motive of impecuniousness brought on by – as yet untraced – demands on Fletcher's purse, he also knew that the Crown had to suggest some reason for why the barrister had suddenly taken to blackmail. Hence he returned to Mike's unfortunate comments about losses at cards.

"Your son has admitted to the fact that you have several times paid his gambling debts. Is your daughter also inclined to such activities?"

"Certainly not," snapped Fletcher, feeling that there was no need to inform the court that he had warned Jenny that he would halve her allowance if she ever acquired gambling debts.

"So you have never paid gambling debts for your daughter?"

"No."

"And what about your other son? Does he also regard gambling in the mess as natural, and ten pounds as a low stake?"

"I have no idea; I have never discussed the matter with him. Currently my conversations with Tom consist entirely of how to improve tank engines, how tanks can be designed to cross rough ground and why this country needs to build more tanks." Fletcher paused. "He wants to serve in a tank regiment, you see."

"I think that we might have gathered that," replied Hilliard, somewhat sarcastically, before returning to the attack. "So, your second son does not outrun his substantial allowance?"

"No."

"And he does not put you to any other extra costs in addition to his allowance?"

The legal experts guessed that Hilliard was fishing in the hope of discovering debts other than gambling ones – perhaps even a paternity suit. What they were not expecting was Fletcher's mordant reply. "As I am not in the position to buy him a tank, no."

"Perhaps we might move off the subject of tanks, important though they are to the country," suggested Mr Justice Hawkroyd, much to the delight of the reporter for the *Daily Post*, who saw the opportunity to write an additional column entitled 'Murder-Case Judge Calls for More Tanks'.

"As your lordship pleases," bowed Sir Reginald. "If we return to the day on which William Forrest died, the typist, Miss Ellis, said that he was mannerless and irritable when she brought in the tea. I put it to you that his worried state of mind was directly owing to your threats."

Patrick Fletcher shrugged his shoulders. "Given that Miss Ellis had said that he was irritable even before he had met me, I find that somewhat hard to believe." He half-turned to the jury, before explaining courteously. "Miss Ellis stated that Forrest was snappy and inclined to blame her for the fact that he was late for his appointment."

"Thank you," snapped Hilliard himself, cross that Fletcher had reminded the jury of that particular piece of evidence. "However, she also said that he was mannerless in the middle of his meeting with you. Surely that suggests that – just as he wrote in his letter to the police – you had threatened him?"

"Quite possibly," agreed Forrest placidly. "Don't forget that, as I said earlier, I had summoned Forrest to see me so that I might investigate the grave allegations which had been laid against him. I should have been surprised if he had given the impression of being pleased with life after being accused of extortion."

"Or, equally, if you had been threatening him?"

"I told him that I intended to prosecute him and to inform the police of his activities. Is that a threat?"

Sir Reginald preferred not to answer this query and instead turned towards the question of Midge's reliability as a witness.

"I gather that Miss Carrington is a friend of your daughter from their mutual schooldays. How long has she known your daughter?"

"My lord, I fail to see the relevance of this questioning," intervened Sir Everard, who could see exactly what Sir Reginald was intending to suggest.

"I am inclined to agree with you, Sir Everard," remarked the judge.

"As your lordship pleases," stated Sir Reginald, with a brief bow. Perhaps I might ask whether the accused has known Miss Carrington long?"

Mr Justice Hawkroyd allowed this version of learned counsel's earlier question.

Fletcher made a brief calculation. "The first time I met

her was when she came to stay with my daughter six years ago."

"So, naturally, as an old friend of your daughter, she will be inclined to do anything to support her friend and to help you?"

"Both Miss Carrington and my daughter have a high regard for the principles of justice. Neither would pervert the course of justice."

"However, is it not the case that some young women who have gained a smattering of knowledge develop rather strange ideas, ones which are often very much at odds with the straightforward principles which the jury will understand?"

"I can't claim to be an expert on young women, but I've never regarded Miss Carrington as being odd. Or do you think that attending a Cambridge college – say, for example, Caius – is inclined to lead to people developing rather strange ideas?"

Since Gonville and Caius had the honour to be Sir Reginald Hilliard's alma mater, this was a retort which he chose to ignore. Meanwhile, tucked away at the back of the court, Midge's supervisor, Miss Harlington, had been bristling at the idea that any Newnham gel gained only a smattering of knowledge. However, she found her anger being soothed at this evidence of sound thinking on the part of the accused. She herself had always had grave suspicions of the calibre of the Caius dons, let alone the specimens which that particular college fondly designated 'students'. A short mental excursus into whether the accused was carrying out the equivalent of an Athenian defendant deliberately attempting to attack one geographical region of the city-state in the hope of endearing himself to residents of all other demes, distracted Midge's supervisor for several minutes. When she returned from the glories of classical oratory to the concerns of the present, she discovered with some annoyance that she had missed the final questions from prosecuting counsel. The evidence of the accused was now complete and the judge chose that moment to call a recess for lunch.

Chapter Forty-Nine

While Fletcher was giving evidence, Midge had been busy. First, she had gone to Barnet, where she had spoken to Weaver. She knew that, since her discovery of his name, the chemist had been pestered by journalists asking to see his poison book and demanding to know how often he sold various poisons. Moreover, the crime reporter, Sutton, had told the defence that Weaver's denials were becoming increasingly weak. Hence Midge hoped that, if she were very lucky, she might just be able to persuade Weaver to give evidence.

Midge was aware that witnesses were not meant to discuss a case amongst themselves and that the prosecution could make much of it if they found out that she had approached Weaver. However, she consoled herself that she could always argue that Weaver had not yet been called as a witness when she spoke to him. In fact, she was actively aiding justice by encouraging him to come forward. For his part, Weaver showed no pleasure at the thought of aiding justice. Once Midge started speaking to him about the case, he tried to bundle her out of the shop. A woman appeared from behind the curtain.

"Whatever are you doing, Zacharias?"

Weaver halted. "Oh. There you are, my dear."

Mrs Weaver seemed uninterested in this obvious statement. "Who is this young woman?"

"She's pestering me."

Midge intervened. "I apologise for interrupting you, Mrs Weaver, but I wanted to tell your husband how important it is to give evidence if he knows anything about the Fletcher case."

Mrs Weaver eyed Midge thoughtfully. "You're Miss Carrington, aren't you?"

Midge nodded. She knew how Mrs Weaver had

guessed – one of the papers had seen fit to describe her appearance and there couldn't be many girls on sticks who went around asking about aconitine. "Yes, I am. Please, Mrs Weaver, if your husband did sell aconitine, it is vital that he tells the court as soon as possible. He could save an innocent man's life."

"I wouldn't be believed," protested Weaver feebly.

"You would."

"Then I'd end up in trouble. I could lose my licence as an apothecary."

"But if you don't give evidence a man could lose his life," Midge pleaded. "You would be a hero if you saved him."

"Never mind heroes," remarked Mrs Weaver with a distinct snort. "If you could risk standing up in court and being laughed at, I don't see why my husband can't. He's a man, after all."

"I know nothing about any sale of aconitine," argued Weaver. "I don't see why I should get dragged into court to talk about it. Leave me alone."

Realising that she had an ally, Midge turned to the woman. "Mrs Weaver, I beg you to help me. Your husband's evidence is vital. The trial is nearly over – if he doesn't give evidence today, it may be too late." With that, she left the shop. A glance backwards showed that the couple were arguing. Midge judged that Mrs Weaver was the stronger of the pair. Would she persuade Weaver to give evidence?

When she had returned to central London, Midge put the Weavers out of her mind. What she intended to do next was far more demanding than talking to a harmless apothecary and she blessed the fact that her uncle had arranged for her to have a journalist guarding her. Beckoning today's bodyguard, Midge explained her intentions.

"I have to go into this building. I know that until now you've kept out of sight, but I want you to come in with me." She swallowed. "I may have to speak to someone on my own, but I'll be much safer if you are in the building, too."

Richards glanced at her, wondering what she was planning to do. "Are you sure?"

"Yes."

Pulling herself together, Midge mounted the steps of Duke's Buildings and pushed open the door of Forrest and Creech.

Davie appeared in the corridor to greet the visitor. When he saw who it was, his eyes bulged. "What are you doing here?"

"I've come to have a word with someone."

"You've got a nerve." Davie's eyes travelled beyond Midge to the reporter. "Who's he?"

"Someone who will see that nothing happens to me."

Davie seemed lost for words, but his glance in the direction of Wynne's office was eloquent. Ignoring the office-boy, Midge went up the corridor. Having signalled to the reporter to wait behind, she opened the door and entered. After closing the door, she turned to the occupant.

"When did you take in the tea, Miss Hurst?"

Unlike Davie, the secretary showed no consternation.

"Well, Miss Carew, what a surprise. Have you decided you want your job back?"

Midge ignored this pleasantry. "You took in the tea, didn't you? It was laced with aconitine. It must have been you."

"I don't know what you are talking about."

"Wynne said that Forrest didn't take tea in the afternoon. That was a lie. He did. He always had tea. He had it with toast and jam. And that was what poisoned

411

him."

"My dear Mary, what an imagination you possess."

"Forrest would have been suspicious if Wynne or Creech had brought in the tea. It's not a man's job. Even Davie objects to doing it. But Forrest would never have questioned a woman doing it."

"And why should I have poisoned Forrest?"

"Because the refugee racket had been uncovered. Because any investigation of that would lead to the tax fraud being uncovered. Because you were probably involved in both."

Miss Hurst surveyed Midge thoughtfully. "And do you possess evidence to substantiate such an interesting accusation?"

"Do you think that Wynne will protect you?" demanded Midge, who was all too aware that she possessed no evidence of the secretary's complicity. "He doesn't like you. He'll never wriggle out of the tax fraud. And his bank accounts are being investigated – as are Creech's."

"Yes, you appear to have dreamed up some account which you found under his desk. How very creative you are, Mary Carew."

"I'm not creative," retorted Midge. "I'm telling the truth."

"And you have come in here to accuse me of being a murderess. How very brave – or foolish – of you."

"I have a well-built journalist waiting for me in the corridor and another three outside."

Miss Hurst gave a dry laugh. "I rather doubt that there are four. One, perhaps, but not four."

Midge flushed and opened the door so that the secretary could see Richards in the corridor. "There's one of them." She closed the door.

Miss Hurst nodded her agreement. "Yes, you have a

guard-dog with you. Perhaps you might tell me what I am meant to do at this point?"

"You could answer my original question – when did you take in the tea?"

"Really, Mary, you must know that I am very busy. I don't have time for this sort of nonsense. I should be grateful if you would leave now before I get seriously annoyed."

"The next people to come asking you that question will be the police, and they will insist on it being answered."

"Indeed? I shall have the same reply to give them."

Feeling as if Miss Hurst had scored all the points in the interview, Midge retreated reluctantly. Once back outside, she turned to the reporter.

"I need to get back to court as soon as possible to give a note to Sir Everard." She gulped. "I've just spoken to a murderess. I don't know if I've ruined the chances of the defence by telling her that I suspect her."

Back at the Old Bailey, Sir Everard felt that Fletcher had given his evidence well. Nonetheless, he still feared that the jury might side with the prosecution; most people automatically assumed that the police would not arrest an innocent man. Moreover, whilst Midge's evidence was useful for suggesting that the dead man had been an unpleasant type involved in criminal activities, there was always a danger that the jury would discount this. If they decided that, no matter whether Forrest had been a scoundrel, Fletcher had killed him, then Fletcher would hang. However, when defence counsel rose after lunch to begin his closing speech, there was nothing in his manner which indicated concern. Instead, he had chosen to tackle the most damaging aspects of the case first.

"Members of the jury, you have now heard the arguments and witnesses for both prosecution and defence.

It is sometimes easy to become confused by the various claims and counterclaims which are put forward in a long court-case such as this and I shall do my best to set out the facts as clearly and concisely as possible."

The press watched with cynical amusement as several members of the jury appeared pleased with this consideration on the part of learned counsel. Naturally, Denys would want to appear reasonable and helpful, but that would not stop him from twisting his arguments round or from selecting the facts most supportive to his case and ignoring or dismissing the more damaging revelations of the prosecution's case.

"The prosecution's case is very clear. One, that my client attempted to blackmail William Forrest and two, that before even waiting to discover whether Forrest would pay this blackmail, my client poisoned Forrest. It is an ingenious argument, but the truth is that the police case against my client was flawed from the start. One feels that m'learned friend has got so used to dealing with petty criminals and cheap crooks that he has forgotten that the inhabitants of Middle Temple are honourable men, dedicated to the pursuit of justice. How likely is it that a man of Mr Fletcher's eminence would stoop to blackmail? Would I? Would Sir Reginald Hilliard?"

A quick glance at Mr Justice Hawkroyd's face warned Sir Everard not to suggest that the noble judge might also be as likely to stoop to blackmail as Patrick Fletcher. Learned counsel moved swiftly on.

"Moreover, in the midst of all these allegations of Mr Fletcher's amateur attempts at extortion, it seems that the prosecution has forgotten that we have clear evidence of blackmail – but from Forrest, not my client. We have heard the evidence of the highly-respected and eminent jurist, Professor Schulmann. In it, he quite clearly stated that it was he who alerted Mr Fletcher to the fact that Forrest was a scoundrelly blackmailer. And it was Professor Schulmann who asked Mr Fletcher for help to put an end to Forrest's wicked trade. How likely is it that my client would try to blackmail Forrest, when Forrest's days as a blackmailer were already numbered? To put it brutally, any attempt to blackmail Forrest was pointless: why blackmail someone whose source of revenue would soon dry up? Moreover, we have heard further evidence from two refugees who were victims of William Forrest. Their statements confirm the evidence of both Mr Fletcher and Professor Schulmann. Again, this evidence suggests that it would be highly unlikely that Mr Fletcher, a man of justice and integrity, would change the habits of a lifetime and resort to sordid money-grubbing and extortion; extortion, furthermore, which had every likelihood of failure.

"As you will now be well aware, William Forrest died from ingesting a fatal dose of aconitine. I shall have more to say about when the poison was administered and how it may have been administered. However, before I reach that stage, I should ask you to consider the following point: there is no evidence that Patrick Fletcher had any access to poison. The police searched his room; they found nothing. The police searched his chambers; they found nothing. Finally, the police searched his house; but still they found nothing. Despite their best efforts, both police and prosecution have singularly failed to show that Mr Fletcher bought aconitine; they have failed to show that Mr Fletcher administered aconitine; and they have failed to show that Mr Fletcher had any need to poison the dead man.

"What is the solution to this conundrum? As you have heard witnesses explain, it was Forrest who had cause to fear Patrick Fletcher, rather than Fletcher who was afraid of Forrest. It was Forrest who feared being reported to the police; it was Forrest who feared ending up being prosecuted for blackmail; it was Forrest who had the motive for murder. Surely it is more likely that Forrest would attempt to murder my client than that my client would poison a man who was already suspected of criminality. This is certainly one solution – Forrest attempted to murder the man who would bring him to justice but, in his worry and excitement, he muddled the poisoned teacups and drank the fatal dose himself. As I say, that is one solution. However, is not self-murder the most likely explanation of William Forrest's death? He faced exposure as a blackmailer who latched on to helpless, desperate refugees. He faced prosecution and professional disgrace. Overcome by fear for the future, might he have seen only one way out – to kill himself?"

A rustling in the court suggested that there were a number of people who were taken with this idea. As Sir Everard had appreciated, although he might point out every inconsistency in the prosecution argument, the problem remained – Forrest was dead; who, apart than Fletcher, might have killed him?

"Other evidence which has been presented to you," continued the barrister, "shows that Forrest was leading a double life. Apparently he was a clever, if not especially scrupulous, solicitor but, underneath this guise, there was also a crook who avoided paying tax and who sold naturalisation permits for money."

Sir Reginald rose at this point. "M'lord, it has not been proved that the dead man sold naturalisation permits," he protested. "Nor has it been proved that Forrest was involved in tax evasion."

"I defer to m'learned friend," replied Sir Everard graciously. "I am afraid that I attempted to simplify the situation for the benefit of the jury. I should, of course, have stated that the office of Forrest and Creech is currently being searched by the police who are looking for evidence of tax evasion and that we have heard from witnesses that they obtained false papers of naturalisation from the dead man, who then proceeded to demand payment for these papers."

No-one in court felt that Sir Reginald had come off better in this exchange. Counsel for the defence smiled pleasantly at the jury, before turning to the question of Midge's evidence.

"Part of the reason that the defence has such a clear picture of the, ah, unusual arrangements at the firm of Forrest and Creech is owing to the generous and brave efforts of Miss Carrington. You have heard the prosecution imply that because Miss Carrington is an undergraduate at Cambridge this means that she could neither be a competent typist nor a reliable witness as to what went on in the office in which she worked. You might bear in mind that very few businesses keep bad secretaries on and, indeed, you heard the witness' own fears that she might have lost her job after a week if she were not of sufficient calibre. You have also heard her fears that the Cambridge authorities might send her down for working during the vacation and the – rather more terrifying – fears that she was working with a murderer. She explained that she undertook this potentially dangerous action because she and her friend, the daughter of the accused, could see no other way by which they could find evidence to prove that Patrick Fletcher is quite innocent of the heinous crime of which he stands accused. Far from being unreliable, I would suggest that Miss Carrington is both competent and loyal.

"Moreover, Miss Carrington's evidence is very important testimony to the fact that the dead man, William Forrest, was mixed up in criminality firmly located in his office, not the chambers of Patrick Fletcher. It is through Miss Carrington's quick-thinking under pressure that we have such a wealth of valuable and suggestive evidence.

The prosecution have stated that so far the police have not found evidence of a deliberate attempt to defraud the Revenue by the issuing of false accounts. However, I ask you – as plain men and women – what other interpretation can there be of what Miss Carrington saw? What was charged in invoices was not being recorded in the account books. And finally, I should ask you to remember how easy it would be for someone to destroy any compromising files. As Miss Carrington pointed out, there are plenty of hearths in Duke's Buildings – what easier than to consign such papers to the all-consuming flames?"

The listening journalists sensed that this must be the crux of the defence case – not that Forrest killed himself, but that he had been murdered by someone else who was involved in the tax fraud. Was Denys about to name an alternative suspect?

"I turn now to the medical evidence," declared Sir Everard. "Dr Brook, the police pathologist, very fairly admitted on cross-examination that the deceased could have drunk more tea some time after he had left Mr Fletcher's chambers. Indeed, you may remember that I raised the fact that the tea which was found in Forrest's stomach contents would be very unlikely to be that tea which was drunk at half past three that afternoon."

Learned counsel coughed. "I hesitate to embarrass you, ladies and gentleman of the jury, but a man's life is a stake. If you give a moment's thought to what happens to you when you take afternoon tea, you will see my point. A call of nature is bound to occur long before seven or eight o'clock. Forrest died with at least a cup of tea in his stomach; where did he drink that tea? Where else than in the very office building where he worked?"

A shiver ran through Midge, who had returned in time to observe the afternoon session. Somehow, Sir Everard's dispassionate tones as he built up the defence case, point by point, made her all the more conscious that she had spent hours and days in the company of a murderer.

"Let me now turn to the letter which Forrest sent to Scotland Yard. You have already heard how the contents are totally at odds with what witness after witness has sworn. Indeed, I cannot improve upon the words of Mr Fletcher who described the allegations contained within it as 'a pack of lies'. However, what I should like to direct your attention to is the question of when this letter was posted. The letter arrived at Scotland Yard on the following day, so it could not have been posted before six o'clock on the night of the death of the deceased. If it had been, it would have been delivered that evening to Scotland Yard. However, you have heard evidence from Miss Carrington as to the office routine. All letters from Forrest and Creech are taken to the nearest pillar-box in time to catch the six o'clock collection. Then the office staff are free to go home and – apart from Mr Wynne, the clerk – they have all sworn that they departed as normal before six o'clock that night. So who was it who posted Forrest's final letter? Forrest himself could not have done so because by six o'clock he had retreated to his room complaining of feeling unwell. He locked the door and did not emerge again. By the time nine o'clock struck, P.C. Roberts and Mr Wynne had broken down the door and discovered Forrest curled up by his desk, contorted in his death agony. Clearly Forrest did not post the letter, but how did it emerge from a locked room and become placed in a pillar-box?"

Sir Everard had predicted correctly that the journalists would seize with gusto upon this tantalising conundrum. They were scribbling furiously and Mr Justice Hawkroyd had to call for order as whispered speculation erupted throughout the packed court. However, counsel for the defence also knew that the jury would dislike such unresolved problems, so he proceeded to suggest an explanation.

"Now, ladies and gentlemen of the jury, locked-room mysteries are all very well in books, where they belong, but you will want to know how this letter – the sole piece of evidence around which the prosecution has built its entire case – reached its destination. Naturally, it did not grow wings and fly, nor was it thrown out of the window in a last desperate lurch by Forrest before he collapsed. Nor, according to Wynne's evidence, did Wynne pick it up and post it. Therefore, the only way in which it might reach a pillar-box is if someone entered the room whilst Forrest lay dead or dying, collected the letter and then posted it. There is nothing fanciful about this solution – all it would take to achieve is a bunch of keys. Moreover, given that no-one has, as yet, admitted taking a cup of tea to Forrest, is it not likely that the person who brought that cup of tea also later crept silently into Forrest's room, ignoring the agonised appeal in his eyes, snatched the letter and retreated as silently as they came? A shadowy figure, who has not yet attracted attention, but one who had reason to strike Forrest down and who attempted to cause the finger of suspicion to point at an innocent man."

This time, the judge allowed a few moments of commotion before he restored order.

"Are you making a specific accusation, Sir Everard?"

"Not yet, m'lord; I am exploring possibilities which appear to have been scandalously neglected so far."

"Then perhaps I might remind you to observe the rules of evidence."

"As your lordship pleases."

Counsel for the defence returned to his speech, but more than one person noted that he now appeared to be playing for time. Dickie, observing with a professional eye, frowned slightly. Why should Denys want to delay matters?

Surely he would have been better keeping his suggestions about a mysterious assassin until the following day? That way the jury would retire for their deliberations full of speculations that one of the other members of Duke's Buildings had killed Forrest. If they were left to consider the matter over the evening they might start to notice that Denys had woven a wondrous web of suspicion from very few facts.

About twenty minutes later, a court official could be seen to enter, bow hastily towards where the judge sat and then pass a small slip of paper to Denys' junior counsel. Wolsey unfolded it, allowed a triumphant smile to spread over his face and then handed the note to Sir Everard. Defence counsel brought his rolling sentence to an end, before turning to the judge.

"M'lord, I have just learned that, outside the courtroom, this very minute, is the chemist who sold aconitine three days before the death of William Forrest. Will you allow him to come and tell the court what he knows?"

Chapter Fifty

The packed spectators in the courtroom craned forward as one. Would the judge allow this surprise witness to give evidence, even although counsel for the defence had already begun his final speech? Mr Justice Hawkroyd added to the tension by deliberating for several moments. Finally, he spoke.

"You say that this witness is prepared to state that he sold aconitine several days before Forrest died. I agree that this might be more than coincidence, but, equally, it might be just that: coincidence."

Seeing that the noble judge was not disposed to admit this new witness at a most unorthodox point in the trial, Denys revealed a little more.

"I agree, m'lord, that the appearance of the witness might indeed be coincidence, but for one point. In a telephone directory at the office of the dead man, a pencil-mark was found next to the name of this chemist."

Sir Everard attempted to keep speaking over the uproar which erupted, but was forced to wait until the noise had died down somewhat before he could continue. "I am sure that Miss Carrington would be happy to resume the witness stand and to give oath to the effect that she saw the mark against the name of Mr Weaver. Moreover, she wrote down the name of this chemist in the presence of two of my legal colleagues who witnessed it, before signing and sealing the envelope in which her statement is enclosed. It is that envelope, m'lord, which I requested that you might keep in case it was necessary to prove that Miss Carrington had indeed alerted me to the existence of Mr Weaver."

Mr Justice Hawkroyd frowned thoughtfully. It was true that Denys had indeed carried out such an unconventional move, and it was true that counsel had also explained that he felt that the evidence it contained was too speculative to be called in open court, but might prove to be valuable if circumstances changed. The judge inclined his head. "Let Mr Weaver be called."

Considering the sensation which the announcement of the chemist's existence had caused, his actual appearance was felt by most of those present to be something of a let-down. The small, rather threadbare little man shuffled forward and peered myopically at the Bible on which he swore to tell the truth, the whole truth, and nothing but the truth.

"Do I understand that you have important evidence to give the court?" asked the judge, who wanted to establish some facts before Denys was let loose to do what he liked with this unexpected witness.

The little man bobbed his head nervously. "Yes, your honour."

"You have a chemist's shop in Barnet?"

"Yes, your honour."

"And you believe that you may have sold the poison which was used to kill William Forrest, of Forrest and Creech?"

"Yes, sir."

"What poison is this and when did you sell it?"

"It was aconitine and I sold it three days before this Mr Forrest died."

"Indeed. And why, when there was considerable publicity in all of the newspapers about Forrest's death, have you only now chosen to come forward?"

Weaver wriggled uncomfortably. He had known that it would end like this. Why had his wife listened to that wretched girl?

"Well?" demanded the judge curtly, hoping that this man did indeed have something valuable to offer. Whilst he, Hawkroyd, would, naturally, do his duty if Fletcher were found guilty, he would greatly prefer not to have to place the black cap over his snowy wig and pronounce sentence of death upon a man who was widely respected as an able and dedicated barrister.

"Well?" repeated Mr Justice Hawkroyd.

"There's been a lot in the papers about the trial and I thought that it might be important."

"That does not explain why you did not come forward before. Were you unaware that the police had asked chemists to check their poison books and notify any sales of aconitine?"

Weaver gulped. "The thing is, your honour, I couldn't check my poison book."

Hawkroyd's face grew stern. "Were you not keeping it properly?"

"I was, sir," protested Weaver. "But... but...," he faltered, "it went missing."

"Missing?"

"It disappeared."

"What do you mean by that?"

Now that Weaver had admitted the worst part, it was easier for him to stumble out the rest of his story. "I did keep the book properly and the purchaser signed the book, just as is laid down, but a few days afterwards the book went missing."

"So, despite the fact that you knew that the police were looking for sales of aconitine and despite the fact that your poison book went missing, you did not consider either of these facts of sufficient importance – or, indeed, sufficiently suspicious – to alert the police? You appear to be very lacking in public spirit, Mr Weaver."

"I didn't think that they would believe me," mumbled the hapless chemist.

"Perhaps, now that you have finally remembered your duty, you might tell the court what else you remember about this sale of aconitine."

"It was a rainy night and I was about to close up the shop when I heard the door open and someone entered, all bundled up in a mackintosh and hat. I served the customer, asked for a signature in the poison book and made up the aconitine."

"This was definitely three days before the death of William Forrest?"

"I think so. Three or perhaps four. It was definitely several days before his death was reported in the newspapers."

"And when did the poison book disappear?"

"I'm not exactly sure."

The judge sighed, wondering how so inaccurate a man could manage to run a business. Perhaps his vacuity explained his general air of shabbiness.

"What were the circumstances of the disappearance – or do you not remember that, either?"

"I do," protested Weaver, stung by the judge's tone. "We've just started a new line in toilet water which my wife was hoping would attract more customers.

"Was anyone else serving in the shop at the time?"

"No; we're quite small, so normally I serve or my wife does."

"Go on."

"The customer asked for a large bottle of the lily-of-the-valley toilet-water. I hadn't finished unpacking everything, so I had to go into the back room to find a bottle. I didn't notice anything odd when I wrapped up the bottle, but when I needed the poison book later on that day, I couldn't find it. I thought that it must have been misplaced, but it didn't turn up again."

It was abundantly clear to everyone exactly why the chemist had not wanted to report matters to the police. Weaver must have delayed and delayed, expecting to find the poison book tucked behind a carton of liver salts or hidden underneath some proprietary medicines. First incompetence, and then concern lest he be reprimanded for carelessness had kept him quiet.

Meanwhile, the judge was satisfied that Weaver could indeed have sold the fatal aconitine, and indicated to Sir Everard that he might question the witness.

"Naturally, we are all very grateful to you for coming forward with your unexpected and important story," stated Denys. "You may, indeed, be said to be in a position to supply the missing link in a baffling murder case."

Weaver looked up gratefully. It seemed that at least one person in the court did not regard him with contempt.

"Can you give a description of the customer who bought the aconitine?" enquired Sir Everard. "Perhaps you might start with hair-colour?"

"I don't have very good eyesight," apologised the chemist, rather weakly. "I didn't really notice. He – or she – looked quite average."

"He or she?" repeated counsel for the defence, conscious of a scrawled note which he had received from Midge, shortly before the court had resumed that afternoon. "This is an important point, so take your time in answering. Do you think that the customer was a man or a woman?"

"I thought it was a man."

"Could it have been a woman?"

"I don't really know. There was something about the walk that maybe seemed a little odd for a man."

"Could you tell the court what makes you think that?"

Weaver scratched his head, dislodging the lock of wispy hair which was normally plastered down over his ear. "I don't really know."

"What about his height and build?"

"I didn't really notice. He looked quite average."

"Was there anything distinctive about his manner?"

"No, not really."

Denys repressed a sigh. Ineffectual witnesses like this were the worst kind: it was irritating to examine them and juries often dismissed their evidence because they sounded so feeble and uncertain.

"What about this person's voice? Was it high- or low-pitched?"

"Quite low, I think." Weaver shifted in the witness box. "I don't really remember. It didn't seem important at the time."

"What about the customer who came in to buy toilet-water on the day that your poison-book disappeared?"

"It was a woman," answered Weaver, relieved to be able to say something definite.

"A woman. Just so. Can you give any other details?"

"Not really. She was wearing a skirt. It might have been tweed."

"And what about her height? Was she average?"

"I think so. I really didn't pay any attention. I was too worried about finding where the toilet-water had been put."

"Could this woman customer have been the customer who bought the aconitine?"

"I suppose so. I don't know."

Grateful that at least Weaver had not condemned the possibility outright, Sir Everard asked a number of other questions. He knew that the chemist was unlikely to give any more detail, but he needed to emphasise that Weaver had sold aconitine – and that someone at Forrest and Creech had known of Weaver's shop.

For his part, Sir Reginald Hilliard listened in fury. How dare Denys sneak a surprise witness into the closing stages of the trial? It was all very well prating on about justice and truth, but the entire affair was damnably irregular. He rose like a warhorse scenting battle, and determined to demonstrate the unreliability of the witness.

"What sort of clothes was this supposed customer of yours wearing?" he snapped, without any preliminaries.

"I don't know," admitted Weaver apologetically. "It was so dark and wet outside. The light wasn't very good and the customer was all wrapped up against the weather."

"But presumably you noticed whether this putative customer was carrying an umbrella or not?"

"I didn't really notice."

"What about his trousers; what colour were they?"

"I don't know."

"Tweed or flannel?"

"I don't know."

"What colour was the mackintosh?"

"I'm sorry; I can't remember."

"Hat?"

"I think so."

"Colour and shape of hat?"

"Nothing distinctive."

"Scarf?"

"I think so, but I can't remember what colour or how it was tied."

Deprived of his next question, Hilliard glared at Weaver. "So, if we are to summarise your evidence, someone whom you cannot describe visited your shop on a day of which you are uncertain and apparently bought aconitine, even although you have now lost the poison book which ought to record the sale. Is that an accurate summary?"

"Yes," nodded the little chemist unhappily.

"Then, with your lordship's permission, I should like to point out to the jury that this so-called surprise witness has produced nothing of value. All he has done is to make a few speculative remarks, singularly failing to back them up with evidence. From his description it is impossible to discern whether he is talking about man, woman or child." Hilliard snorted. "This witness is just another of those sorry specimens who seek notoriety and come forward with unlikely evidence or confessions of guilt to crimes which are attracting public attention."

"I'm not," protested Weaver, before involuntarily shrinking under the glare of prosecuting counsel.

With Weaver's sensational evidence finished, Sir Everard shot a satisfied glance at the clock. Hawkroyd would be bound to call the day's proceedings to an end, while still leaving him the following morning to conclude the defence speech. Denys' speculations proved to be entirely accurate and the jury were dismissed for the evening. As the crowds streamed out of the courtroom, Jenny turned to her friends with an almost radiant expression.

"Surely the jury must acquit my father now?"

"Let's hope so," commented Ronald soberly.

"But they must!" protested Jenny. "Here's a new witness who swears that he sold the beastly stuff *and* he's linked to Forrest and Creech – the only reason that anyone had heard of Weaver is because Midge saw his name in the directory in the office." She turned to Midge. "We owe you everything."

"Steady on," warned Midge uncomfortably. "Mr Fletcher isn't free yet."

"Exactly," agreed Ronald, hating to disappoint Jenny, but feeling that he ought to bring her down to earth. "There's always a chance that the jury will think that Weaver's appearance is just a little too convenient for the defence."

Midge cleared her throat in an embarrassed fashion. "I hope I haven't done anything disastrous, but I went to the office today."

"Forrest and Creech?" asked Ronald in horrified tones. "What on earth were you doing? Why didn't you let me come with you?"

"I had a reporter with me; I was quite safe."

"But why did you go?" demanded Jenny. "Have you spotted the murderer?"

"I think it was Miss Hurst. I'm sure she took in the poisoned tea. I went to challenge her." Midge's face fell. "She just laughed at me. She kept calling me Mary Carew and denied everything."

Jenny's face fell. "Blast. I hoped..."

"Of course you hoped she'd give something away," agreed Midge. "So did I." She sighed. "I know Weaver's evidence suggests that – at the very least – a woman was involved in stealing the poison-book, but unless Miss Hurst loses her head I don't see how we can prove it was she who killed Forrest."

"And that may be too late for my father."

Chapter Fifty-One

Sir Everard Denys was well aware that the jury might distrust Weaver's convenient appearance and he went into court the following day ready to emphasise not only the value of Weaver's evidence, but also the weakness of the prosecution case. Having carefully pointed out that whoever stole the poison book from Weaver's shop did so after Patrick Fletcher had been arrested, he reiterated the arguments which he had made on the previous day regarding the medical evidence, the tea and the locked room.

"Every time we look for an explanation of the killing of William Forrest we return to his own office. Where was there a criminal enterprise? At Forrest and Creech. Where was there persecution of the innocent? At Forrest and Creech. And where was it most likely that Forrest was fed a cup of tea laced with aconitine – tea which is shown by the medical evidence, but which no-one is prepared to admit having brewed? Again, at Forrest and Creech. Both police and prosecution have neglected the obvious, straightforward explanation and have, instead, preferred the sort of exotic suggestion to be found in thrillers. We have tax fraud, extortion and a direct link to the chemist's shop which supplied the poison. All of these facts – and I stress the word 'facts', members of the jury, for these are facts, not the bizarre concoctions preferred by the prosecution – all of these facts, I repeat, point directly to the office of Forrest and Creech. There is no link to my client. Patrick Fletcher is on trial for his life but he has not committed tax fraud, he does not prey on refugees and – search though they might – the police failed to find the slightest trace of aconitine connected to him."

Sir Everard paused, then spoke in his most serious tones. "Members of the jury, you will all have seen the statue of Justice outside this building; blind Justice who guards and protects us all, without fear or favour. We only need to look round the world today to see how important it is to preserve the impartial traditions of British justice. Here, the weak and the lowly can appeal to justice and be heard. Here, justice is decided by twelve good men and women true. Here, justice is not decided according to political affiliation. You have only to think of the extremely moving statement of Herr Lipinski to realise the significance of these points. He was willing to appear in this court – even at the very grave risk to his own life – so that he might serve the cause of Justice. He thought it more important to expose a wicked and unscrupulous crime than to consider whether he might be sent back to Germany. That, ladies and gentlemen, is true devotion to those very ideals which lie behind our system of justice, and I should ask you to bear in mind such dedication when you begin your deliberations.

"The real criminals in this crime are those who were associated with Forrest in his evil actions. Hunt for his killer amongst them and set my client free as an innocent man, his reputation restored for all to see. He is innocent; Forrest and his crew of criminal associates are the guilty ones."

Sir Everard made a deep bow to the jury, before sitting down. There was a short silence in court, during which Jenny sent Midge an agonised look. Midge squeezed Jenny's hand, hoping that none of the jurors would think that Jenny's expression suggested that she thought her father guilty. She glanced at Ronald, but his face was expressionless. Privately, the junior barrister was wondering whether Sir Everard's speech would strike the jury as a little florid but, on the other hand, the case seemed to lend itself to remarks such as his final ones.

Counsel for the prosecution restricted himself to a

short restatement of his case, deliberately lowering the emotional tension. He concluded with a reminder that the jury had to do their duty, no matter how unpleasant it might be. Then all eyes switched to the judge as he began his summing up. He started with an explanation of the phrase 'reasonable doubt', before turning to the evidence as it had been presented. Fletcher, in the dock, was listening intently, but not so intently that he could not see that Jenny looked as if she could not take many more minutes of careful, forensic analysis. She would have to bear up a bit better if she ever presented a case in court but, he supposed with a hidden dry smile, presumably the circumstances were somewhat unusual.

Meanwhile, Denys was occasionally scribbling notes on his pad of paper. Anyone who noticed assumed that he must be providing himself with aides-memoires should there be an appeal, but Wolsey was close enough to see that the numbers suggested that counsel for the defence thought that there was just a shade of a chance of an acquittal. Certainly, Hawkroyd's summing-up seemed fair. Indeed, when it came to the key defence witness, Wolsey thought that the old boy was actively generous. Junior defence counsel had half-wondered whether Miss Fletcher's friend had made up most of her evidence, but his lordship seemed to have believed every word of it.

"The prosecution has cast doubt on whether someone working in a busy office could really have managed to gain access to a large amount of incriminating information and to have carried out the names thus discovered disguised by means of cryptograms. You have heard the witness, Miss Carrington, explaining how she could create such cryptograms quickly enough. Doubtless you will be helped in your decision as to the likelihood of her achieving this in the offices of Forrest and Creech by her demonstration in court.

"Miss Carrington also explained how she was struck by the similarity of names which she discovered on two separate lists. You have heard her give examples of these names and you have also heard evidence from Herr Lipinski which would appear to substantiate her assumption that these names were connected with some activity which needed to be kept secret. The prosecution have suggested that there may have been an element of collusion between witnesses for the defence, but I should also remind you that Herr Lipinski gave evidence despite his very considerable fears that he will be returned to Germany for doing so. Moreover, Professor Schulmann is a man of rectitude and honour." The judge allowed himself a dry snort. "The current, ah, authorities in Germany may not recognise Professor Schulmann's qualifications, but I have no hesitation in assuring the court that he is a jurist of very high reputation in legal circles."

The judge then turned to Weaver. His caustic assessment of the man's powers of observation was entirely accurate, but served to puff out Jenny's flickering hopes. If Hawkroyd had clear doubts about this final witness, then the jury would be left still wondering where the poison was purchased and, by inference, they might wonder whether the accused had somehow got hold of the aconitine secretly.

Mr Justice Hawkroyd's voice continued, separating facts from conjectures, and sending each weaving in and out of each other, nodding and dancing as bobbins controlled by an expert lace-maker. However, Jenny was no longer observing which holes he discerned or what delicate patterns he made – she had stopped taking in his words, which had turned into a meaningless blur of ascending and descending pitch. Finally, the movement of the jury as they rose to go and begin their deliberations roused her.

"Is there any hope?" she asked when the junior lawyers crossed over to join her, John and Midge.

"There'll be nothing to complain about on appeal," declared Dickie.

The look which Jenny shot him made it clear that she would be unlikely to contemplate dinner with Dickie in the near future.

"Sorry, Jenny," he stammered. "What I meant was, Hawkroyd's given a good summing-up for our side."

"Do you think it'll go to appeal?" demanded Jenny.

Ronald could see that Jenny was looking distinctly ravaged. He guessed that she had probably not slept properly and saw no reason to add to her worries. "You never know what the police may find. They'll be bound to look into all this odd stuff about the poison."

In fact, Ronald was more correct than he knew. Groves had no intention of letting extortion and tax evasion to flourish under his very nose, but he had seen no need for precipitate action until the previous evening when Midge had unexpectedly arrived at the Yard and had insisted on speaking to him. The arguments which she had put forward had shaken some of his confidence that Fletcher really was guilty of murder. Hence not only were the police busily interrogating Zacharias Weaver in even greater depth than he had faced in the witness box, but Inspector Groves had gone to visit several addresses. At two of these he had made an arrest. At the third address he had drawn a blank, but had consoled himself that the ports were now alerted and that it was unlikely that anyone would escape the country. As for the murder, the judgement on Fletcher's guilt or innocence now lay in the hands of the jury.

An hour went by.

"What the devil can they be doing?" demanded John.

Ronald took pity on one who lacked the professional

calm appropriate to those who were regulars in the halls of justice.

"Juries don't like to race back; it makes them feel that they haven't taken things seriously enough."

Another hour passed. This time it was Midge who wondered what was happening and James who supplied an explanation.

"Quite often you find one juror who is difficult and won't agree with the others. I didn't like the look of that cadaverous man – he's exactly the sort to spend hours explaining why an obscure part of Leviticus can provide enlightenment, not only to this case, but to life in general."

"Or," suggested Dickie as he lit yet another cigarette, "there's a lawyer or a medical man on the jury. Educated men are the worst. They take command and insist on going through the case point by point."

Midge frowned. "Aren't they meant to?"

"Ye-es," admittedly Dickie reluctantly. He shot John a rather unfriendly look. It had not escaped his notice that John appeared to be deeply enamoured of Jenny. "I had one jury with a don on it. He refused to believe that my client had accidentally struck a man in the face with a broken beer bottle."

"Most unreasonable," snapped John.

"Oh, quite," agreed Dickie, with unfailing good humour. "I fully expected my client to go down for twelve months hard labour, but why take the best part of two hours to decide what was palpably obvious?"

By the third hour, even Ronald had lost some of his professional calm. "If they don't hurry up, the deliberations will last until tomorrow."

"Yes," nodded James, wondering what was causing the delay, but fearing that it was not a good sign.

It was nearly four hours after the judge had finished his summing-up when there was stir at the back of the court. The clerk appeared, spoke to the judge and made a signal to one of the warders. Shortly afterwards, Mr Fletcher was brought up into the dock, his pallor now showing clearly. He remained standing as the jury filed in. Mr Justice Hawkroyd turned to the foreman.

"Are you agreed upon a verdict?"

"Yes, my lord."

"And is it the verdict of you all?"

"Yes, my lord."

Jenny was conscious of a lurching in her stomach. What would the next answer be? Black cap or freedom?

"And how do you find the accused, guilty or not guilty?"

"Not guilty, my lord."

The judge turned towards Fletcher, but the foreman was not finished. "And we'd like to record that we think that Herr Elsner and Herr Lipinski ought to be naturalised as they have served the cause of justice better than anyone else has."

Hawkroyd bowed towards the jury. "I am sure that your comments will be widely reported in the press and thus brought to the attention of the relevant authorities." He turned to the dock. "Patrick Fletcher, you have been tried before a jury of your peers and found not guilty. You walk from this court a free man, cleared of all suspicion." As cheering broke out from several exuberant spectators, the judge added, "I need hardly say that this will prove to be a popular verdict with many people, particularly those who know of your unswerving devotion to justice."

"That makes it quite clear what old Hawkroyd thinks," muttered Ronald to Jenny. "And it'll be all over the press."

Jenny hardly heard him. Instead, she was wishing that it

would not be hideously unprofessional to thank both judge and jury for their decisions.

Later that evening, there was an exceedingly jubilant gathering in Fletcher's chambers. Denys had somewhat solicitously suggested that the barrister go home and rest, but Fletcher had shrugged off this advice.

"Certainly not, Everard. I am eternally grateful for what you have done for me, but I must thank people in chambers. If I know Thomson, he'll be waiting for me. And how could I not thank Miss Ellis in person for her very spirited defence of me?"

Thomson was indeed waiting for Fletcher. Indeed, he appeared to want to treat the barrister's return as something of a regal procession, but Fletcher hastily asked for everyone to assemble in his room. Jenny was hovering at his elbow as her father began to speak. He first thanked everyone for their loyal support, before making a few comments about the case.

"There were moments," admitted the K.C., "when I rather feared that I was going to be convicted. As a barrister, one is all too inclined to see potential problems which may not even have struck the prosecution. I gather, however, that I was not alone in seeing problems. Junior members of these chambers appear to possess a highly-developed awareness that clear-cut proofs are very useful when attempting to demonstrate that a prosecution case is wrong." He coughed. "I understand that such exploratory activities were, at times, somewhat unorthodox, but doubtless Parry's experiences will stand him in good stead with his future clients."

"Absolutely, sir," James murmured urbanely. "Nothing like sharing an anecdote about the local clink."

"And," continued Fletcher, "I trust that any infelicitous questioning on the part of Miss Fletcher will be overlooked as the natural concern of an unqualified pupil who has not yet reached the maturity of one called to the Bar."

Jenny blushed. Mike, standing on the edge of the crowd, stared at his sister in some surprise, but became distracted by his father's praise of Midge's undercover work. As Mr Fletcher drew his remarks to a close, he turned to Midge.

"I should like to hear how you worked out who the murderer was."

Midge shivered. "I still can't believe that it was Miss Hurst. Under her stuffy exterior, she was *nice*. She was kind to me. How could she be involved in something so foul?"

Fletcher smiled rather sadly. "'Nice' people can stoop to making money in nasty ways. But do explain your deductions."

Midge tried to present things logically. "It was obvious that the murderer must have known a lot about whatever was going on. How else could Herr X's evidence have been undermined so neatly by the appearance of his children? And I firmly believe that Lipinski was attacked to prevent him from giving evidence – after all, the attack nearly succeeded. That meant that the killer was either one of the refugees or someone who had been involved in the racket. I always thought that it was much more probable that crooks had fallen out than that a refugee had decided to kill Forrest. After all, if a refugee had wanted revenge, he could have left London and then reported Forrest anonymously."

"Unless," pointed out Ronald, "he thought that the police would do nothing."

"I did bear that in mind," agreed Midge, "but I couldn't understand why a refugee would want to harm Mr Fletcher's case. Moreover, once the evidence of tax evasion turned up, I was even more certain that the murderer must have belonged inside Forrest and Creech. I simply couldn't believe that two different crimes had originated in the same office, but were organised by two different sets of people." She frowned. "I did wonder whether Forrest had killed himself and that his letter was a warped revenge upon Mr Fletcher, but it didn't seem very credible. I shouldn't have wasted any time over it."

"My dear Midge, at least you thought that I was innocent – it was more than the police believed."

Midge blushed. "I'd hardly have thought anything else." She moved on hastily. "Both the tax fraud and the false papers required a lot of documents to be signed, which made Davie an unlikely collaborator. He could have been working with Forrest, but I didn't see why Forrest would have invited him to join and Davie hadn't been there as long as the refugee racket had been running."

"He could have discovered something and then forced his way in," suggested James dubiously.

Midge looked embarrassed. "I don't want to be rude about Davie, but whilst he might have wondered about a stream of Germans visiting the office, I honestly don't think that he was well enough educated to have spotted a tax fraud. He couldn't read or write very well and something Miss Hurst said gave me the impression that he was another person who'd been employed on the lowest possible wages because he wouldn't be able to get another job easily."

"An ex-criminal?" suggested Ronald.

"No. Miss Hurst didn't like it when I spoke Suffolk at her. Davie was clearly East End and he once boasted to me that he'd never been registered by the state." Midge shrugged. "That must mean he didn't go to school. I can't say I liked him one bit, but I suspect he's never been given much of a chance. Goodness knows where he picked up the education he has acquired."

"So with Davie ruled out, that left three people," commented James. "What made you decide that Miss

Hurst was the master-mind?"

"Creech was clearly involved in whatever was going on – he had details of a bank account hidden away and then he had an argument in German with one of the refugees. However, he can't have been the person who bought the aconitine – Weaver said that the customer was of average height, but Creech was tall."

"And Wynne?" John asked.

"Wynne was far more suspicious of everything I did. In fact, I was scared of him."

"I'm not surprised," agreed Jenny.

"I was sure Wynne didn't trust me," continued Midge, "and he was clearly up to his neck in the tax fraud – it couldn't possibly have been carried on without his knowledge. Davie also told me that Wynne had had a number of meetings with the German-speaking man whom I'd seen. Even so, that didn't necessarily mean that Wynne was the murderer. Nor did it explain how he had got Forrest to drink the aconitine. Sir Everard showed how Forrest had probably drunk an additional cup of tea in his own office and I couldn't help remembering how it's always women who bring the tea. That meant one of the typists. Mr Sutton said that my predecessors had been investigated practically back to their cradles and were utterly free of suspicion. That left Miss Hurst. Wynne wouldn't have demeaned himself by bringing tea to Forrest, but for Miss Hurst to do so would have been perfectly plausible."

Fletcher agreed with this summary. "I don't suppose that Forrest would have wondered too much if Miss Hurst appeared with a cup of tea, even if it was normally the job of the junior typist."

"Was it Miss Hurst who typed those letters which the police said were copies of the ones that Forrest sent to Daddy?" demanded Jenny.

"I expect so." Midge suddenly grinned. "It must have been very frustrating for a trained typist to have to type with two fingers so as to ensure that a typewriter expert would swear that a complete amateur had typed them."

"Clever planning," commented Ronald approvingly. "No wonder she wasn't spotted."

Midge sighed. "I should have been able to work it out earlier. After all, I knew everyone who was involved." She glanced apologetically at Fletcher. "And it was a horrible risk to go and tackle her outright."

"Indeed it was," responded the barrister. "I am appalled that you put yourself in danger like that."

Midge shook her head. "I didn't mean the risk to me – I had a stalwart reporter waiting in the hallway. What I meant was the risk of giving away too much." She coughed. "The thing is, Jenny said something about how it would look a very guilty action if someone were to flee. I rather hoped that Miss Hurst might. And she did – I didn't know whether to be pleased or worried when Groves told me."

"Why did she flee?" asked Jenny. "After all, she'd stuck it out a long time."

"I kept pointing out that Wynne didn't like her and that he would drag her into any prosecution for fraud. She must have known that was true." She sighed. "It took me a long time to convince Groves regarding the point about the tea. If he'd acted sooner, the trial might have been halted."

"I doubt it, my dear," commented Fletcher. "The evidence may be enough to convince us, but it certainly wouldn't have been regarded by the Crown as conclusive – especially not before all of the various frauds have been sufficiently proved." The K.C. smiled at Midge. "You have no need to apologise for anything. If it hadn't been for you, I'd have been found guilty. As for Miss Hurst, I should imagine that she is probably on the continent already.

Anyone who was clever enough to carry out that crime, with all the planning that was involved, is bound to have foreseen the need to flee."

"It doesn't matter," exclaimed Jenny, hoping that what she was saying would prove to be true. "You're free and nobody can possibly think that you did anything wrong. Even the judge said so!"

Finale

Chapter Fifty-Two

Fletcher had smiled tolerantly at Jenny's optimistic hope that no-one would regard him with suspicion for having been in the dock, but the next morning a close reading of the newspapers suggested that the press had presented a remarkably positive assessment of his involvement in the Forrest case. The *Universal Record* castigated the police for jumping to conclusions, while the *Morning Post* produced a weighty editorial arguing that 'one of England's most highly-regarded K.C.s has suffered because he came to the aid of the dispossessed and persecuted' and that 'only the good sense of a British jury' had saved him.

"Rather unfair on Hawkroyd," the highly-regarded K.C. commented, as he tossed the paper over to Jenny. "Hilliard could legitimately claim that he summed up in my favour."

"And so he should," declared Jenny pugnaciously, but her father was not listening. He had slit open an envelope and was reading the enclosure with a wry smile on his lips.

My dear Fletcher (began the letter),

I trust that you will believe me when I say how pleased I am that the jury found you innocent. I took no pleasure in prosecuting you, and I hope that you, your son and Miss Fletcher will forgive me for the somewhat rough handling which I gave them in the witness-box. Moreover, I sincerely hope that Miss Fletcher – as one who intends to become a barrister – will be able to explain to her friend that no malice lay behind my cross-examination of Miss Carrington. I fear that Miss Carrington may have been left bruised from her encounter with our adversarial system of law, but, perhaps, her feelings may be assuaged somewhat by learning that I thought she made a cool and competent witness who materially assisted the defence – indeed, more than any other witness.

> *I remain etc,*
> *R. N. Hilliard.*

Jenny sniffed dismissively. "It's all very well apologising now. He oughtn't to have attacked Midge as he did."

"Really, Jenny, what a feminine response," teased her father. "I thought you wanted to be a barrister."

Jenny shot him a look which would have stopped a dragon in its tracks, but Fletcher, whose skin proved to be tougher than scales, merely laughed.

"It was Hilliard's responsibility to cross-examine Midge properly, just as Denys asked very searching questions of the prosecution medical expert. Midge was our expert on Forrest and Creech; would justice have been served if her story wasn't checked?"

Jenny frowned. "I suppose not," she admitted reluctantly.

"Would you expect Hilliard to let Midge off being questioned because she has been ill? From what I've seen of your friend she wouldn't thank you for that." The barrister sighed. "It's an odd world nowadays, Jenny. In my young day, women were to be protected and shielded and treated like fragile jewels; but here are you training for the law and your friend has saved my life."

Jenny walked to the other side of the table and put her arms round her father.

"Never mind, we can still be nice," she stated as she kissed his cheek.

Fletcher laughed. "And since I'm clearly such a dreadful father that I haven't bought you any hats or jewellery recently, why don't I repair that omission today?

Earrings or a bracelet, my dear?"

"A gel," drawled Jenny, "can never have too many earrings."

It had been agreed that Midge and John would come for dinner that evening. The way in which John kissed Jenny confirmed to Midge that he was distinctly keen on her. A few minutes later, Jenny dragged Midge off into the dining-room.

"I need to tell you something," she began.

"John?"

"Yes." Sounding very embarrassed, Jenny attempted to explain. "It was when Herr X's children turned unexpectedly. I was distressed and didn't stop to think." She hesitated. "Midge, I am sorry, but I really do like him. I'm not hurting you for the sake of a casual flirtation."

"Is it that obvious?"

Since to answer 'yes' would be disastrous, Jenny produced a convincing 'no'. "I only noticed because I've known you for years and years."

"John's known me for just as long."

"I'm a woman," pointed out Jenny incontestably. "We notice more than men do. And he hasn't said anything to me. Honestly, Midge, I feel like a traitor, but..."

"It's all right. The trial was what really mattered. And we'd better get back or your father will be wondering what we're talking about."

Jenny swallowed. Midge was being very decent about it, but she was clearly upset. For a moment, Jenny thought about referring to Ronald's unexpected concern for Midge's safety, before deciding that it would sound patronising. She shrugged. Midge had only had one term in Cambridge. That hadn't given her much chance to meet a nice chap – maybe John could be prevailed upon to introduce her to some. But for the moment, it sounded as

446

if they had better concentrate upon discussing the trial.

When they returned to the drawing-room, Fletcher poured them each a glass of sherry. Then, much to Midge's surprise, the barrister presented her with a diamond bracelet and matching pair of earrings.

"I can't possibly...," began Midge in shock, but Fletcher insisted.

"My dear girl, you saved my life. I want you to have something."

"We did consider a diamond collar for Bertie," pointed out Jenny, glad to move off the subject of John.

"Bertie's a boy," argued Midge. "He can't wear diamonds." Then she blushed, as she realised that Jenny was joking. "Sorry. I wasn't thinking."

"Put them on," urged John.

Midge was busily admiring the play of the light on her bracelet and hoping that she was not looking at it too greedily, when Jenny's father handed her a fat letter addressed to Miss Carew, care of Sir Everard Denys. The letter had been opened and she looked up at Mr Fletcher rather nervously.

"Yes, it is for you," he commented soberly. "I think that you ought to read it."

Midge picked up the sheets rather as if she expected them to bite her.

Dear Miss Carew (I find it difficult to think of you as otherwise),

Well, what a surprise you turned out to be. There I was, thinking that you were a rather dim country girl, and you turn out to be a bluestocking with your head chock-full of Latin and Greek. Of course, Wynne took full advantage of your supposed status, smirking about his cleverness in offering you such a low wage and being sure that you wouldn't find anyone else who wanted to employ a girl who

447

couldn't walk properly. It appears that you have had the last laugh. But you won't be interested in that. What you'll want to know is what really happened.

You were quite right that Forrest was running a tax fraud from the office. It was very straightforward and just as you – or Miss Fletcher – suspected. Accurate invoices were sent out, but inaccurate accounts were filed. Exceptionally easy to carry out and it must have netted Forrest a hundred pounds a month. Obviously, Wynne was in on the act as well, although he was less discreet than Forrest – did it never occur to you that his gold watch and smart clothes cost more than a clerk in a not-especially large firm could afford? Or did you assume that all men waste their money in an attempt to convince themselves that they are more important than they really are?

Never mind that. The point was, I became suspicious and, after I discovered what was going on, I saw no reason why I shouldn't share in the proceeds of their tax evasion. Forrest was livid at the thought of having to give me a cut and claimed that I could have no evidence. I pointed out that I didn't require old invoices – one mention to the Revenue of my suspicions and they would check up on every account that had ever been created. After that, Forrest caved in pretty quickly. (In fact, the fraud was confined to a few firms since it was much easier to keep track of the substituted accounts when we knew which ones were involved.) I made it clear to him that I was not interested in blackmail and that I would not raise my demands beyond a set percentage of the profits of the fraud. It did worry me for some time that Forrest gave in so easily – I was afraid that he might decide to murder me rather than keep paying me. On reflection, I suppose that's what first gave me the idea of murder – and it certainly warned me that Forrest would not stand up to any firm questioning by the police. So, about that time, I started to make certain preparations in case things went wrong and I fell under suspicion as well. I don't intend to go into them in detail – suffice it to say that they have enabled me to reach my current address abroad safely.

Our tax evasion went on quite happily for several years, but Wynne grew greedy. It occurred to him that a solicitor has access to a number of important documents; moreover a solicitor's signature is an excellent guarantee of a document. Given the situation in Europe, it was obvious that there must be a good number of people who would give almost everything they owned to escape to Britain. All we had to do, Wynne claimed, was to supply false naturalisation papers. This began promisingly, although we had to bring Creech in on it as well. Your Mr Lipinski was the type of man we were after – he could pay a large sum and then be left well alone. But, again, Wynne grew greedy. He saw how he could exploit less well-off refugees: although they could not provide a large, one-off sum, they could be made to pay a regular sum every week. He didn't tell me the details until he had arranged everything, but he worked it out quite well. He even managed to add in a few men like Elsner who had bought their papers from other sources.

Obviously, a large number of people trailing in and out of the office every Friday might start to attract suspicion, particularly as they would be bound to arrive after the office had ostensibly closed. Hence Wynne designated several refugees to collect what was owed from a larger group. One of them was Yannonov, whose name you discovered. Yannonov protested, but he didn't have much choice, not least because Wynne told him that he'd expose the entire group to the police if he didn't co-operate. Wynne always was more ruthless than Forrest – he told Yannonov to regard himself as a rate-collector.

Then, as you know, one of the Jews squawked. It's always a danger when you are dealing with people, rather than papers. Next, Forrest received a mysterious telephone call from your Mr Fletcher summoning Forrest to Fletcher's chambers. Forrest didn't want to talk about it, but I had put through Fletcher's call to Forrest and I knew that important and respected barristers like Fletcher don't mix with rather shabby and distinctly non-respectable solicitors like Forrest. It was sheer chance that I was working late that night and I don't mind admitting that I got the wind up. In fact, as it turns out, I was quite correct to worry. I didn't know whether Fletcher had discovered about the refugees or the tax fraud, but I didn't intend to go to gaol along with Forrest. Hence the aconitine (which I had learned about, purely by chance, when I read an article about famous crimes of the nineteenth century).

I had a few days grace before Forrest's appointment so I hunted around for a place run by the sort of incompetent fool that Weaver was. His small, fly-blown shop was a godsend and Barnet is not a place where I was known. All I had to do was wait until Weaver was serving alone and I had the necessary poison. A few days later, I returned and stole his poison book. I'm still rather proud of remembering to do that. It confused the police no end. The incriminating file of letters I planted in Forrest's room when he was out seeing Fletcher – I'd typed them on Miss Peters' machine at various points over the previous week just in case they were needed. If nothing else, they would have bought enough time for me to make a getaway. As it was, they helped cast suspicion well away from the office.

Forrest was nervous before his interview with Fletcher and when he returned he was ashen-faced and frightened. I knew that he was not going to listen to my urgings to ignore what Fletcher had said. I told him to abandon the refugee racket and go back to tax evasion. I told him that there wasn't enough evidence to prove anything. However, he wouldn't listen to me; he was trembling and kept insisting that Fletcher was a man of integrity and that he daren't challenge him, because no-one would believe him. That was when I had my brilliant idea.

Of course, I'd already planned to kill Forrest if necessary – but that wasn't the brilliant bit. What was, I think, very clever, was to persuade Forrest to write a letter in his own handwriting accusing Fletcher of blackmail. The police might have suspected that the typed letters hadn't been written by him, but they certainly couldn't claim that about a handwritten letter. Forrest believed me when I said that it would buy him time. Whilst he was writing it, I brought him a cup of tea into which I had put the fatal dose of aconitine. He was thirsty and drank it quickly. I slipped out again unobserved, with the cup and saucer hidden in my handbag. No-one saw me leave, but I hadn't expected them to – Creech (always something of a sleeping-partner until Forrest died) had departed early and Wynne was attending to business elsewhere. Miss Peters and Miss Hemming were too busy seizing the opportunity to talk about hats to notice how long I was out of the room.

I had told Forrest that I would return later and help him to prepare a plan of action. I told him lots of rubbish — I said that I would help him to escape the country if he wanted. I think I even said that I would marry him if necessary since a wife cannot be forced to give evidence against her husband. He seemed quite touched by my loyalty, so I emphasised again that he mustn't leave his room until I came back. I said that I didn't want Wynne interfering because he'd stop Forrest's chances of escaping. I was surprised that he agreed so readily, but he didn't trust Wynne much more than Wynne trusted him.

Naturally, I had no intention of returning to the office; I'm afraid that your clever defence barrister was just a bit too clever about that. I'd already taken the letter with me — Forrest wrote it quicker than anyone anticipated because I dictated it to him and, of course, he wasn't actually ill at that point. I deliberately didn't post it before six o'clock, partly because I didn't want Miss Peters to see me posting anything when we left the office together, and also because I didn't want the police showing up that evening, as they might have done if they had received it in the last delivery. Of course, I wasn't to know that Wynne would discover the body before the morning. He hadn't believed Forrest when he claimed that the interview with Fletcher was unconnected with either tax fraud or the refugee racket. From something Wynne let slip later, it was clear that he'd thought that Forrest was staying late to destroy papers before he fled from Fletcher's wrath. Wynne had intended to catch Forrest in the act and force the truth out of him. He must have got a considerable shock when he discovered that Forrest was himself destroyed.

Oddly enough, although I knew that it would be a terrible risk to return to the office and perhaps be seen there, I had not anticipated having such a strong desire to go back and find out whether Forrest was dead yet. It was a dreadful strain waiting and I nearly fled the country that night. However, when I went into work the next day, all was as I had planned. Indeed, things had gone even better than I had hoped, because the police soon arrested Fletcher and were reluctant to believe his story. Nevertheless, I didn't let myself relax, which was just as well. Wynne was suspicious. I don't think that he ever really believed that Fletcher had killed Forrest, since the alleged motive was completely untrue. Then Wynne discovered that Creech had been trying to cream off more than his fair share of the profits. They had a blazing row, which was very convenient for me, because from that moment each thought the other was the guilty party. Wynne even accused Creech of taking his false passport, although I imagine that was your doing. All the same, just like you, I had to be very careful what I said to anyone in the office. That was why I didn't fight too hard to keep Miss Peters or Miss Hemming. It was much better – I thought – to have someone fresh who could know nothing about the murder. Instead, I got you!

The refugee racket was clearly dead in the water by this point, so Wynne told Yannonov and the others that they had paid off their debts. I doubt whether any of them believed it, but we couldn't take the risk of any nosy parker spotting the connection. Indeed, Wynne was extremely suspicious that you were late leaving the office on the very day that he intended to bid goodbye to Yannonov. Then you met Yannonov one day, when he came round to check with Wynne that he really had finished demanding money.

Foolishly, it seems, I discounted Wynne's fears. However, I did take pains to ensure that I knew where Elsner's children were – we'd been keeping a watch on Schulmann since he was our best chance of working out who had spilled the beans. Wynne was furious that Elsner had escaped from his clutches and had to be restrained from attacking him – he'd already tried to get rid of Lipinski by thrusting him under a bus. I had a much better scheme and it nearly paid off. If Elsner was one of those who had squawked, what better method of undermining his claims about wickedness in our office than if he could be shown to be under an enormous debt of gratitude to Fletcher? All I needed was to send a hasty message to the children telling them that they must flee from where they were living and to go to Fletcher. I wasn't sure whether they would do what I wanted, but they did. It appeared obvious that Fletcher had bought his testimony – the police certainly believed he had.

Despite these precautions, I felt unsafe. Something – instinct? – told me to beware. So, immediately I heard that you had not turned up for work, I put arrangements into operation. And then when you accused me to my face I realised that things were definitely finished. I left five minutes after you did. No waiting within the long arm of the law for me! I had suspected that the game couldn't go on forever and my savings are easily realisable, not tied up in traceable bank accounts. I hope that I shall not be found, but there are other – swifter – poisons than aconitine, so I doubt that I shall swing on the gallows.

Reading over what I have written it occurs to me that you may wonder why I – apparently so upstanding and careful – broke the law. Naturally, the money was a large attraction – you have seen how badly paid typists are, despite their importance. But another reason was the thrill. In a strange sort of way, I enjoyed making plans and carrying them out. Maybe it would have been different if I'd married and had a family, but I doubt it. Men boast about having power; I just liked the chance to do something interesting. Would I have let Fletcher hang? I hope not, but I'm glad I wasn't put to the test. In any case, I always assumed that his sentence would be commuted to imprisonment – the legal profession tends to look after its own, as I've seen from the sidelines.

Well, my dear, don't gloat too much when you read this – Mary Carew wouldn't.

Yours sincerely,
Annabel Hurst

There was a pause when Midge finished reading the letter out loud. Then John spoke.

"What a cold-blooded, callous woman! Thank goodness you didn't fall into her hands."

Midge shivered. "The irony is that she was playing almost as big a part as I was. No wonder I was scared." She sighed. "It's dreadful, but in some respects I don't want Miss Hurst to be arrested."

"She killed a man and showed no pity for the people from whom Wynne was extorting money," pointed out Fletcher grimly. "I don't think that you should have much pity for her."

"But," declared Jenny, attempting to lighten the atmosphere, "it just shows what happens when women aren't allowed to do interesting jobs."

The K.C. looked at his daughter quizzically. "Are you suggesting that if you don't get called to the Bar, you'll end up in the dock?"

"Not precisely," admitted Jenny, before adding happily, "But think how much chaos an entire generation of bored women with trained minds could cause. Midge could forge manuscripts and I rather fancy starting with jewel heists before moving on to bigger things."

John laughed. "Midge might be called in to investigate the said heists. Perhaps it would be safer to let other people buy you jewels."

"Ah!" declared Jenny, pretending to be frightened. "If you're going to put Midge on my track, rather that Groves *et al*, then I may have to reconsider my future career."

"What about it, Midge?" asked John. "Are you going to strike terror into the breasts of criminals? Will you pursue Scotland Yard or Cambridge?"

"Cambridge," answered Midge firmly. "Solving crimes may be like teasing out a particularly interesting translation, but it's definitely Cambridge for me."

Finis

ALSO AVAILABLE IN THE MIDGE CARRINGTON MYSTERY SERIES

Blood on the Backs

An undergraduate crashes to his death from the roof of Trinity College, Cambridge. Did he fall or was he pushed? Midge's cousin John is forced to turn to her for help when one of his students is accused of murder. Meanwhile, Midge faces her own problems – her college disapproves strongly of her getting involved in another murder and there is the complication that, although she is in love with John, he loves Jenny, her closest friend.

The second in the Midge Carrington mystery series.

ALSO AVAILABLE IN THE MIDGE CARRINGTON MYSTERY SERIES

My Enemy's Enemy

When Ralph is sent to investigate a supposed outbreak of gloom and despondency in a Suffolk regiment, he consoles himself that he will be closer to Midge. However, when the colonel is shot dead, it suddenly appears that there is much more at stake than imaginary Fifth Columnists dreamed up by the regimental padre.

The latest in the Midge Carrington mystery series.

Printed in Great Britain
by Amazon